English Winter

Swords of Resilience Book 3

J.A. Stein

J.A. Stein Publishing

Book Cover by Venom Co.

Edited by Gail Delaney

Map by J.A. Stein

ISBN (Paperback): 979-8-9864908-5-4

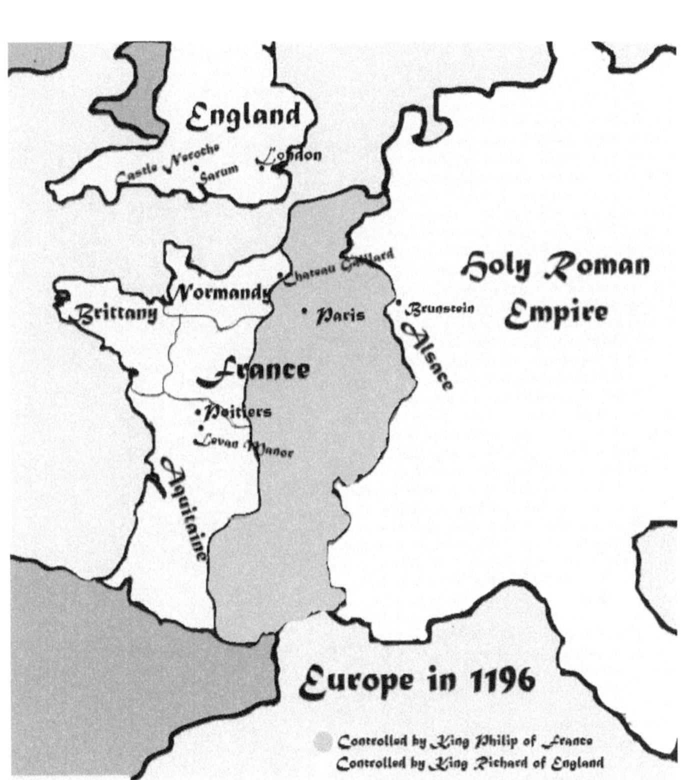

England
Castle Neroche
Sarum
London
Normandy
Brittany
Chateau Gaillard
Paris
Brunstein
Holy Roman Empire
Alsace
France
Poitiers
Levan Manor
Aquitaine
Europe in 1196
Controlled by King Philip of France
Controlled by King Richard of England

Chapter 1

November 1199

Levan Manor, Aquitaine

The wind caressed her face with a thousand needles. The cold sting of winter burned her eyes, making them tear, and yet she leaned into it, reveling in it, enjoying the pure sensation of being alive. Lady Eleanor de Levan did not have to urge her horse, Noir, faster, for he could feel her desire. He leaned into the bridle, lengthening stride, nostrils flaring in the cold air. The danger of a gallop on frosted earth was not enough. Eleanor let her reins slide through her fingers onto Noir's neck, closed her eyes, and threw her arms open, embracing the wind.

They were flying, for no reason but that they could.

Eventually the field they galloped across came to an end, and Eleanor had to pick up her reins, slowing Noir. He obliged, but not without a toss of the head in protest. They were on the rise of a hill, not far from Levan Manor. Around them lay Eleanor's estate, her hard-won inheritance, which though now brown with dormant grass and leafless trees, still was beautiful in early morning. The light was a silvery grey, highlighting a low-level haze in the valley before her as if it were a magical curtain. The icy wind blew her cloak and hair around her, but she was not cold. The exhilarating power of the horse beneath her and the strength it took to stay in harmony with him had her muscles as warm as if she stood before the fire.

Noir's whinny cut the quiet morning, answered by the distant call of his stablemates back at the manor, which lay behind them, nestled between harvested fields and pruned vineyards. Eleanor laid a hand on the big horse's neck to reassure him, and he settled. They were used to each other by now, so in tune that they could read each other's minds. They both needed the outing, even in the cold, to calm their overactive personalities. There were no battles or tournaments for Noir, no long journeys that took him across kingdoms. Eleanor felt the restlessness in him. Though perhaps, it was only a reflection of herself.

The past year and a half were the longest she had stayed in one place since she'd left her uncle's castle of Brunstein as a scarred, desperate teenager. At first she had accepted her assignment as lady of the manor at her childhood home with relief. It was what she had fought for years to enjoy, after all. Not to mention, she had a son to raise, a husband to please, and a household of servants dependent on her. All her dreams had come to pass, so why was she so restless, like the horse beneath her that wanted to push on, run further, try harder? Try harder for what? What more was there to gain? She had everything she had dreamed of.

Eleanor stroked Noir's neck, murmuring to him. At least he still made her feel alive and strong. He granted her freedom from her responsibilities at the manor, if only for a moment. Alas, even now, they should return home. The chill of the late November air was biting through her cloak, and her face had shifted from the sting of needles to plain numbness. It was cold for this early in the season. Perhaps it would be a long winter. That was no matter; they were ready for it. The newly built granary at the manor was brimming full, the manor was well-stocked, the villagers had built their own huts, and even the pigs had food set aside for them. Let the wind blow.

In a smooth motion, she turned Noir for home, but instead of galloping, she let him walk on a long rein, his stride swinging, ears pricked. The closer they got, the more she felt the weight of her responsibilities. They weren't even that overpowering, just constant. She straightened in the saddle, reminding herself to be grateful, as they all had made great sacrifices in order to place her in this position. Even now, her husband Alec was in England for the first time in years, checking on the estate he had been honored with and never seen. Eleanor wondered how he fared. Was his dream coming true as well? The political climate in the wake of King Richard's recent death left some doubt, but Alec was a suave, likeable man. Surely, he was building the foundation with the new King John that would keep them in favor for years to come.

Noir lifted his head, suddenly alert, and Eleanor followed his gaze. A rider galloped across the field between them and the manor. She shortened her reins. Eleanor watched as the galloping rider slumped forward in the saddle, then straightened, then slumped, and finally fell to the ground. Eleanor pressed Noir into a canter in the direction of the rider. The riderless horse continued to run headlong into the distance.

As they reached the place the rider had fallen, she slowed, standing in her stirrups to spot the person. He wasn't hard to find, a man flat on his back in an ice-fringed puddle of mud. He looked unconscious, eyes closed and arms splayed. Then his limbs jerked, enough to splatter the mud. Noir shied a step away. The man was still, and then again the limbs jerked. This time, his eyes opened wide, and he stared at Eleanor. What was wrong with him? A sort of illness? She dismounted and approached, but stayed out of arm's reach.

The man groaned as another spasm shook him. A white foam appeared at his mouth. Poisoned, perhaps? Eleanor took a step back, the compassion in her warring with caution.

"La—lady El—inn—" He gritted his teeth and groaned again. "Warn...you know...he knows...over—." The man squeezed his eyes shut, a hiss issuing from his lips as his jaw clenched in pain.

Eleanor took a step towards him. "What happened? Who are you?"

"Poison!" the man forced out. He trembled a moment, then coughed, and then seemed to be calmer. Eleanor took another step towards him. The man gave a shuddering breath, and then his eyes flew open, meeting hers with a steady, fierce gaze she had only seen on tournament fields and in the eyes of warriors. She stood her ground, though her hand involuntarily reached for the dagger on her hip. "Overheard," the man said clearly. His eyes widened, his voice softened to a whisper. "Raganor coming."

With a last shudder, he was dead.

Eleanor took a panicked step backward, reaching for Noir to steady herself. She looked around wildly, but there was no one in sight. The man's horse was grazing at the edge of the field as if nothing had happened. She had a dead body in front of her, and the name in the air of the grandfather her husband had told her to fear.

She swung back onto Noir, trotted over to catch the stranger's horse, and then galloped back to Levan Manor, spare horse in tow, to sound the alarm to lock down the manor. It was a country manor, not a castle, but they had thick doors, high windows, and stone walls. They had a chance to protect the manor if she could get her people inside. Her heart hammered in her chest as she galloped into the courtyard. Cottage doors were flung open at the sound of hooves. She looked around her at the wide eyes of men, women, and children. She had to protect them.

"My lady, what's wrong?" Gregory the Hunter asked.

She swallowed, looking around the expectant faces. "Prepare for an attack," she said firmly, with more confidence than she felt. "Everyone, and your animals, into the manor. Take whatever you can use as weapons."

The villagers scurried into action, panic in their expressions. Raids between lords of estates such as hers were not uncommon, though it had been years since this piece of Aquitaine had been disturbed. The villagers had enough stories from friends of friends to feel fear.

"Who is coming?" Gregory asked, standing his ground at her side.

Eleanor looked over his head towards the horizon. "I don't know. And I don't know when. But suffice to say, we have been warned."

Chapter 2

Chateau Brunstein, Alsace

Lord Raoul of Brunstein's first sign that something was amiss was when his spy never reported back. The man had communicated with the regularity of a lunar cycle for years, regardless of weather, up until a few days prior. Raoul had returned to Brunstein, wondering if the weather was at play or if the man had finally met some mishap on the long road from Aquitaine. The second sign something was amiss was the arrival of a letter, dated a month prior, with a signature Raoul had never seen in his life and had hoped he never would. The third sign was the speck of light in the dark valley beyond his fortress walls.

The ease with which a single flame could cut darkness never ceased to amaze Raoul. Even now, as he looked out his tower window, the glow of a single torch could be seen far in the distance. It was as loud an announcement as a red pennant waving on the battlefield or a horn blaring during a hunt. *Here I am. I am coming.*

Raoul stood in the highest tower of the castle, his father's old study, and waited while the rider approached. The flame bobbed just enough to indicate that the rider pressed on in a steady canter, unrushed and efficient. Only a skilled rider would travel at night at such speed, even with the light of a torch. Sir Simon of Bavaria was one such skilled rider, and Raoul would bet his inheritance that it was he who approached in the dark of night. He was a warrior of a class few could rival. Thankfully, Raoul was also of that class. It was equally good that Simon was an ally.

He could see the horse now, a dark body, unadorned but for the basics of saddle and bridle, the shadow of a rider on its back. Simon liked to travel modestly and alone, though most men with his noble bloodline rode with entourages for protection, or at the very least a squire or two. He claimed he didn't need protection, but Raoul knew from experience that what he didn't like were others slowing him down. Privacy was another concern, and at times like this, it all combined to equate a great convenience. They would be able to speak alone, and no one would know they had spoken at all.

Simon disappeared from view as he rode into the courtyard. Raoul turned away and looked around the tower room. It was bare but for a table, once built within the room, now too big to carry down the spiral staircase. Even the hearth was swept clean of ash. Two bloodstains on the floor—one small, one large—marked the event that had led to the room's abandonment. Raoul's gaze lingered on the larger, picturing with perfect clarity how his father had lay sprawled, dead. He could still see it as if it was yesterday, not almost two years ago. He hadn't been sad then, and he wasn't sad now. The power shift that Montag's death had caused still lay heavy on his shoulders, and it likely would continue to do so for the rest of his life.

A firm knock on the door drew his attention. Had he been staring at the stain long enough for Simon to enter the castle? Such distraction was why he'd shut the room. It was just as well. This conversation with Simon could not be overheard. The reason Montag had used this room as a study was the fact that it had the highest degree of privacy in the castle. Nothing above it but the roof, only the staircase below it, and only air beyond the stone walls surrounding the tower; there was nowhere for spies to hide.

Raoul answered the door, and Simon stalked in without greeting. He pulled off his expensive leather gloves and scanned the room, frowning slightly at the cold hearth. Raoul closed the door behind him.

"I didn't know you had a grandfather," Simon said bluntly. He spun towards Raoul, his face expressionless as rain-washed mud. He was older than Raoul by a decade, his hair already grey at the temples. And though Raoul was taller, he knew Simon was not one to pick a fight with.

"I didn't know he was still alive. Apparently he is." Raoul crossed his arms and raised his chin. "I take it you got a letter, too."

Simon pulled a piece of parchment from a pouch on his hip and handed it to Raoul. Raoul already knew the contents, as his own was identical. Raganor le Brun had signed it as if he were their long-standing leader, not a stranger that had appeared from the Far East.

Simon's voice was grim. "We have been summoned."

"I know—"

"There will be another initiation, to replace your father."

"I was trying to let it die out...that is what we agreed at the last meeting. We would let it end with us. All of us, the whole Order, agreed."

"Some are changing their minds." Simon pointed to the parchment. "I have been told he is traveling, convincing each member of what The Order could be. Apparently they did far more when *he* was in power. They reached far higher."

Raoul rubbed his forehead. "I am tired of the bloodshed."

"As am I. I have five sons." Simon met Raoul's eye. There was a flicker of sadness there. It was rare for Simon to allow it to show, but Raoul had known him his whole life, had worked hard to prove he was an ally, not a threat, and thus he earned the occasional glimpse of humanity when Simon felt strongly enough about something. Raoul knew without explanation how much Simon had at stake if The Order continued to induct members.

"So you agree with me? You want to end it?"

"Yes. We need to keep the others on our side. If an initiation commences, we have no choice. We must follow through."

Raoul inhaled through his nose. He looked down at the scrap of parchment. "We have until the spring equinox."

"We don't have until then to act, though."

Raoul sank onto the edge of the table. He'd expected Raganor to return. His father Montag had not spoken of the man often but when he did, the image he painted was grim. It was the rare topic on which he'd sensed Montag's insecurity, maybe even a little fear. "If he has sent this, then he is already here, in Europe." Raoul slapped the parchment down on the table.

"He is watching you." Simon looked pointedly at Raoul. "I also have people watching him. I know where he is, and what he plans. I am hoping you can explain to me his motive, for that I do not understand."

Raoul's eyes snapped up to Simon's. His own spies had lost Raganor's trail months ago. "Where?"

"He is in Aquitaine, asking about a woman named Eleanor. My source may have been confused, but he said she is a knight."

"He's looking for Eleanor." Raoul's blood ran cold. For years he had feared this, and now it was happening. Le Brun was back and looking for the one person in the world that he should never find.

"Who is she?" Simon asked.

Raoul laughed coldly. "Simon, you know her, though you have never met." Simon still looked confused, so Raoul shook his head. "Lady Eleanor de Levan, the knightess. She is my cousin, my father's bane, and if Raganor is already in Aquitaine, he has found her. If he has found her, he will soon have the very thing he needs to not only control The Order, but to keep control for generations after his death."

"She's the one—"

"Yes. Her son is the heir."

Simon reached forward to lean on the table next to Raoul, his wide eyes studying the knots of the wood as he digested this news. Lost in his thoughts, Raoul stared at the bloodstain on the floor. For all his cousin had been through, she still didn't know what was coming. She didn't know why Montag had made the decisions he had. Raoul did, though he had hoped he would never have to share. Eleanor only knew that terrible things had been done to her, and she had grown hard and independent as a result. It was better to live with anger and the assumption you've been wronged than to live in cold fear all your days from something you couldn't prevent from coming.

Simon broke the silence, his voice tight, "We need a plan."

The two men locked eyes, determination resounding between them. And then Raoul began to lay out to his unlikely ally all the ideas he had come up with over the past years. He had prayed he would never need to use one of them, but now it seemed as if they may need to set them *all* in motion.

"I will begin by flying the Le Brun crest from the keep." Raoul crossed his arms and walked to the window, watching out over the darkness blanketing the tree-tops below him. If Raganor's spies were watching Brunstein, let them watch the old stag Montag had banned snap in the wind. Let them tell the old man that his grandson knew he had returned and supported him. He doubted Le Brun would trust him—he hadn't lived to old age by making mistakes. And yet, the offering would be noted, and perhaps Le Brun would be just distracted enough to miss the other threads Raoul—and Montag—had been weaving. After all, it only took one thread, pulled the right way, to unravel an entire tapestry.

Chapter 3

Eleanor winced as she stepped in chicken manure, then scraped her shoe against the stone of the manor floor. At least it was only chicken manure, and not that of a cow—or worse, a pig. The manor was filled with crying children, bickering spouses, and the stench of an un-mucked barn. Her immaculate home had turned from refuge to prison. She strode past a cluster of bewildered hens, shooing them with skirts lifted out of the refuse of filthy rushes. Down the stairs she went, but the state of the kitchen was not much better. The cook was in a rare mood, banging pots and grumbling to himself. Eleanor pushed past him and out into the sunlight, not caring if it was still cold and her cloak was indoors.

She took a deep breath of fresh air, steadied her nerves.

"How long will this keep up, my lady?" a soft voice rose from her left.

Eleanor looked down to where her maid Collette sat on a bench, cloak tight around her as she nursed her youngest child. Eleanor pushed a wisp of hair from her forehead, then looked out over the estate. The messenger that had dropped dead had been buried where he fell; Eleanor didn't want anyone to touch him for fear of contagion, poison or not. Once they'd rolled him with spades into the grave, she'd covered him with a blanket after studying his face, as if she could have forgotten the man, his dying moments etched in her mind forever. She was certain she'd never seen him before, which only added to the mystery. And he had no identifier on his person or horse. Though everything he had was well made, showing he was no poor peasant, it was all plain and unremarkable. He could have come from anywhere.

That had been two weeks ago.

The first days with the manor locked down had been accepted with tense determination by the entire household. They protected their families and their most valuable possessions, their livestock. By the end of week one, the novelty had worn off and the inconvenience was made clear. By week two, after receiving no further threat, not even a passing traveler, everyone, including Eleanor, was frustrated. They wanted to go back to their homes. The animals wanted to be outside. The hall needed to be cleaned.

Eleanor felt like a fool for cooping them up in the first place. She'd acted on the word of a stranger. And yet, how had the man known her—and her grandfather's—name?

She racked her mind for how to explain the situation to Collette, and just as she was about to offer words, they both heard the rumble of a cart and looked up.

A humbly yet neatly dressed man, bundled warm in layers of wool, waved to them. Beside him ambled a donkey pulling a cart brimming with oiled-canvas bundles. The man smiled brightly and stopped the donkey in front of the women. "Bon Jorn!"

"Bon jorn," Eleanor answered tentatively. "And you are?"

"Name's Percy Miller, purveyor of the finest wool in Christendom. Would I be able to speak to the lord of the manor?"

"I am the lady of the manor," Eleanor said bluntly. She brushed her hands down her dirty dress. She was suddenly aware that she looked more like a peasant who'd woken up in a barn than a noble woman. She lifted her chin.

The merchant didn't miss a beat. "Ah, my lady, excellent. Please, come, look at the wool. Feel how soft." He went to the back of the wagon and opened a bundle. The donkey cocked a leg to rest, his long ears drooping low with fatigue and boredom.

Collette raised an eyebrow at her.

"It's not a good time, sir," Eleanor said. "Perhaps when you pass through next."

"Ah, but I never pass through twice. It's a great wide world out there, and I intend to travel it far and wide. This may be your only chance to purchase such a fine fabric as this. Or perhaps you would prefer something finer…a silk, perhaps?"

Eleanor couldn't help but smile a little. If she were to even touch a silk in her current state, she would ruin it with dirt. Surely, that mistake would force her to buy the man's wares. "Not today. Could you tell me though, how are things in the countryside?"

The man shrugged. "Not sure what you mean. Quiet. Not a lot of travelers willing to brave the elements as I."

"And Poitiers?"

"Lovely city. The nobility there bought quite a bit of my fabrics." He began to get the sense he wasn't going to make a sale and closed his wool bag.

"No armies on the roads?"

The merchant looked at her curiously, but remained silent. He leaned his hip against his wagon and crossed his arms.

Eleanor pursed her lips. "How much for a roll of wool?"

"What color?"

"Something plain. And very warm."

The merchant smiled and told her the price, revealing a roll of dark brown-grey wool that appeared worth every penny. At least he was an honest trader.

Eleanor nodded. "I'm not in need of wool at the moment, but perhaps we could trade a few yards for a hot meal?"

The trader hesitated, weighing his chances, then relented. "Fair enough, if you have hot wine as well."

"We do. Collette, could you fetch this man a plate and a skein of wine?"

Collette nodded and shouldered her baby, disappearing back into the manor.

Eleanor turned back to the merchant. "No mercenaries?"

"None." He shook his head. "No word of conflict in the taverns, not anywhere I've been. And I've been from London to Harfleur to Fougères to Poitiers..."

Eleanor felt her chest tighten at the mention of her late friend's home city. Even the passing of years had not erased the residual shock of losing Edmond de Fougères. She pushed the memories aside. "So nothing out of the ordinary?"

"Not that I've seen. Most folk seem like they're settling in for the winter. Came early this year. I wanted to be further south by now, get into the Mediterranean, before it snows."

Eleanor inhaled. Collette appeared with the food, which steamed in the cold. Eleanor pulled a coin from the pouch belted to her waist and placed it in the merchant's hand—the food was merely a tip for the information.

"Thank you, my lady." The merchant saluted her. He placed the wool in Eleanor's hands, and she hugged it to her. With a cluck to his donkey, they were off again, on to their next destination. The merchant ate as he walked, turning back once to lift the flagon of hot wine in thanks.

"What did he say?" Collette whispered.

"He says all is quiet." She gritted her teeth. "And I believe him." She didn't believe that the dead messenger was a liar though. Raganor was coming. Perhaps not soon. Perhaps not with an army. But he *was* coming.

She laid a hand on Collette's shoulder. "You can all go home. I'll tell everyone."

Collette's broad smile lightened her face, and she ducked inside to tell the cook. Eleanor followed her and smiled as he slammed a pot and said, "About time."

Eleanor ascended to the main hall, set her wool on a vacant table, and approached the hearth, her back straight. "Everyone gather!" Her voice carried with authority around the vast space. Her people quieted and listened. "The threat has passed for now. We must stay vigilant; report anything suspicious to me. But you may return to your homes."

A cheer rose, then suddenly everyone was talking at once. They dispersed with eager steps. Belongings were fetched. Eleanor's sister-in-law Marie approached, her youngest child in her arms. Her oldest—Godfrey—and Eleanor's son, Benec, trailed not far behind.

"Has it really passed, Eleanor?"

Eleanor dropped her voice. "No. But for now we are safe. Something is still coming, I just don't know what or when."

"Any word from Sir Alec?"

"No." Eleanor gazed around the room, biting her lip. "Marie, I didn't send for him. Or Wilfred. They have important work to do." She wasn't sure if she was a fool to not send a messenger for reinforcements two weeks ago, but in light of this false alarm, she would have been embarrassed to call the men home. It would have made no difference.

To her relief the other woman nodded with understanding. "They promised to be home before Christmas."

Eleanor squeezed her arm. "And they will be."

Benec gave her skirts a tug, and she reached down to pick him up. At almost two, he was a handful, but thankfully he had his cousin, who was only a few months older, to play with. He wrapped his arms around her neck, and she breathed him in, grateful for the warmth of his little body in her arms.

She pressed her lips to his brown hair, then turned back to Marie. "We're going to be fine." She believed it.

Chapter 4

Harfleur, Normandy

S ir Alec Earnblaec frowned at the grey outlines of the buildings before him, the damp enveloping him like a wet blanket. Only minutes off the ship and the chill already crept into his bones. It was about as cold as it could be without freezing. Snow would have been a relief from the inescapable drizzle. He pulled his hood up over his head and changed his stride to an irregular dance between the worst of the mud puddles. Already the wet was leaking into his boots, and though his feet were not yet cold, he knew as soon as he stopped walking, they would be.

The smells of fish and woodsmoke filled his nose, with an underlying note of sewage forcing him to shift his gaze warily to the river on his left. The docks of the port city of Harfleur were quiet today, the residents locked into their wood and plaster houses near their fires, hiding from the weather that only seasoned, or perhaps desperate, men traveled any distance in.

Alec was certainly a seasoned traveler, or at least he had been until he'd settled into a rhythm with his wife and son that had limited his reach to a small county within beautiful Aquitaine. He wasn't quite desperate yet, but the mission he was on was urgent. The king was dead. Prince—no, King—John had ascended the throne, and unfortunately, Alec's recent meeting with the new king had not gone well.

Alec had someone to see before he could go home to his wife.

A cart rattled up the muddy street, and he stepped off to the side to allow it to pass. The driver didn't look up, his head tucked down against the dreary mist. Alec wondered if the man knew that the King of England was dead, and the new king ruled. Had they shouted the news on every streetcorner, the heralds yelling themselves hoarse, barraged with questions? Did the people mourn? Or was it just a passing observation to them, as they put their heads down and leaned into the yokes of the labor that would put food on the table for another day?

Eleanor told him the common people would hardly notice. But in Alec's world, everything had been turned upside down. The drum of loss pounded in his temples, a headache threatening. He pressed his fingertips to the spot, feeling only partial relief. He needed to get some food into his body. The journey across the channel had been rougher and longer than usual. As if on cue, the smells of roasting meat blew on the breeze. He glanced up at the sign of a tavern, then shifted his gaze further ahead, to the long road that would carry him out of town. He gritted his teeth and passed the tavern. He would have time later to seek comfort in food. It would be better enjoyed after the message burning in his mind had been delivered.

The road turned to cobbles, and he picked up his pace. Normally Alec would casually glance into windows as he passed, wondering what life was like for people who did not spend months of their life on the road and had enough stability to accumulate material things, even if those things were simple furnishings and blankets. Alec had slept in borrowed beds for decades now, and beyond his sword and his crested ring, he owned nothing of sentimental value—except maybe the green ribbon he had tucked in the pouch on his belt. Eleanor...just the thought of his wife made his heart—and other parts—ache. The sooner he finished this business, the sooner he could return home. He hurried past, leaving the peasantry to their own doings.

He ducked into a side alley, again sidestepping mud and refuse. A small sign hung over the door of a wooden townhome, part of a line of haphazardly connected structures that stretched the length of the dim alley. The sign showed the voluptuous figure of a woman. Alec stopped in front of the door, then looked up at the sign, then down at the pile of rubbish to the left of the door. Was this really where she had moved to? His hand brushed his sword, its presence comforting, and then he pushed open the door. He had to duck his head to cross the threshold. He gave his eyes a moment to adjust to the dim light of the room beyond as the door clicked shut behind him.

The room was small, dark, and yet comfortably furnished with cushioned chairs and tables wide enough to dance on. It was also empty at this time of day. Alec pushed his hood back from his head as his cloak dripped on the wide-planked floor.

A door opened down the hall, and Alec took a step sideways to look. A board squeaked, and a half-asleep woman startled and let out a yelp. With a hand to her chest, she leaned against the wall.

"Oi, you scared me," she said, then straightened, pulling her shawl tighter around herself. Below it, she wore only her shift. "Madame's out on her weekly errands. We'll be open at dusk if you want to come back then." The woman held herself rigid, her young face hard with an unapproachable distain.

Alec averted his eyes, scanning the rest of the room, as if who he was looking for would appear. "I'm meeting someone. A woman with tan skin, black hair, and a Germanic accent. She told me I could find her here."

"The Raven? She's here." She shifted her shawl. "She expecting you?"

Alec gave a short nod.

The woman pushed away from the wall and turned up a flight of stairs. She reappeared a few minutes later, her frown deeper. "She says you can come up." Her hands went to her hips. "We're not supposed to conduct business without the Madame here. You try anything funny, I'll skin you alive."

Alec smiled. "No worries, my lady. I know what the Raven herself is capable of."

The woman pursed her lips, looking him up and down. Then she pointed her chin to the stairwell and took a step back. "Last door, end of the hall."

Alec tipped his head in thanks and went up, taking off his sodden cloak in the process. He tread down the hallway as quietly as he could, then knocked softly at the end door. A familiar voice bid him enter. He pushed open the door and closed it behind himself.

The room was bathed in candlelight, and the woman known as The Raven was lighting a last taper from another before setting it down as well. She turned to him, and he couldn't help but acknowledge her beauty. She was dark in a way that set her apart from other local women, her eyes deep pools of gold-brown that she had mastered control of, showing men only what she wanted them to see of her thoughts. She could scorch you with that gaze, or she could see right through you. She was older than Alec, but she had not aged as long as he'd known her. Clad in only a shift, she plucked a few pieces of clothing off a chair and gestured to it. After dropping most of the clothes on the bed, she shook out a dress and pulled it over her head. She turned her back to Alec and pulled her silken, raven-black hair to the side.

"Lace me?" she whispered.

Alec's fingers deftly tightened the laces. They were silent until he reached the last one, at the base of her back. "Why are you still here, Giselle?" He heard the tightness in his voice and hoped she heard it, too.

She laughed. "I've only been here a few months. How often do you think I should move?" Her accent, Germanic with a lilt of something else, added a music to the words. Or perhaps that was just how artful she was.

"I mean, doing this. This establishment is worse than the last. You could get a position in a castle, be a ladies' maid. Marry some rich merchant."

Giselle let her curtain of hair fall over her back and turned away, knotting the final lace herself. Her eyes flashed with a spark of anger. "Alec, I don't need to be rescued."

He shook his head and slouched into the chair she'd offered. She took a drink of wine and paced the room. He'd tried arguing with her in the past. She was as independent-minded as his wife, and probably smarter than the two of them combined. Giselle offered the bottle to him, and he took a drink. His eyes flicked up to her in surprise. The wine was a good, expensive variety.

Giselle smiled. "Do not mistake my living conditions for poverty. You, of all men, know I am playing a far greater game than most."

"You play a dangerous game. You know, the woman downstairs offered to skin me alive if I hurt you."

"She's a good one." Giselle's eyes grew sad. "She *should* be rescued." She took the bottle from Alec. "I'm working on it."

As she took a drink, Alec watched her. Those liquid pools of her eyes twinkled with challenge. He knew Giselle occasionally helped get girls out of the trade, though she herself seemed locked within it. He'd granted her freedom, but the allure of what she had always known and the vast coin it won her was too great. At least she now worked for herself, and not for those vile men in Alsace. It would be a waste of words to linger on the subject, so he changed it. "How long will you stay here?"

"Not long." She scrunched her nose and looked around. "Look at this place."

Alec didn't need to scan the room a second time. The place was vile. He kept his gaze on Giselle. "Where next?"

"Maybe a castle. I hear London is nice. But you'd know all about that now, eh? How's the king?"

Alec frowned. "He is no leader as his brother was. His kingdom is fracturing around him while he beds his latest mistress. His nephew, Arthur of Brittany, has made a grab for the crown."

"Hmm, perhaps I should set my sights on Paris instead?"

"King Philip of France supports Arthur. There may be a war."

"Well, that is news, isn't it?" She settled onto the bed and leaned back against the headboard thoughtfully. "Who's Arthur?"

"The teenage son of the late Prince Geoffrey."

"The prince that was killed in a tournament?"

"The same." Alec hesitated. "His claim is legitimate. For a while, King Richard had named him as heir. Only a year or two ago he started indicating John as successor, which needless to say, John has taken to heart. He's been crowned."

"Then the matter is settled."

"It's never as simple as that. A claim is a claim, and the support of the King of France means something."

"And who do you want to be king?"

Alec's eyes flicked to Giselle, who looked at him with a sly smile.

"I will support whoever the greater powers say is king," Alec replied carefully.

"You're learning." Giselle sat up and leaned towards him. "You haven't asked me anything. A good espier trades for such weighty news."

"I know you always like to receive before you give."

Giselle smiled and leaned back against the headboard. "I met someone interesting, a man with an Alsatian accent. He was quiet, polite. A little boring. But I mentioned I knew someone else with his accent, and he started to ask a lot of questions. Described a man that sounded an awful lot like Raganor, though that's not who I originally referred to."

"Who did you refer to?"

Giselle waved a hand. "Alec, you know where you found me." His mind flashed to a roadside inn in Alsace. "I referred to a list of men with Alsatian accents. Anyway, I finally pulled the name out of him, and he was indeed looking for old Raganor. I told him Raganor was in Poitiers, and he departed as if I had offered him a chest of gold. Then another man came a few days later, and he was looking for the Alsatian. His accent was a bit more Germanic, more northern. We had a good long conversation, flipped langues a bit, had a little fun. He left, but then last week he returned. I asked if he found the man he'd searched for and he said no, but he found someone else whom his employer wanted more."

"Who?"

"Wouldn't say, but based on what he did say, I have a feeling he found Raganor, which means the old man *is* still lingering in Poitiers. The German wouldn't say who his employer was either, try as I could."

Alec inhaled. Why was Eleanor's grandfather not moving on? "Did he say where in Poitiers he found Raganor?"

"No. If that's even who he searched for. Either way, I'm not going to linger and let that man lead Raganor here."

"Send word that you're safe after you move."

"Yes, Mother." She rolled her eyes.

"Giselle—"

"I'll be fine, Alec." She reached to him and laid a hand on his knee. After an awkward moment she removed it. "How is your wife?"

"She was well when I left. I miss her."

"I bet you do. She's prettier than you described. Did you tell her about us?"

"I said we're friends."

Giselle shook her head. "You're still a fool, Alec. You better tell her all of it before someone else does. It's more harmless if you're honest now."

Alec narrowed his eyes at Giselle. "I have been nothing but faithful to her—"

"My bet is that's not the entirety of what she asked. Bold move, showing up with her like you did last summer. She took it well. At least outwardly." Giselle rose. Their meeting was over.

Alec glared at her. She, as usual, was right. Eleanor had asked if he'd ever partook of Giselle's services. He'd answered that *we are only friends*. Past tense answered with the present. That probably didn't constitute as a full answer.

Giselle cocked her head to the side, as if reading his thoughts. If she could discern them, she didn't comment. She turned away and began blowing out the candles. "I'll send word if I learn more. But I'm done with Raganor, Alec. Darkness surrounds him." She avoided his gaze, but he could sense from her posture just how much her history with Raganor le Brun haunted her. She'd left Poitiers not long after Alec had told her Raganor was there, and even now intended to skip to another country entirely.

"Are you alright, Giselle?"

She hesitated, only the light of the last candle illuminating her expression. That hesitation told Alec everything, though the determination with which she closed off her expressions proved she could not yet be dissuaded to leave the life of seduction and secrets she had long lived behind. "I am always fine, Alec. Go home." She blew out the last candle and they were plunged into darkness. Alec felt her hand on his chest as she pushed him the last step out the door, and then there was a quiet click as she closed it. He stood there a long moment staring at the bare wood, wondering what more he could do for her, then left the brothel.

As always, Giselle's information had proved invaluable. Raganor was lingering in Aquitaine. Had he yet found Levan Manor? Why he was there at all was still a mystery, likely one that would only be solved by speaking to the man directly. If Alec was brave, he would ride south by way of Poitiers, and look for Raganor himself. It may be time to settle this once and for all. Alec pushed his hunger headache aside, eager to ride on and get home in as few days as possible.

The further south he rode, the more convinced he was that he needed to meet Raganor face to face. Monsters didn't look so scary when you saw them in the daylight, just like a king somehow seemed less like a king, more human, when you could see the sweat beaded on his brow or the food stuck in his teeth. Perhaps Raganor would be the same. When he arrived at Poitiers a few days later, he searched. Every tavern, brothel, and way house had the same answer.

No one had seen Raganor le Brun. He had vanished yet again.

Chapter 5

December 1199

Levan Manor, Aquitaine, France

Levan Manor was peaceful as Alec rode into the dark courtyard. The earliest pinks of dawn were just beginning to light the horizon, and even the roosters were still sleeping. He put his horse in the stable, the new arrival waking the other equids. They nickered a greeting, asking for breakfast. A stableboy appeared, his eyes bright despite the hour.

"Welcome home, Sir Alec," he said politely.

Alec gave him an encouraging smile and allowed him to take over his horse's care. He gave his other horses a look over—all well—and then headed into the manor.

He was exhausted, but sleep was not on his mind.

His pulse quickened as he pushed open the door to the lord's bedroom, a private sanctuary under the eaves of the manor's roof. Eleanor was curled in the middle of their bed, his pillow clutched to her chest, her dark brown hair tangled around her.

If there had ever been a doubt that she was the woman he was meant to be with—and there hadn't been—it would have been erased. She was his, through and through. He felt himself drawn to her, wanting to protect, cherish, love her as if drawn by an invisible thread. There was a physical need, after so long away, but this was more than lust.

It was a need to be one.

She was his second half.

Alec's lips traced a trail of kisses up her bare shoulder to her neck, feather light. As he moved, he watched her slumbering form. She shifted just slightly into him, so he tucked himself behind her and cradled her body to his own. She stirred.

"I love you," he whispered.

She made a noise between a moan and a sigh, refusing to open her eyes. But her fingers interlaced with his as she pulled him around her like a blanket. Her sleepy recognition encouraged him. He again kissed her shoulder, and when she still refused to stir, he gently freed his hand that it could roam the rest of her body. She was clad only in her shift, which was bunched up to her waist from what appeared to have been a restless night. It allowed him access to the places he had missed the most.

Despite her half-sleep, her body revealed she had missed him, too.

He propped himself on his arms over her, and she rolled onto her back, eyes still firmly shut. He kissed her lips. At first they were still, but as his lips teased she woke enough, probably in a dream, for them to follow his with a gentleness they rarely were patient enough for when awake. He smiled to himself, pausing to gaze down at her. Even now she tried to curl into him, her head tucking into the crook of his elbow. He gently kneed her legs apart and lowered himself onto and into her body. She moaned, eyes fluttering only slightly. He kissed her again, and she kissed back, a little more awareness in her movements now. They stayed like that a long moment, then he started to move.

As the tempo built, Eleanor woke. Her hips rose to match Alec's, and her eyes flew open to lock on his, to meet his challenge. After the wave crested, they lay together, Alec again trailing light kisses across her lips and jaw. Her arms tightened around him to hold him still.

"Good morning," he murmured.

"Uhm."

"Did you miss me?"

"Uhm, hmm."

He chuckled.

"I had longer to sleep, you know."

"I couldn't wait."

"Hmph."

Alec moved to get up, but Eleanor locked her muscled legs around him and pulled him tight. "No!"

He laughed again but yielded to his wife. "So you did miss me?"

She kissed him in response and sighed into his shoulder. "How was England? The voyage?"

Alec propped himself on his elbow and frowned. "We have a lot to talk about. But later."

"That bad?"

"Pretty bad." He kissed her forehead. "May I get dressed now?"

She shook her head and latched onto him, adding her arms to their entanglement. "I haven't seen you in weeks. And I have that time before I need to get up still…"

"Insatiable—"

She kissed him hard. In a movement, she rolled them both, still joined, that she now sat astride him. "I love you, Alec Earnblaec." Her fingers caressed his jaw as she studied him with a sober expression. Then they lost themselves in their kiss, using their time well.

Eleanor knew it would come as soon as they left the confines of their room. Sure enough, it did, that metamorphosis of an affectionate husband and wife into civil partners managing two complicated, distant estates. It was subtle, perhaps so much so that Alec didn't feel it. She did though, as he dropped her hand to reach for the plate of ham and eggs that Collette set before them. She could see his eyes roaming the hall, checking on each tenant, on the manor's orderliness. It must have met his approval, for he refocused on his food as if he hadn't had a real meal in weeks. She understood. Long days of travel were hard and getting good food in winter, even with a full coin purse, could be challenging.

She gave him a few minutes, picking at her food, wondering how to reveal all that had transpired in his absence, then asked, "So how were things in England?"

Alec took a swallow of ale to wash down his food. "Depends which part you are referring to."

Eleanor set down her food. The tension in his body, though his posture remained casual, warned her of the gravity of his news. "Start with the king. Did you meet?"

"Only briefly." His eyes flicked to Eleanor's, then back to his plate. "He is not King Richard. We are not in his favor."

She frowned. "We will be as loyal to him as we were King Richard. Surely he assumes that?"

"King John assumes nothing." Alec hesitated, as if debating if he should tell her something. He paused to meet her eye. "Lady Gwen was at the White Tower in London. She warned me that your uncle and the king were once friends. Because of the circumstances of Lord Montag's death, she feels the king is keeping an even closer eye on us."

Now that was a connection she hadn't anticipated her uncle having. Alec leaned towards her and whispered, as if to sink the point in deeper, "I did not discuss it with Gwen, but this Order your grandfather and uncle were a part of...it may still have other members."

"Like King Jo—"

"Yes," Alec cut her off, his eyes flicking towards the tenants around them, though they seemed oblivious to their conversation. "Though I cannot say for sure without proof."

Eleanor understood his caution; they were likely being watched from within. It would not be the first time someone in their household betrayed them. She pressed her lips into a line and let her gaze roam, wondering who it could be this time. Meanwhile, Alec began telling her about his estate, the great castle there, how organized the castellan was, how well the old household from Neroche had settled in, how much they raised in trade each year. She began to feel self-conscious of her own small estate, which though now showing a meager profit, did little to compare to the grand estate in England that Alec described. It was obvious where his pride lay. How could she voice how much Levan Manor meant to her after all they had gone through to reclaim it? Her thoughts wandered back to the threats surrounding them, until Alec dropped a bag of coins in front of her with a solid clunk. She stared at the heavy bag, then raised her wide eyes to meet his.

He smiled at her. "The earnings from the estate, after taxes, after leaving enough behind for maintenance until I return. Eleanor, I feel like real nobility now."

She couldn't help but smile. "Alec, you've always been real nobility."

"You know what I mean."

Their eyes met, gazes laced with just a hint of sadness. She knew all too well what he'd felt as a poor noble; she'd been one herself most of her life. For years she had chosen that path, living in hiding. Alec had almost lost everything, his family smeared by the accusation of treason. Even after revenge and the reinstatement of property, Alec had not forgotten those years he had been forced to live as a knight-errant.

Alec lurched into another confabulation about his many plans for his manor. Eleanor felt as if she'd burst.

"I received a messenger about three weeks ago," she blurted.

Alec froze, his mouth open mid-speak. Slowly he closed it, the lines on his face sharpening.

Eleanor met his eye, her hands fisted at her sides. "He died after telling me Raganor was on his way."

Alec straightened, that warrior's fire rushing through him in a transformation Eleanor never grew tired of watching. "You didn't lock down the manor?"

"I did. For two weeks. No attack came. No armies have been spotted."

He again scanned the room. He would not see evidence of the barnyard the manor had been those weeks. It was cleaned as well as new again, the rushes fresh and strewn with mint. To his credit, Eleanor could tell he now recognized this. He turned back to her with greater respect.

"Who was the messenger?"

"We don't know. We buried him where he fell, across the fields. He was sick from something, likely poison, but we didn't want to chance the plague."

"Nothing on him? A ring? Letters? A sword?"

"Nothing you can't find at any market in Christendom. Even his horse is as plain a rouncey as can be."

"You trust his message?"

"I did." She hesitated. "But no attack came. Now I don't know what to believe. We couldn't live in fear forever." A defensive edge entered her tone. What else could she have done? Maybe Alec would have sent out a search sooner, looking for the source of the warning. She hadn't thought of that at the time, only the protection of her people.

"No, you made the right decisions. On all accounts."

The shouts of children echoed from the stairwell. Alec turned and smiled as several of the household's children ran into the hall, laughed as they settled onto the benches at one of the long tables, and helped themselves to breakfast. Fair, round-figured Marie emerged after them, one toddler clutching her skirts as he waddled towards the others, falling occasionally, another on her hip sucking his thumb, and a babe swaddled against her chest. Eleanor's face lit up as she reached out her arms for the nearly two-year-old child on Marie's hip.

"Benec, sweetheart, look who's home," she said as the boy reached for her. Eleanor gave Marie a grateful look, then turned Benec in her lap towards Alec. He brushed the boy's cheek with a finger. Bright blue eyes, like her own, blinked at him. Benec didn't reach for Alec as he did Eleanor, but he didn't fuss either. "Did you sleep well?" Eleanor cooed.

Benec turned from Alec to start reaching for food off their plates, most of which he would likely throw instead of eat. Eleanor caught his fingers and gave him something he could chew.

Alec stared. "I think he gets bigger every time I see him."

"Of course he does. If he's going to take after you, he's got quite a long way to go." Eleanor smiled.

Benec began fussing until Eleanor set him down, then toddled on wobbly legs towards the other children. When he reached them, two of the older ones pulled him up onto the bench with them. Marie and Wilfred's little boy Godfrey wrapped his arm around Benec as if they were brothers. Eleanor leaned her chin on her hand, watching them with contentment. She looked over to smile at Alec, only to see he too stared at the children, his face an unreadable mask. When he felt her gaze, he quickly turned back to his food.

At that moment, Wilfred stepped into the hall. Marie let out a yelp of joy and ran into his arms. Alec rolled his eyes. Eleanor shot him a knowing look as she pushed away from the table. She thought his half-brother's passionate romance was as overexaggerated as he did.

"Wilfred, welcome back," Eleanor said as he approached, his wife on his arm. He released Marie just long enough to give Eleanor a brief hug.

"Good to be back. Seems there's a full-on reunion today. How was England?" Wilfred's smile didn't fade as he turned to Alec.

Alec grumbled into his food. "Long story."

Wilfred turned back to Eleanor, an eyebrow raised. She shrugged.

Marie clung to Wilfred's arm. "We were under siege for two weeks!"

"What?" Wilfred turned to his wife, eyes wide.

Marie began to regale him of the exciting manor lockdown as she led him over to the breakfast table. Eleanor and Alec were again alone. Eleanor let her head fall into her hands, the weight of the encroaching dangers pressing from all sides.

"I thought with Montag and Lezay dead, I would finally be able to stop looking over my shoulder every few minutes. Oh how naïve I was."

Alec reached across the table and pulled one of her hands into his own. That simple touch was all she needed as reassurance.

"Eleanor—I've been thinking about this since we saw Raganor—do you think your cousin Raoul would tell me more about this Order? If your uncle and Lezay were part of it, I'm sure he was, too. Maybe he could tell us more about Raganor. I tried to find Raganor, in Poitiers, but he's moved on. If that messenger died trying to tell you Raganor is coming…that's not something I'd discount."

"I can't act as if we are under siege forever—"

"I know. I'm not saying that. I think I should go to Alsace. Speak with Raoul."

Eleanor pursed her lips. She knew perfectly well that Alec didn't like her cousin and childhood friend, Lord Raoul of Brunstein. The man had appeared fickle when they last had met. Now, as word had it, he was reigning over his land in Alsace with the same fearless power as his father Montag before him. His connections were deep. Surely, Alec was right and Raoul knew things. But what did that matter? It wasn't worth the long journey to have that knowledge.

Eleanor gave her head a firm shake. "Alec, I'm not going back there. I swore I'd never set foot in that castle again. Every time I go back I add horrible memories."

He caressed the hand he still held with his thumb, sending a pleasant shiver through her. "I'll be back before you know it."

"No, Alec. You are staying here for the winter."

"Eleanor, I refuse to be caught unaware. We need answers."

She pulled her hand away, glaring. "You just got back. You are not going to that place without me. And I'm not going."

"I won't be long—"

"No!" Her voice carried across the hall, and the tenants quieted. She dropped it an octave as she pulled the words from deep within. "I do not ask you to stay because I can't handle things alone. I just don't want to. The threat is real, and it has not passed. Give me the winter with you."

She knew what she was asking. There was quite a lot of money to be made by him continuing to travel, offering his services to the Norman lords as they prepared for the feud between King John and Arthur of Brittany. He had his own estate in England to maintain, after all. He could go there, be free of her family debacle. Alsace aside, there were plenty of places for him to be other than her little manor.

Meanwhile, she had a duty to her liege lord to run this place. It was her responsibility, and asking for help seemed selfish and weak. He was right; she would be fine alone. Still, her intuition had burned since the messenger had died in front of her. More was coming. She longed for Alec to stand beside her. Willingly. Though perhaps willingness was too much to ask. His posture said he was still ready to leave, to insist it was more important to speak with Raoul than winter in Aquitaine. That cut her in a way no sword could. She averted her eyes, steeled herself for the rejection that was surely coming. When she spoke, bottled pain shook her tone in a way it had not in years.

"Be careful how much you force me to be independent."

Alec studied her, that muscle in his jaw working. "Unless the king calls me away, I will stay."

Relief flowed over Eleanor like the welcoming heat of a hearth-fire. "Thank you." She leaned clear across the table and kissed his bristled lips. "Take today to rest." She picked up their plates and headed towards the kitchen, looking over her shoulder a last time.

While Wilfred was busy talking to Marie, his two children crawling in his lap, Benec slipped down from the bench and toddled towards Alec. Eleanor tracked Alec's gaze as he watched the little boy fall, pick himself up, and continue on the seemingly long journey between tables. At last he made it to Alec's side, looking up at him with big blue eyes. Alec met the gaze with a slight smile, then lifted the boy by his armpits onto his lap. Benec wrapped his arms around Alec's neck. Alec was so surprised he didn't move, then curled his own strong arms around the child.

Eleanor turned away, blinking quickly, a smile twitching at her lips.

It was nice to have Alec home again.

Chapter 6

"Oh, Lady Eleanor, not yet!" Marie caught her hand and pulled her back towards the hearth, where a crowd of villagers was gathered, drinking, laughing, and talking. Someone had even procured a lute to accompany the bawdy songs that occasionally rang out from part of the crowd.

"You have fun." Eleanor withdrew her hand gently. "I have a bit of a headache."

Marie pouted playfully, then with a "Feel better!" danced back towards the group.

Eleanor smoothed the folds of her skirts, watching as the former maid, now nursemaid, looped her arms naturally around Wilfred. He laced his fingers into hers without breaking his conversation. Alec was engrossed in his own discussion. Benec was fast asleep with the other children in Wilfred and Marie's room off the main hall, an arrangement decided when he'd returned to Levan Manor as an infant. It had enabled him to be close to his wet nurse, and now he enjoyed being close to his cousins. Eleanor was not needed, headache or no. And though her head physically felt fine, the thoughts swirling in it were not.

As she walked up the stairs she rubbed her forehead. Never one for crowds, she was greatly out of practice. The day had been busy, but good. The gathering in the hall was well deserved. The past year had practically been solitary confinement in the absence of tournaments and busy castles brimming with people. At times she missed the excitement, the charge of human emotion in the air. Then, nights like this, she remembered how much she enjoyed solitude.

"Never content, are you Eleanor?" she muttered to herself.

She sank onto the edge of her bed and slouched forward, elbows on her knees as she studied her hands. Her father's pewter ring was on her right thumb, Alec's wedding band on her left ring finger. Callouses from working the manor farm and years of sword practice etched her palms. She was an anomaly if ever there was one. She could play the role of ladylike beauty, a humble peasant, or deadly warrior.

Though she didn't get to be that last role anymore.

The hours of listening to Alec and Wilfred's adventures were what had done her in, she thought. They had seen so much over the past months, met so many new people. Alec had even met the king for goodness sake. Traveling across kingdoms, feeling alive with adventure, was what she missed. When she became a knight, that was how she imagined her life. Hours on a powerful horse, seeing new places. Occasional fights for good causes. A comradery with fellow knights that knew no boundaries.

Instead, she was the perfect lady of the manor. Organized, kind, strategic, fair, reliable.

That is good, she told herself. Yet somehow it still didn't feel like enough. No one wanted to listen to stories about how the lady of the manor made a deal with a busy local tavern to supply all their wine for a year, thus guaranteeing the manor income. No, it was far more exciting to hear about meeting the king or squashing rebellion at some remote castle. As a lady and mother, she should be content, as Marie was. But no. That role was complicated even on days when she wasn't lost in frustrations.

Laughter rang from down below. Had anyone other than Marie even noticed she was gone? Better if they didn't. They deserved their fun. All of them had worked hard for it. They would have had a harvest celebration well before now if the threat of attack hadn't come on like a black cloud. She sighed, then rose to look out the small attic window, where a warm firelight glow flickered on the branches of the trees. She watched it for a moment, the visual reminiscent of nights along the road, a campfire the warm reprieve of the day.

There was a shout outside, and then another. She frowned. There should be no campfire. Were the villagers taking the party outside? She sighed and returned to the main hall, ready to chastise whoever was burning firewood unnecessarily. It seemed like most of the group was still by the hearth. She slipped down the stairs to the lower level, then opened the front door. Eleanor froze, blood draining from her face, before reeling back with the quick heartbeat of panic. The granary, which stored all their hay and grain for the winter, was ablaze.

She shouted into the manor, then ran, her thoughts narrowed with the rush of fear. Two men had already started throwing buckets of water on the spreading flames.

Within seconds, the men in the manor rushed to draw buckets to douse the flames, Alec and Wilfred among them.

"The children?" she shouted to Wilfred as she hefted full buckets in either hand.

"All safe with a few of the women," he called back, throwing water on the fire and running back to the well.

For a moment, she thought they would manage to put it out. Then the flames took off with a whoosh as the straw mound caught. Alec took hold of her upper arm and pulled her back. Her heart thudded as the roar grew louder. The wind picked up, the fire pulling the air around them with hungry appetite. She headed again towards the well, panic rising. They couldn't lose everything they had grown this year. A whole harvest—

Alec again took hold of her arm, and she shook him off in impatience. He reclaimed her shoulder, firmer this time, and pulled her to face the direction he pointed, towards the manor. There was a man dressed in black walking up the front steps.

"Who is that?" Alec asked.

Eleanor scanned the scene. Almost all the household and villagers were outside, fighting the flames. In the chaos, she couldn't identify each one, but it was odd that anyone, save one of the women, would be heading into the manor. And most of the women were fighting the fire, skirts tucked out of the way, arms straining from the weight of their buckets. She looked back as the man in black slipped through the manor door.

Without discussion, she and Alec both sprinted toward the manor. She pushed through the door first, scanning the room. The man in black was at the foot of the stairs to the upper level, but when he saw them, he turned and sprinted toward the kitchen.

"Marie!" Eleanor called out. She took the stairs two at a time as Alec rushed after the man into the kitchen.

Marie appeared, her eyes round with worry.

Eleanor pushed past her into the room where the children slept, each curled in exhaustion and oblivious to the excitement outside. Benec lay back-to-back with his cousin in his trundle, thumb in his mouth.

Eleanor pulled herself away, laying a hand on Marie's arm. "Bar the doors. Someone was here." Marie nodded and followed Eleanor out. Eleanor listened for the sound of the board sliding home across the door, then turned her focus back to the fiery scene before her.

Alec met her, his sword now belted to his side. She wished she had grabbed hers while she'd been in the manor. Alec's jaw was tense with exertion, a bloodlust thrumming just below the surface. "He rode off. You didn't recognize him?"

"I couldn't see." She looked down the road the man had ridden, but all was dark and quiet. Before her the fire cracked, another part of the granary catching. Pursuit of the man would have to wait.

A few dozen buckets of water later, and Eleanor threw her empty bucket down with fury, the bright flames lighting the dark night like the fires of hell. They might as well be. They had swallowed everything the manor needed to make it through winter. A whole year's worth of work, two years' worth of building, gone in a few hours. Every beam of the granary was now ablaze.

Alec joined her, setting his buckets down to wipe soot from his face. The black streak only smeared more. Their bucket line had broken as the villagers realized their fight was futile. They were breaking off one by one to watch the inferno.

"Augh!" Eleanor's fury pierced the night. Nothing was in there that could have started a fire. The chimneys of the manor were far away, as were those of the cottages. No stray sparks. That was why they built the granary there.

This was no accident. She propped her hands on her hips and glared at the fire, which seemed to rage higher beneath her gaze. The timbers cracked. The smell of woodsmoke filled her nose, but she did not feel warm and at home as she usually did with that smell. She sweated from her exertion, only to have the sweat chill her back as she stood apart from the raging heat before her.

Wilfred joined them, standing at Eleanor's other side in breathless amazement. "I'm sorry, Eleanor. It's no use."

"I know." She wiped at a tear of frustration. The soot on her finger burned her eye, only making it tear more. She blinked rapidly, her hand falling back to her hip. "At least no one is hurt." She glanced up at the manor. The children were all safe, with Marie watching over them. She could see her profile in the window, watching. She scanned the crowd, counting heads. All here. And no sign of the man who'd gone into the manor. Now they all stood by and watched the flames lick the sky, sparks drifting like a cloud of fireflies.

"Who would do this?" Wilfred asked, his eyes still locked on the flames.

Before she could answer, her attention was seized by a falling beam, a shower of sparks exploding around it.

Though Eleanor longed to sink to her knees with weariness, that was not something a lady did. She had to be strong for her people. They would look to her for what to do. She gritted her teeth. This was the second time the manor—or at least part of it—had been burned since she had inherited it. That was not a good impression for the greedy lords circling, hoping the now-productive land would be reassigned.

The flames grew hotter, and they all stepped back. The household was starting to turn to her, their expressions dour. Eleanor motioned with her hands for them to gather around. They approached in somber bunches until they were gathered in a circle, the heat of the fire warming their backs, the smoke ingrained in their clothes and skin following them like a woody perfume in the crisp December air.

"Everyone all right?" Eleanor looked out over the bobbing heads, her heart breaking with their downcast faces. "Tomorrow we will salvage what we can."

"It won't be enough," a man grumbled, kicking the dirt.

Eleanor sighed. "No, it won't. But we will work something out."

Frustration lined grim faces. They knew, as did she, that their chances of finding enough hay and grain to keep their animals and themselves fed for the winter were slim. It had been a meager harvest across Aquitaine, and though Eleanor had been confident and proud that her manor had enough for winter, things were now much more difficult. Would there be enough? Could she buy more? Anyone that had hay or grain would want a premium price at this time of year. Perhaps there was a merchant in Poitiers with money to lend, but he would demand interest, rightly so. She rubbed her forehead, then turned back to her household, her friends.

"We will assess the situation in the morning. What matters now is that we keep this fire from spreading to the other buildings." To punctuate her statement, the roof of the granary fell in, shooting flames into the air higher than the roof of the manor behind them. Eleanor swallowed. Fear flickered in the eyes of the household as they watched. The fire seemed to quiet after that though, and one by one the villagers turned back to their lady.

"Is this what you warned was coming?" someone in the crowd asked.

She hesitated, then admitted her fear. "I am afraid so. And we must be ever more vigilant. This may not be the end of their attack."

She swallowed. Would her villagers leave? These were free men and women, not serfs. They'd been brought on to rebuild the manor, and many had stayed. Now how long would they last with limited food and a threat of violence hanging over their heads?

"We will stand with you," Gregory the Hunter called out, his wife Collette at his side nodding.

"As will we, my lady!" another pair of tenants called out.

The call repeated around the courtyard, until Eleanor's eyes blurred with tears. She exhaled a shaky breath, fighting to hide her emotion. She had never dreamed of such loyalty, such respect. These were her people, and she would do anything in her power to give them the life they were working so hard for.

"Thank you. All of you." She straightened. "We will get through this." The fire cracked behind them as if to argue. Eleanor gritted her teeth, willing herself to believe her own words. "Spread out. Keep full buckets with you. Watch for sparks. It's going to be a long night."

They dispersed with stoic faces.

She turned back to Alec and Wilfred. Wilfred still watched the fire, frustration lined in his face. Alec watched her, his eyes sparking with his own unspoken fear and anger. As she held his gaze, she thought of the conversation they had had that morning. How much should they say in front of Wilfred?

Wilfred's face was alight with the fire's glow, lines casting shadows that aged him beyond his twenty years.

Eleanor spun in a circle, taking in the stone manor with its newly cut beams that had turned from ruins to house not long ago. The cottages of her village, which was ever expanding as the manor started to prosper into a productive, lucrative estate, stood only a short distance from the blazing granary, which up until an hour ago had been the second largest structure on the property. Now it was a pile of blue-flamed coals. They had worked so hard to establish this, to make this place not only a home but a prosperous asset. The past summer had given Eleanor hope as to just how successful they could be.

After a long silence, the only sound the crack of burning wood, Wilfred turned to them. "You left, running into the manor. What happened?"

"A stranger thought he could sneak in while we were distracted," Alec said, his voice edged. "And when he saw us, he ran out the kitchen and rode away."

"Who?"

"Now that's the question, isn't it? My guess is he's the one that did this."

The dying messenger's face flashed in Eleanor's memory. The stranger had ridden to his death to warn her of this. Months ago, in a brothel outside of Poitiers, she had been told a story of a man who liked to burn things. The man that had sprinted away was not old Raganor. But it was well known that the well-connected man did not work alone.

Had Raganor le Brun, her grandfather, found her manor at last?

Chapter 7

The wreckage of the granary looked no better in the daylight. Remnants of smoke drifted in the winter air, the mid-morning light a cloudy grey that echoed Eleanor's mood. They had lost a great deal. It was going to be difficult, if not impossible, to resupply at this time of year. Eleanor kicked a smoldering piece of wood, and it landed in a pile of ash, what once had been grain.

Eleanor stood alone before the rubble, her eyes stinging from exhaustion and smoke. It was a few hours past dawn, and the villagers were asleep. They deserved their rest after the long night keeping watch over the fire. By some miracle, it had not spread. Eleanor was grateful for the moment of solitude as she attempted to process what had happened. She had only a few hours to come up with answers to the questions that surely raged in everyone's minds

Why? How? What's next?

She'd mulled such questions over in her mind all night, even in the few hours in which she attempted sleep after the fire was tamed. She did not like any of the options at hand. The arsonist had her attention. His willingness to harm left her with a lump in her stomach.

She hugged her arms to her sides, her cloak pulled tight against the icy breeze. The air smelled like snow. She heard the door to the manor open and close behind her, and turned just enough to see who it was. Alec. She sighed. At least he was home for all this. Had the arsonist known? What if it had been only her, and Alec and Wilfred were not by her side last night? Would the perpetrator have lit more fires, destroyed everything?

What would he have taken from inside the manor if Alec hadn't seen him?

Alec came up behind her and put his arms around her shoulders, his lips pressing into the back of her head.

"Not what you expected to come home to, is it?" Eleanor said quietly.

"No. But it could have been worse. Everyone is fine."

"I know." She sighed, leaning back against him. "Thank you for your help last night."

"Of course."

"Do you…" She hesitated. "Do you think someone followed you from England?"

"I usually notice if I'm followed. But I thought the same thing. The timing is strange. I suppose someone could have followed Wilfred home as well."

"That's true." She sucked in a breath. "Alec, you know how Raganor likes fire?"

"Yes."

They stood in silence a long moment. They had learned that Eleanor's grandfather had used burns to punish, as well as in some kind of dark ceremony. The use of fire to destroy was not exactly his signature, but it certainly ran along the same theme. Burn to purge.

"Why not just come out and tell us what he wants?" Eleanor asked. "Why terrorize and destroy?"

Alec was silent. Eleanor pulled away and turned to him, studying his thoughtful expression.

"Maybe he wants more than we would be willing to give."

Eleanor gestured to the granary. "They just destroyed a year's harvest. Our income! What do they gain from that? How can we afford to give anyone anything now?"

Alec gazed at the smoking ruins. "The fire was a distraction."

Eleanor's eyes narrowed. A pit settled into her stomach.

Alec took a deep breath. "What we learned a few months ago about Raganor, and what Montag told you the night he died—" He bit his lip. "What if Montag taking our son wasn't just for his own reasons? What if there was a driving force behind his actions?"

Suddenly Eleanor felt nauseous. She thought back to how her uncle had kidnapped Benec, via a trusted maid, as soon as he was born. She never wanted to feel that panic and grief she'd woken from childbed fever into again. "Like The Order?"

Alec nodded.

"You think they want to kidnap him again?"

"It would make sense, wouldn't it?"

The edges of Eleanor's vision danced with stars, and she realized she wasn't breathing. She gasped, filling her lungs, but then doubled over, hands pressed to her sides. When she stood, she felt as if every nerve was on fire with the force of the blaze the night before. She looked to the smoking ruins, then back to Alec, then back to the manor that housed her son.

"Who are they? And what could they possibly want with a child?" She steepled her fingers and pressed them to her lips. "I don't have time to figure this out, do I? Raganor knows we're here."

Alec reached for her, and she let him fold her into his arms. "We're aren't going to let Benec go."

Her body remained rigid. "They already took him once."

"It won't happen again. We'll hide him."

"Where? Raganor found us. We should have just spoken with him when we saw him in Poitiers. Maybe then this would all be cleared up."

The sound of hoofprints drew their attention to the courtyard. Alarm softened to relief on seeing Wilfred.

"Good morning," Wilfred said tentatively, glancing from one to the other before dismounting. The tension was palpable. "Did I miss something?"

"Where were you?" Alec demanded.

Wilfred patted his big chestnut horse, Harlequin. "I couldn't sleep, so I followed the tracks of our arsonist."

Alec straightened. "And?"

"He's dead on the road about five miles down. Skull is split like he fell from his horse. And before you ask, yes, I'm certain it was him. He was dressed in black, no item by which to identify him. The horse is gone. It reminds me of how Marie described your messenger." Wilfred raised his eyebrows at Eleanor.

She nodded. "Sounds like it. What did you do with the body?"

Wilfred pursed his lips. "I didn't touch it." He crossed himself. "May God forgive me, but I didn't want to draw any more attention to this manor. You've had enough dead men as of late. Add more, and people are going to start talking."

"Wise," Alec whispered.

"So, before someone else falls over dead, any idea who we are dealing with?" Wilfred slipped from his saddle, twisting his reins in his hands.

Alec hesitated, then turned to Wilfred. "We found out in the beginning of the summer that Eleanor's grandfather, Montag's father, is still alive. This is his doing.

And he may want to kidnap Benec. He may be part of the reason that Montag kidnapped the boy in the first place."

Wilfred's eyebrows shot up. "What is wrong with your family, Lady Eleanor?"

She shook her head and studied the ground.

"Well, why would he want a little boy?"

"We don't know," Eleanor said quietly. She kicked a rock. "It is hard to fight against a ghost you cannot see." She couldn't bring herself to say more, her mind roiling with emotions.

Alec explained, "His reputation precedes him as a devil. And when I went to face him, he disappeared." He turned to Eleanor. "We need answers. We need to speak to Raoul. There is no one left to ask but him."

Eleanor inhaled, then turned to Wilfred. "Alec and I need to go to Alsace, to Brunstein. Maybe Raoul can tell us why Montag—and now my grandfather—was so keen to abduct my child." Eleanor bit her lip. It was a lot to ask, but there was no one she trusted more than Wilfred and Marie. Her gaze flicked to Alec and then met Wilfred's eyes. He blinked, brow furrowing at the intensity of her expression. *Yes, this is how it must be done.* She took a deep breath, knowing what she asked was no small request. "If you and Marie are willing to make the journey, I think Alec's castle will be the safest place for Benec. And for Marie and your children. And Marie's family is there." She bit her lip. "It is a long trip, particularly in winter. But you are the only one who can get him there."

Wilfred looked from one of them to the other. "This is drastic. You need to tell me who your grandfather is. Most people like their grandfathers." He shrugged. "And their uncles for that matter, though I don't blame you after meeting that one. Montag wasn't exactly young himself, so how old is this grandfather? He must be ancient. Is he really a threat?"

Alec answered. "He is one of the most powerful men I've heard of. Like a king, but he is not bound to the duties of a king. He is wealthy, and he has extensive, dangerous connections. And he is not afraid to take his power through murder. The dead man in the road failed, which I'm sure is the reason he is dead. The earlier messenger learned too much and was poisoned." Alec met Wilfred's eye, as if to drive this knowledge home. "He has spent most of his life in the far east, but we saw him in Poitiers just a few months ago. And yes, he is old. I estimate him to be maybe seventy or eighty, but he is strong, sharp minded, and dangerous. And most importantly, he has allies and spies, and I cannot figure out who they are." Alec clenched his jaw in telltale frustration. "Trust no one, Wilfred. It doesn't matter their title or station or gender. Raganor will use anyone."

"Raganor? Raganor le Brun?" Wilfred's eyes went wide.

"You've heard of him?" Eleanor asked, her brow furrowed.

Wilfred swallowed. "I met him. When I was a few days north of here. He bought me a drink at a tavern. He appeared to me a perfect gentleman."

Alec cursed under his breath. "I should have told you about him sooner," he muttered.

"What did you talk about?" Eleanor grabbed Wilfred's arm.

"Nothing out of the ordinary. My family, what I do, the weather. I'm sure I mentioned both of you, but it's not like he was asking anything most people don't already know. You're famous."

Alec and Eleanor's eyes locked. Whatever Wilfred had said, it had led Raganor to them. Judging by how Wilfred twisted his reins, he now realized this, too.

"What else?" Alec said quietly.

"He went on for a long time about Jerusalem. I was fascinated and asked a lot of questions. He answered them all."

"Of course he did," Eleanor whispered.

Wilfred shook his head, scuffing the ground with his heel. "I'm so sorry. I didn't know."

"Not many would," Alec said quietly.

Eleanor began pacing, biting her lip. If only Raganor had sent a messenger, and not an arsonist. "Wilfred, please get my son away from here. Away from France.

Away from—me." She turned away, towards the charred building. "Please, protect him. I must speak with Raoul. He must know something. And I will not let Benec go back there, to the nest of my enemies. Maybe that is what they want. They want us to come asking questions and drop him right into their hands."

"There are more men than Raganor after Benec?" Wilfred asked.

"Raganor's spies," Alec said smoothly. Eleanor knew they spoke of The Order, but it was also true that the old man had people working for him.

Wilfred accepted this explanation. He met Eleanor's eye, inclining towards her to indicate his sincerity. "You know I will protect him. We will go to England."

Eleanor gritted her teeth, emotion rolling through her. She straightened her spine and inhaled, then let the tension out slowly with a single nod. It must be.

Alec continued where she could not. "The rest of the household has the option to stay or go. It will be a rough winter here. If Raganor is truly after us and not the land, they will be safe.

His words rang true among the three of them, though no one liked the idea of leaving. Eleanor inhaled, raising her chin with what she hoped was a spark back in her blue eyes. "It's only for a few months. We'll reassemble everyone in March, when the ground thaws." She smoothed back her hair from her temples and turned, a piece of her heart cracking deep within her, faith shaken as to why she could never call a place home for long. She felt Alec and Wilfred's eyes on her, and guilt settled into the pit of her stomach. It was not only her own life being pulled to pieces, but the lives of everyone around her.

And that, she would not allow to happen.

Chapter 8

Chateau Brunstein, Alsace

Raoul's new spy was proving to be very useful. After only a few weeks, the espier had sent a vague note, signed with his symbol and no name. The note only read, *He's in Harfleur. Messenger not found, assumed dead.* It told Raoul what he needed to know. Raganor was still in Aquitaine, and his old informant would not be coming back. Best of all, the man knew how to write a concise note and hire travelers to deliver it doused in women's perfume. He was still on Raganor's trail then.

He took the note and threw it into the fire, where it flamed bright for only a second and then vanished. Simon had promised he could trust this man, and Raoul had no choice but to trust Simon. He knew Simon had his own men continuing to watch Raganor. It was all a layered web of individuals that others could barely trust and yet they trusted them because there simply was no other way.

"Raoul, dear," a gentle voice called from the doorway. "Dinner is about ready. Come, before it's cold."

Raoul turned to the elderly woman and smiled. "Be right there, Madame Brigitte."

She shuffled away with a slight limp. Her arthritis was bothering her again, and still she kept the rest of the staff in line. For goodness sake, she kept Raoul in line. If she hadn't continued to hover over him like a worried grandmother, making sure he ate and slept, he probably would have starved years ago.

Raoul followed her into the hall, where the household had already assembled to eat. A plain-clothed knight entered the far end of the hall at the same time. Their eyes met and brows furrowed. Raoul met Simon halfway across the room.

"Back so soon? At least you came in time for dinner," Raoul said.

Simon kept his voice low. "I'm going to stay for a few days. Eleanor de Levan is on her way *here*."

Raoul didn't bother to ask how he knew. Simon's network of informants was as deep as his grandfather's. "How soon?"

"Maybe tomorrow. The messenger said he wasn't far ahead. He had to switch horses a few times. They're coming in fast."

"They?"

"Sir Alec Earnblaec is with her."

"Lovely." Raoul rubbed his temples. He had a certain dislike of Eleanor's new husband. He was an arrogant, nosy man. Though he claimed to have fallen in love with Eleanor, Raoul had a deep sense that there was far more to the man than what met the eye. Alec was a hard person to read, and he was very good at reading others. The visit to Brunstein wasn't going to be purely social. He was going to be looking for and at everything. He wouldn't find much, as Raoul was used to protecting his secrets. "News of Raganor?"

"He's in Harfleur. Didn't your man tell you?"

"Just checking." Raoul smiled.

They settled down to eat, Raoul's mind grasping for what had driven Eleanor to return to Brunstein. Something had happened, and word had not yet reached Alsace.

When the servants were well away from the head table, Simon leaned into Raoul's ear, his voice dropping to a whisper. "Could they ride as fast as they are with the child? Are they bringing him here?"

Raoul thought for a moment. They were both skilled riders, and though carrying a small child on horseback that long was dangerous, he wagered it was possible. "Why would they?" He thought harder, taking a sip of his wine. "And yet if they didn't, where is he?"

"That's what I was thinking."

"Do the others know they are coming?" Raoul had a sinking feeling. He trusted no one, and their allies could turn Eleanor and Alec for their own agendas. Until Raoul gained control of The Order, everyone was scrabbling for power, quietly though. They couldn't let Raganor know.

Simon shook his head. "I doubt it. My men are far better than theirs. If they do find out though, they will be excited. They think they still have a claim to her. And their hatred of Alec is obvious."

Raoul leaned back in his chair, watching across the room. *Eleanor, do you know what you're walking into coming here?*

Chapter 9

Alec felt Eleanor's tension increase the closer they got to Chateau Brunstein. If he watched her, he could see her roll her neck, shift her weight in the saddle, or fidget with her reins. He didn't need to watch. He could feel it roll off her in waves like a fever. It made his stomach clench, and he caught himself fidgeting with his armor and equipment as he rode.

"For goodness sake, Eleanor, you need to stop."

She reined up, shooting him a curious look.

"You're making *me* anxious. Just breathe for a minute and calm down. We still have a few miles to go."

Her posture deflated, and she rubbed her brow with her palm. "It's the first I've been back since—"

"I know. But Montag is gone. Lezay is gone."

"That's not it. We left Benec so far away, and this is how it was last time. I was riding this same road, with no certainty for my future. I was so angry then that I couldn't process it. But now...I remember everything, Alec." She pressed a knuckle to her trembling lips. "We should all be dead. All of us."

"But we aren't."

"Why?"

"Because you're tough."

Eleanor was quiet. She took a breath. "I killed a man, Alec. I killed my own uncle."

"Like you said, he would have killed all of us." Alec watched her. "Should I stop correcting people when they assume I did it? Do you want me to shoulder the blame? I will."

"You have enough lives on your conscience," Eleanor said quietly. "You don't need to rot in hell for my sins, too."

"I think God knows the truth. The rest of the populous—"

"Alec." Eleanor shook her head, and he let the conversation drop. They turned their horses down the road again, letting the rush of a steady canter clear their minds.

Minutes later the massive chateau loomed above them. Pennants hung from the towers in Raoul's red and black colors. The Le Brun crest blew proudly from the central tower.

"He's resurrected the old family crest." Eleanor pointed. "Interesting."

Alec studied the flag. It was Montag's black diagonal stripe over red, only with a black stag's profile in the center.

Though the stag did not have the detail of eyes, it appeared to be looking right at them. Alec felt a prickle of warning run up his spine. Why would Raoul have brought back the stag? Was he allied with Raganor?

"Montag's crest was certainly easier to draw for tournaments," Eleanor mused. "Though you have to admit, the stag is—powerful. I wonder why Montag got rid of it?"

"To separate himself from Raganor," Alec said quietly. "Now your cousin has invited him back."

Alec pulled his gaze from the pennant and turned his attention to the big iron gate that creaked open in front of them. They had already been spotted and welcomed. There were men on the walls, watching them, but they seemed at ease. No weapons were drawn. One man raised a hand in greeting.

Alec nudged Eleanor gently as they neared the gate, noting she was getting nervous again. "We enter by the front gate today." It was a much grander entrance than their shuffle through the caves behind the chateau had been when they'd last entered—more like invaded—Brunstein.

Eleanor felt as if her heart would leap out of her chest as they halted in the familiar courtyard. Not much had changed over the years. The water trough was in the same place. The squires had been known to induct the younger boys by dunking them in there a time or two. Now it was filmed with a layer of ice. The stables were to the right, and she half expected Old Michel the groom to step out, before she reminded herself that he had died years ago, protecting her. Then there was the castle before her, full of passages both wide and narrow, rooms within rooms. She'd escaped twice. Now she was entering on her own free will.

Every fiber of her body screamed against it.

It's only Raoul, she reminded herself. Though, when she'd last seen him, he was a skeleton of a man holding a sword against her, threatening to kill them all. He'd let them pass then. Was he still of the same mind?

She had to assume he knew their grandfather was back. Raoul was Montag's son after all. He had resources.

He was flying the stag.

"Eleanor?" Alec's voice called her from her thoughts. He held Noir's bridle; his own big bay horse was already handed off to a groom.

She debated turning and fleeing, but then the past few weeks in the saddle, away from Benec and her household, would be in vain. She owed it to them to seek answers. Her fear was only in her head, the real threat behind her in Aquitaine. She dismounted.

She took a shaky breath and led Alec to the entrance of the castle. Raoul emerged before them, his tall, lean figure notably filled out from when she had last seen him. His hair was streaked with gray, and yet his face held the familiar features she'd known since they were children. He was greatly changed, but then again, so was she.

They stood awkwardly in front of each other for a moment, and then Raoul opened his arms, his expression softening. "Welcome."

Eleanor took a shaky step and then accepted his embrace. She hugged him tight, and he her, as the years of unspoken grief welled between them then dumped, leaving them lighter. Eleanor stepped back and smiled.

"Madame Brigitte has been feeding you well."

Raoul laughed. "She may not be the cook anymore, but she certainly makes sure we are fed. Come. You are just in time. Dinner is about ready, and I am sure we have a great deal to talk about. You must be starving after that long journey."

"You know it well," Eleanor replied. She gestured to Alec. "You remember Sir Alec Earnblaec?"

Raoul shook Alec's hand. "As if I could forget. Welcome."

Raoul graciously tapped a barrel of Burgundian wine, and platters were filled with steaming food. The smells of roast venison, carrots, and baked apples drifted in the air. Alec and Eleanor sat with Raoul at the head table.

"You look well, Raoul," Eleanor said quietly, watching him.

"You as well, cousin," Raoul smiled. She was as pretty as ever, and though he doubted it was possible, she looked even stronger than she had two years prior. He reached for another pheasant leg. "The estate is flourishing. Allies are secure. The coffers are full. What more could a man want?"

"A wife," Alec said quietly.

Raoul didn't miss the bite in the comment. He gave Alec a hard look, and Alec met it readily. He might as well learn the truth. "I will not marry," Raoul said, a finality in his voice that gave Alec pause.

"Why?" Eleanor asked. "You are free now."

"I will never be truly free, Eleanor." He meant the words philosophically, but realized even this was too much to tell Alec. Already he leaned towards Raoul like a ravenous dog.

"The Order's hold is too strong on progeny, isn't it?" Alec asked.

Raoul froze, the food in his mouth suddenly a tasteless rock. Of all the things he thought they knew, he had not expected they would know about The Order. He forced himself to swallow.

Alec leaned back in his chair and crossed his arms, studying Raoul as if he'd already said yes.

Death to all who admit our existence, echoed in his mind as if it was again shouted on initiation day. He focused on his pheasant and took another bite. He had an urge to glance at Simon, who sat discreetly across the hall with a group of traveling merchants, but he didn't dare, knowing Alec would notice. "I don't know what you're talking about," Raoul finally replied. "More meat?" He handed the bowl to Eleanor.

Eleanor shot a worried glance at Alec but took the bowl. "Raoul, something has come to our attention. A rumor—"

Alec cut her off, impatient. "Your grandfather is back. And he's meeting with King John."

Raoul again went still, his wine glass halfway to his lips. This last bit was news to Raoul, unless of course Alec was bluffing. Everyone at the table seemed to hold their breath a long moment, but then the journey resumed of wine to lips. He took his time setting the cup down. He leaned back in his chair, eyes narrowed as he studied them both. "Is that why you're here?"

Alec kept an unblinking eye on Raoul, searching for some twitch of admission. Raoul met the gaze, refusing to give it to him.

"What do you know about Montag's Order?"

The twitch Raoul tried to hold in was more of a jerk, complete with a stiffening of the spine and a rapid blink. He masked his countenance within a second, but it was too late. Alec and Eleanor simultaneously inhaled a sharp breath and shot each other a look. Apparently, they now knew it was true. There was an Order. Moreover, they knew Raoul was part of it, just like his father. Alec gave Eleanor's hand a reassuring squeeze. He honed his focus onto Raoul.

Angry at himself and for Alec's relentless interrogation, Raoul broke eye contact entirely, focusing on the plate of food before him. Each bite seemed impossibly thick to chew, so he took smaller tears of the meat to keep the illusion that he was occupied. Alec took a long drink of wine.

"You know your grandfather is alive then?" Alec asked.

"Of course. I am Montag's son, am I not? As if he would let me forget…"

"Did you know he's returned from the Holy Land?"

"No," he lied, testing if he could fool Alec. He didn't look convinced, though he did look curious.

"Raoul, why did you re-hang the stag?" Eleanor asked quietly. She, unlike the two men, had not resumed eating. She watched Raoul as if stunned, her hands fisted on the table on either side of her plate.

Raoul met her eye, then looked quickly away. He swallowed his pheasant. "So he knows, when he returns, that I am not his enemy." He reached for more food, then suddenly dropped it, looking at Eleanor. "He's not a man to be trifled with, Eleanor. Stay away from him. Keep your son away from him." He looked to Alec, debating if he should add a warning for him too, then decided otherwise. "Where did you see him?"

"In Poitiers, last summer." Eleanor still sat like a stone. "We didn't talk to him."

"Neither of you?" Raoul looked pointedly at Alec.

Alec shook his head. "He looks like Montag. I recognized him. We left."

Raoul frowned at Alec, picking his teeth with his tongue. If what they said was true, they might yet be unknown to the man. "Keep it that way. You'll be fine."

Alec shook his head. "That's where you're wrong. Someone tried to burn—did burn—Levan Manor. A man entered the manor, then fled. The fire devasted the granary. The warnings are coming to us from all sides, and what I don't understand is what he wants. I would ask him myself, but now I can't find him." He leaned towards Raoul. "We need to know what this Order is, and who is in it. Who do we need to watch out for?"

Ah, so that is why they came. Raoul shook his head. "I won't tell you that. I won't tell you who. You already knew it exists. You should pretend you don't know even that." *Death to those outside this circle that know.*

"Montag was a member. Was he high ranking?"

"There is no ranking."

"But blood—family blood—is important to them."

Raoul didn't answer. They knew too much. Who had they spoken to? He looked away. There would be blood, always more blood, before investigations were over.

Alec continued, "And they are only powerful men. Men with money, resources."

Raoul leaned back in his chair to let Alec talk. Perhaps the details Alec relayed would reveal who had broken the circle.

"And to tie such powerful men together there needs to be rules, ceremony…rituals?"

Raoul frowned.

Alec frowned himself. "This must bind you all like brothers. And yet you never invited your best friend to join. Why?"

Raoul was unfazed. "I don't have a best friend."

"Of course not now. He's dead by your father's hand. Edmond?" Eleanor flinched beside Alec, but he met Raoul's glare. Alec was cruel to do that to Eleanor, even as an attempt to shock. Alec could not be ignorant as to what Edmond had meant to her, how important that bond of friendship had been in their youth. Still, he was relentless. "Why wouldn't you insist such a close friend join their ranks? He even apprenticed under Montag."

"How do you know he wasn't a member?" Raoul fidgeted. He was stalling.

"He wouldn't be dead if he was a member."

Raoul had to hand it to Alec, he was smart.

"I think...I think whatever this is was too dark for Edmond, and you knew it. You didn't want in yourself, but because you were 'of the blood,' your father forced you. You kept the secret well, Raoul. Edmond never even knew about it, did he?"

"How do *you* know?"

Alec smirked. "I really have no idea if your grandfather and King John are meeting. But you did not counter that, which means this Order defies all borders. That makes it more powerful than a kingdom. Am I wrong?"

If he knew that, he really did know too much. And that put everything in jeopardy. Raoul broke. "They are extremely powerful, Alec. And if word gets out you have breathed a word of their existence, you and your family are dead, as is everyone you talk to. So be careful who you push."

"Are you threatening us?" Alec's muscles tensed, the will to fight visibly rising like a wave in a narrow channel.

Raoul shook his head. "They'll have my head on a stake next to yours for not turning you in, but no, I will not tell anyone that you know. I just warn that others will not be as kind." Raoul thought a moment. "You are right, they are more powerful than kings. Some are kings, but that doesn't matter like you'd think. And yes, it is a brotherhood bonded...in ways you don't want to imagine. My grandfather has returned. And he has a very narrow taste." Raoul glanced at Eleanor, a worried expression on his face. "I heard stories about your parents..."

Eleanor leaned forward eagerly, but Raoul didn't continue. If she didn't know that, he wasn't going to be the one to tell them. He shook his head.

Alec quietly added, "I already told her. About her father...Jerusalem."

Raoul's eyes went wide. "Where did you get that story from?"

"Can't tell you. You'd kill them."

Raoul shook his head in awe. "Then you know why Raganor would be interested in her."

Alec cocked his head to the side. Raoul surmised Alec perhaps did not yet know Eleanor's—and her child's—importance. Alec's mind was beyond that, as he asked, "Will he want to kill her...or have her join them?"

"I don't know." Raoul shrugged. "The child of his blood and his enemy must be a monster in his eyes. And yet he's fascinated by monsters."

"When you talk to him—"

Raoul cut Alec off. "We don't talk. You see the pennants flying from the tower? I brought back the stag, so he'll know from a distance I mean him respect and peace. That way he'll never step foot here in Brunstein. He must have the lives of a cat to even be alive, much less traveling, at his age. I've only heard the stories of him that my father told, and they were never in a good light. I hope he stays far from here. So no, I won't be talking to him."

Alec and Eleanor were silent, watching Raoul, who calmly took a long drink of his wine. When he set the glass back down, he fixed Eleanor in a hard look. "Stay ignorant of the Order, and Raganor will stay ignorant of you. I've done my share to warn you. I've broken my vow to tell what little I have. I won't reveal more. Do not ask."

"I understand, cousin," she replied gently. Alec frowned as she reached across the table to touch Raoul's hand. "Thank you."

Raoul sighed and poured them all more wine. "Here's to better conversation," he toasted, and they downed the succulent juice in absent thought.

Chapter 10

Raoul slipped into the deepest cellar of the castle and shut the door. The room had a damp smell to it but was spotlessly clean. He raised his torch, his eyes adjusting in the dim light to make out the shadow of a man across the room, a second torch on a sconce behind him. Raoul crossed until they stood across from each other, a stone slab between them—the altar they never spoke about.

"You didn't mention she is so pretty," Simon said with a sly grin. He perched on the edge of the slab, a hand casually on the hilt of his sword. "I thought all the fuss was exaggerated, but now I understand. How much do they know?"

Raoul considered protesting his lack of respect for the place, but decided it wasn't worth the battle. He crossed his arms. "Too much. They know The Order exists. They know Raganor is alive, suspect he is in a position of power. But other than me, they have no idea who the members are, and we need to keep it that way."

Simon nodded. "I'll follow them. No sense sitting in a castle being bored." He hesitated. "Are the stories about the two of them true? Alec a tournament champion? And Eleanor as good with a sword as a man?"

"She killed my father."

"True." Simon narrowed his eyes in the darkness. "Where is the boy?"

"They sent him to England."

"Damn."

Raoul nodded solemnly. He had to hand it to them, Eleanor and Alec were smart. Even without knowing what the danger was, they were taking the precautions necessary to prevent it. This time though, they may have taken the wrong one.

"So we get to him in England." Simon crossed his arms, deep in thought.

"Our English member is too powerful. If the child makes it there, he is out of our reach. It will be up to Eleanor and Alec to keep him safe."

"As it should be."

"I wish we could tell them what they face. *Who*."

Simon slapped the altar beneath him. "Don't you dare. If anyone slips one word, we're all dead, probably on this slab of rock."

"I know. But it is very hard to keep this from her after all she's been through."

"You love her." Simon smirked with amusement.

"Like a sister, yes, I do."

Simon shook his head and stalked past Raoul to the door. He hesitated, his hand on the handle. "What about her husband?"

"What about him?"

"You know, if our plan fails, one of them *must* die. You either break her heart or your own."

"I know," Raoul said somberly.

Simon again shook his head. "Your father raised you no differently than the rest of us, Raoul. How did you get to be so emotional? It's dangerous."

Raoul straightened and glowered. "It is more dangerous to not feel anything at all, like you." Even as he said the words, he knew they weren't entirely true. Simon would not have lingered at Brunstein for days if he wasn't emotionally invested in the events unfolding. He was faking a tough visage to hide his fear, for the truth was, Simon's nearly-grown sons were as much an interest to The Order as Eleanor's.

May this ring of blood never be broken, echoed in Raoul's mind. Well, to Hell with all of them. He intended for it to shatter. Starting with the Le Brun bloodline first. Montag of Brunstein would never have an heir. Raoul could at least ensure that.

There was another bloodline that could be weakened. But they were allies, so it would have to be done carefully.

He frowned at the floor in front of him, weighing the risks and benefits.

Simon narrowed his eyes at him. "What are you thinking, Lord Raoul?"

"The risk of *me* telling her is too great. If the others find out and follow the code—if I am dead—then Raganor will not just want but *need* the boy. It puts the Earnblaecs in more danger. But if someone else tells her, someone we trust yet can afford to lose—"

"You want me to tell the Lezays she is here?" That knowing smile crept onto Simon's lips.

Raoul felt as if a fist clenched his gut. It was a risky plan for all involved, and yet it may allow Eleanor to gain her explanations. "Eleanor and Alec will pass Leuwenstein on their way west."

"And the obnoxious Lezay son won't keep his mouth shut." Simon tilted his head to the side. "Even if Raganor finds out our ring of secrecy has been broken, our newest member won't be much of a loss."

They eyed each other.

Simon stood abruptly. "I'll ensure they run into each other. After that, I wash my hands of whatever happens." He hesitated. "Is it worth the risk—to our plan, to her, to The Order—for her to know more?"

"She—they—won't stop looking until they do."

Chapter 11

Eleanor had followed Madame Brigitte into the kitchen after dinner. The vast room, stacked with stores on one half and a cupboard of dishes and pots on the other, was warm from the cooking hearth. Eleanor now stood in front of the fire, the coals throwing a comforting heat. It was amazing how fire could both comfort and destroy. She reached her hands to the flames and rubbed them together. Though she was considerably warmer than she had been when they arrived, days in the cold left a lot of thawing to be done.

Madame Brigitte rocked by the fire, watching Eleanor with a content expression on her lined face. "I always hoped you'd be back one more time. I missed you so."

Eleanor smiled at her over her shoulder. Madame Brigitte was as close to a grandmother figure as she'd ever had. They'd already shared a joyful reunion. "I missed you, too."

"How is your little boy?" The corners of Madame Brigitte's eyes wrinkled with her smile.

"He is good. Growing fast. Too fast. He's always in motion with the other children. Very curious. Perhaps a little too brave."

"All good traits for a knight." Madame Brigitte smiled at the thought.

Eleanor rotated at the fire. "I'm almost afraid to get too close to him, knowing what dangers he will face when he grows up, how hard his life will be. Does that make me a bad mother?"

Madame Brigitte didn't change expression, didn't hesitate in her rocking. "You are already close to him, regardless of your fears. You came here and risked everything to rescue him, and now this journey, too, is based on his protection. You cannot shelter him from the storm that rages, Eleanor. You can give him the tools he needs to survive it. And one of those tools will be the unconditional, unfettered love of his mother."

Eleanor felt her expression soften. "I miss him. I hope it was the right choice to send him away." She pressed an errant brown lock of hair from her face. "By the way, thank you for all you did for him. Without you—"

"Shh. What else could I have done? It was a pleasure." The corners of her eyes crinkled with joy. "He looks like you."

"That's what Alec says, too." Eleanor thought for a moment. "What happened to the maid that brought him here? Marin?"

Madame Brigitte slowed her rocking. "Your uncle brought him here, my dear. Where he got him from, I don't know, for he was not gone long enough to ride all the way to Aquitaine." She pursed her lips. "I have lived with this family a long time. I have seen many things. It is my job to keep my eyes averted, lips sealed. But I will tell you this…I do not think you need fear your maid's return. Montag always hated a traitor, even when that person worked for him."

A prickle ran up Eleanor's spine, despite the warmth of the fire. "Then do you know what happened to a young squire named Lance? He supposedly followed my uncle from England. He had been Alec's squire."

"We never had a squire by that name here at Brunstein."

Eleanor let her breath out in a whistle. Just as she thought she had found Montag's humanity, he appeared even more monstrous. "Was he always—like he was?"

Madame Brigitte narrowed her eyes.

"You helped raise him, didn't you? As you did my mother?"

"Yes." The rocking grew quicker, then tapered off, then stopped. The old woman leaned forward in her chair, her grey eyes boldly meeting Eleanor's. "No one blames you, child, for that night. If we could have made him listen, we would have told him it was coming. You are half Le Brun yourself, your mother's daughter through and through. If you weren't, you would not have left on your wedding night. We—the household—knew you would return for the boy. You did what you had to, what we expected." She leaned back, still holding the steady gaze. "Now, you ask if he was always a monster. No. No, he was a good child. Raganor—" The chair started rocking again, the tempo quick. Madame Brigitte crossed herself, her lips in a thin line.

"What about him?" Eleanor prodded.

"In everyone there is evil. In some, it sinks its roots down deep, like a black oak centuries old." Suddenly Madame Brigitte stood. "I'm going to bed." She hugged Eleanor tight. "If I don't get to speak to you again before you leave, know that you are a blessing, and I wish you many long, happy years."

Eleanor hugged her back, and tears welled in her eyes. When would she return to Brunstein? Madame Brigitte would not live forever.

The old woman pulled briskly away, wiping her eyes, and shuffle-limped to her room off the back of the kitchen. Eleanor watched after her, eyes blurred. She then looked around the empty kitchen. How many of these pots had she scrubbed until her knuckles were red? How many buckets of water had she hauled from the cistern? Alone within the sleepy halls of Chateau Brunstein and wide awake, the memories beckoned.

Alec would never have let a man wander freely through *his* castle. He made a mental note to remind his own castellan of such when he returned to England. Raoul was too trusting, letting an outsider knight wander his halls. Perhaps he was overconfident in the castle's defenses, with its maze of corridors and thick walls. That aside, Alec was not one to waste such an opportunity once it was presented.

Alec had left Eleanor and Madame Brigitte in the kitchen, then walked the long bailey wall, enjoying the sunset view. Geographically, Brunstein was built in an excellent location, with a cliff behind it and yet high enough on the rise to see far into the distance. A siege here, in hindsight, would have taken months, if not years. It was fortunate Eleanor had known about the passageway to the cave in the belly of the castle. Their quest for Benec two years ago had been over in a matter of days. As Alec counted their blessings, he had explored the stable—Raoul had an excellent herd of horses, perhaps worth breeding a mare to—and then returned within the castle to wind through corridors to discover storerooms, armories, and finally, a narrow doorway to a spiral staircase up the tallest tower of the keep.

He'd followed that stair, hand on his sword, his heart pounding, only to find a bare room with two bloodstains on the floor. He'd squatted down, placing his hand on the smaller of the two, remembering his closest brush with death. Standing there again seemed surreal, and yet he felt strangely alive. His pulse beat solidly in his chest. His bones and muscles obeyed his commands. He smelled the mildew and dust that laced the air, the creosote that drifted down the unused chimney. He felt the chill of the winter wind as it rattled a window across the room. He was alive.

And now he wanted to find Eleanor.

She was no longer in the kitchen. Fatigue was kicking in—after all, they'd ridden hard for weeks to get there and now he'd spent hours climbing stairs in his explorations. The household members and Raoul were nowhere to be found. Just as fear was beginning to rise, he spotted her, staring down the hall with torch in hand, her back to him.

"Eleanor?"

She turned, face awash in anguish.

He was at her side in a matter of strides. "What's wrong?"

She only shook her head and looked down the hall again. "Memories..." she whispered.

"Good or bad?" It was a silly question, he knew. From her expression, they were pretty horrible.

"Both..."

"Come. Let's go to bed."

She didn't move. "It's harder here." She turned back to him, eyes pleading. "Do you want to know?"

No, I don't, his head screamed. He brushed a strand of hair gently from her forehead. "Do you want me to know?"

"I think you should." She took a deep breath, then slowly moved forward, the torchlight flickering across the contours of her face. Outside a thick wooden door, she stopped. "This is where I spent my wedding night. My first wedding night. This room." She didn't open the door. She faced it and closed her eyes, swallowing hard. What horrors was she reliving? Alec wondered and yet was glad she didn't share. "Raoul said he distracted Lezay by convincing him to search all the rooms in this hall. There's only three. He held him longer than that. I don't know how, but he must have. And I got away." She opened her eyes, the light surrounding them shaking with the tremor of her hand. "You may not like Raoul, but he saved me that night, Alec. He told me years ago that he has scars from the punishment Montag gave him. I got away."

"You saved yourself, Eleanor. You're the one that fought back. You were brave enough to run, and to keep running into a world you knew nothing about. Don't underestimate the role you had in your own escape."

Eleanor closed her eyes, took a deep breath, and then turned from the door, her expression once again veiled. That worried Alec more than her tears. He knew his wife was strong. He knew she had it in her to return here, that it was worth it to find answers as to who continued to threaten them. He also knew that there was a lot of memory and emotion tied to this place where she had grown up, perhaps more so than Levan Manor. And here the memories were not all happy. She was pushing them away again. Was it better to bottle them or dump them out? He wasn't the one to advise her. He did not know what she had gone through, which he suddenly realized was his own fault. He'd never asked.

Eleanor pushed open another door and entered, placing the torch on a sconce within. "This is the room for nobility. Raoul said we may stay here. I guess we qualify as honored guests now, don't we?" Alec followed into the warm, cozy room where a fire burned in the small hearth. Eleanor poured them both glasses of wine from a decanter on the side table, then began pacing back and forth in front of the fire as she drank hers.

Alec settled into a chair and watched her. The way the firelight glowed on her skin gave her an ethereal beauty, a beauty men would kill for. That he had already killed for. He felt the lust rise in him as he watched her and didn't bother to conceal it. She was his wife after all. She absently undid the pins holding her hair, and it fell in dark waves to her waist, as it had when they had first met. Alec had to shift in his seat. She still had no idea what she did to him.

Suddenly Eleanor turned to him. "Is our son safe?"

"With Wilfred watching over him? Of course. Eleanor, come here."

She took a step towards him, completely distracted by her own thoughts. "We should leave for England. Tomorrow."

"We've only just arrived." He caught her wrist, pulling her in front of him. Finally, her eyes locked on him, rounding with a mild surprise. They widened even more as he guided her hand to where his thoughts were. Her mouth made a little O, and she froze.

Alec released her as he leaned back.

Normally Eleanor would catch on to his ideas, meeting his parries in the most elaborate dance two human bodies could undertake. Tonight, she looked as if she fought herself. She shook her head and backed away.

"What?" he again caught her hand, gently pulling her back to him. He knew it was coming without her elaborating. She was going to turn him down, pull into herself again like some recluse. He could not hide his frustration. He was at least going to make her voice her reasons.

"I can't do that—not here—not where it happened. I can't, Alec. I can't—"

"Shhh." He pulled her into his arms. He'd hoped they were past all this; she hadn't pulled away from him in months. He sighed. Some scars were still deep. He felt one of her tears wet his shoulder and shifted her so he could see her face. "Eleanor, you are safe now. Why do you give him this power over you?"

She shook her head. "I hate it. But being in this place...everything feels like it happened yesterday. You don't know what that's like."

Alec frowned, furrowing his brow. Slowly he set Eleanor back on her feet and rose to lean against the mantle of the fireplace, staring into the flames. "Is that what you think? That I don't know what it's like?"

"Of course you don't," she muttered, wiping her eyes and steeling her back.

A thousand thoughts rushed through his mind. He wanted to fight her, to scream the lists of wrongs that had been done against him, the things he had seen and done that kept him up at night. He clenched his jaw, curling his fists against the solid beam of the mantle.

Without turning to Eleanor, he spoke. Though he willed his tone patient and gentle, it rang in his ears as a flat, cold line. "To be wronged is to live, Eleanor. And though we may wish to avoid it, to live in the romantic tales of the troubadours, we cannot. That is not how this life works, and for every person the struggle is *different*."

He heard her settle into his vacated chair. Her eyes burned into his back. He toed a log deeper into the fire with his boot, watching the flames spark higher.

Alec frowned, debating how to explain without forcing her walls higher. "Lezay murdered my father. His body rots in an unmarked grave mere miles from here. Tonight I was in the room where I faced my closest brush with death. You think I don't feel anything? You are not the only one with scars, Eleanor." He whirled to face her, crossing his arms before him. She was staring at him, a stunned expression on her face.

The fire cracked in the silence between them. Alec debated saying more, then decided he'd already spoken too much. He turned away, toed off his boots, dropped his travel-dirtied breeches, and made for the bed. He heard Eleanor approach long after he had buried himself under the blankets. She sat on the edge and laid a hand on his shoulder.

"I didn't know your father was buried so close to here," she said quietly. A long silence held between them. "We should go there tomorrow."

He didn't respond. Lezay had taken everything from him, the same as he had Eleanor. His emotion, now that he had spoken the words aloud, was raw in his throat. She would hear it, think him weak.

Yes, he knew how she felt.

She crawled into the bed next to him, curling against his back, which he kept towards her. "Alec, what is the hardest thing you've faced in this life?" she whispered into his skin.

"This isn't a competition, Eleanor."

"You want me to understand; I'm asking. Not to compare, just to know."

Alec sighed, debating. His parents' deaths had been difficult, but that was something everyone dealt with. He had fought many fights, suffered injuries, taken lives. Knowing what Lezay had done to Eleanor on top of what he'd done to his father had made his blood sing for revenge for the better part of a year, and that long wait had been rough. There was one claim though, one claim that still wracked his soul every time. But no, he couldn't tell her that. He couldn't hurt her like that.

"Tell me."

"It's nothing, Eleanor."

She pulled on his shoulder until he faced her. "Tell me!" Her eyes, like deep pools of the sea, begged.

Still he hesitated, though he sat up, hope of sleep abandoned. She twined her fingers into his.

"Please," she pleaded again.

"You told me our son isn't mine. Now I wonder every time I look at the boy." He saw the shock register on her face and instantly regretted saying anything at all. He had guarded his feelings and secrets closely for years. If only there was an art to expressing them as there was to extracting them from others. He was terrible at it if there was. "Forget it." He shrugged. "It doesn't change anything. He's mine." He gently pulled her with him onto the bed, kissing her, hoping to make her forget the entire conversation.

Alec felt her lips follow his, her hands pulling him in tight. He pulled away only when he felt something wet on his cheek. Sure enough, her eyes brimmed with unshed tears.

"Alec, I'm so sorry. If I could change the past—"

"We can't. If we could, I would have fought harder for you in the first place. I would have been the man you needed me to be, instead of letting you rely on Edmond to heal you."

She kissed him again, twining her body around his. He settled next to her, content just to hold her as his mind fended off sleep with a torrent of thought. Alec laid a wrist across his forehead, staring at the ceiling as he listened to Eleanor's quiet breathing beside him. He had to master his thoughts or there would be no rest.

Chapter 12

Eleanor pulled herself from the warm covers, careful not to wake Alec. It was no easy task: the man seemed to be on alert even in sleep. Yet the journey to Brunstein and late-night conversations led him to slumber deeply. Eleanor wished her dreams would let her rest. She had been awake for a while, mind racing. Now that the dawn light cut through the room, she yielded to it. She dressed, wrapped her cloak around herself, and headed through the castle. There was still one place she felt obligated to visit while they were at Brunstein. With that obligation met, perhaps she would never have to return.

Montag's grave was in the churchyard with the rest. The little stone chapel was tucked down the valley from the castle, outside the great walls. It was positioned like a guardhouse, not that it was used as such. Eleanor suspected it had been strategically built there so that any visitors were granted the illusion that the Le Bruns were religious. As part of the Holy Roman Empire, they were expected to be. Yet as long as Eleanor had been at Brunstein, there had never been a priest in the little building.

She pushed open the door, and the hinges squealed in protest, cutting the quiet morning. She winced. But all was quiet again. Light streamed into the little room through colored glass windows, a kaleidoscope of colors covering the bare floor. Really, the whole room was bare, with only a crucifix hanging on the wall over the altar. No benches, no tapestries. No dust. Someone within the manor was maintaining the chapel. Eleanor mused over whom for a moment. Perhaps it was a joint effort, and the souls of Brunstein had not been as corrupted by Montag's ruthlessness as she imagined. At least the building was not being used for storage.

No, Montag would never have allowed that. Appearances wouldn't allow for it. And perhaps there was something he believed. Eleanor crossed herself and closed the door, the hinges squealing yet again. She had so many conflicted feelings about Montag, she didn't know where to begin. She turned into the churchyard. If only stones could talk.

Raoul had covered the grave with a massive slab of stone, Montag's effigy artfully etched into the surface, the image of a knight with sword held to chest. The mighty knight of the image lay far more somberly than Montag ever had in life, yet the skilled artist had managed to replicate the broad shoulders and stern expression of the warrior.

A chill breeze blew Eleanor's cloak around her, and she pulled it tighter. The rays of morning light cut through the trees, making the frost on the grass sparkle. The shadows of the branches overhead danced across the stone, a single beam of sunlight illuminating the name at the bottom of the stone. Lord Elfric of Brunstein, MCXCVIII. Eleanor crossed her arms, frowning at the words. Had Raoul thrown the last insult after all, reminding the world that the mighty Montag was no more than mortal Elfric? At least he had not written the Le Brun surname, which Montag had stopped using long ago.

Eleanor backed to a bench beneath the big oak tree and sat. She felt as if she should cry but had no inclination to do so. She'd killed the man. Had he really protected her? If he had protected her, she would not have been forced to marry Lezay. Or had Montag been so afraid of what Raganor would do that he felt Lezay's cruelty was the lesser evil of the two? She mused on that for a while. If Raganor had orchestrated her father's death, and been willing to destroy his own daughter, perhaps he was as ruthless as the stories Alec and his friend told. The burning, the murder involved with this strange ceremony...was that only the start of the darkness? How much darker did Raganor go?

The leaves rustled next to her, breaking her trance. She looked up at Raoul. His face was as impassive as ever, though he sat next to her, casually leaning forward with his elbows on his knees. They sat in silence until the morning began to warm, the sun inching higher to melt the frost into mist. The birds chirped in the tree. It was a beautiful morning. It was a strange morning to be sitting at a gravestone.

Finally Eleanor broke the silence. "You know, my parents have no stones. My mother wanted to have one carved for Father, but she fell ill before she could find someone to do it. And then Montag rushed me out of Levan Manor so quickly, we barely had time to put my mother in the ground, much less carve a stone. I think I remember where they are buried, but I'm not entirely sure." She straightened her back, rubbing her neck absently. "What you did for him is a nice tribute."

Raoul remained silent.

"Raoul...I am sorry it was by my hand. He was your father—"

Raoul shook his head so vigorously that Eleanor quieted. "He was my father in name only. He spent so much effort as my mentor—my lord—that fatherhood was lost on him." He pursed his lips in thought. "Are you sitting here because you want to forgive him? Or are you trying to forgive yourself?"

Eleanor inhaled. "Alec told me some things. I understand now why Montag was how he was. But to negate all he did to me, to all of us, is impossible. Still, if the human side of Montag was broken because of his past, if in his mind he thought he was raising us to be strong by being hard, and if he brought me here to keep me from Raganor—" She gripped the edge of the bench with her hands, the ice numbing her skin. "Then the guilt of being his bane is so much worse."

Raoul turned to her, his eyes narrowed. "Forgiveness does not negate the wrongs done to us. He carried that weight on his own soul. Forgiveness gives us the power to look past those wrongs and move on."

Eleanor's eyebrows went up, and she stared at the stone slab. The breeze swirled around them, rustling leaves. "Will you forgive me?" she whispered.

"Already have."

She hesitated, allowing that to sink in. "Did you forgive him?"

"Yes."

Eleanor's sharp intake of breath cut the morning air. "With all he's done to you—to your mother—" She bit her tongue. Alec had warned her not to speak of Raoul's mother.

"Yes," Raoul said without hesitation. "If I did not, I would become as bitter and isolated as he was. And then what kind of man would I be?" He thought for a moment. "Forgiveness is the most powerful thing, Eleanor. It is a cornerstone of Christianity for a reason."

Her eyes flicked from him to the chapel. "You...you're the one that's maintained this place through the years."

Raoul shrugged.

Eleanor bit her lip. "And you—you know about your mother?"

Raoul gave a sad smile. "Lezay 'let it slip' years ago that she was alive. Montag almost hit him. But I don't know where she is. The two of them took that secret to the grave."

"Do you want to find her?"

"I don't know. After all this time, if she's made her peace, I don't want to ruin that. And now that Raganor has returned, it could be dangerous for her. If she's even still alive." He looked pointedly at Eleanor. "I don't know how Alec found out, but you need to keep Alenor a secret. Do you understand?"

She nodded.

Raoul turned back towards the tombstone. "Alec has ways of finding things out that he shouldn't."

Eleanor didn't know what to say to that, so she remained silent.

Raoul scuffed the ground with his boot, sending sparkles of ice crystals into the air, only for them to melt as they resettled on the ground. "Raganor is still dangerous, Eleanor. He is powerful. If what I hear is true, he has no conscience to check like the rest of us do. That is why my father banished him. It is why he hid my mother, and he tried to hide you. It was why, when you were too old and independent to be hidden, he gave you to a monster he thought would keep you out of Raganor's hands. And Lezay would have. I don't know if Montag underestimated Lezay's depravities, or if Raganor is that much worse. And he had other reasons for your marriage." Raoul chewed his cheek, choosing his words. "What do you know about your parents in relation to The Order?"

"My father was part of the ceremony and escaped. Alec said there was a rumor Raganor had him killed in a tournament."

"I can't confirm Raganor killed him, nor from what I know could my father. But if he was part of the ceremony, he should have been dead. And that means you should never have existed."

"Why would my existence matter?"

Instead of brushing off the question with the expected *It doesn't*, Raoul looked pained. "I can't say."

"Why? Raoul, what does Raganor want? If he wants me dead, why didn't he just kill me instead of burning my granary?" *Let him take it out on me, not my people.*

"I can't say."

"Can you say what I'm supposed to do next? My home is threatened. I fear my son isn't safe—is anyone I love safe?"

"The less you know, the better." Raoul lowered his eyes as if pained.

Eleanor rubbed her forehead. She was tired of warnings, tired of not knowing where to look for the danger. "You know more, and yet you will not help me understand."

"I am sorry. When I can, I will explain everything. But not here, where ears are listening. Not now, while so much is at stake. Where are you headed next?"

"I can't say," Eleanor said sarcastically and kicked the ground with her heel.

Raoul rose. "I really am sorry. Trust me, if I could speak about it, I would, but it is too dangerous. I wish you would stop pursuing The Order and Raganor. Hide if you must. Go to England." He looked around the sparkling grove. "But I know your husband better than that. He will want to keep looking. Be careful. Take your time here. I will tell Alec where you are. He's likely tearing apart the castle looking for you. I don't know whether to call it love or insanity, but the man is certainly loyal to you."

Eleanor smiled faintly.

"Take care, Eleanor. Remember my warnings." He turned away.

"Raoul?"

He hesitated.

"You don't have to be completely alone. I may be frustrated, but you are family. And you have never given me reason not to trust you. I am here for you, too."

The corners of his lips turned up to a demi-smile, and he bowed slightly before briskly walking back to the castle.

Eleanor turned back to the stone slab. Emotions rumbled from deep within her. She gripped the edge of the bench, her nails digging into the frosty wood. She held her breath, trying to force the forgiveness out. But the wrongs were still too great. She stood, gliding up to the foot of the grave.

"I will try, Uncle. But I still need to understand some things." Feeling the need to leave at least something in memorial, she took a silver coin from her purse and slipped it between the stone and the ground at her feet. It wasn't as much as he'd given her mother when her father had been killed, but it was something in tribute for that kindness.

She would be careful as she sought understanding of The Order and her uncle. She would be patient, observant. The question remained whether she had time to wait for answers before the next deed was done against her.

Chapter 13

A light snow covered the road, hiding the slick places. Alec and Eleanor rode slowly, letting the horses find their footing. After a few miles on the road west, Alec reined up. A stone cairn stood a slight distance off a lightly beaten path.

"This is it."

They halted and Alec dismounted. His horse followed behind him as he approached the stones. It had been several years since he had stacked them here, where a farmer had indicated that the man that wore the Earnblaec signet had been buried. The stones blended with the leaves and brush around them, particularly with the light snow covering, and for that Alec was grateful. He had feared someone would disturb the grave, but it was as abandoned as he had left it.

He felt an urge to kneel, but he pushed it away. There was only a pile of stones here. His father was long gone. No sense marking the place to other travelers now. He inhaled the cold air, letting the steam of his breath out in a puff. He turned to Eleanor, who was mounted on her horse behind him, watching.

"What was he like?" she asked quietly.

Alec glanced back to the stones. "Big man, as tall as me. Quick to laugh. Handsome I suppose. He had a way of telling stories that could keep a room of strangers on the edge of their seats."

"He was a knight?"

"Of course." Alec shrugged. "He fought a lot in his youth for King Henry, so by the time tournaments were becoming popular, he had no interest in chasing more brutality. He may have competed in one or two tournaments, but otherwise he kept to Castle Homme."

"Was it his choice to go on pilgrimage? Or was he sent?"

"Oh, that was his choice. He had talked about it for years. When my mother died, I think he was even more determined to go. He felt he needed to do penance for his sins against her...his adultery. She really was heartbroken when she found out about Wilfred's existence. But it was after she died that he made his plans. I don't know if he wanted to specifically go to Jerusalem or one—or several—of the other holy sites. Of course, the king and everyone else supported it. How could they not support a Holy Mission?"

The whole scenario still made Alec grit his teeth. Penance or not, Sir Alfred of Homme had left him with the management of an entire castle, when Alec should have been out fighting and honing his skills and reputation. Then he never returned while rumors did. Everything had been taken away by the very king who had agreed to let Sir Alfred go on pilgrimage. When Alec had tried to protest, to explain to the stewards in London that his father would never have abandoned his men in the Holy Land, he was too much of a nobody to gain an audience. Yes, for as much as he respected his father, there was lingering bitterness there.

Alec vaulted back onto his horse. "There's a tavern just down the road. We can stay there tonight. I'll warn you, it's a bit rough." He smiled at his wife, knowing she wouldn't object. Rowdy crowds of men were far more familiar to her than the quiet life at the manor she'd been living the past year.

Eleanor rolled her eyes, smiling slightly. But Alec saw her pull her hair back into the hood of her cloak. She knew the game.

When they arrived at the tavern, it was bustling with men. The stable was practically full, and the main room was crowded with men deep into a flowing barrel of ale. The stench of ale and sweat laced the air, but the smell of roast meat made their stomachs growl. Eleanor followed Alec closely as he pushed through the crowd with his large frame, keeping her chin down under her hood.

"Do you have a room left?" Alec shouted at the tavernkeeper. He placed a coin on the counter that was replaced with two ales.

"Just one." The tavernkeeper's eyes flicked to Eleanor. "Your friend need one, too?"

Alec shook his head. "We'll be fine." He put another coin on the counter.

"Up the stairs and to the left. Fourth door. Another coin if you want to eat."

The innkeeper pocketed the money, and Alec nodded his thanks as he was handed two bowls of stewed meat with root vegetables. He handed one to Eleanor and pushed off towards the lone vacant table furthest from the big blazing hearth. They sat, and Eleanor slumped back in her chair, eyeing the crowd from under her hood. To anyone watching, she looked like a young man, her breeches worn and boots travel-dirty. The thick wool of her garments hid the rest of her figure, and though it was warm in the room, she left the cloak on to hide the face that was all too obviously feminine.

She sipped her stew, her red, wind-burned lips blowing on the broth occasionally. "This place always this busy?"

"It was when I was here last, too. They have fantastic ale." He toasted her, smiling.

Eleanor gazed around the room.

"Not a woman in sight, either. Not even a serving maid."

"Nope. Can you imagine this crowd with a woman around?"

At that moment there were shouts as a fight broke out a few tables away. Alec felt for the sword at his side, but relaxed as friends of the combatants quickly pulled them apart. His eyes scanned the rest of the crowd. A few farmers laughed at a large table on the far side of the room. A few other travelers were amicably chatting over their ale. His eyes lingered on the table near the fire, where three well-trimmed men sat with swords next to them. One looked to be about Alec's age, late twenties, while the second man's grey beard proved him older. The third man seemed to be somewhere between the two in age and less active in their conversation. He had dark hair and a long scar across his cheek. By their fine clothing, the three were obviously nobility. Alec tapped Eleanor's toe under the table. When she looked up from her stew, he inclined his head towards the men.

She nodded. "I saw them, too. They watched us when we came in. I didn't see any heraldry though."

"You don't recognize them?"

Eleanor shook her head and took another sip of stew. "This is fresh. And hot. You should eat."

Alec continued to watch the men through the course of their meal. They were absorbed in their own conversations, and despite the loudness of the room, no further excitement had broken out since the scuffle. "More ale?"

Eleanor nodded. She leaned back against the wall, slouching again comfortably. Alec was always amazed at how she could change her persona to match the situation. His regal Lady of the Tournament, slouching in a tavern. He reminded himself it was how she had survived. He scooped up their mugs and took them to the bar. He lingered with the tavernkeeper a moment, chatting about local news as the man poured the ale. When he turned around, his smile disappeared. The old nobleman was seated at the table with his wife, and her posture was now queen-straight, though her face was still obscured by her cloak.

Alec flinched as a hand slapped his shoulder. Spilled ale ran down his hands.

"He's just talking to her," the young noblemen said from beside Alec, casually leaning his elbows back on the bar. Alec cursed himself for not paying better attention. Were his instincts that out of practice, or were these men that good?

"Who are you?" Alec frowned at the short bearded young man. He was dressed in black, with a silver chain hanging around his neck and down into his shirt.

"Sir Elfroid de Leuwenstein. Pleasure to meet you." He held out his hand, which Alec ignored. His hands were full of ale anyway. Elfroid smirked as he let it drop again. "You aren't from around here, are you?"

"England," Alec said shortly. He watched Eleanor, nerves on edge. It looked like the conversation was very one-sided, and Eleanor was the silent one. His eyes flicked over Elfroid. There was no mistaking it. The man had the same close-set eyes and round-cut jaw. If Sir Rothulfus Lezay had been younger and taken enough care for some personal grooming, this man would give the image. He had to be a relation. Alec felt the energy tingle through his body from toes to fingers, his senses heightening. He trusted his well-practiced voice to stay steady. "And how are things in Leuwenstein these days?"

Elfroid smiled, watching the conversation going on at the table across the room with as much intensity as Alec. The scar-faced nobleman had stayed at the table, watching everything intently, sword only inches away.

"Oh Leuwenstein...it's a bit cold this time of year. But that's all of Alsace for you. What brings you all the way from England?"

"Work."

"For who?"

"The King of England."

"Which one?" Elfroid's eyes twinkled.

Alec squinted his eyes at the man, weighing his options. "There is only one."

Sure enough, Elfroid furrowed his brow, looking away from Eleanor's table. "I thought—"

Eleanor suddenly stood up, her hood falling to reveal her fuming glare. Alec pushed away from Elfroid, working toward his wife.

She pounded her fist on the table. "I don't care what arrangement he had! That arrangement was not with me, and I am not bound to it!" Her voice rang out clear and musical despite her fury. Alec groaned inwardly. So much for hiding the fact that she was a woman. Every eye in the room was now turned to her. Some patrons stared open-mouthed.

"It would be beneficial to the boy, and to your family—" the noble began.

"What family? I have not had family in ten years!"

Alec set the mugs of ale on the table with a loud thud, sloshing more of the liquid out. The grey bearded man didn't flinch. He glared at Alec with a cold stare from close set eyes. "You must be the brother," Alec ventured.

Eleanor was still standing, visibly shaking, her hand on the handle of her sword.

"Now, my lord, you have upset my wife greatly. She's not a woman you want to anger. You may have heard of her? The Knightess?"

The man's lips curled up in a smirk. "Lady Eleanor de Levan. You didn't disguise her well, Sir Alec Earnblaec. From the detailed descriptions my brother once gave me,

I spotted her straight away. I wondered when you two would venture back to Alsace. What luck that you stopped right in my favorite tavern."

Alec kept his gaze on the bearded man before him and frowned. If this was true, he'd led Eleanor into a lion's den. Now he had to lead her out. "Which brother of Leuwenstein are you?" Alec asked. He fought to keep his hands at his side and not smash the man's face.

"Sir Roric Lezay de Leuwenstein. I believe you met my son, Sir Elfroid?" The son had stepped up to the table, shadowing Alec.

Alec ignored Elfroid. "What does he want?" he asked Eleanor.

"Our son. Just like Montag warned."

Roric gestured across the table. "See, even *he* tried to explain the importance of this contract to you. And you murdered him for it."

"It wasn't murder," Eleanor and Alec said in unison.

Amusement lit Roric and Elfroid's faces.

Alec took Eleanor's vacant seat, effectively putting her behind him. He pushed one of the ales towards Roric. "Let's talk." It was just as important that the rest of the crowd went back to their own conversations. The tension had to deescalate.

Eleanor balked. "Alec, are you—"

He held up a hand to silence her, and for once she obeyed. He stared Roric in the eye, challenging. "Answer for a question. Question for an answer. You go first." The room was beginning to chatter again, despite frequent glances their direction.

"Where is Eleanor's son?" Roric glowered.

"Safe. Why do you want him?"

Roric sighed and resigned himself to explaining. "Montag and my brother long wanted to unite Alsace by uniting our families. It would be an exceedingly powerful union, giving us control of an area as large as some kingdoms. With it, the ability to control the trade routes. We could be the wealthiest family in Europe."

"Well, they failed with Lady Igraine; they failed with Lady Eleanor. You need a new plan. You aren't taking my son."

"How sure are you that he is yours?" Roric smiled maliciously as Alec blanched.

"How dare you insinuate—" Eleanor tried to cover.

Elfroid cut in, holding up a finger to silence her. "We know about Edmond. Everyone knows about Edmond."

Eleanor stilled.

Alec gritted his teeth and stifled a curse. This conversation was about to end with blood all over the room if he didn't get a handle on it. "My turn," he said calmly, tempering his anger. "Do you know Eleanor's grandfather has returned?" He tilted his head, curious. If the Lezays knew about Raganor, they likely knew about The Order.

Roric frowned. "Yes." He hesitated, then did not elaborate. "Why are you here in the dead of winter?"

Alec stroked his jaw, watching the two men in front of him. Eleanor laid a hand on his shoulder, and he took it as his permission. "Looking for Montag's Order. I guess we found you." He shrugged casually, then hope soared as he watched the men glance at each other in shock. They didn't know how to react, and that was his answer. He'd found two more members of The Order, and as suspected, they had been bound by familial ties.

"We will kill your cousin for telling you about us." Elfroid openly glared at Eleanor.

"Oh, he didn't tell us about you. But you just told us about him. So I guess that means you'll be the first slated to die?" Alec smiled. "How is it done? Ceremonially?"

Elfroid started to nod before Roric gave him a hard glare.

Alec leaned back. They were easy fools after all.

"Why would you want to find us?" Roric asked. His expression had gone serious, the frivolity of the conversation gone.

Eleanor cut in. "I want in." All three men gave her a glare that could wither a flower in spring, but she didn't flinch. "I'm the only one in my family that is knighted and not part of whatever this is. I want in."

"Do you know what that would entail?" Roric snarled.

"Tell me." Eleanor took a step forward, the heat of her body against Alec's back.

The men exchanged a look. Roric then focused on Eleanor, rising from his seat. "This is not the place to speak of such things. Come to Leuwenstein. Then we can talk."

"Absolutely not." Alec stood to face him, effectively blocking Eleanor.

He didn't like the way Roric looked him up and down. He was being judged like a horse at auction, his purpose and usefulness weighed.

"Why would you stop here, Sir Alec? Do you not know how close you are to Leuwenstein?"

Alec gritted his teeth. "I visited my father's grave. This was the closest place for travelers to get out of the cold." He looked at Eleanor, allowed a softer look to show in his eye. "Well, we will be on our way by morning." He'd leave now if it wasn't howling with cold wind outside.

Roric shook his head. "You must come to Leuwenstein. We have things to discuss that can't be spoken of here." That sharp gaze didn't waver. "Well then, you two go to bed and get warm. We will talk tomorrow."

He didn't like the assuredness in those last words, as if it was a guarantee that Alec and Eleanor would stay long enough to finish whatever conversation Roric had in mind. They had nothing more to say, and they certainly weren't going to ride to Leuwenstein to speak more. And Eleanor, for that matter, was not going to join this order.

That conversation would be held privately in their room, which he had already paid for. With permission to be excused granted—not that he was of a mind that it was necessary—Alec clasped Eleanor's arm and guided her through the crowded room, the eyes of the men following them. In their room, they barred the door behind them.

Eleanor sank onto the bed. "I told you I hate Alsace. A whole family of Lezays. It's like a nest of vipers. What the hell are we doing here?"

Alec watched through the window, his own nerves still on edge. A porch roof below promised an alternate escape route, if necessary. "It was a mistake. I am sorry." He let the thin curtain drop and sat next to her on the bed. "Why did you say that you want to join them?"

The sounds of the people downstairs echoed through the floorboards. Eleanor straightened, the warrior within her shining through. "If I need to join them to find out why they keep threatening my son, I will. I am tired of warnings without substance. I am tired of being told to fear every shadow, every dark corner. I want to know what I am up against. And you know that I will do anything to protect that boy."

Alec gave her a long look, gauging her. He sometimes wished she were just a woman, that she was content to manage a manor, raise babies, and welcome him home. But she never had been that, as hard as she'd tried to make peace with that life. Just as he had lived a nomadic life, she had done so tenfold. It had left its mark in the form of a restless sense of adventure, a desire to always be striving for something, accomplishing more. Was that a fault or a gift? It was more than Alec could judge. It was the same fire that had made him fall in love with her. How could he now say that it was wrong?

Alec reached for her, and took her hand. "I promised you I would protect you both. So if you choose to go forward, we do so with caution. We will find our answers. And then we will return to Benec."

Alec unbuckled his sword. As much as he wanted to be done with Alsace, he had a feeling it would not let go of them easily. Eleanor appeared behind him, her hands snaking across his chest. He felt her worry through her touch. Alec closed his eyes, then stepped back and snuffed out the candle. With their swords next to their hands, they curled together in the small bed and tried to get a few hours of rest, exhaustion and caution warring within them.

Alec's eyes fell closed. *First light.* They would leave before the Lezays could sleep off their ale.

Chapter 14

The blood pulsed in Alec's veins like a smith's hammer. It made his temples throb, his nerves burn, and the world seem both oddly sharp and out of focus at the same time. He lay still, cheek pressed into straw-strewn dirt, and got his bearings. His ears strained, but he could not hear a sound other than a peaceful grinding. Even in his mind, that did not make sense, but somehow the sound was reassuring. He blinked his eyes open, and slowly his sight began to sharpen. He had a lovely view of a manure pile and beyond that, the underside of a bench. A horse snorted. The grinding sound was horses chewing their hay.

Alec pushed off the ground, his head aching as if it would split in half. He sat there for a moment cradling it, fighting back the waves of nausea. When that subsided, he worked to piece together what had happened. Where was he? He gritted his teeth and forced his eyes open again. It took a moment, but he recognized the stable. He was at the inn in Alsace.

That thought sharpened his senses another degree. He turned to look at where he and Eleanor had tied their horses the night before. That stall was empty. He pushed to his feet, stood for a moment with hands to his knees, breathing deep as the nausea washed over him again. His pulse pounded harder, the thump in his skull an easy indicator, but now every beat seemed to bring alive his senses, to restore him to himself, to restore his thoughts. It was the same wave of awareness that washed over him before he entered the tournament ring, only now all that energy was not focused on a fight, but one question. Where was Eleanor?

He looked around. There were scuff marks on the dirt floor, and an overturned bucket of grain. He walked to where the horses had been. He'd come down here with her. They'd been ready to leave. Then what had happened? He put a hand to the back of his head, felt the lump. On the ground was a single drop of blood, splattered on a blade of golden straw. It shone in the morning light like a scarlet torch in darkness. Not his.

Alec felt for his sword at his hip as he ran out of the stable. He grabbed at air. The sword was gone. He reached for the short knife he kept in his boot and was reassured to feel it's presence. He spun around in the courtyard. There was no sign of anyone. How long had he been unconscious? He cursed. His horses were gone. His wife was gone. He was stranded in the middle of the enemy's lair.

They had been careful. He again questioned his instincts. Why had he not sensed the men that attacked them? For as much as he wanted to find fault in he and Eleanor's awareness, no matter how he wracked his brain, he could find none. They had taken every precaution as they left their room that morning. They hadn't even come down the stairs. They used the window. They'd been quiet.

Were the Lezays that much more skilled, stealthy and patient?

The tavern yard was still quiet. And Alec recognized that the sun was barely over the horizon. That gave him some relief. He had not been unconscious long. He strode to the tavern.

Alec slammed open the door. The main room was dark, only the light from the hearth flickering across the tables and benches, their shadows dancing like monsters in the dim light. Alec wasn't afraid of those kinds of monsters. He was only afraid of the ones that possessed human intelligence. And there was one seated in the darkest corner of the room, only the whites of his eyes showing in the firelight.

"Where is she?" Alec bellowed, not caring who he woke. His attention was again sharp as bloodlust thrummed through his veins as if it was a tournament day.

The man chuckled. "She's home, Alec."

Alec strode toward the man, drawing the knife from his boot in a smooth motion. "You tell me where she is, you bloody ass." Now he could see that it was the elder Lezay, the brother of Eleanor's former husband. Roric did not seem concerned at all by the furious knight or blade headed his way. He lounged back comfortably, a pint in his hand.

Roric gestured towards an empty chair. "Have a seat, Alec. We have much to talk about. I tried speaking earlier, but you weren't listening. Do I have your attention now?"

Alec clenched his jaw but stayed his hand, knowing full well this man was the secret to finding Eleanor as quickly as possible. What were they doing to her? He did not let his mind linger on that thought. The agony of it was too great and served him no purpose. He needed information to move forward. He didn't sit, but he quieted himself enough to listen.

The man swirled the contents of his cup, and Alec's heightened senses picked up an earthy note; it wasn't ale. Alec eyed the cup suspiciously, and as Roric followed his gaze, he smiled.

"I'd offer you some, but the mix is a bit hard to describe." When Alec didn't respond, Roric sighed, his expression bored. "She's alive, if that's what you're wondering."

"She better be more than alive. If you or your men lay one hand on her—"

"Oh, we've laid many hands on her," Roric said casually. The narrowing of his brow belied that he was studying Alec's reaction, trying to provoke him, so Alec remained motionless. Roric continued, "She put up quite a fight, as you can imagine. My son almost had a gash to match his late uncle's."

"What do you want?"

Roric leaned forward. "I want you to listen." His voice changed to a harsh whisper. "You are meddling with things you have no business in. Questions that should not be answered. You need to *forget* the questions you blasted all over the room last night, go back to your cozy little manor, and keep your head down."

"Oh, so now you're concerned for our welfare? A warning? Really?"

"I mean it, Alec. *My* family is not the enemy."

"Then why did you steal my horses? *And my wife?*"

Roric shook his head. "So you would listen. Do I finally have your attention?"

"No! I'm a bit distracted by the fact that *you took my wife*," Alec bellowed. The innkeeper shuffled in from a back room, carrying a candle against the darkness of the early-morning light, which illuminated his furious look. Alec watched that look fade to fear as he noted who was making the racket, and the man silently shuffled back to his quarters.

"I just want to talk, Alec," Roric said more quietly.

"Well, go ahead then. What is so important?"

"We need the boy. Name your price. We will give you whatever you want: money, horses...maybe even titles. We own plenty of land here in Alsace. Just admit the boy was fathered by Rothulfus before his death."

Alec snorted. "There is no chance of making that story believable. Unless you'd like the world to assume your brother raped Eleanor sometime between when she was on my arm and when she was making a mockery of him in tournament? I suppose that might be possible, given his reputation."

"They were married," Roric protested.

Alec raised his eyebrows. "And since when does that mean anything? You might still be in awe of your big brother like a child trotting on his pony to keep up with the hunt, but Rothulfus Lezay raped Eleanor once, and the only other times they saw each other, she was the one with the blade pointed at him. She is the one that watched him die. No one, I repeat, no one, will ever believe they ended up in the same bed again."

Roric frowned, eyeing Alec with caution. Alec could tell his words had hit home, and the man believed him. He was recalculating.

"Sir Alec, I know my brother's injuries in the melee were not fatal. He died from a clean gash across his throat. A thin blade, most likely, like a dagger. Funny, the dagger he always carried was not on his person when they recovered the body. It is rare these days, for someone to actually die in a melee. With recent advancements—"

"If you're trying to blame me for something, spit it out."

Roric leaned across the table, his eyes dancing in the firelight. "I know you killed my brother, even after the melee had been called in your favor. If that knowledge comes out, you could be tried for murder. Your friend King Richard may have been a witness to protect you last year, but now he, too, is dead. It is your word against King Philip of France. And whose side do you think he will choose?"

Now it was Alec's turn to be silent, calculating. He was careful to veil his thoughts. When he spoke, he spoke slowly, letting ice sink into his tone. "There were many witnesses, both English and French. There was a great deal going on. Swords flying. Hooves pounding. Lances cracking. You will never prove his injuries were more than casualties of a brutal melee, even if his body had not already been eaten away to bone by worms."

Roric leaned back again, his knuckles white as he grasped his cup.

"Where is my wife, Roric? I had no issue with you or the rest of your family until you took her. My conflict was with Rothulfus Lezay, and that is settled. I am not a man you wish to have as an enemy."

Roric's frown grew deeper. "Let us mentor the boy. Train him to be a knight. You will see him on holidays, the same as any other young man apprenticing. Just like you and I were raised."

Alec furrowed his brow. "I don't understand the importance of such a young child. He's not even two years old. He can barely speak! You have a son of your own, grown and ready to take on the Lezay legacy. Let him marry and have sons of his own!"

"He has sons of his own," Roric said blankly. "How do I explain?"

"Start with the truth."

Roric shot Alec a glance. "Eleanor's son needs to be my brother's heir."

"He's not."

"For The Order...please...I can't explain further. But to have an heir that is both Lezay and Le Brun blood—ugh, I can't say more." Roric looked genuinely frustrated, as if checking his words was forcing him to swallow his own tongue. He looked away from Alec, studying his mug. His shoulders dropped. Alec saw the moment of distraction as an opportunity to attack the man, but attacking would not accomplish anything. He was no murderer, particularly while he was in the enemy's land. He clenched his fist.

"I will not sell my son to you for the twisted purposes of this secret order that until today, you denied exists."

"You already knew. And Eleanor's right…she's blood…and a knight. If she insists, we may be forced to accept her. That's why we took her."

"If it's her *choice*, then why did you attack us?"

Roric chuckled. "Your wife is a fierce woman, Sir Alec. And she obviously hates my family. Your impatience left us no choice. And technically, she already knows too much to have a choice. Didn't Raoul warn you?"

If Raoul had told them *this*, then perhaps they would have understood what they were trying to avoid. Alec gritted his teeth, weighing his options. "I can't let my son mentor with your family. Eleanor would never allow it. So now what?"

"I promise you, if you let him mentor with us, you will be richer than your king. We have deep treasuries and deeper connections. Think about it."

Alec, so accustomed to faking his wealth with good armor and horses, was not untouched by this statement. His only possessions of value were his wily tongue and skilled sword arm. And his wife and horses, both of which were currently in another man's keeping. He was well aware that he would not retain his youthful vigor forever, and society did not care for old war heroes unless they had an estate and a full treasury to back them. He could not hide the stiffness in his spine as the wheels in his head turned.

Roric noticed. With a bemused smile he said, "You might as well go nurse that headache. I'll take you to the castle to collect Eleanor tomorrow. Then we will speak more, as I originally requested."

Alec snorted. "Delay? While my wife is in the hands of her rapist's family? We go now."

"It's a long ride. And you don't have a horse."

"Get me one."

Roric smiled, amusement lighting his eyes. "Tomorrow. So you both have time to think. It will be here soon enough."

Alec towered over the older knight. "Sir Roric, so help me God, if your son or anyone else lays a hand on my wife, I will kill each and every Lezay until your family tree is as dead as that log in the hearth." He pointed as the log cracked loudly to punctuate the promise. "Can you account for the actions of the men keeping my wife enough to warrant staying here even one breath longer?"

Roric rose with Alec, meeting him eye for eye. "You really do need time to think. We ride in the morning."

With a groan of frustration Alec pushed past Roric. It was not the stairs and the beds beyond he moved to though, but the empty kitchens in the back of the tavern. There he took bread and ale, pacing all the while. The innkeeper entered, expression grumpy in protest, but again shuffled back to his quarters when Alec sent a coin flying at his head.

How could he have let this happen? He would keep his promise if they hurt her. He steeled himself, visualizing the men dead, their wives dead, their innocent children dead. He lingered on that image, pausing in his feeding. He had never killed a child before. He didn't relish it. Boys grew up to be men though, and men sought revenge, if Alec himself was any example. It would have to be complete. He chugged the rest of the ale, willing his mind to quiet, that he could rest even a few minutes before the ride tomorrow.

He should have listened to Eleanor. Alsace was cursed to them.

Alec strode back out of the kitchen, catching Roric off guard enough that he could grab him by the scruff of his shirt. He dragged him from his chair and pushed him ahead of him out the tavern door. Roric must have sensed the fragile control Alec had on his emotions. When Alec said for the second time, "We ride now," Roric agreed.

Chapter 15

Déjà vu it was called. Already seen.

Eleanor had already seen a man disarm her. Overpower her. To make matters worse, he had shared the same face, only older, as the man who now had her bound and seated rather uncomfortably in front of him on his saddle. For a moment present and past had blurred together, and her focus had waivered. That was why she had failed. The Lezay family had taken possession of her dagger a second time, as well as her person.

The throbbing in her head grew worse as consciousness sharpened, and she felt every step of the horse beneath her. The saddle pinched the front of her legs, yet she dared not shift, as her backside was literally in Elfroid's lap. His arm was wrapped tight around her, his other hand holding the reins. Could she take those reins and push him off? She subtly moved her wrists. Tied. To the saddle. Surely he knew how dangerous that would be if the horse they were on decided to spook and dump them off; Eleanor would be dragged to death. Perhaps he didn't care. She gritted her teeth and looked around as best she could with lidded eyes, feigning disorientation. Noir was being led by the scarred man, as was Alec's horse.

The older man, Roric, was gone. It was just the two men, odds she could handle if she could work the knots free. She worked her wrists back and forth as they rode, resting back against Elfroid, as much as she hated him. Let him think she was weak; let him think that he was keeping her in the saddle and she didn't know where she was. At least he kept her back warm in the frigid winter breeze. The radiant sun that made the dusting of snow sparkle offered little warmth.

The men rode in total silence, which Eleanor mused at. They were either angry at something, or the scarred man literally never talked. A waft of onions suddenly drifted through the air and Eleanor stilled, every nerve firing at the memory of Lezay. Suddenly she wasn't sure if it was Elfroid behind her or Lezay, and the thought made her head spin, a wave of nausea washing over her. She fought the heat, trying to breathe deep, but the anxiety only grew worse. She twisted in the saddle, looking back at the man pressed behind her. His eyebrows went up in surprise.

Eleanor, despite her circumstances, had never felt such relief. It was Elfroid. The other man was eating something on a piece of bread as he rode. That was likely the source of the onion smell.

"Good morning, pretty one," Elfroid's voice rumbled against her back.

She could shift now, which she did awkwardly. It took away some of the pressure of the saddle, but she became even more aware of the man behind her.

"Be careful how much fidgeting you do there, darling." Elfroid chuckled. His voice didn't sound like Lezay's at least. Far less deep. But it held its own mocking, dangerous tone.

"Where are we?" Eleanor grumbled, subtly working at the knots at her wrists again.

"Almost to Leuwenstein." Elfroid pointed down the valley, and there ahead was the massive castle Eleanor had heard so much about, yet never visited. His hand covered hers as her movements on the knots became more frantic. "You won't undo those, darling. I learned from a fisherman."

Eleanor squirmed, trying to flick away his hand.

Elfroid chuckled, but he released her. He nudged his horse into a canter, and Eleanor had to stifle a groan as the ride became even more uncomfortable.

"You know, I could have ridden my own horse," she pointed out.

"And have you run off on your own? No chance. We know you better than that."

Eleanor gritted her teeth until they finally slowed to a walk at the castle gate. It was already wide open for them, a garrison watching as they entered. Pennants flew from the grey stone towers, their bright red tails ironically cheerful against the greys and whites of winter. Eleanor had to crane her neck to see up to the top of the castle. It was massive, a sister-fortress to Brunstein. No wonder her uncle and Lezay had been such friends; there was obvious wealth here.

The horses halted, and Eleanor felt her energy surge. She would only have one chance to escape, and it would be in the seconds where she was untied from the horse yet still mounted. She would have to move quickly.

The scarred man dismounted and handed his horse to a groom; Elfroid did the same. The groom held the reins, but that would not be a problem. Elfroid untied the knot that held her wrists to the pommel, but left the rope that bound her wrists together. That too was managcablc, and as the saddle knot came loose, Eleanor kicked the horse beneath her with all her strength. The beast lurched forward, knocking over the groom. She kicked again and the horse skittered off, pulling the reins from the groom's hand. Elfroid made a dive for the flapping leather straps but missed. Eleanor looked back the way they had come and urged the horse forward, turning it with her legs.

They cantered down the road towards the gate, gaining speed as they went. The horse was spooked now, the flapping reins adding to his anxiety. All would have been well if the gate had been open, but Eleanor's eyes widened in panic as she realized it had already been shut. She leaned back in the saddle and said "Whoa!," praying that the horse would listen to a seat aid despite his panic. He didn't, and they barreled towards the gate. At the last second, the horse ducked to the right, and Eleanor lasted only a few strides before the sharp, unbalanced turn threw her off. She rolled and quicky found her feet, grateful for years of practice in falling. Her shoulder ached, but it was nothing she couldn't push through.

She looked around wildly for a smaller gate, a doorway out of the fortress to freedom. Instead, she saw Elfroid, the scarred man, and a dozen men from the castle garrison, all with swords drawn. They circled her, closing in with all the caution one would use to approach a wild beast. Her heart pounded. The look in Elfroid's eyes echoed so much of Lezay's sick evil that it sent her into a panic in which she would fight them off or die trying. Fleeing had not worked, so as the men approached, they were each greeted with blows from feet, elbows, knees, and tied fists. It did not matter if they threatened with blade; she ignored the blades. If they wanted her dead so be it; she would go with a fight. History would not repeat.

But the men did not want her dead, they merely wanted her subdued, so despite their weapons, they avoided using them, taking the brunt of the violence from the crazed woman. Only when Elfroid tackled her to the ground did Eleanor yield, sobbing out her exhaustion and panic. As

Elfroid helped her to her feet, she made one more grab for his dagger—really, *her* dagger. He caught her in time, pinning her to his wiry body with a surprising strength, her bound wrists in a grip that bruised her.

"Enough!" he shouted in her ear, patience spent.

Eleanor flinched and stilled herself, her muscles shaking from exertion.

Elfroid released her enough to take hold of her arm, carefully placing himself out of reach of her elbow. His grip was again strong enough to bruise; he obviously didn't trust her. "Let's go."

She followed him into the castle, carefully mapping the layout in her head. They stopped outside a door in one of the towers, where panic started to overwhelm her again. She pulled back. "What do you want from me?"

Elfroid pulled her tight against him as the scarred man opened the door before them with a key. Together, the men forced her inside the small room, which was sparsely furnished with a heavy framed bed and a three-legged stool. A chill draft drifted from the window. Elfroid gave the rope around her wrists a sharp yank as he looked around the room. His eyes settled on the iron sconce which was bolted into the stone wall. He pulled Eleanor across the room like a stubborn dog.

Eleanor's eyes went wide in panic. "No, no, no! What do you want?" Eleanor screamed. She pulled away, feet and elbows again thrashing.

"Hurry up, Heinrich," Elfroid whined.

The scar-faced man shot Elfroid a glare. Perhaps he didn't want to be named? Eleanor registered this only barely, as she continued to writhe in Elfroid's arms. Soon enough her bound wrists were secured to the wall, and Eleanor's hands were stretched up above her head until only the balls of her feet touched the ground. She tried to kick the two men that circled her, but without sufficient leverage from the ground, she was powerless. She stopped fighting, glaring at them.

"I am a noblewoman. When my countrymen hear about this, you will pay."

"The king of England is too busy to meddle with petty matters. Particularly yours."

Eleanor fumed but bit her tongue. He was right. She could protest her treatment, but if and when the events came to trial, it would be pointless. Who knew what would happen between now and then? "You intend to keep me here forever?" she asked sarcastically.

"Only until we're bored with you," Elfroid smirked. The implication wasn't lost on Eleanor. Elfroid drew his dagger. "My uncle told such stories of you…" He hooked the knife through the laces of Eleanor's tunic, and the sharp blade cut with ease. The unraveling of the strings awoke in Elfroid's eyes a new joy, and Eleanor swallowed. It was her worst nightmare coming back to life. She concentrated on her breath, willing her mind to stay clear as panic again threatened to overtake her.

"Elfroid…" Heinrich said and cleared his throat from across the room.

"Don't speak," Elfroid shot. He cut her tunic down the middle, the green fabric yielding to the sharp blade with no more than a traitorous hiss. Eleanor closed her eyes, keeping perfectly still. Breath in, breath out. Her shirt was next, seam by seam until it was in pieces at her feet. A tear leaked from her eye as she willed her mind out of the room, back to warm, cozy Levan manor. She thought of her son, hopefully warm in bed, and prayed that no matter what happened, he would never fall into the hands of these men as they so desired. She squeezed her eyes shut, clamped her legs together.

"Now, let's go," Heinrich growled.

Eleanor opened her eyes to see the older man grab Elfroid by the arm. Elfroid was staring at her with one of the most conflicted expressions she'd seen on a man. Not quite lust, but desire mixed with some kind of deep hatred. She shivered. There was murder in that gaze. It lingered until Elfroid followed Heinrich's pull, and the men left the room. Heinrich returned a minute later.

Eleanor tensed in fear yet again. "Please, let me go," she pleaded one more time, but Heinrich did not speak. He reached above her and undid the ropes that were tied to the sconce, holding the knot at her wrists firmly in his big hands.

"You dare to strike me again, woman, and I will leave you tied until Roric returns. You understand?"

She nodded. After another moment's hesitation, Heinrich hastily undid the knot and retreated from the room before Eleanor could even rub her wrists. She heard the solid click of the lock behind him. Knowing it was futile, she tested the door anyway. It didn't budge. The window was far too narrow for a body. She was trapped.

Her upper layers of clothing were a useless pile of rags. Eleanor grabbed a blanket from the pile on the bed and pulled it tight around herself, the stress shaking her body with a tremble that made her teeth chatter. Any minute Elfroid would be back and take what he wanted, whether that be her body or her life or both. Eleanor doubted he would even know which he wanted until he was in the moment.

Eleanor belted out a scream of frustration. She cursed Lezay. She cursed Alsace. She thought about cursing Alec for bringing her back here, but that wasn't quite fair. She'd had a choice, and she'd insisted on coming along. All this for secrets no one was ready to part with. She let the tears flow, checking back the sobs that threatened to break through, knowing that if she fell apart completely, she would be that much weaker when Elfroid came back.

She had to be strong, ready. She had to think and to save her strength.

They would come back.

Chapter 16

T he bloodlust thrumming in Alec's veins was what kept him on the boney, ill-tempered horse he'd been forced to ride all the way to the gates of Leuwenstein castle. It loomed above them like a granite tombstone. Fitting, for the Lezays.

Grooms emerged to take their horses as the wind picked up, its icy fingers warning of a change in weather. Alec glanced around, taking in every detail. The serfs stared at him with cold disdain, then turned back to work. Nerves tingling, he followed Roric into the castle.

"Come, let's get a drink," Roric offered.

"I want to see Eleanor."

"She's preoccupied."

The fragile chord restraining his anger snapped. In seconds, Alec had the man by the throat and thrown up against the wall. "I'm done with the games. I will spill your blood in your own house if you don't show her to me. Right. Now."

"Oh, but that would make such a mess." The voice came from further down the hall. The son.

"Are all Lezays so casual about death?" Alec asked as he drew his dagger.

"Death is part of life," Roric smiled. "Elfroid, why don't you take our guest to his wife?"

"Certainly." Elfroid pivoted and strode back the way he had come. His eyes glinted maliciously as he stopped to glance back at Alec. "Coming, Sir Alec?"

Alec cursed under his breath, sensing a trap but unable to avoid it. He glared at Roric, then followed Elfroid in a circuitous route through the castle. It seemed Leuwenstein was as much a maze as Chateau Brunstein. Or perhaps Elfroid was trying to disorient Alec intentionally? Finally, they emerged at a door somewhere in a tower of the castle, and Elfroid took out a key.

"You locked her up? Roric said she wasn't a hostage."

Elfroid smiled, tossed Alec the key, and disappeared down the stairwell. In a rush, Alec unlocked the door and threw it open, the sight greeting him stopping him in his tracks. The room was small and drafty. Against the wall was a small bed. Directly center was a narrow paned-glass window with a wide sill, on which his wife sat staring out at the snowy ground below. It would have been a peaceful picture if they were at Neroche or Levan Manor, but they were in Leuwenstein, and Eleanor, if her bare shoulder gave any indication, was dressed only in a blanket. Alec fought down instinctual jealousy, which was replaced by a more sickening fear that the Lezays had again violated her, which turned to a fist-clenching anger. When she didn't turn to face him, his fears deepened into a full-blown panic; what had they done to her?

"Don't just stand there, Elfroid," Eleanor said with a bravado Alec knew she worked hard to fake.

His heart pounded. "I'm not Elfroid."

Eleanor whirled towards him, one hand grabbing at the blanket as it slipped down her shoulder. "Alec!" She slid off the windowsill and was in his arms within a second. His arms wrapped around her, his hands trembling.

"What did they do?"

"Nothing," she whispered into his chest. One of her hands clenched the blanket at her neck, her other twined around his waist, pulling him in tight.

"If they did nothing, then where are your clothes?" His anger surged to a roar, blood rushing in his ears. They had been with her.

She laid a hand on his cheek, forcing him to meet her eyes. "Alec, they did not touch me. I am fine." She glanced at the open door behind him. "Eager to get out of here though. How did you get in?"

As much as he wanted to believe her, he knew the reputation of the Lezay family all too well. He studied her with narrowed eyes until she stepped back in frustration and dropped the blanket. At least she was still dressed from the waist down. Her wrists were bruised, perhaps chafed by rope. She had a dark bruise across one shoulder blade. Otherwise she was un-marked. That didn't mean much though. He knew there were ways to scar that did not leave a mark.

Eleanor pulled the blanket back up, wrapping herself tightly in it again. "Satisfied?"

"I don't understand."

"I'll explain later. I want to get out of here. But we have to talk to them first."

"Talk? Eleanor if I so much as enter the same room as them, I may kill them."

"Don't kill them. I know what questions to ask. We have to talk to them, and then we will leave. How did you get in?" she asked again.

Alec frowned, emotions warring. "I came through the front door. With Roric." He stripped off his cloak and tunic, pulling both over her head. "Let's go, but then you better give me answers."

Dressed in Alec's clothes, Eleanor pulled the cloak tight around her. She eyed Alec's naked torso. "Now you'll be cold."

"Don't worry, I need to cool down if you expect me not to fight my way out of here. Now explain, quickly, why we aren't running out of this castle right now."

"That's what they expect us to do."

Alec raised an eyebrow.

"We're going to go to the main hall, sit down, and enjoy dinner in the warmth. With the Lezays."

Alec again debated how ill his wife was. He reached out on impulse and felt her forehead. Cool.

"We're going to talk. We're going to get as much information as we can. I am going to ask a lot of questions, and for once you are going to have to do more listening than asking." She hesitated. "They brought us here to talk in private, and that is what we will do."

"Mm-hmm." His hands ran over the top of her head, feeling for a lump or cut that would indicate a head injury. Sure enough, there was a slight bump. Perhaps that was it. "Why did they have you half naked, Eleanor?"

"To scare me. It worked. For a while. Are you listening?"

Alec nodded. "You want me to sit down to dinner with a bunch of men I'd like nothing better than to kill. And to keep my mouth shut, too."

"Yes."

Alec pursed his lips, debating. "If they so much as put a finger on you, it will be a bloodbath. Do you understand?"

"Fair enough. Make sure you throw me a sword." She smiled, cupping his cheek in her hand.

Unspoken understanding passed between them. Alec had a thousand things to say to her, but the itch in his sword hand was too great a distraction. He gestured towards the door, and Eleanor led the way. As he suspected, Elfroid had taken him in a circuitous route.

They emerged into the main hall far more quickly than it had taken to reach the tower. His fury at the Lezays heated anew. Perhaps it was good that he was bare chested in the chill of the hall. He would need all the help he could get to cool his temper. He squared his shoulders. If he was to be exposed, let them judge him. Now at the age of thirty, he had aged better than most and was fitter than he had been when he'd entered his twenties. He'd been fortunate to avoid major injuries; only the faint scars of scuffles traced their constellations on his torso and arms. He knew he was taller than the rest of the men. Let them judge if they wanted to test his strength.

He prayed they did not scrutinize Eleanor as closely.

A wave of heat washed over him again as he remembered at least two of them had seen her half naked. He sought out Elfroid, and he glared with the fury of a chained beast waiting for permission to attack.

Every head in the room, few as there were, was locked on the couple as they approached. The three noblemen were seated at a table near the hearth while a few servants drifted around the hall serving their lords. Eleanor led the way to their table, where after an awkward moment, Roric cracked a smile and yelled for a servant to add two more plates. Eleanor and Alec sat down across from him.

Alec gauged reactions as Eleanor clasped her hands on the table before her, bruised wrists on display. Roric's gaze flicked up and down her, his brow furrowed, though his lips forced a gracious smile. His eyes lingered on the bruises, and his smile faded. Elfroid had not taken his eyes off Alec, meeting his challenging gaze. Alec clenched his fist beneath the table, willing himself to be patient. The third man, who Eleanor had mentioned was named Heinrich, was as stoic and silent as ever. Finally, Roric gestured to the food before them and helped himself to a full plate.

The meal commenced, the tension palpable. The hall was so quiet they could hear each other chewing. Though Alec had little appetite, he forced what nourishment he could into his body. He would need his strength for what was to come. When Eleanor and Roric had finished, they stared at each other, each nursing a goblet of wine. Alec finished his plate, nerves alive as he waited.

"How do you like the wine?" Roric asked.

Eleanor shrugged. "I'm afraid I'm partial to the Aquitanian varieties. My estate produced an exquisite red this year." The stare down continued. "I want to know why you kill," she blurted. Alec straightened.

Roric looked unperturbed. "I'm afraid you'll have to be more specific about what you mean. We are knights after all."

"Murder is the purpose of The Order, is it not? Death and knowledge, reliant on each other. Do I need to go ask my grandfather himself the details? I have some fine stories to tell him now, don't I? I wonder if he would care that you threw his granddaughter naked into a tower prison?"

"Don't..." Elfroid said, immediately silencing himself as glares shot his way. He clenched his jaw so tightly Alec could see the muscles strain.

Roric glared at Elfroid. "You did *what* to her?"

Alec leveled his gaze at Roric. "I warned you, Roric." Internally, he noted how Eleanor had determined that Raganor was not part of whatever the Lezays were orchestrating. It was a small consolation.

Roric turned his attention back to Alec. "I assure you, my son will be dealt with appropriately."

"Why don't you let me determine appropriateness?" Alec offered.

"All of you, shut up!" Eleanor slammed her fist on the table. "You *kidnapped* me to talk, so let us talk. Let's try this again, and I will be specific. Did The Order kill Lord Edmond of Fougères?"

Roric leaned back, his expression curious. "That's not the name I expected you to bring up first." He met Eleanor's eye, gaze steady. Alec clenched a fist, biting his tongue. Roric shrugged. "Edmond's death was carried out by members of The Order because your uncle ordered it."

"So you *are* assassins. Why Edmond?"

"Montag was looking for you. Always, he and my brother were looking for you... like an obsession. Edmond was a clue, until he got in the way." Roric sipped his wine, and there was pause. He seemed to make some sort of judgement on Eleanor, for he nodded once with an amused finality. "I assume you have been warned that knowledge of The Order can get you killed?"

"Yes."

"Edmond learned less than what you already know. We worried he would tell King Richard."

Alec's gaze shifted to Eleanor, who sat straight and still, her fist clenched. Roric had all but told them they would be murdered. It was time to go. Still, he'd promised to let her ask the questions, and she looked like she was far from finished. Alec went back to studying their hosts. He would give her as much time as his intuition allowed.

Eleanor's brow was furrowed as she watched Roric. "I'm too valuable for you to kill. I realized that this morning during a fight. But before you tell me my value, tell me—did the same happen with Alec's father?"

Roric twitched and coughed on his wine. "I can't say."

Alec found that interesting. They'd admitted Edmond's murder. What was Eleanor onto? The words left Alec's mouth before he could stop them. "Why did Lezay kill my father?"

"He didn't," Elfroid muttered. Roric and Heinrich glared at him. "What?" Elfroid looked around the table. "Father, she wants in. Certain things we can tell her, prepare her for."

Roric frowned deeply, studying Eleanor.

"He's going to tell us to let her try anyway. Why delay?" Elfroid asked.

"You've outstepped your place, son. In more ways than one."

"If you thought it was so easy to bring her here, you should have done it yourself. I only did what I had to." Elfroid glowered. "Woman's a fiend..." he muttered.

"And you *had* to strip her naked? We will talk later." Roric's tone left little room for argument. He stroked his beard, then faced Eleanor again. "If Alec steps outside the hall, I will tell you what you want to know. But you must swear that you inquire based on a desire to enter our guild. Once this information is passed, you will have only two options. You join us, or you die. Most would choose ignorance over those two options."

"I'm not leaving," Alec said bluntly. He was highly aware that the question his life had revolved around for years was as yet unanswered. Had there been a motive for his father's death?

"For what it's worth, we are taking great risk ourselves by discussing any of this." Roric's posture alluded to his inner doubts on continuing. "That is why we needed you to come here, to Leuwenstein. And it is why we will only speak to Eleanor."

To Alec's horror, Eleanor said, "Alec will leave. I need to know."

The look Eleanor shot Alec had him struggling to bite his tongue. He shook his head. Perhaps it was her head injury. She wasn't thinking straight. Raoul, blast him, was right after all, and they never should have continued to ask questions. That was on Alec; he was the one that had pried at the tavern. And yet somehow, even when they'd stopped and tried to leave, the actions of the Lezays alluded that they did want to spill secrets. It was enough for them to attack and kidnap.

Eleanor again ordered him away with a touch of her hand to his arm, a point of her finger. "Alec, go."

The room was silent as Alec stared at her, weighing the situation. Eleanor met his gaze, and Roric glanced between the two of them, a knuckle to his lips in amusement. Elfroid shifted uncomfortably, and Heinrich leaned back in his chair to take another long swallow of wine. The servants stepped out of the hall, leaving the room silent but for the cracking of logs in the hearth.

Alec turned to Roric, his fists clenched at his sides. "I want my sword."

Roric pursed his lips, then gave a subtle nod to Heinrich. The man produced Alec's sword from the bench next to him. Alec's fingers closed around the sheath, decisions laying heavy on his mind. With a slow inhale, he handed the sheathed blade to Eleanor, rose, then spun on his heel and stalked out of the room, hands clenching and unclenching in fury. Elfroid followed him, closing the huge door to the hall shut with a smirk.

The thud of the door echoed like a drum.

Eleanor was not afraid, for she had realized in the tower that they needed her alive. They needed her untouched, and thus far, Roric's behavior had proven she was right. Elfroid may hate her, but he could do little more than intimidate her. That shifted the power back to her. Just as in a tournament, when she could tell the other opponent was out of tricks, out of strength, and she was going to win, she felt that confidence surge.

"You're a bold one," Roric said quietly. He observed her with his chin in his hand, an echo of respect in his eyes.

"I have no choice but to be. If I do not get the answers I seek, I will continue to be harassed and kidnapped, like a baited bear for your sport. You don't want me to die, so the game can continue."

Roric smiled slightly. "You are a unique woman, Lady Eleanor. Yet I wonder if you truly want what you seek."

"I feel I have no choice." And she meant it. She'd been harassed enough over the years. Kidnapped, married off, her son taken, belittled, hidden, her home burned...when would it end? To protect Benec, she would do anything, whether it be to send him to England or bind herself to this horrible group. She took a deep breath. "Will this nonsense cease if I become one of you? You are bound to protect each other, are you not?"

"Yes. You would then be protected."

"And my son?"

"We have only ever wanted to protect him, albeit what we have in mind may not be the same as your desires."

"Like how Montag thought he was 'protecting' me by marrying me to your brother?"

"Yes."

"And how you felt it was necessary to kidnap me and strip me naked?"

Roric held up a finger. "They were only to take you. Elfroid will face his punishment."

"How can I trust that?"

Roric looked to Heinrich, who nodded once and rose, drawing his sword and plunging the tip into the fire. Eleanor moved her hand to the hilt of Alec's sword, but did not draw. Heinrich's attention was not on her, but the blade.

Elfroid shot out of his seat. "Don't you dare. I am not some child that needs to be scolded, Father." He glared at Roric. "You weren't here. You didn't see how she fought. I only meant to scare her, and it worked. She is docile now."

"You were to treat her as a guest, Elfroid." Roric gave his son a disappointed frown, then turned to Eleanor. "You may do it. It is part of our oldest custom. Burn the flesh to purge the soul. Elfroid, take your tunic and shirt off."

Eleanor clenched her fists on the table, unsure of what to do. Elfroid was already undressing, furious and yet yielding. Heinrich checked the red tip of the sword then placed it back in the hearth. She had been told stories of this, but she did not want to see it firsthand. She did not want to burn someone, even a monster like Elfroid.

"Consider it the first test," Roric offered. "If you cannot do this, you will not be able to fulfill what is necessary to join The Order. How badly do you want answers? Or are you willing to entrust us with your son's safety blindly? For that is what you must do. You do not know what you are up against. We do."

Eleanor swallowed.

"We know about you," Roric continued. "In addition to assassinations, we work for knowledge on those around us, for those in power. Why do you think Raganor was in Poitiers last summer? He knew you would be there. Why do you think he knows about Benec? Men have been watching that child since the day he was born. The Order's network is deep. What no one seems to know, and I intend to find out, is if you are strong enough to do what will be asked of you."

Eleanor looked at Elfroid, who smirked at her with such a challenge she found herself rising to her feet. Even when she circled him, he continued to eye her as if she would falter. Heinrich drew the red-tipped sword from the fire and handed it to Eleanor, its handle warm in her hand.

"One touch," Roric said unemotionally. "Anywhere." He averted his eyes.

Elfroid's smirk changed back into a glare, but he turned his back to Eleanor. There was a small smattering of scars there, maybe five or six. At least Elfroid had not gone through this often. Eleanor took a deep breath and touched his shoulder with the hot tip of the sword, her arms holding it steady. He flinched and let out a hiss of air through his teeth. She counted to three—which seemed like an eternity—then removed it. The smell of burned flesh filled the room. She pointed the sword tip down, and took a step back.

Elfroid straightened, rolled his shoulders, and then pulled his shirt and tunic back over his head. He and Heinrich returned to their seats as if nothing had happened.

Roric opened a hand, indicating her place at the table. "And now you and Elfroid are even. We may continue."

Eleanor leaned Heinrich's sword against the table and returned to her seat.

Roric continued, his eyes sparkling. "Now, remember what I warned you. You will only have two options from this point. Leave now if you want a third."

She straightened. For Benec, she would do this. She must. She could not live with an unnamed enemy always seeking her.

"Very well then." Roric smiled. "There is still more you may not learn until the ceremony, but I *can* tell you this. We are descended from thirteen ancient lines. Those men were each powerful in their own lands, but when they came together, they were equals."

"Like King Arthur and the Knights of the Round Table?" She thought of the troubadours whose stories circulated at tournaments.

"That story was inspired by us, though it is far from the truth. After knowledge of our existence escaped, we implemented a policy by which all those who knew of us either died or joined us."

"You must have many members."

Elfroid and Heinrich looked away.

"We never allow over thirteen." Roric took a slow sip of his ale. "All descendants."

Elfroid leaned towards her over the table. "We have one opening, Montag's. I took my uncle's place after his death. The initiation involves a death. And you're going to be the one to execute."

Eleanor paled. "That is murder."

"It's sacrifice," Heinrich said solemnly.

The three of them looked at him, but he was as immobile as if he hadn't spoken, staring at a knot in the wood.

Roric explained, "The sacrifice also has to be a knight from one of the bloodlines."

Eleanor furrowed her brow. "But if you have members of each line, doesn't that mean the sacrifice would be related to someone there?"

Elfroid shrugged. "Sometimes a son, or a cousin. At the very least, a best friend's son. You should have kept your nose out of this."

Eleanor's heart began to pound as understanding dawned. "And that is the purpose for which you wanted my son? To sacrifice him to this barbaric, evil—"

"No. We want to protect him. He is going to be the most powerful member of all," Roric said.

"Someone to finally replace Raganor," Elfroid added.

"He is our heir," Heinrich said quietly.

Eleanor looked from one man to the other. "Why him?"

Roric took another long drink. "There is a legend you should know about. To keep the thirteen bloodlines pure, they have long been said to be cursed if ever they cross. For centuries, members would try to marry the daughters of their allies, trying to make a dual bloodline that would sway the balance of power within the order in their favor. Those marriages always proved fruitless."

The table was quiet for a moment.

"You are a Le Brun. The Lezays are of a different branch. When my brother Rothulfus married you, he hoped to break the curse, gain the power of your dual-blooded child."

"He failed," Eleanor said quickly. Though she began to understand why they continued to ask her to name Benec as Lezay's heir.

"He did. But your child is no less important."

"I don't understand...he is not a Lezay."

Roric smiled, his eyes twinkling. "That is the beauty of it. He never had to be. *You* are the dual-blooded child. When your father escaped the ceremony and married your mother, it broke every rule we had."

Eleanor's heart pounded.

"Tell her the rest of it," Heinrich said quietly.

Elfroid leaned forward, his eyes malicious with their own kind of sparkle. "You were right when you questioned if The Order had anything to do with the death of Alfred of Homme, Alec's father. He was not just an assignment, like Edmond. He was the sacrifice in an initiation."

Eleanor gasped and shot a look at the door Alec stood behind. If he overheard this now, he surely would unleash his fury. "But he overheard Lezay bragging in the tavern—"

"My brother was there, as were we all, except Elfroid who had not yet joined. But Lezay was not the initiate then. He did not deal the last cut." Roric said quietly. He paused for his words to sink in. "I think you will realize who joined us during that time, but that is not important. You are missing the most important detail."

Eleanor thought for a moment, and then it dawned on her with a horror that made her skin prickle. "Three? If Alec is his father, then my son is of *three* bloodlines?"

"In all the centuries, that has never happened." Elfroid smirked. "So how sure are you that Alec Earnblaec is the father of your child?"

Roric held up a finger to his son, who tempered his enthusiastic prodding of Eleanor's deepest doubts. "You should decide who you really *want* to claim the father of your child to be. For if he is an Earnblaec, he is both even more valuable and in more danger."

Edmond's face rose in her mind with such clarity it took her breath away. It was possible. She'd always known as much. Yet to take fatherhood from a man who had given so much to her—it would devastate Alec. Eleanor felt nauseated. She sat with her head in her hands for long minutes.

When she looked up, Elfroid watched her emotions with the same hungry fascination he'd shown as he undressed her in the tower. She checked herself, aware he was not the fool the others treated him as. He leered at her. "You should also know that we consider your husband a murderer. We know he killed my uncle in the melee. After Montag had surrendered. That is murder."

"My horse kicked him..." Eleanor said weakly.

Roric shook his head. "Your horse didn't make a clean cut across his throat."

Eleanor closed her eyes, trying to remember. She'd been weak from blood loss. Montag had made the same claim when she'd spoken with him before her ordination. It was likely true.

"Because of this," Roric explained, "Alec is not our choice to fill Montag's vacant chair. It is you."

"Welcome to The Order." Elfroid chuckled. "Kill or be killed."

Her eyes flashed open. She needed time—space—to process all she'd learned. It was time to leave. She stood. She met each man's eyes in turn.

"When?" she asked.

"The spring equinox." Roric offered.

Only a few months away. Her brow furrowed. She still didn't understand why two-year-old Benec was so desired, and she told them such.

A slow smile crept on Roric's face. "Don't you see? As a dual—or even tri—blooded young man, plus as the great-grandson of Raganor our leader, he is certain to take control on Raganor's long-awaited death. That is more power than any single king can wield. If you knew our members, you would understand. Though you must wait to join to know them." Roric pointed a finger to the table, gesturing to punctuate his words. "Whoever raises the boy will have his loyalty. They will condition him to be the heir they want. *We* would raise him as an Alsatian, with a strong desire to build the empire we have started. Your grandfather would likely twist him to continuing the more grotesque traditions of The Order. There are others, too, all with their own agendas. If your cousin dies childless, which he seems determined to do, and if your son dies before he is knighted as some members desire, a power void will be created." He shook his head, face suddenly somber.

Heinrich explained. "None of us want that. Thus why your son must be raised to prepare him for what is to come."

"And if he does not want to join at all?" she asked. Of course she didn't want her innocent boy to join a group of murderers.

Roric met her eye. "If he lives to adulthood and is knighted, I promise you, someone will tell him about us. And he will be offered the same choice we just offered you."

Join or die.

Eleanor left the hall before the emotion within her burst, the whisper of her movement like the ghosts of her past that refused to stay dead.

Chapter 17

Alec's flesh pebbled in the cold air, and he resumed pacing. He replayed what he had been told about the Lezay family, about his father's death, and about Edmond's death. The list was short. Roric had taken over running Leuwenstein, even while Rothulfus Lezay was alive. Roric was a gifted lord. They were rich, and they seemed to get richer every year. Their massive castle was proof. Beyond that, most of the control of Alsace fell to Montag, or at least it had. Now Raoul was lord. Eleanor seemed very curious about the death of Alec's father, and he didn't know why. It was a highway murder, nothing more. Lezay had admitted to it. Lezay had paid. Edmond had been tortured to death as Lezay had attempted to find Eleanor. Perhaps she was trying to give that death another reason, that she would not feel like the catalyst for her lover's demise.

Alec's mind went to dark places as he paced the hall. The past welled up like a great spring of despair. He did not yield to it though. He let it feed his anger, his resentment.

He allowed the walls of defense to rise around his battered heart, the heart he'd only let one woman into. If something happened to her now, how could he move forward?

Finally Eleanor emerged from the hall, approaching Alec with brisk steps but not meeting his eye.

"Well?" he prompted, his tone short.

"Our horses are in the stable. Let's go." She handed him his cloak. He ignored it, still glaring at her. She held up the sword instead, and that he took and belted around his waist as he stalked ahead of her and out of the castle. Grooms already had their horses saddled and ready, as if they had known exactly how this escapade would transpire. Eleanor's blades were even tied onto the saddle, and their saddlebags were packed with provisions. A maid came running out of the castle after them, a bundle of clothes in her arms, which she offered to Eleanor with a blush and downcast eyes. Eleanor took the clothes with a quiet "thanks," but did not dress. Instead she mounted her horse, the bundle in her lap.

Alec didn't speak, just mounted his destrier and followed Eleanor out into the countryside. His mind raced with questions, yet another part of him was relieved to put as much distance between them and the Lezays as possible.

In answer to his unspoken thoughts, Eleanor said, "We'll go to Abbey St. Catherine. We should get at least partway there before dark." She pressed her horse up to a canter, tucking the cloak tighter around her.

Alec gritted his teeth and followed her. "Are you going to tell me what's going on? You were locked in a room like a criminal for a day, and all you want to do when I free you is be alone with those men. What is wrong with you?"

"I told you, it was a test."

"And was it worth it? Did you pass?" He could not hide his bitter tone. He had never felt this kind of anger towards a woman, and he didn't know what to do with it.

"Yes."

Alec grabbed her reins at that, pulling both their horses to a halt. She snatched them back angrily but did not kick her horse forward.

"What did you do, Eleanor? What did they do to you? You tell me now. You are my wife."

"I'm fine."

"It's more than that! You're running into the wilderness only half dressed. Tell me what happened! What was your payment for their secrets?"

Eleanor backed her horse away from him. "There isn't always a cost for answers, Alec."

"They had you naked. Alone."

"But nothing happened."

"I don't believe that."

"What do you want me to say? They tied me up and took turns with me. All of them. They left me alone in the dark only to come back and do it again. And then to steal their secrets, I asked them to take me right on the banquet table, while you stood outside the door. Is that what you want to hear?"

The face of another woman, a gorgeous, dark-complexioned prostitute, flashed behind his eyes with such clarity he had to blink it away. He felt as if a rock settled in the pit of his stomach. "Is it the truth?" Alec asked quietly.

"No!" Eleanor looked at him with exasperation. "I told you, nothing happened. And do you really think I'd sell my body for information? What kind of person does that?" She shook her head and kicked her horse down the road, missing the shocked look that flitted across Alec's face. "I'll let you get dressed when we get out of sight of the castle!" she shouted over her shoulder.

As he rode off after her, he finally believed her. She had told him about her first marriage bed years ago, willingly enough. She would not lie about this. Her words stung though, for reasons she did not realize. Perhaps she had not sold her body for information, but in the past, Alec had. Yes, he knew what it was like to play the nobility with all you had. There was so much Eleanor didn't know about him. She didn't ask. That was probably his own fault; when they'd met he'd tried to charge her for secrets, the price a kiss, a caress, a moment alone. Did Eleanor think she'd still owe him if she asked?

Alec thought of the secrets he still held. He urged his horse faster, his heart racing in time with the hoofbeats.

The heat of his muscles flexing with his horse's kept the icy wind at bay, at least for now. Eleanor was probably right not to question him about his past. There was too much he didn't want her to know.

Alec and Eleanor did not speak the rest of the day. He let her guide them down the road into the west, following the sun. They stopped only once, to let the horses drink and to pull their clothes on. Her teeth had been chattering so loud he could hear them from a distance away, but he did not offer warmth. She was ignoring him with a rigidity to her spine that might as well have held up a fortress. He'd been grateful to take back his own clothes, his body numb with cold. His body temperature was just beginning to stabilize when the sun began to fall, and they made a modest camp just below the crest of a rocky ridge.

Eleanor stood with her back to Alec, arms clasped tight around her as she stared over the cliff to the glistening valley below. The setting sun cast her with a red light, the tendrils of her dark hair drifting in the gentle wind like flaming coals. Alec hesitated, for a moment in awe of the raw beauty that had always entranced him. Then he gritted his teeth and stepped forward, reminding himself she was no goddess, but human...his wife.

As the snow crunched beneath his feet, she spoke, and he froze in his tracks as if she really did have a magical power. "Does it hurt, you think, to die?" The words were as soft as a whisper, yet spoken with firm clarity.

Alec again hesitated, wondering where her thoughts lay. "I suppose that depends on the manner of death."

"Oh, I don't mean what leads to the death. That's always some form of bodily failure. Injury, illness, age…all of that hurts. But what about the part where the soul rips from the corporeal form? You think if the rest happens fast enough, that death wouldn't hurt? Or is that tear from the body the worst? Does time slow with a fast death, and you feel it just the same as someone that dies over months?"

"Eleanor, what are you talking about?" He eyed the cliff below her feet, the stunning sunset washing the snow-covered trees below in hues of orange and pink, the shadows below their branches dark fingers reaching up from the depths. "Can you come back here? Please?"

Eleanor seemed to break from her trance and turned to him, carefully stepping away from the edge. She still clutched her arms around herself.

Alec frowned as he fell under the full force of her glare.

"You made it fast."

"I what?" His eyes widened.

"For Lezay. He would have suffered. What Montag said before he died was true…it was you. You made it fast. They told me."

"I…" he gaped at her.

"I suppose I knew all along. I couldn't see. But I heard." She leveled her gaze at him another moment longer as he remained speechless. Then something in her softened. She frowned. "I thought we wanted him to suffer?"

Alec let out a slow breath. The image of Lezay lying there, struggling for breath, his pathetic hands scratching for his dagger to do what his eyes pleaded Alec to finish. He was a dead man; he wanted a warrior's death. Hate had left Alec longing to watch the long, slow process as the man struggled. But Eleanor had been bleeding out behind him, and their witnesses were closing in. "I did it so we could move on, Eleanor. Both of us." He took a deep breath. "You would have spent every day looking over your shoulder for him, and I would forever be wishing to do exactly what I did, which was to avenge my father." Alec closed his eyes to the vision of Lezay's blood pulsing from his throat onto the grass, the light in his eyes fading as his pupils stared into Alec's face with a confused mess of shock and relief.

Eleanor stared at him, her expression unreadable even to Alec.

"Eleanor…if you want to philosophize on death, wait until we see Wilfred. He'll talk to you about it all day. But if you want the reason why I dealt our enemy a mercy blow, that's it." He turned back toward the horses. "I'm not going to talk about it again."

"Alec…" the fear in her voice caught him off guard yet again. "I found out what the initiation is."

He blinked, stunned. No one had ever surprised him so many times in such a short amount of time. Either his nerves were in tatters or hers were. Likely both.

Eleanor sighed and pulled her cloak tighter around her, facing the sunset.

Alec swallowed and approached her side.

"We were right, their network of spies runs deep. And the men involved are more powerful than we anticipated." A tear glistened at the corner of her eye, though it could just be caused by the cold air. "If we are both dead, they will have Benec." She took a deep breath and glanced around them. "Are you sure no one has followed?"

They were deep within the forest, far from the next village, still a few miles from the Abbey St. Catherine. They had seen no tracks other than those of the wild animals of the woods.

"I am sure. We are alone." Alec waited patiently, then pressed a hand against the small of her back in reassurance.

"I don't know where to begin. There's so much."

"Start with you first." He didn't hide the pleading from his voice. "What happened when they took you?"

Alec listened, anger rising and falling as she gave her account of her capture. As she spoke of how she'd lost her upper layers of clothing, he had to close his eyes, teeth gritted against the image of another man gazing at his wife.

Eleanor pressed on, unable to look to Alec and instead staring off into the distance. "He wanted to lose control, to hurt me—lord knows what stories his uncle told him—but Heinrich wouldn't allow it. By the time you arrived, I had realized I had a certain power. They need me. They can't kill me. They could probably hurt me, but then they would answer to a more powerful man."

"Your grandfather?"

She nodded. "When Montag was alive, I think he was their leader. He had control. That both kept me protected and opened the door for the Lezays, well, particularly Rothulfus Lezay, to test his control. When Montag died, the Lezays lost prestige. And they want it back." She rubbed the back of her neck. "I suspected, since they won't kill me, that keeping you out of that room would in a way protect you. It did."

Alec could tell she was still holding something back. "Protect me from what?"

She shook her head and looked away.

"Eleanor, you know I can keep secrets." If only she knew to what degree.

She pursed her lips and then nodded once, making a decision. "The Order is based on bloodlines, as we suspected. The ceremony involves murder, as we feared. The participants must be knights, though some are nobility higher than knights. They refused to name names. Their rules are very strict."

"How many members can there be?"

"Thirteen." Eleanor inhaled then unleashed a flood of words, as if once stopped they could never start again. Alec grew cold as she explained about the bloodlines and how they chose sacrifices. She exhaled a steaming breath into the cold air. "They said there is a curse on those who try to blend bloodlines. They've tried to do it many times, and those couples always end up childless."

A hawk called from overhead, distracting them both a moment, its belly golden with sunlight.

"Eleanor, why would Lezay marry you, since he knew you were a Le Brun? The curse would continue."

"I am more than a Le Brun. I am a Levan." She inhaled. "My parents were the only ones that ever broke the curse. I am the first progeny of two bloodlines."

"Your father was intended to be the sacrifice..." Understanding lit his face. The story was true then, without a doubt. Years ago, Sir Enric de Levan had escaped The Order's clutches.

She nodded. "It is why they were so mad that my parents married. It's likely why he was killed, to ensure I was the only child that was created. By my blood being two lines, I am somehow dangerous to their balance of power. If Montag had not taken me, I likely would have been killed as well. I should not exist." She hesitated, then said to herself, "That is what Raoul tried to tell me..."

Alec inhaled, digesting this information. It made sense, as much as he disliked it. "But that still doesn't explain why Lezay would want you."

"It does, though. Don't you see? I'm the one that broke the curse. They hoped to do it again. And if he could add his bloodline to the mix, that would be three. That would make my child the most powerful member The Order had ever seen. That is why, even knowing that it's not true, they want me to pretend Benec is Lezay's."

Darkness was falling over the valley below them now, the temperature dropping. A chill ran up Alec's back, and he turned away from the rays of light to stare at Eleanor.

Her lips pressed in a frown, thoughts obviously still rushing through her mind.

"Roric explained that part of things to me as well. Is that what you want to do?"

"Heavens, no." He noted in the way her eyes flicked to him that she was holding something back. With a subtle shake of her head, she added, "He is yours."

The sun fell, and the last rays of light lit the clouds in a final glorious show.

"It's like the night we first met," she whispered, watching the sky.

Alec nodded. How far they had come, and how far they still had to go. He swallowed. Alec wrapped his arm around her and kissed her on the forehead. Her arms circled his waist.

"It was nice to have someone save me this time," she murmured into his chest.

Alec closed his eyes, and when he opened them he was taken by a passion and possessiveness that took his breath away. He kissed her until their blood ran hot, then led her to the edge of the forest, where their thick blankets had been set beside their fire for the night. He stacked the fire higher, the flames catching, light flickering through the forest. Then he laid his wife down with a desperation in joining that felt as foreign to them both as a new lover.

Chapter 18

A few miles from the Abbey of St. Catherine, Alec noticed they were being followed. At first it was only a prickle on the back of his neck. Then he could hear hoofbeats, just a few steps off from the rhythm of their own horses' footfalls. They traveled on the main roads. Of course there would be other riders. Still, Alec could not shake the feeling that whomever was behind them had followed the same path for too long. Not to mention, the rider seemed to hover just out of sight, the same distance away. The odds of that were slim.

Eleanor glanced over her shoulder, twisting in her saddle. She stared behind them a long moment, then turned ahead, frowning. Alec smiled to himself. She was as aware as he.

"Something wrong?" he asked.

"No. I just…" She looked behind them again, then turned back. She rode straight ahead for a moment, then twisted to give Alec a narrow-eyed look. "You noticed too, didn't you?"

Alec smiled. "You're good. Now stop doubting yourself."

Eleanor let out her breath in a whistle. She moved to look behind them yet again.

Alec hummed a low note. "No. Now that you've noticed, don't show him that we know he's there."

"Who is it?"

"No idea. He's been following for a while though."

"You didn't tell me?"

Alec shrugged. "Wanted to see how long it took you. If he had come closer I would have said something."

Eleanor rolled her eyes.

They rode in silence a while longer, their senses honed towards the sound of the rider's progress. He and the abbey came into view at the same time. He was closing in, likely noting their destination lay a short gallop ahead.

"Listen...we run for the abbey. Whether he stops at the abbey or not, we have him outnumbered." Alec discreetly looked backwards under the guise of adjusting his saddle. The man had come no closer, hovering just within their line of sight. "He is likely just a traveler. But under the circumstances..."

Eleanor nodded slightly.

"You ready?"

She smiled.

They nudged their horses into a steady canter. Alec glanced behind them. The rider was continuing at the same leisurely pace. That was a good sign. Eleanor met Alec's eye and tipped a little more forward in the saddle, asking Noir for more speed. The big horse gave it freely. Within no time they reached the walls of the abbey. Eleanor slipped inside, turning her horse into position next to the wall, out of sight. She drew her sword as he tucked his own horse against the opposite wall. He waited, ears straining, for the sound of pursuit.

It took a long time before they heard hoofbeats. Several times he longed to step out from the shadow of the wall and check the rider's status, but he forced himself to stay. When the sound finally came, it was slow and steady. His fingers curled around the hilt of his sword, nerves alive. The man came into view, hood pulled down over his head against the cold. The notes of a song drifted on the breeze, and Alec realized the man was singing to himself, in rhythm with his horse's footsteps. When he noticed Alec, there was no sign of alarm. The man merely waved a hand in passing and continued down the road, passing the entrance to the abbey.

Alec released his grip on his sword. He rode a few steps to where he could see the man round the next bend of the road. When he returned to the abbey, Eleanor's expression was just as baffled as his.

"Was he singing?" she asked.

"Yes." Alec looked over his shoulder and shook his head. "None of it makes sense to me. Why didn't he catch up with us earlier? He waved, but he didn't say a word. Just kept on singing."

"What language?"

Alec frowned. "Latin, I suppose." A good, neutral language for any country.

Eleanor looked off into the distance, as if she could see the rider through the trees beyond the abbey. "We should rest here, at least for the night. If he is following us, he'll either make himself known or we will face him tomorrow. With full bellies and fresh horses."

Bells tolled from the tower above their heads, making them both flinch.

"Prayers are concluding," Eleanor said softly.

Alec looked to the sky, where the sun was tantalizingly close to the crest of the hills. Evening was only a few hours away. He sighed and dismounted. She was right, they needed a break and refreshed horses. Eleanor followed suit, and led her horse to the water trough. She cracked the film of ice, allowing Noir to drink.

She looked up at Alec with a nervous shine in her eyes that had been absent when they'd been running from a potential attacker. He narrowed his gaze, willing her to explain. She brushed off her breeches and tunic and took a deep breath, facing the abbey.

"Let me speak with them first."

Alec nodded. This is where she had run to, when she'd fled Lezay. How fitting they return, given their second escape from the Lezay family. The last time they had ridden to Alsace, they had stopped here, but they were in such haste that she had gone in and out and they'd been on the road within minutes. Now they were asking to spend the night. Many religious houses would offer lodging and food in charity to travelers, though they could also be defensive, protective of their secluded lifestyle. They weren't sure which to expect.

"I'll be right back." Eleanor squeezed his hand and then headed to the massive doors, her long strides carrying her with the grace of a cat.

Alec turned to his horse and patted him on the neck. He loosened both horses' girths, still aware that they may have to run from the strange traveler. He was not yet comfortable untacking completely. Satisfied that the horses were drinking and content, he propped himself against the trough and waited, his arms folded and his stomach rumbling.

Eleanor looked up at the high façade of the abbey's church. It was modest compared to some, but still beautiful in its detail. It was hard to believe that it had been over twelve years since she'd run through the night to Abbey St. Catherine. The stone walls encircling the gated courtyard seemed fit for a castle, but the gates were thrown wide open in welcome to anyone who passed by. The space within was immaculate. No trace of manure, loose straw, or even a stray weed graced the wide expanse that led to the modest doors of the sanctuary where the nuns welcomed those who sought refuge.

Unlike when she'd galloped in with resounding hoofbeats and screamed for help years ago, her entry was quiet today, and the nuns did not come rushing out of the sanctuary. Still, she knew they had been called by the bells, and she waited patiently in the entryway, studying the intricate stained-glass windows. The one above the door held her eye, a woman with long hair kneeling at a man's feet. Her glass tears fell onto them as the man's hand stretched out to her in a reassuring gesture.

"Mary Magdalene at the feet of Christ," one of the nuns said from beside her. She stood motionless, studying the window with as much attention as Eleanor, as if seeing it for the first time.

Eleanor continued to frown at the window. She studied Christ's outstretched hand. "She followed him all the way to the cross, didn't she?"

The nun nodded. "She was the first to see him alive after the resurrection, even before his disciples."

"Why would he let her follow? Demon-possessed, wasn't she? Why would he want a woman like that?"

The nun's voice lightened with her smile. "He heals all. I believe she was greatly changed after they met."

Eleanor's frown deepened, her eyes running up and down the full image.

"My dear, Mary Magdalene is the very image of the most powerful gifts Christ gave us." She turned towards Eleanor, and Eleanor was forced to meet the elderly woman's intense gaze. Her eyes sparkled with light from within a lined face. "Forgiveness. Peace. Hope." The words lingered in the air like a perfume, and the woman's lips curved into a gentle smile. "Welcome back, Lady Eleanor."

Eleanor straightened, her eyebrows raising with surprise. "You remember me?"

"I never forget a face, my dear." The nun took her hand and gave it a gentle squeeze. "It has been a long time."

"Sister...Sister Catherine if I remember correctly."

"The same." Catherine squeezed her hand again, then released her, gliding across the foyer deeper into the abbcy. Eleanor followed. "Don't confuse me with the saint our dear abbey is named after though," she warned, holding out a finger. "I am far from a saint. Though I try my best to redeem myself."

"Yes, my lady."

Catherine stopped abruptly. "Oh, dear. None of those titles here. Just 'Sister' will suffice." She continued walking, her pace brisk for her age. "You will join us for dinner, I hope?"

"If you'll have us." Eleanor lengthened her stride to keep up. "My husband is with me. We are just passing through. I reasoned I should stop—"

"Finally. We have much to discuss. Word of your adventures has reached us."

"Really?"

Sister Catherine stopped, and Eleanor scrambled not to run into her. She tilted her head to one side. "Where is your husband?"

"In the courtyard."

Sister Catherine pursed her lips in thought, then strode back towards the entry door with an even brisker pace. She snapped her fingers at a passing nun. "Sister Margaret, set a table for a male guest in the front entry." The sister nodded and hurried off. Turning towards Eleanor, Catherine explained, "We do not allow men to dine with us. Nor will we allow their bellies to go hungry."

"Oh, that's fine. I can eat with him as well."

"No. You eat with us."

The finality with which she spoke the words left Eleanor without argument, her mind spinning. They pushed through the front doors. Alec glanced from one of them to the other, his brow furrowed.

"Welcome, Sir Alec," Sister Catherine spoke. "You are hungry. Come."

She led the way back inside, and Alec shot Eleanor a questioning look. She gave a subtle shrug.

Sister Catherine gestured toward his newly set table, a plate high with steaming food at the ready.

"Thank you, Sister. You are too kind." He bowed.

"You are welcome. Lady Eleanor will dine with us, and then we shall give you rooms for the night."

"That would be wonderful," Alec said. He settled in to eat, only to be met with a sharp look from Sister Catherine. He set down his food, crossed himself, and folded his hands to pray.

Eleanor followed Sister Catherine down a short hall, emerging into a room with a long table set in the center. Though there was a fire to the side of the room, it was not much warmer than it was outside, and the women's breath showed as they turned their faces to look at Eleanor. The expiration mixed with the steam rising off the bowls of bread and lentils that sat upon the table. The sisters whispered amongst themselves, standing behind their chairs.

As Catherine took her place at the head of the table, they grew quiet. She gestured for them to be seated, and there was a noisy scraping of chairs as the sisters sat. A chair and plate appeared as Eleanor was granted a place next to Catherine. They bowed their heads for a long prayer, then the sisters dug into the food before them.

The sister to Eleanor's right gave her a large spoonful of mucky-looking lentils. Eleanor tentatively took a bite and was pleasantly surprised to find they were deliciously herbed. The hunger from the road caught up to her, and she devoured her food within minutes.

Sister Catherine eyed her with amusement, picking at her plate a bite at a time. "So—what brings you back to Alsace? You look well."

"Traveling from Brunstein." Eleanor took a sip of the watered-down wine.

"I'm surprised you would go back there."

"Did you know Lord Montag is—" Eleanor hesitated and chose a more decorous word than *dead*, "—passed?"

There was a flicker in Catherine's eye that was immediately masked. But years of living around Alec and watching how he read people left Eleanor with no doubt that there was a flicker. "I have heard that. There are rumors of how, but that is not a conversation to hold over dinner."

"I visited my cousin."

"Ah, the new Lord of Brunstein."

"Yes, Sister."

"That is a long journey."

Eleanor laughed. "All I seem to do is take long journeys." She smiled to herself, watching the nuns down the table. Many of them spoke with each other and ate, though a few had turned their attention to her conversation. "Really, I have wanted to come back here for some time. I never got to thank all of you. Yet now here you are feeding me again. How will I ever repay you?"

Catherine smiled. "It is not us who wish to be repaid. Merely carry the kindness forward to the next person who needs it."

Eleanor nodded. "Of course. Yet still—"

"Eat more," the sister on Eleanor's side added more lentils to her plate, smiling ear to ear. She was younger, Eleanor's age, her cheeks round with flesh. "I hope you'll tell us some stories of your adventures." Her eyes flicked towards Sister Catherine. When no disapproval was hinted, she plunged ahead. "What's it like to wield a sword?"

Eleanor laughed loudly, drawing the attention of half the table. She checked herself but still could not help but smile. "I suppose it's...exciting? I can't believe you've heard about that."

"Oh, we hear lots of things. You are said to ride a horse bigger than any man's."

"And faster!" another sister chimed in.

"I thought she would be taller," a lanky sister further down the table admitted.

"Goodness. What else have you heard?" Eleanor blushed.

"You were knighted by King Richard himself. Is he as handsome as they say?"

"Was, you silly goose! He's dead."

"Right..."

"What was it like to sail to England?"

"I heard you helped crown the King of Germany."

The voices threw other tales, both true and false, towards Eleanor. Some made her laugh, some wince. She admitted what she had to and set the record straight for others. All the while Sister Catherine finished her dinner slowly with a smile of amusement, the corners of her lips meeting the deep lines of her eyes.

"I heard she killed Lord Montag."

An instant hush fell over the room as every head turned towards a petite, middle aged woman at the far end of the table. It was the first she had spoken, and the first Eleanor had noticed her. Her face was heavily lined, though the skin did not seem as transparent and spotted as Catherine's. Could she possibly be younger? She must have been a beauty in her youth, the angles of her face smooth and proportionate. Her lips still held the plumpness of youth, though they were rimmed with deep frown lines.

Sister Catherine could not hide her shock, and Eleanor's brow furrowed as she tried to fathom why. The statement remained unaddressed as Catherine quietly whispered, "Sister Mary?"

Sister Mary glared at Eleanor in a way that sent goosebumps up her arms. Her lips remained locked in a tight line. Still, the nuns stared.

One of the older women cleared her throat, cutting the silence. "Sister Catherine, may I be excused for prayer?"

The request echoed hastily around the room.

"Yes, yes. Go," Catherine said, still visibly shaken.

There was again a loud scrape of chairs, and the hall was suddenly empty but for Eleanor, Catherine, and the mysterious Sister Mary. The three held their seats.

Eleanor's glance flicked back and forth between the two sisters. "Have I offended? If so I'm sorry—"

A firm shake of Catherine's head silenced her. Her eyes were still on Sister Mary, and Eleanor followed the gaze to meet Mary's glare once again.

"My Sister, after all this time, you break your silence?" Catherine asked.

Mary was silent.

Catherine sighed, finally turning to Eleanor. "She took a vow of silence years before I came to the abbey. I have never heard her speak."

"Never? How long have you been here?"

"Twenty-four years."

Eleanor's eyes went wide. She looked at Mary. The woman, despite her age, held her back straight and chin high. Suddenly Eleanor noted the shape of the nose, the angle of her cheekbones, and gasped. The similarities to Raoul left no doubt in her mind, but she dared not say anything in front of Sister Catherine. Did she know who Mary *really* was?

There was a shift in Mary's face as she noted Eleanor's recognition. Confusion, doubt, a trace of fear, and yet still a fiery glare of anger.

"What is it, dear?" Catherine asked.

"Sister Catherine...may I speak to Sister Mary? Alone?"

Catherine looked even more confused. "My Lady, she does not speak. I doubt she will again, now that words have passed her lips."

"We will manage. Please."

"Fine, then, if you wish." She stood and took her leave, shooting several curious glances back at the two women seated at opposite ends of the massive table.

Eleanor took a shaky breath. She debated approaching the other woman, but decided against it. That glare promised too much fire. Instead she said quietly, "You must be Lady Alenor of Tielo."

Sister Mary sat in silence, then let a slow smile turn one corner of her mouth.

Eleanor let out a breath of relief. "My God, you are alive." Eleanor hesitated, the shock hard to process. It was as if she sat across from a ghost. How many stories had she and Raoul shared of their dead mothers? And here was Alenor—her aunt—alive. She took a deep breath. "Alec—my husband—told me what Montag did to you. We didn't know if it was true. We couldn't tell if you were still alive or buried like the rest of the world has believed for all these years. *Is* it true? You are so close to Brunstein…no one ever knew?"

Sister Mary looked away.

"Sorry. I ask too many questions." She sighed. "I did kill Montag. If you still loved him, then for your sake, I am sorry to cause you pain. You see, I had to protect Alec…and my son."

Sister Mary's eyes shot back up to her. Eleanor was surprised into silence, then even more so as the woman spoke, her voice raspy from lack of use.

"You have a son?"

"Yes, Sister."

"Where is he?"

"Safe—"

"Do not let them take him."

"What?"

Silence echoed.

Eleanor's heart pounded. She'd been warned so many times about the boy, and yet here it was again coming from a woman who had not spoken in over twenty years. She stood and moved closer to Mary, then sat next to her.

"How is my son? Raoul…" Mary asked quietly.

"He is well. I saw him a few days ago."

Mary shook her head. "What kind of man is he?"

Eleanor took a sharp breath. She thought for a long moment. "He is a good man, Sister. He is tall, like Montag. With his dark hair. But he has your nose. More finely featured like you, I suppose. But he is a good man." Eleanor hesitated. "He is working hard to be different from his father."

Mary leaned back in her chair. "He has a wife? Children?"

Eleanor shook her head. "He swears he'll never marry. And I believe him."

Mary lapsed into silence again. Relief softened her features. A strange reaction, Eleanor thought.

Eleanor pressed on. "You should know, Sister, that my mother thought you were dead. Montag lied to her for years. She named me after you." Mary's eyes flicked over her, no judgement hidden. She appeared not to approve of Eleanor's attire, but that was nothing unusual. "It was Lezay who suspected you were alive."

"Sir Lezay visited me often."

This took Eleanor by surprise. "Really?"

Mary nodded once. "He would come when he traveled, and as such we could not turn him away. He always found a way to cross my path. He had a sick sense of humor, taunting me with updates on my son. Refusing to let me forget Montag's betrayal. I had been silent before then and remained silent after, with even more resolution." She sighed. "Until now."

"That must have been so hard for you."

"My sisters and the Lord gave me strength."

The silence lingered in the room a long moment, both women lost in their thoughts.

"Sir Lezay told me Raoul joined them." Mary brushed down the skirts of her habit.

"So you know about The Order then?"

"You can tell all sorts of secrets to one who has taken vows of silence."

Eleanor sucked in a breath. Would Mary tell her more of their secrets?

Mary looked over her shoulder to a great stained-glass window, where the light of the setting sun amplified the colored glass. This image was one of a woman kneeling at the foot of the cross. The nun's plain habit seemed to glow with fire, giving her a fierceness that her expression reflected. "Do you know if it's true—did they induct my Raoul?"

Eleanor swallowed. "Yes, Sister."

Suddenly a tear glimmered at the corner of Mary's eye. "I prayed so long..." She closed her eyes and inhaled, and when she opened them, she turned to Eleanor, the fierceness in her gaze even stronger than before. "Now I will pray for his soul. I will pray he never sires a child. And I will pray they never find yours."

"They want my son."

"I know. It is why Montag is dead, is it not?"

Eleanor studied her carefully. "Do you know the bloodlines of the members? Whatever you can tell me will help me protect my son."

Mary shook her head firmly. "If I knew more, I would have saved my own boy."

"But he's—" Eleanor cut herself off. Raoul wasn't fine. He was bearing the burden of this secret organization, even if it meant he would live life alone. And if the stories about The Order were true, then Raoul had been forced to dance with evil. The dark look in his eye made sense to Eleanor now. He was working to atone for his sins, because he was a good man. But who knew when that list of sins would get shorter, with a group that dark and powerful breathing down his neck? It had to be a horrible way to live.

And she had told them she wanted to be part of it.

Eleanor exhaled. "Fair enough. Thank you." She thought for a moment. "Why didn't you escape? Warn Raoul? Why not seek out Raoul now that Montag is dead?"

"These walls are not a prison, Eleanor. I do not need to escape. I remain here for my own protection, or at least I did for all these years. I have no desire to depart now. As I told your uncle years ago, I am a bride of Christ now, and these women my family. I could not leave them."

"Do you want to meet your son?"

Mary straightened. "He thinks me dead. I'm not sure I wish to be anything more to him. I would be a disappointment. The dead hold so much more power over memory than the living."

Eleanor couldn't believe that. "If my mother were alive, I would want her back." She paused. "Lezay told Raoul you are alive. Much like he taunted you, he taunted Raoul and Montag. Raoul didn't know if Lezay could be believed. He doesn't know where you are."

Mary smiled sadly. "Keep it that way."

Eleanor hesitated again, not sure how she felt about that request. She wanted to argue, but sensed that would be a waste of Mary's few words. "Sister Mary...did you...did you recognize me when I came years ago?"

"How could I not?" The older woman leaned towards Eleanor. "It was I who stitched your wound, much like your mother stitched mine. I spoke no word, so you would neither have known, nor remembered me. But I paid your mother her due."

Eleanor brushed a tear from her eye. The memories of that night were a fitful blur, but she remembered the soothing hands of the woman that had pieced together the skin that Lezay had cut. She had hurt her with needle and thread, but she had healed her. She had given her the chance to finish her escape and live. It was Lady Alenor, all this time.

"Did you love him still? Montag? I am sorry...so sorry—"

"Shh, child. I loved the man I married. The man you killed was someone else. And I came to terms with that a long time ago."

Alec was on his feet from the moment the sisters exited the dining hall. Though they filed past him at the far end of the corridor, he did not miss their averted gazes, their hushed whispers. He could not blame them for their modesty. Still, he could not help but compare the quiet, solitary demeanor of the women to the rowdy, boisterous behavior of the all-male tavern they had eaten in only days before. It was as if women and men were different animals entirely. He stood ignored, a road worn traveler in a field of black habits. Only Eleanor was able to blend so easily from world to world.

The nuns disappeared, and he was again alone. He began pacing as he waited for Eleanor to emerge. It was odd, that she had not been among the Sisters. His nerves fired, his mind too well aware of the last time they had been separated.

Sister Catherine was the last one to appear, and the pale, worried look on her face set Alec's nerves on edge even further. His hand fell to the hilt of his sword on instinct.

He brushed only air, as he'd left the sword by the front door as was expected. He forced his hand to relax again, feigning nonchalance. She walked over to him, her hands folded before her, rosary clenched in white knuckles.

"What's wrong?" Alec asked, meeting her a short distance from his table.

Catherine turned to him, her eyes wide, as if she'd seen a ghost. "I have never seen one of my sisters break a vow of silence, but Sister Mary just did. She is in there speaking with your wife."

Alec's eyebrows shot up. This was not the answer he expected, and curiosity replaced his wariness. "What did she say?"

"She would not speak in front of me again, but she blamed Lady Eleanor for killing Lord Montag. How could she say such a thing? Of all the things to say after all this time...to speak a lie..."

Alec inhaled and pursed his lips. "Sister Catherine, that is not a lie."

Catherine crossed herself. "Mon Dieu..."

"How would Sister Mary know? So few know—"

Catherine was too distracted to answer his question. "She's lived here longer than I. I have never heard her speak—never!" Her wrinkled face had taken on a new firmness and vigor, her tone sharp. "How I wished she would speak when I first came...to have some solace for my own abrupt transfer. I came to understand she is a solitary soul. She keeps to herself. No, I do not know how she would know such a thing." She frowned. "Poor Lady Eleanor, to kill her uncle…what came over her?"

"She saved my life that night." Alec met Sister Catherine's gaze as she looked over him with such intensity it seemed to see into his soul.

She pursed her lips and began to pace. She shook the rosary as she emphasized, "Oh, I have so many questions for Sister Mary!"

The quiet tap of Eleanor's shoes sounded from the corridor, and she appeared, a hand absently running through her hair as she thought. When she looked up at the pair before her, she smiled.

Sister Catherine rushed to her. "What did she say?"

Eleanor took Catherine's hands in her own and met her eye. "She wants you to know she loves you all like family. But she warned that she will continue in her silence once again. She hopes you all will respect that."

Catherine could not hide the disappointment from her face, but she nodded. She pulled Eleanor into a hug. "Whatever she had to say to you, it must have been important."

Eleanor made no further indication of what had been said, only smiled in what Alec knew was the most reassuring look she could manage.

Catherine sighed. "Well, how long will you be staying? At least the night I hope?"

"We'll move on in the morning," Eleanor replied

"Very well then. You wish for provisions?"

Eleanor handed her a few coins. "Just enough for a week."

"This is too much." She held up the coins, weighing them.

"The rest are for the abbey." Eleanor closed Catherine's fingers around the coins, and pushed them back to her. "It is only a small portion of the debt I still owe you all."

Catherine cupped Eleanor's cheek, smiling gently. "Well, let's get you settled." She led the way down the corridor to two tiny rooms in a separate wing of the abbey. Even travelers were kept separate from the sisters' solitary lives. Alec and Eleanor thanked her, and then went back outside to tend to the horses. Ches and Noir looked up at their riders, ears pricked as they chewed mouthfuls of hay provided by the sisters.

Eleanor kept tight to Alec's side as she stroked Noir's forehead. "She's alive," she whispered. "Lady Alenor is here."

"You're sure?" Alec froze, his saddle hovering over his horse's back mid-heft, his eyes wide.

"Positive." Eleanor pulled her own tack. "She said Lezay knew about her all along, which fits with your friend's story and what Raoul told me. She warned us about The Order, about them wanting our son. I think the Lezays were telling the truth." Eleanor turned away from her horse to face Alec, her voice still hushed. "I don't think anyone here knows Sister Mary is Lady Alenor of Tielo. And she wants it to stay that way."

"She has Sister Catherine's head spinning." Alec managed to remove his tack and took a brush to his horse's back, wiping away the crust of dried sweat.

"I can only imagine. She really didn't say much, but what she did say—" Eleanor inhaled. "I think she still loved Montag in a way, but she knew he had changed. She didn't blame me for his death."

"Does that help?"

"A little." She studied the gate of the Abbey. "I tried to talk her into seeing Raoul, but I don't think she wants to. She's afraid of what he would think of her." She took another armful of hay and set it before the horses. Satisfied with their care, she turned to Alec. "I will keep her secret for now, but I have a lot of emotions tied into Raoul's ignorance. If my mother were alive, I would want her back from the dead." She quickly looked away, wiped her hands on her breeches, and started walking back into the abbey. "We need to get to our son. I need to know he is alright."

Chapter 19

Alec did not sleep well that night. Perhaps it was Eleanor's absence from his bed, a propriety in the abbey despite their status as a married couple. She was close enough. He could hear her bed shift when she rolled over during the night, only a thin plank wall between them. Their rooms were more like closets, with only room for a body-wide plank shelf as bed and a few feet to stand next to it. Perhaps it was the small space that had him on edge. Perhaps it was the bean-heavy food, which left him with a gurgling stomach. Or perhaps it was the feeling in the air, that sense that something else was coming.

Was it the mysterious traveler?

Alec laid awake a long time, staring at the heavy, roughhewn beams above his head, ears straining through the wall for Eleanor's breath, which at times reached him in the moments of total quiet in the manor. Then a board would creak, a window pane rattle, and he would lose that anchoring note. The wind was picking up outside. Would it snow? It was certainly cold enough. He pulled his cloak and blanket tighter around him. The abbey was not much warmer than the bare ground had been the night before. It was the stone. Everywhere, stone. The cold sank into it, and only a roaring fire could fight that rooted chill. The fires here only burned in the common areas.

Was he growing soft in his old age? A few years of having a home, and already he was expecting hearth-fires, clean beds, and hot food. Spoiled, that's what he was. What had happened to all the years on the road, sleeping in ditches and on horse blankets, eating what he could buy with what little coin he had? Alec squeezed his eyes shut. He'd done that plenty, and he'd won himself a few beds as well. Though they were far from clean.

Giselle. She'd been right. She'd told him she never passed on false information, but he'd been hesitant to believe the tall tale she'd extracted out of Rothulfus Lezay himself. Lady Alenor of Tielo was alive, some twenty-seven years after she was supposed to have been buried. What were the implications of this? Who else had disappeared, and yet could resurface from the dead? He blinked at the dark ceiling. Was everything Giselle had told him true?

How do you extract this knowledge from a man? he'd asked. *It's not about being loved*, she'd whispered, tracing his jaw with a finger, *it's about being needed.*

A door opened and closed somewhere deep within the abbey, and Alec gave up on sleep. He had no idea what time of night it was, but he pushed off the bed, pulled on his boots, and adjusted his clothes. The cold air bit into him, pebbling his flesh. As quietly as possible he strode to Eleanor's room and cracked the door. She was fast asleep, blankets pulled firmly around her as if she was in a cocoon. He closed the door softly and headed back to the main hall.

A dim grey light illuminated the stained-glass windows. Dawn must be on the horizon, but the cloud-cover delayed the light. One of the sisters crossed the corridor behind him, heading in the direction of the kitchens. She froze mid-yawn to stare at him, then quickly jogged away. Alec smiled a little to himself and headed out of the manor.

The winter air warned of snow; the wind stung his face. The horses still stood tied, their eyes closed, Noir's hind leg cocked in rest. He walked up to Ches and patted his neck. The horse blinked at him, a low nicker sounding from his chest. That woke Noir, and the fiery black horse pushed his nose towards Alec, demanding breakfast. Alec set hay in front of them both.

Snowflakes began to fall, the light, tiny crystals that alluded to a heavy snow to follow. He walked to the gate and looked out at the countryside. Their tracks from the day before were still visible in the half-frozen mud. They would soon be covered if this snow lasted. Where had the mysterious traveler gone? Alec pursed his lips, thinking, then hastened back to Ches and began to saddle up.

Within minutes, he was swinging up on the horse's back, his sword belted to his hip. Noir let out a whinny of protest as Alec rode out, but Ches was eager to go. The man's tracks continued on after the bend, clearly visible in the mud. The snow was starting to fall faster, the light getting brighter as the sun rose behind the thick cloud-cover. Alec scanned the ground, allowing the horse to move faster as the tracks became clearer. He would follow only to the river, to where Eleanor had told him the road divided North and South, and see where the man had gone.

His nerves fired, awareness of the situation reaching out like the thread-like roots of a plant. Still, his horse was the first to alert him. Ches lifted his head just a fraction, his eyes locking on something ahead. Alec saw the man standing at the crest of the hill, his horse turned towards him in the middle of the road. Alec's hand went to the hilt of his sword, and he hesitated at the bottom of the hill. Ches pranced, spooked by the stranger that had appeared through the curtain of snow. The rider at the top of the hill flung his cloak aside, revealing a sword at his hip. He made a big show of removing it, sword belt and all, held it out to the side, then dropped it.

Alec frowned. It was a gesture of neutrality, and yet it was obvious the man had waited from the day before, probably had camped nearby. Alec had no interest in disarming himself in the presence of the stranger, but he rode up the hill at a steady walk, his own sword still in its sheath. He pulled up, a horse length abreast of the man.

The stranger lifted his chin, revealing a short grey-speckled beard on a face not much older than his own. He smiled, though it was not a warming smile. In Langue d'Oc laced with a thick Germanic accent the man said, "It is good to finally meet you, Sir Alec Earnblaec."

Eleanor groaned as she woke, the opening and closing of doors somewhere in the abbey alerting her that morning had arrived. Exhaustion had overtaken her, and she had slept far more deeply than she had in weeks. She sat up and stretched, awareness coming in with an energy she'd missed. Her muscles had recovered from the hours in the saddle, and better yet, today they would truly get moving towards Benec. No more detours. No more questions. Just a few days of long rides and they could be at the coast, and a few days after that they would get to Alec's new castle.

She listened for Alec in the closet-like room next to her, but it was quiet. She knocked on the wall as she pulled on her boots and sword. "Alec, you up?" No answer.

She sighed and went over to his room, pushing open the door. He was gone. His bed was made and all of his possessions gone as if he'd never been there. Eleanor pulled her messy hair from its ties, ran her fingers through it, and braided it as she walked. She nodded to the Sisters in passing as they began to head to the chapel for morning prayers. The abbey seemed quiet, the day running as usual as dawn rose. She pushed out the front door and was greeted by a gust of wind that whipped snow into her face like a fistful of needles. She burrowed into her cloak, pulling it tight.

Ches was gone. Noir nickered to her, his mouth full of hay. Eleanor walked towards the gate, looking left and right for Alec, but could not see anyone. Already the snow left a thin layer on the ground, just enough to mask any tracks he may have left.

A ride for pleasure in this weather? Slim chance. And yet if there had been some kind of threat, wouldn't he have woken her? In a huff she went back into the manor, searching out Sister Catherine.

She found her in the entryway, already on alert.

"I am sorry, Sister, but I have to go. Are those provisions ready?" Eleanor asked, hearing the concern in her own voice.

"Yes...but don't you want to break your fast with us?"

"Alec is gone. He must have felt the need to check something. I don't know why he just left—" She shook her head, words failing her. It was embarrassing not knowing where your husband disappeared to while you slept. She could only hope she masked the anger that simmered in her gut.

"I'll be back in a moment," Sister Catherine said gently, then walked away in a swirl of habit.

Eleanor went back outside and tacked Noir, who pinned his ears and took even bigger mouthfuls of hay. He knew his time to eat was limited, the time to work coming soon. Eleanor waited with the horse at the door of the abbey.

Sister Catherine emerged with the supplies, her face bowed to the wind. "Are you sure you want to ride out in this?"

Eleanor looked over her shoulder at the gate. If Alec was coming back, wouldn't he already be back? "I have to." She took the provisions with a weak smile and tied the bundle onto her saddle. She turned back to Sister Catherine and on impulse gave her a hug. Catherine's boney arms held her tight, then released her.

"You are always welcome, Lady Eleanor."

"Thank you. For everything." Eleanor gave her arms a final squeeze, then mounted her horse. She turned back towards the abbey a last time, noting a second nun standing outside the door, arms folded in front of her. Their eyes locked a moment, and then Sister Mary raised a hand in a parting salute. Eleanor raised a hand in turn and smiled, then tucked her head into her cloak and rode out, turning right out the gate and heading towards the river, already suspecting what Alec had wanted to know, and praying that he had found answers and not an ambush.

It did not take long to find him. She'd barely ridden a mile when she spotted two figures at the top of the next hill, deep in conversation. She trotted on, the snow stinging her eyes as it now fell in fat flakes, covering Noir's black mane in white.

The riders separated as she approached, the stranger cantering down the far side of the hill, while Alec turned back towards her. Anger roiled through her, and she forced herself to bite her tongue. He wasn't used to working with others, she reminded herself. She didn't have the energy to start another fight.

Still, the sarcasm laced her words as she asked, "Secret meeting?"

Alec frowned at her, but did not comment on her tone. "I wanted to see where he turned at the river before the snow covered his tracks. But he was waiting for me. We spoke." He pursed his lips. "He *was* following us, and he admitted so openly. He is going to continue following us all the way to Paris. An escort, he called it."

"That does not make me feel better."

"He disarmed before I ever approached him." Alec glanced over his shoulder towards the crest of the hill and frowned. "He is friends with the Alsatian lords and is traveling to Paris. He claims to not want any trouble, as long as we keep moving."

"A friend of the Lezays?"

"And Raoul. Otherwise I would worry more." Alec shrugged. "He was too honest with me. That's the thing that concerns me. That, and his name is Simon."

Eleanor thought back to the story Alec had told her months ago of a squire boy of her uncle's named Simon. Her mind told her it was only coincidence. There were, after all, a lot of men named Simon. She'd met many over the years. Still, the proximity to where that story had taken place and the recent events left her with doubts.

Alec turned his horse back to the crest of the hill. "I was going to return to the abbey to get you." He gazed over her traveling attire and what she hoped was a warning expression.

"No need," Eleanor said cooly. She could unleash her frustrations on him. But it was an argument they'd had before. What hope of change was there now? Better to just ride on and get to Benec as soon as possible. Which required energy. Which could not be wasted in petty arguments.

Alec remained oblivious as she rode along next to him. "His accent was Germanic. And he knew me on sight alone. Whoever he is, I get the impression that he knows what he's doing." When they reached the top, Alec stopped.

Eleanor noted a scabbarded sword partially concealed in the snow. Alec looked around warily. Eleanor's own attention peaked, but she felt nothing to cause concern. The horses were relaxed. The wind had even died down, the snow now pouring down on them in fat flakes.

Alec seemed satisfied as well and dismounted. He dusted off the sword and handed it to Eleanor so he could remount. "Odd, that he wouldn't pick this back up. I understand disarming to gain my trust, but no one leaves a sword like that behind."

Eleanor rubbed more snow off the hilt, studying it. It seemed familiar, which was impossible. Ice was already forming in the engraving in the round disk at the end of the hilt. She scratched at it with a fingernail. It broke free in one piece. Her eyes went wide.

"Alec..." she whispered, reaching out with a hand towards him, grasping at air until she finally made contact with his forearm. She squeezed. "Alec, this is Edmond's."

The artisan's engraving was lined with gold, the kind of craftsmanship a knight chose for his favorite, most used weapon. In that image was the letter E. That itself meant nothing, as many knights held names with E. But this E she remembered. She had stared at this hilt as she fell to sleep in the arms of the knight it belonged to, her bare back pressed against his naked torso. This was undoubtably the sword of Edmond de Fougères.

Chapter 20

Alec hated Edmond de Fougères. He'd hated him when he was alive, roiling with a jealousy he had not concealed. He'd hated him when they fought in tournaments, the injuries the man inflicted as much blows to Alec's pride as his corporeal form. And now, even though the man was dead, Alec hated him all the more because he refused to just stay dead and fade into nothingness.

He also hated the fact that he hated him.

Edmond was tied to Eleanor's past, and not just as an illicit affair a few years ago that maybe he could convince her to forget, but in years and layers of childhood friendship that were far harder to erase. And now, with Edmond's sword clenched in her hand, Eleanor was asking questions that revealed her mind was still pained by the death of this ghost she had once promised Alec she'd buried. He knew she couldn't fight those memories. He felt her pain. That's what love did to a person. And that was why he hated that he hated Edmond. He could not bear anger towards a dead man whose unresolved death was still torturing his wife.

"How did he get it?" Eleanor asked from beside him for the tenth time, her voice tense as they rode through the snowstorm, cloaks held tight around their chins.

"Perhaps he stole it. Who knows what they did with the body. They may have just left it lay, and a common thief took the sword and sold it in a tavern." Alec felt as if he had to offer up something, as unlikely as it sounded. Her mind was circling around and around back to the sword. She knew as well as he that any commoner caught with a knight's sword could expect to lose a hand, if not more, for theft.

"Right. That could be it," Eleanor agreed quietly. She seemed as eager to accept the unlikely excuse as he was to give it. She shifted in her saddle. "I think we should get into the Vexin tonight, ride through the woods tomorrow. Maybe we can shake Simon off our trail in there."

When he hadn't been distracted by Eleanor's theories of Edmond's demise, Alec had been stewing over this very dilemma. The snow was proving to be relentless, and though they'd covered several miles by road, the snow was the wet, thick kind that soaked through wool and packed into snowballs in the horses' hooves. When their horses started slipping, they took turns dismounting and knocking out the packed balls of ice, particularly on the hills. There was no inn in sight, nor would there be for many more miles. They were in the frontier between Alsace and Paris. Towns were a hard day's ride in between, and the weather was hindering their progress. Their best bet was to find a partially sheltered place to camp and build a fire. That is, if they could find wood dry enough to burn.

Alec asked Eleanor, "Do you know of anywhere? An outcropping of rock where we can at least get out of the wind?"

She nodded, wincing as her horse slipped with a hind foot and caught himself with a grunt. Both Noir and Ches had their heads bowed into the onslaught of snow, their thick manes crusted in a layer of ice. "Not far." She glanced up, and Alec followed her gaze.

Their escort was within sight, waiting perhaps a quarter of a mile ahead, his own head bowed into the snow. He kept Alec's nerves on edge, and prevented them from relaxing their awareness for even a moment. Edmond had died in an ambush. Who knew what Simon was capable of? Alec and Eleanor met each other's eyes, their expressions grim. The man had claimed he would escort them only to Paris. But what would he do if they didn't go to Paris at all? Years ago, Eleanor had skirted north, into the forest, avoiding the roads. They could do so again.

With a last look at Alec, Eleanor cut onto a side trail that was little more than a deer path into the forest. The trail cut down into a moderate valley at a gentle slope, the old trees here grew so dense the ground below their branches was nearly clear of undergrowth. The snow was only a thin layer. She urged her horse into a trot, letting him find his own pace and footing as they worked down the trail. Before long, Alec could see an outcrop of rock and hear the gurgle of a stream. It was like a silver ribbon cutting through the white of the snow. He couldn't help but be in awe of its beauty.

Eleanor shot a look behind him, her face planted to a frown. Alec didn't have to turn to know that Simon had followed them and closed the distance. He heard the rocks slide and sticks crack as the other man's horse scrambled down the hill. Eleanor dismounted below the outcrop of rock and patted her horse's neck.

It was a perfect spot to camp. The rock had just a bit of overhang, enough to shelter them from the worst of the wind. Water was right there, which the horses eagerly stuck their noses into and drank. The site was also commonly trafficked, as evident by the circle of stones surrounding a small pile of burned wood. Fallen branches indicated that no one had cleared the site in several months, yet it still held a feel of a well-used stop along the road.

Eleanor pulled a branch to the side of the clearing, making more room under the overhang.

She glanced up at their incoming escort. "You think he's going to share camp with us, too?"

Alec watched as Simon took the last bit of trail down into the base of the hollow, then tipped his head and moved downstream to another outcrop of rock that was more exposed but still offered some protection. "Looks like he's going to keep to himself." He gritted his teeth. Being at a distance made him harder to keep an eye on. It would have been easier if he camped with them, and yet Alec had no desire to invite him over.

Eleanor seemed to share the sentiment. She loosened her horse's girth but did not fully untack the horse. They tied their horses to trees conveniently located near the overhang of rock, then set out to collect the driest wood they could find. Thankfully, down in this valley there was just enough, and within an hour they had a smokey fire flickering under the overhang and could stretch out to attempt to dry their woolen layers.

So practiced was their rhythm in travel that they hardly had to speak as they went about their camp duties. They each saw what was needed and acted. When Alec looked over to see Simon still struggling to light a fire, he realized how nice it was to have a partner whom he could work so smoothly with. He reached out a hand to Eleanor and pulled hers to his lips, kissing her knuckles. She raised her eyebrows in surprise.

He smiled at her. She hesitated, then her lips curved up. She sidled closer to him, and he wrapped an arm around her.

Slowly the fire's warmth began to penetrate their damp clothes. They kept it stoked high, allowing the wet wood to dry and light. Their clothes began to dry, and by nightfall the snow slowed. They ate from the provisions in their saddlebags, drank heartily from the stream, and settled down as if it was just another night traveling to a tournament.

Eleanor was asleep in his arms and Alec was staring into the hot coals of the fire when a stick cracked in the forest next to them, and Simon appeared. He smiled as he stepped into the firelight. Alec did not return the smile. He nudged Eleanor awake but did not rise. She sat up, blinking with the alert wariness of a warrior.

Simon's smile faded. He approached their fire, his hands visible and empty. "Your fire looks so inviting. I had a horrible time starting one today. The wood is so wet." He reached his hands towards the flames. "I hope you don't mind."

Alec rose to a seated position, his arms draped over his knees. He minded. But Simon hadn't come over for the fire.

Simon ignored the tension in the air. "Where will you go from Paris? Back to Aquitaine?"

"Of course," Alec replied quickly, though it wasn't the truth.

Simon smiled, his eyes sparking from the flames before them. He appeared to have caught the lie. Who was he really?

"You left your sword," Alec said carefully. What explanation could the man offer? He reached beside him to the trio of swords and lifted Edmond's by the scabbard, the gold E shining in the firelight.

"Wasn't mine." Simon's lip curled up on one side of his mouth.

"We know," Eleanor whispered. Alec stole a glance at her. She was tight as a bent sapling, her body tensed to fight. "Where did you get it?"

Simon turned his full attention to Eleanor for the first time. Apparently he made the same observation as Alec, as he withdrew his hands from the heat of the fire and let one settle on the hilt of his sword. He tilted his head to the side, studying her. "They say you fight like a man. They call you a knightess. Is it true?"

Eleanor trembled, not from fear. Only a fool would miss her narrowed eyes, clenched fists. Simon was no fool.

He continued, "How did a little lady like you kill the great Lord Montag?" His eyes flicked over her from head to foot. "I've been following you for miles. My curiosity has been peaked. The two of you are not deserving of your legendary reputation. You ride slow. You build fires, telling everyone around where you are."

"We have nothing to hide. We are only travelers."

"Ah, but you aren't." The grin crept back into Simon's lips. "Everyone wants you. Her. I could be warm in my castle right now if it wasn't for you two." Simon smiled, his eyes never leaving Eleanor's face. "You do look like your mother."

"I know."

"Your father, too. He had the eyes. So blue that even men noticed them. It was impossible not to." He bit his lip as Eleanor grew still. "You aren't going to ask me how I knew them?"

"I already know," Eleanor breathed.

Simon narrowed his eyes at her. He clearly hadn't anticipated this, and could not conceal the surprise in his features. "How?"

Eleanor looked grim. "Once upon a time, a squire boy in my Uncle Montag's manor was embarrassed by little Edmond de Fougères and asked to kill him. Now Edmond is dead, and you have his sword. There is too much coincidence. You must be Sir Simon of Bavaria."

A tremor ran up Alec's spine. The source of this story, Giselle, would be in danger if Eleanor said more. Though Eleanor didn't know that. "Rothulfus Lezay used to talk, Simon. He told a lot of stories about Montag, and you were included in some of them."

Simon seemed to think about that for a moment. The fire cracked in the quiet that surrounded the three of them. Still, his eyes lingered on Eleanor far more than Alec was comfortable with. She was meeting Simon's eye, answering the challenge.

"He talked a lot about you, too," Simon said, his voice dropping to a rougher timbre.

Alec felt a wave of anger run through his veins. "Well, I hope you're warmer now. We'll see you in the morning."

Simon's attention turned back to him, and a smile slowly returned to his lips. "Till the morning, then." He walked back into the darkness of the forest to his own cold camp.

Alec turned to Eleanor, who still looked ready to fight. "We'll keep watch in turns through the night. I don't want any surprises."

Chapter 21

E leanor stared into the fire for a long time, thoughts swirling like the flames in front of her. Occasionally she'd poke the fire, releasing a shower of sparks that drifted into the trees around them. Simon was right, they were lighting a beacon each night to tell people they were there. The fact that they had not yet attracted highwaymen was a miracle, though perhaps aided in that they always stayed out of view from the main road, as they did tonight. And it was too cold even for hardened criminals to venture far from shelter.

She listened to Alec's soft snoring. At least he would be partially rested tomorrow.

She prodded the fire again. Snowflakes down, sparks up. The ice coming down was not enough to cool the fire, much like telling herself all was well was not enough to quiet the anxiety roiling within her. She was caught in a nightmare that would not end, in a constant state of alertness. Oddly enough, those warning seemed to do the most damage. Roric and Elfroid had used force to get their point across, and she had not yet had time to reconcile those emotions. Then their peaceful layover at the abbey had been highlighted with more warnings and then Simon's introduction. She would feel much better when Benec was in her arms, and she knew he was safe. Then they could take steps to keep it that way.

Eleanor rose and crossed their campsite to the pile of wood they'd stockpiled. It was amazing how much cooler it was just a few steps from the fire. She shivered, loaded an armful of wood and with her back turned to the forest, added it a branch at a time to the fire. The fire hissed and cracked as steam rose. In a few minutes, these wet branches would be dry enough to burn. She reached out her hands to the flames.

The leaves rustled behind Eleanor, and she spun, dagger in hand, arresting her strike mere inches from Simon's neck.

He looked down at the blade with wide eyes, which slowly rose to meet hers. He smiled.

She frowned.

"I just want to talk to you." Simon lifted his hands. He tipped his head towards Alec. "Away from him." He held a finger to his lips, then beckoned her back towards his camp. He walked away, expecting her to follow.

She looked at Alec, then back to Simon, who was disappearing into the forest as silent as a deer. She sheathed her dagger and followed. She would keep her distance, but curiosity was getting the better of her.

Simon waited in a clearing halfway between their two camps, a massive fallen tree next to him. Eleanor could still see her fire, just a stone's throw away. If she called out, Alec would wake.

Simon chuckled. "Knightess...you are no knight."

She smiled to herself. He would find out if he tested her. Her nerves were raw, and she was in the mood for a fight. Her hand shifted to the hilt of her dagger. Perhaps she should have brought the sword as well.

Simon must have seen the challenge in her posture. "No." He gestured to the huge log. "Sit. We're talking like civilized people. Then you can go back to your husband."

"Civilized people would talk around a campfire...while my husband is present."

"My questions are for you, sweetheart. And you're going to want to hear what I have to say." He straddled the log, facing her, and sunk his dagger partway into the punky wood. He placed his hands on his hips, smirking as her eyes locked on the blade between them. "Eyes up here."

She glared at him. "What do you want to know?"

"How did you know who I am?" Simon tilted his head to the side.

"Alec told me stories about when you were my uncle's squire."

"And who did he hear them from?"

She swallowed, imagining Alec's gorgeous female friend. "From Lezay I think."

"Lezay wasn't around much the year we went to Blackstone."

"Maybe Montag told him."

Simon leaned toward her, his hands resting on either side of the dagger. "Let me tell you a story of my own. Once upon a time, I rode through Aquitaine alone, my last quest before I was knighted. When I returned to Alsace, I stayed at a brothel a day's ride from Brunstein. I wanted a good night of sleep and a woman's company before I had to settle into my responsibilities as a knight. There was a beautiful girl there, only a year or so younger than I, that provided the utmost service." His eyes sparkled. "She had the fiercest eyes, skin the color of a light bay, complete with a silken black mane."

Eleanor's heart pounded. He was describing Alec's friend.

"I laid with her all night. I was high on excitement from my journey and my coming ordination. We drank wine by the bottle. I told her all sorts of things, things I told no other. I told her Montag had given me permission to kill little Edmond; I only needed to wait until he was man enough to be worth killing."

Eleanor sucked in a breath, which made Simon smile.

"I returned to her often over the years, whenever I was passing through. Her skills only improved with time, though I learned to control my tongue. Then one day, a few years ago, she was gone." Simon straightened, his gaze still locked on Eleanor. She tried to keep her face impassive. "Her friends told me she'd run off with another knight. They said she had talked too much, pressed the wrong man for secrets. No one has seen her since."

Eleanor sank onto the log, her legs suddenly weak at what Simon was alluding to. She kept her eyes locked on the dagger, tantalizingly close to her reach, like a test.

Simon smiled. "But stories that no others should know have reached Alec's ears, which means only one thing. She is alive. He has found her. And if he has pulled out her secrets, *he has been with her*."

Eleanor closed her eyes. She'd suspected as much, but Alec had assured her that he and the prostitute were only friends. A gut feeling told her Simon spoke the truth.

Simon rose and stepped next to Eleanor, one knuckle grazing and resting on her neck as gentle as a caress. "She trades in secrets, Eleanor. An answer for a question. A question for an answer."

She couldn't hide her inhalation of breath, and Simon must have felt it through the contact of his solitary finger on her neck. His hand fell to her shoulder, gentle, reassuring. She was too stunned to shake him off. After all her insistence that he be honest, all his requests that she trust him, Alec had lied. Her head argued that Simon could be lying, that information could be passed without intimacy. But her gut—and what she herself had witnessed of their easy familiarity—screamed that Simon's story was the truth.

Simon's hand still lay on her shoulder like a hot brand. He continued, "I only wonder what he's told her about *you*. The truth is, Alec deals in secrets, too. If he plucked that story out of her, he offered her something in return. People like that are made for each other. Nothing is ever free." As if he sensed the truth in that, he paused. "I am sure she told many more stories. I am boring in comparison to the other tales she's harvested over the years. That is why she had to run from Alsace. I wonder if it was Alec that helped her..."

Simon returned to straddling the log, the blade of the dagger once again between them. His absence brought the chill of the winter air back. Her hand shifted to her side, only to brush an empty sheath. She looked up at Simon with alarm. He placed her dagger next to his in the punky wood.

Eleanor stared at the blades as they shown in the moonlight. Simon was a master manipulator. Perhaps one of the best she'd met. How could he not be, after having grown up under her uncle's tutelage? She had to play better.

"I've heard you called the English Winter. I think you're not so hard to thaw as they say."

Eleanor blinked rapidly, focusing back on the moment. "What do you mean?"

"Well, there was sweet Edmond. Your reaction to his sword leads me to think you loved him. Then this Sir Alec—you care enough to be jealous of a prostitute. Most interesting of all, you have not fought me. For someone said to be so icy cold, it's like you long for a little heat."

The offensive insinuation certainly created heat, and she was grateful for the darkness that concealed her blush. If he made even the slightest move, she would show him ice in the form of a steel blade.

"What's her name?" Eleanor asked, changing the subject.

Simon smiled, eyes sparkling in the dim light. "Giselle."

She would confirm that with Alec later. She met Simon's gaze. "Is that all? Can I go?"

"I suppose. Though I thought you would be more curious about Edmond. Perhaps I am wrong, and you weren't lovers after all. What a waste, if that was the case."

"There is nothing to be curious about. Raoul told me my uncle killed Edmond. Now my uncle is dead. Though I am still curious as to how you got Edmond's sword."

Simon laughed, genuinely laughed, and Eleanor stilled. What had she missed?

"Montag didn't kill Edmond. How would Raoul know? He wasn't there. Surely he told you that."

Raoul *had* admitted as much. He and Edmond had been best friends. Even Montag had had the heart to keep Raoul out of it. Though Raoul had known. "And you were?" It seemed as if a whole crowd had been witness.

"Yes. How do you think I got his sword?"

Eleanor stilled, nausea rising.

Simon pressed on. "There was a group of us, and it was on Montag's order. Montag took his time questioning Edmond, mostly about you. It was a waste of time. Lord Edmond didn't say much. He didn't have to. We already knew he was working as an espier for King Richard, against our own, so his death was already ordered. Answers about you would have been a bonus. But Montag fulfilled his promise to me."

Eleanor felt the stab in her chest as if it were a real blade. "You — you're the one that killed him?"

"I dealt the last blow." Simon shrugged.

She leaned forward, one arm over her stomach, another on her forehead. She felt dizzy. For years she had felt as if Edmond's death was her fault. Without her, her uncle would have left him alone. No. He'd been marked by The Order all along. *Not the time, Eleanor.* She focused her gaze. The dagger was within reach. Alec was within earshot. Simon's words repeated in her mind, and she caught his casual admission; Edmond was doomed to die for his work for the king, not just for knowing her. Before that could sink in as a consolation, Simon plunged ahead.

"Word at the tournaments was that Edmond bedded you before Alec. That your son came a few months early."

"Where did you hear that?" she stalled. Though her affair with Alec had been the scandal of the year, precious few knew her feelings for Edmond.

Simon only smiled. "We know everything. We know you aren't certain of your son's paternity—"

"You leave Benec out of this."

"*I know* if you were as loose as your reputation implies, Giselle would have found you sooner, well before Alec started hunting you down. She would have taken Montag and Lezay's bounty for herself. You do realize that's what he did to find you, right? Hunted."

Eleanor was silent. She again knew in her gut that what he said was true. She'd always known.

He mistook her pained silence for shock. "Oh, you didn't know. It was no chance meeting in Sarum, sweetheart. He was looking for you. Him bedding a woman that knew your secrets, your family's secrets, was no coincidence. He was looking for a woman like Giselle, who could lead him to you. It's no wonder that when he found her, he took her with him. He never let her go."

Eleanor stood, and Simon looked up at her from astride the log.

"I know the Lezays told you what it means to The Order if you insist the boy is Alec's. That is why so many are searching for him."

Eleanor seethed, glaring at Simon.

"I'm not a bad man, Lady Eleanor. I'm honest to a fault. If you want to be free from the liar that revealed your secret to the world and dragged you back to Alsace and even now is living off your income, your manor, then come with me. Your mother once called me a prince." He smirked. "I may be a seventh son, but I have a castle, a full household, and a life that would keep you more than comfortable." He paused a moment, scanning her up and down. "A real man would protect you. This is the second time in mere weeks that you've been taken from under his nose. Just wait until Le Brun and his men enter the game."

Eleanor's gut clenched. Simon knew too much. She knew without a doubt that he was yet another member of The Order. And by that she knew what game he referred to.

"Eleanor?" Alec's voice bellowed from their camp.

Simon pointed towards the campfire that flickered not far away. "After you talk to Alec and confirm everything I just told you, if you want to come away with me, you can. Consider it at least."

Eleanor laid a hand on his shoulder, looking into his eyes. "Simon…" She discreetly reached for the dagger while running her hand from his shoulder to his cheek, that she could caress that small patch of bare skin with her thumb. "I thank you for telling me all this." Her hand shifted to the back of his head, fisting his hair to pull back his head as she brought up her blade with her other hand. The blade shown in the moonlight against his neck. He looked up at her, and to her amusement, smiled. "I would never betray my husband for the murderer of my friend, even if he has a dozen whores hidden away. Now, you stay away from me, and you stay away from my family. Run home and tell your master you followed us like a good dog." She smiled. "And if you threaten me again, this blade will not stay clean."

She released him and strode into the woods. Simon chuckled behind her, but his footsteps moved away, back to his own camp.

Alec stood next to the fire, sword drawn, his eyes flashing like a man ready to fight. Relief flooded over him when he saw her, and she instantly felt guilty. For what, she didn't know. It wasn't her fault Simon's words were reverberating in her ears.

"Where were you?" Alec asked a little too roughly.

She looked from him to the horses and back. She absently spun her dagger in her hand. "Who's Giselle?"

A rock settled in the pit of her stomach as Alec's expression fell, his shoulders tightening. Apparently Simon *was* honest to a fault.

Chapter 22

Alec ran a shaking hand over his face, rubbing the bristle on his chin a long moment. After discerning she was fine, he was now the one that was not fine. Eleanor knew about Giselle. And if she knew, that meant Simon knew. And if Simon knew, Giselle was now in danger. And he had absolutely no way of warning her.

He began with a burning question. "How does Simon know her name?" There were reasons he hadn't told Eleanor his ally's name. Precious few of her clients knew that name. The majority of men knew her as The Raven, and that is how they were told to speak of her. Giselle—from what Alec knew—was her actual name, one he had waited years to be gifted with.

Eleanor folded her arms across her chest. "He partook of her services."

Alec inhaled through his teeth. Of course he had. Who else could Giselle have gotten some of those stories from? She sourced her information directly. And she had spent many years in Alsace.

"Where is he?" Alec scanned the woods for Simon, wondering if he eavesdropped out of sight. He could not speak freely. And if Eleanor's expression was any indication, he needed to in order to placate her.

As if in answer, Simon rode past them up the trail to the main road without so much as a wave.

"Alec...you better start talking." If Eleanor wasn't furious yet, she was getting there. The mistrust was laced into her features like a pattern in a tapestry. There were stories there, good and bad. If he didn't shine light on them they would fade to one confused furl of colors that meant nothing.

He gritted his teeth. "You have met Giselle. She was the woman in the tavern last summer."

"I guessed as much," Eleanor said in an icy tone.

Alec swallowed. That cold tone could well be what had given her the nickname English Winter. "I have known her many years."

"How many?"

"She introduced me to Lezay. That is how I heard about my father's death. And about you." He inhaled slowly. "That was what, five years ago?"

Alec rubbed his forehead with his wrist.

"You need to understand, the men Giselle attracts are naturally tight lipped. Lezay may have boasted when he was drunk, but he wasn't dumb. He wouldn't have told some of the things he told if he wasn't coaxed somehow, and there are only a few things strong enough to loosen smart men's tongues. Lust is one. And for men of certain proclivities that cannot be satiated by a normal woman, or even a normal prostitute, a gorgeous woman willing to fulfill their darkest desires can hold a certain power." Alec bit his lip. "They would go to her, hot with their own thoughts, needing the body satiated to find a calm. When she was through, and they were gasping for breath, she offered a listening ear, promising the utmost secrecy, for whatever they needed to work through. And by such she learned their secrets."

"Did she do that to you?"

The blunt question shot through Alec like a blow from a lance. At the time, he had barely noticed he was talking. He had been too distracted by the lithe body in his arms, her sweet perfume, her full lips. It was only hours later that he'd realized he had told Giselle about his quest for his father, which until that point he'd kept to himself. The next day he saw her again, and she told him about Lezay's boastful story. Alec had confirmed the information easily by seeking out the older knight, Sir Rothulfus Lezay. The ease of her truth had won his loyalty. He only realized later that she wanted something more from him. And he was fine with that.

He had enjoyed it.

Eleanor turned away from him. She'd read it all in his face. "You told me you were only friends."

"We are now. Have been since I met you. I have not been with her like that in years."

"But you still visit her."

"I do. We share information."

Eleanor scoffed.

"It is a partnership, Eleanor. It wasn't easy keeping her from Lezay. He wanted her dead once he realized what she was doing. For goodness sake, you know he told her about The Order! That in itself should have equated death. So yes, I tell her what she needs to know to stay safe. And in turn, she tells me what I need to know to keep *you* safe."

Eleanor kicked the ground, then stilled, staring at the line of brown earth now etched in the snow. "She was with Lezay?"

Even in the dim light, Alec could see Eleanor's face pale. "Often."

"Then she..." Eleanor swallowed.

Alec could only guess what her former husband's sexual proclivities had been, but they had been intense enough to make Eleanor run for her life. "She is very good at what she does," Alec said gently. From what he knew of Giselle's offerings, his own experiences with her were tame. Even so, they were still vivid in Alec's mind even years after the acts. The woman had risqué desires of her own.

Eleanor sat down by the fire, her head in her hands. Alec watched her a moment, and when she didn't move, he walked over to her and sat down beside her.

"I have a past, Eleanor. Just like you. I don't know what to tell you and what not to. I prefer we focus on the future. But I also want you to trust me. I will tell you anything you want to know."

She propped her chin on her arms, gazing at the fire. "An answer for a question, question for an answer," she mumbled.

"Not with you. You get whatever answers you want." He reached a hand to the small of her back, feeling the warmth of the fire on her cloak.

After a long moment she sighed. "I feel like a fool, not knowing when I met her that you two had been intimate. But to ask you for a list of women—it would likely be pages long, wouldn't it?"

Alec inhaled.

Eleanor shook her head. "No, I don't want to know. It's in the past, as you said. Though if there's anyone else I know, maybe you should warn me before we see them again."

"Gwen," Alec spit out. He closed his eyes, his jaw tight. "Lady Gwen of Sarum."

When he opened his eyes Eleanor was staring at him, her expression unreadable.

"She was the last one. The only other one you've met. And no, the list isn't pages long. But you should know that."

"She's married."

"Yes." Alec looked away, his face flushing in the cool air. "To your liege lord..."

"Yes." He closed his eyes again. "He knows."

Eleanor's eyes widened. She turned back to the fire.

"It was only once. She used me. I used her. I wanted information about you. She was suspicious of you, you know. That is why she allowed you to come with me so easily. I was to report back as to who you were. I didn't, for the record. She didn't know you are Eleanor de Levan until you revealed yourself at that tournament."

Eleanor swayed slightly, pressing her eyes closed. "Then it was the night I met you...after the tournament at Sarum."

"Yes. And not since," he emphasized. He longed to reach for her, but feared it was too soon.

She was silent a long while. Slowly, she turned to look at him, her expression pained. "So what are you using me for?"

"Nothing. Not now. You know that."

"Right. My role in your revenge is complete. Your father's murderer is dead."

"This has grown so far beyond that."

She nodded slightly, then stood. She turned her back to him.

Her abrupt change in demeanor alarmed him, and yet he didn't know what to do. "Eleanor—"

"I need time, Alec," she said sharply, throwing her rolled blanket on her horse's saddle with a little more force than necessary. Noir snorted, and she patted him in apology. "There's only one thing I asked of you last summer: the truth. Though you haven't outright lied, these omissions feel the same. You've misled me. I *have* to be able to trust you. You know, Simon offered to take me home with him. And the horrible thing is I would go, just to be anywhere but here. And yet he killed Edmond, so that would be wrong on a thousand levels—" She cinched Noir's girth and shot Alec a look over her shoulder. "I am going to ride ahead, and start compiling my list of questions. Then we can play your question and answer game all the way to the coast." She mounted, and Noir moved off with a mere cluck. She twisted in the saddle one more time to yell over her shoulder, "Since we're telling the truth, you should know you killed the wrong man. It wasn't Rothulfus Lezay that killed your father." Then she straightened and trotted up the embankment just as the first rays of dawn cut through the clouds into the snowy valley.

Alec stared after her in stunned disbelief. She was wrong—she had to be. He'd heard the claim from Lezay's mouth himself. As had Giselle. Why else would Alec have spent years of his life seeking revenge? His blood rose in a wave of anger. After all he had done for her—he'd just rescued her from Leuwenstein Castle for goodness sake—for her to taunt his father's demise was reproachable. He was tempted to let her ride to the coast by herself. He stood, collected their few possessions, and doused the fire with snow. Then he rode after her, the tension in the air following him like the lingering smoke from the fire.

Chapter 23

*H*e *lied. He lied.* Her mind chanted with the pound of each stride as her horse cantered away from their campsite. Rays of dawn warmed her back. She'd let Alec catch up later. All she knew was that she could not be next to him. An omission, intended to mislead, was as bad as an outright lie. And Alec was full of them. Between him and everyone around them giving her half-truths, she was ready to scream. Maybe it would be better if she did. Get it out of her system.

Hoofbeats suddenly sounded directly behind her. Noir spooked and shied, but Eleanor held him true. At first she expected to see Alec, but it was not. There was a masked man on a plain horse, and judging by his ragged appearance, he was one of the very outlaws she'd been grateful to avoid.

Eleanor cursed under her breath. Apparently, her intuition had been warning her. A thought of outlaws had not even crossed her mind until the night before and now, sure enough, here one was.

Though Noir was fast, Eleanor had no desire to push him and risk injury in the slippery snow. She drew her sword and prepared to fight. The rider matched his horse's stride to Noir's. Eleanor saw him reach for her bridle, his arm outstretched. She swung the sword, but he moved away just in time. He moved his horse back behind Noir, then rode up close, almost clipping Noir's heels. His nasty rouncey took a bite of Noir's rump, and Noir threw a buck with a double-barrel kick. This both slowed them to the point where the rouncey ran into Noir and threw Eleanor forward in the saddle.

She gripped mane and straightened herself. A second rider emerged from the woods, and she gritted her teeth. She swung hard at the man that was again trying to ride up next to her. He withdrew, only to be caught on the opposite side by the second rider. His friend? A sword flashed and the man let out a scream. No. The other man was someone else entirely.

The outlaw lost control of his horse, and the little rouncey bolted from between the two destriers. Eleanor pulled Noir back, wishing to avoid both riders. The second rider kept pace with the outlaw until the outlaw's rouncey slipped in the snow and went down. The man sprawled in the snow, still, as the rouncey slowly rose to its feet and shook off snow. The other rider dismounted and with the flash of a blade, slit the outlaw's throat.

Eleanor was taken aback at such ruthless efficiency unfurling before her eyes. She stopped Noir a short distance away and stared. The second rider wiped his blade with a handful of snow, then straightened. As he turned, Eleanor could finally recognize Simon, the bloodlust sparkling in his eyes.

She backed Noir a step.

Simon approached, the blade of his sword still pink with bloody snow.

Eleanor raised her own blade in warning. The look he gave her was not unlike that which she'd seen in knights fresh from battle.

The corner of Simon's lip turned up. "You think you can fight me?"

Eleanor's grip tightened. *Stay on the horse, no matter what*, Alec had once told her.

Simon raised his arms and let out a roar from deep within. It made the hairs on Eleanor's arms stand on end, but battle-hardened Noir snorted and reared, striking out with the same blow that had once disabled Rothulfus Lezay. Simon sidestepped, but then swung upwards at her.

She was ready. Their blades collided with a ring that resounded through the forest.

"You may defend, but can you fight? Can you wield the blade to *take a life*?"

Eleanor narrowed her eyes.

Simon again attacked, and Eleanor drew on her months of pent-up fury and frustration to give him a battle worth remembering. Even through her anger, she sensed he was staying his hand, testing but not desiring to kill. Was this, too, yet another mockery of her? She used her position on Noir to drive his sword away, and with the force of the blow, she sent his sword spinning into the snow behind him. She stilled her hand a mere inch from Simon's neck, her body shaking.

Simon met her gaze with a challenge in his own, yet his posture was as relaxed as it had been when they'd spoken the night before. "Again, you defend without taking a life."

"That does not make me weak." Eleanor glared.

Simon gestured to the man sprawled in the snow, a spray of crimson blood surrounding the corpse. "Could you have done it?"

Eleanor shifted her gaze back and forth from the corpse to Simon's intense gaze.

As she did so, he closed the distance, letting her sword now touch the wool of his cloak. "You think you are tough. You think you want to join us. You don't even know *what we are*." He turned his back to her, the timbre of his voice falling deeper as he studied the corpse. "This is what we are. Blood and death."

Eleanor straightened, realization beginning to dawn. Perhaps this was no mere outlaw. Was there a tie to The Order? "Who was he?"

Simon knelt beside the corpse, patting the man's clothing. He located a dagger, studied the hilt, then rose. He held it to her.

She couldn't see but still, she was hesitant to dismount. "Who?"

"This was one was Raganor's. Likely assigned to take you captive." Simon threw the blade into the snow at Noir's feet. "I just saved your life. You already disarmed me. Get off your beast and look for yourself."

She considered pointing out that he'd attacked her, but she had enough training to know that if Simon had wanted to kill her, it would have been a far more intense fight. She swung her leg over Noir and slipped to the ground to retrieve the dagger. It was plain. Her grip tightened on the pommel. Was this yet another trick to make her vulnerable?

Simon watched her with narrowed eyes. "Raoul's espiers travel with no mark. He learned the technique from his father, who learned it from his father. The sign of a Le Brun is nothing. And this man was not Raoul's."

"How can you be sure?" Eleanor didn't want to think of her cousin trying to harm her, and yet he had been vague while so many others spoke freely. He had to be hiding something.

Simon's eyes raked over her from head to toe. They lingered on the dagger in her hand. "Raoul believes you are the future of The Order. He would never try to hurt you."

Simon abruptly turned back to the corpse. He mumbled to himself, "She's a fool to not know it." Louder, he asked, "Where's dear old Alec, anyway?" He ruffled through the dead man's clothes a second time. He appeared to come up empty handed but for a small coin purse.

"I'm sure he'll be along," Eleanor said quietly. She studied the plain hilt of the dagger. Even the most basic of smiths could have forged it. That observation alone reminded her of the two men that had died near Levan Manor. Had the messenger been one of Raoul's men? The arsonist Raganor's? Or had Raoul burned the manor to drive her north to Alsace, into this elaborate dance of threats and warnings she and Alec had been navigating since they arrived? Who else was he allied with? "The Lezays—" Eleanor pursed her lips, bitter memories surfacing at the mere mention of the name.

"They work with us."

"The Order."

"No. Us. Raoul and I." Simon rose to his feet, demonstrating just how much taller and broader he was compared to her. She wasn't cowed. "We—"

The sound of hoofbeats interrupted him, and Alec emerged into the clearing, sword drawn. He took in the scene with a furious expression. "What happened?"

Eleanor was at a loss for words, her mind still reeling from the revelation that Raoul was working with not only Edmond's killer, but the *Lezays*. No wonder he had been vague. No wonder he was flying the stag! Was he secretly working with Raganor himself as well? Eleanor's desire to get out of Alsace grew stronger by the second. Even that wouldn't be enough. She wanted out of all of France.

Simon's voice drew her to the immediate situation. "Outlaw." Simon let a hand fall to his empty scabbard, then slid it around to cross his arms.

"Which one of you killed him?" Alec asked.

"Him." Eleanor looked away, sheathed her sword, and handed the dead man's dagger back to Simon. "Now what?"

Simon tucked the dagger into one of his saddlebags then searched the snow for his sword. "Now nothing." He found it, dried it with the edge of his cloak, then sheathed it.

"The body—" Eleanor protested.

"Will be found." Simon shot her a look. "You think we keep our identities secret by reporting every body we leave behind?" Simon mounted his horse.

With a last look at the corpse on the snow, Eleanor swung back onto Noir.

"I'm returning to Alsace," Simon said to Alec. With a look at Eleanor, he frowned. "You now know what you're dealing with." After a heartbeat he added, "Don't hesitate. Or you will not survive." With a nod at Alec, Simon pressed his horse into a canter and headed back in the direction of Leuwenstein.

Alec sheathed his sword and glared at Eleanor. "Another dead body at your feet and no explanation?"

"Simon says he was one of Raganor's men."

"And he just happened to rescue you in my short absence."

Eleanor shot a look over her shoulder as she rode away. "Yes."

She was still mad. The brutal death she'd witnessed didn't change Alec's half-truths. If anything, she was annoyed *he* hadn't come to her rescue. Not that she needed him. Even without Simon, she would have been just fine. So she pressed Noir into a canter, heading away from Alec once again.

Now, instead of his footsteps pounding, *He lied, He lied*, they said *Get home, get home, get home.* Her son was waiting for her.

Chapter 24

Raoul clenched his fist around the stoneware mug so hard his knuckles began to cramp. He glowered at the man seated across the table from him in the busy tavern. It did not matter that the man was his senior. He was a fool that had ruined their intricate plan for a petty game of his own.

"Roric, do you realize what you have done?" Raoul asked through gritted teeth. He sat with his back arrow straight and leaned forward towards Roric just slightly and dropped his voice. "Now that she knows, there will *have* to be an initiation. Raganor will tell the other members she knows, and they will *insist* on it."

"She wanted in," Roric protested. "Who am I to deny someone *of the bloodline*? I feel like that's an unwritten rule. And she meets all the requirements."

Raoul cursed under his breath and slammed his mug on the table. Ale sloshed over his hand and he shook it off absently. "You are so eager for her to die."

Roric leaned forward. "Not her. *I* think she'll go through with it. She'll pass. And if she does what I think she'll do, then *he* will die."

Raoul drank the last dregs of his ale and slammed the cup again, earning a few strange looks from the men at the table next to him. Of course Roric would want revenge on the man who killed his brother. Roric could not admit to Lezay's wrongdoings, or that the melee was a fair fight. He could not admit that Alec's last blow had been a mercy kill to spare a monster a life of pain.

How would this play out? Eleanor, if she could go through with it, would be inducted. Alec would be dead. If she went through with it, she was not the woman Raoul thought she was, and she would be too corrupted to sway to his side. Thus Raganor would still be in power. They would still need more members, and the cycle of initiations would continue. Who would be next? Likely one of Simon's five sons.

"She won't do it." Raoul shook his head.

"But who else would be an eligible sacrifice?"

Raoul let Roric think a long moment, running through the genealogies. The foreign members either already had sons in The Order, did not have male progeny, or had sons too young for knighthood. Raoul and Simon already knew this. There was no one but Eleanor, a rare female knight, and Alec. Raoul narrowed his gaze as Roric's eyebrows went up at this realization. It was a trap set as tight as any snare, so invisible even the trapper had stepped in it.

"Congratulations. You've made certain that one of them will die. And if your gamble is wrong, and they go to their graves together, as lovers, then you realize the power Raganor will wield until his dying day?" Raoul's fingers itched to throttle Roric, but fortunately at that moment the tavern door blew open to allow the cold wind and another plain-clothed man into the tavern. Roric was spared—for now.

Simon spotted them easily, and the look in his eye showed all the fury of Raoul's thoughts. He covered the room in a few long strides, his hood falling back to reveal an expression that could melt an ice-capped mountain. He shoved aside a patron whose chair was in his way, and then flipped Raoul and Roric's table on its side, the better to access Roric and grab him by the throat. Cups and plates clattered on the floor, spinning to their resting places across the room.

"You arrogant swine!" Simon spit out. "We have waited patiently for years to undo this, and now you have ruined everything!"

Raoul casually brushed crumbs from his lap. "We just came to the same conclusion ourselves, Simon. Care to sit down?"

Simon glared at the wide-eyed Roric and shoved him back. He righted the table and leaned against it with his hands, remaining on his feet. The patrons around them, at least those still left in their seats, edged their chairs away discreetly, lest they be subject to the next outburst.

Simon's voice became a breath, barely audible over the murmurs around them. "My son will be the next, if one of them doesn't take the place. He'll be knighted this summer."

Roric shook his head. "I'm sorry. I thought there were others, from abroad."

"That's the problem with you Lezays. You act, and then when you are wrong, you think you can just apologize and we forget. We don't." Simon shook his head.

Raoul inhaled slowly. "It's done now. They know. And the others will know they know, so there will be an initiation. We can only help prepare Eleanor and Alec."

"Your cousin is rather adept at taking care of herself. I'm sure you can ask Elfroid about that," Simon snarled.

Raoul tilted his head to the side. "What do you mean?"

Simon smiled maliciously as Roric swallowed. "The whole of castle Leuwenstein is talking about how Eleanor fought twenty men in the courtyard and then was imprisoned in a tower. The maids can only speculate, but her clothes were found shredded and she was seen walking around wearing Alec's tunic, while he walked around half naked."

Raoul had heard of anger that blurred the mind to where it only saw the color red. Something about the blood rush was theorized. He'd always believed it to be an over-exaggeration, as he'd been in plenty of fights, taken plenty of lives, and never seen in only one color. Now though, looking at Roric's thin-lipped expression, he knew the expression was true. The room had grown red with his anger. He rose slowly, hands fisted at his sides. Simon took a step back, allowing him free access, and then for the second time that night, the table in the tavern went flying. It was followed by a fist to Roric's jaw that loosened teeth, split Raoul's knuckle, and would leave the man with a mark for weeks to come.

The tavern grew deathly quiet. The patrons around them staggered back from their tables, giving the men space. More space was not needed, as Raoul was done. He was done with all of it. He was done with partnering with the Lezays. He was done with the shady, back-stabbing conversations. He was done working with men who thought a woman's only purpose was for their own pleasure and advancement. As he watched Roric stretch his sore jaw and spit out blood, Raoul resolved that if it was the last thing he did, The Order would be destroyed beyond any further resurrection.

He spun on his heel, throwing his cloak over his shoulders.

"Raoul—" Simon called.

Raoul hesitated at the door, a full tavern of guests staring at him.

"Alec found Giselle," Simon finished.

As if that just wasn't the apple in the fat pig's mouth. He slammed the tavern door and headed into the night.

Chapter 25

"Benec!" Eleanor shrieked as she jumped off her horse and scooped up her child. The boy looked bewildered but didn't pull away from her fussing. She whispered in his ear and poked him in the belly, a fit of giggles suddenly erupting from the boy as he smiled and reached his hands to her. He twined his arms around her neck as she picked him up. Noir followed quietly behind her as she approached Wilfred, beaming.

She hugged him with her free arm. "Thank you." She could not hide the emotion from her voice. For days they had pushed on through bitter cold to get to Alec's manor in England, worrying all the way about what they would find. She had lost sleep many nights as she worried if Wilfred, Marie, and the children had made it to Alec's castle. Now, here before her was the proof that they had avoided all the threats that rose from winter fires. Thank God, Benec was fine. He was healthy, he was strong, and he was unhurt. She would have to think long and hard on how to repay Wilfred for keeping the boy safe.

Wilfred gave her a last squeeze and released her, his smile understanding.

"The children traveled better than we expected. They loved crossing the channel. Thankfully, we had good weather. You have a nice castle, Alec." Wilfred looked up at his half-brother, who was still seated on his horse, watching the scene before him with a hesitant curiosity. Eleanor kissed Benec's soft cheek, her eyes on her husband. She could almost see the weight of their conversations in Alsace playing in his mind. They were still both hurting from those conversations.

Alec looked up towards his castle, then back to Wilfred. "How long have you been here?"

"About a week, maybe two. It's slow traveling with the children. Did you make it to Alsace?"

Eleanor hugged Benec tighter to her. "We made it," she said quietly. Benec squirmed and she had to soften her grip.

"That sounds like a story." Wilfred furrowed his brow.

Alec dismounted and approached Eleanor and Benec, laying a hand on the boy's back, then turning to Wilfred. "We'll talk later. Anything eventful here?"

"No. All has been quiet. Collette sent word that they were able to buy enough grain with the coin you left, so as far as I know, everyone from Levan Manor is safe for the winter."

Alec still appeared distracted. "Is my steward Thomas around?"

"Somewhere in the castle, yes." Wilfred began working his way into the castle, a three-story square, wood-framed keep. It wasn't huge, far smaller than Sarum, but still was larger than Eleanor's little manor in Aquitaine. "He's been accommodating. Seemed surprised you were coming back so soon after you'd been here."

"Well, I wasn't planning on it," Alec admitted.

Marie appeared at the entryway, her children in tow as usual. Her belly looked curiously round, and Eleanor suspected she was again with child. Eleanor smoothed down her skirts, suddenly aware how flat her own figure was. Two years…maybe the curse The Order spoke of had merit. But that would mean Benec was not Alec's. She lifted her chin, forcing her thoughts back to the present.

The younger woman beamed at them, shifting her baby. "Welcome!" Marie said.

Eleanor awkwardly embraced her, the children creating a bit of an obstacle between them. Benec squirmed and Eleanor put him down, and he headed off after his little cousin into the manor. "They're getting so big," Eleanor said. Even a month away was too long—her little boy had changed even in that short time.

"If only we could hold time still," Marie mused, then smiled. "Come. I'll show you the castle. Unless you'd rather the lord of the manor show you around?"

Eleanor looked back to Alec. He smiled his lopsided grin. "What?" she asked. He took a slow step towards her, and she furrowed her brow. "Alec...wha—" She shrieked as he scooped her into his arms.

"I am carrying my wife across the threshold." He smiled. As if she was weightless, he carried her up the staircase to the castle door.

Eleanor wiggled. "Really? There is nothing wrong with my feet." On one hand she was amused, the other furious. Wary of knocking them both over, she acquiesced.

"I know."

True to his word, Alec carried her across the threshold and set her on her feet. He planted a lingering kiss on her forehead.

"Welcome home," he breathed.

Eleanor didn't know what to say. The dimly-lit, chilly hall didn't exactly have a homey feel to it, at least not like Levan Manor had. There were tapestries and pennants hanging along the walls, but they were not familiar. They were not Alec's, nor her family's. She felt as if she was in a stranger's house. When she looked at it from that perspective, it seemed better. The place was tidy and clean. There was obvious pride in maintenance. That had to be the doing of the castellan, Thomas Rivers, whom Alec had spoken about.

Thomas himself appeared, his face stern and manner stiff. "Welcome back, my lord." He bowed neatly. "I trust you had safe travel?"

Alec and Eleanor shared a knowing look. It had certainly been an eventful journey.

"It went well enough. All well here, Thomas?" Alec asked.

"Yes, sir. When you've settled I will be glad to report all that has transpired."

"Perhaps this evening." He pulled Eleanor toward him. "Allow me to introduce my wife, Lady Eleanor de Levan."

Thomas bowed to her.

Scarcely before Eleanor could address the castellan, Alec took her by the hand and pulled her forward. "I think I'll do the grand tour, Marie."

Marie's cheeks flushed as she smiled. "Take your time. We'll tell the kitchen to start preparing dinner a little early." The children ran screaming gleefully down the hall.

Alec's warm hand pulled Eleanor forward. She felt the shift of tension in his body, noted the spark in his eyes as they locked on her. She could only hope that look was not as obvious to the others. Marie's giggle and Thomas's averted eyes indicated it was.

Alec showed her the defenses, the arrow slits and crenellations. He showed her the buttery, where they sampled the estate's ale. He introduced her to every servant they passed, greeting each one by name. They seemed surprised he remembered them all. There was a reunion with tenants from Neroche in the main hall, then it was down to the store rooms and up to the top of the square keep, where there was a view in every direction of the beautiful countryside. They stood there for a while, taking it in.

"How much land?" Eleanor asked. It was pretty, with flat fields cut neatly and stone-walled pastures of sheep and a few cows. There was only a thin crust of snow here in England, just enough to make the ground look clean and white.

"As far as you can see." Alec squeezed her hand.

"A dream come true?" she asked quietly, then looked up at him.

He looked out and nodded. "Aye. Better than Castle Homme, actually."

"I am happy for you, Alec. I really am."

He looked down at her sideways, brow furrowed. Then he straightened.

They both knew that as much as he wanted her to feel like all this was hers, it never would be. Levan Manor was her home.

She was glad her household was keeping up with things while they were away.

The thoughts swirled, made worse with impending exhaustion. The past month of stress and travel had caught up to her, and she wanted nothing more than to crawl in bed and sleep an entire day away.

Maybe after she saw Benec one more time.

As if in answer to her heart's plea, Benec and Godfrey ran across the courtyard below, scattering chickens in their wake. Wilfred strode casually after them towards the stable, an apple in hand. Eleanor smiled to herself. Wilfred still had a soft spot for Noir.

Alec gently pulled her arm and led her away. That bold, lustful look was still in his eyes. Eleanor was aware that he had not shown her the lord's chambers yet. Though she knew what he wanted, she wasn't sure how she felt about it. He'd stayed true to his word and given her time to consider everything that had been revealed in the forest of Alsace. He'd offered to answer her questions, but she had stayed silent, wondering which ones she wanted answered. A part of her suspected though he claimed he would answer all, there was a limit to what he would tell her. She wanted to make sure she got what she needed. And there were some things she would rather never know about her husband.

All of this roiled in her mind as Alec led her to the heavy door that marked the lord's chamber and pushed it open. She looked around as he closed it behind them and barred it with a soft scrape of wood. Then he stood leaning against the door, letting her take in everything. There was a massive canopied bed in the center of the room, the headboard carved with an ornate scene of horses galloping. The pillars of the bed curled upward in a beautiful twist to the heavy curtains that hung above the thick mattress. The rest of the room was hung with intricate tapestries, mostly of day-to-day scenes, and a hearth burned hot. In the corner was a large chest, as intricately carved as the bed, and on the opposite wall was a table and chair. It was every bit as magnificent as Lady Gwen's room in Sarum.

Eleanor sucked in her breath and turned to Alec. "Feel like real nobility?"

He pushed away from the door and stepped towards her. "Like real nobility." He cupped her cheek in his palm, caressing it with a thumb.

Eleanor closed her eyes to the sensation. It was comforting and made her heart pound. She wasn't ready, and yet she didn't want him to let go. She wanted to scream and could hardly breathe.

"Whatever reasons you have for still being mad at me, I want to make them up to you," Alec whispered.

She felt the heat of his body now, felt his breath on her lips, and then the bristle of his jaw was there and he was kissing her. The world spun behind her eyelids, which remained pressed tight. Her skin warmed, and then she reached for his neck, his hair, pulling him tighter, kissing him back, pressing her hips into his.

She gasped as he pressed her back a step. Alec ran a finger down her neck, along her collarbone, and then slipped her tunic off her shoulder. She knew she smelled of sweat and horse, her traveling clothes badly needing a wash, but so did he. He leaned forward and kissed the bare skin. She trembled, aware of how much control Alec had in that moment. She was locked in a room with him, in his castle, as his wife. There was nothing he couldn't do to her. If she told him she was still mad at him and didn't want this, he didn't have to stop. He had a right to her, to this.

Just as her other husband once had.

As his hands ran down the curve of her hips, up to the small of her back, up to a breast and down to her buttock, Eleanor grew lost in sensation. With a kiss as soft as a feather, he brushed her lips with his. His fingers worked the strings to her tunic, and then piece by piece the clothing began to fall. This was her chance to challenge his power, to tell him to stop. Would he listen?

Alec circled her naked body, tracing fingers over her as if she was made of fine marble. His touch burned her alive as she flinched away only to press into him, her body begging for more. The sensations grew overwhelming, almost too much. He ran his hand lower, and she jumped as he traced his fingers over the very core of her tensed energy.

It was in that moment that she knew she would yield to him, no matter what he asked. She missed him; she needed him. He was a part of her, and only when they were this close, skin to skin, could she feel complete. That thought terrified her, and yet she knew it was true. How had she let herself get so close to another person? This had started as a mere marriage of convenience. It was now beyond the lustful love she had always pictured; it took trust to yield like this, to be this vulnerable. *Love trusts.*

Alec began to undress.

They stood together, two naked forms in the middle of the ornate room, caressing each other until their flesh pebbled from the cold. Then Alec guided her back to the bed, and she stepped willingly, though her heart pounded, mind raced. What would he do if she relinquished control, allowed him the power to guide? Usually they met each other halfway, a silent dance of communication and challenge that created a beautiful passion. What if Alec had no limits? *As with Giselle.*

Alec pressed her onto the bed, pulling her wrists over her head. Then he kneed her legs apart, and she yielded to him, body conflicted between the tenderness of his caress and the sharp thrust that searched for release. The tension built within her. Alec's hands tightened on her wrists, and she opened her eyes, meeting his. He stared down at her with a spark in his eye, watching her expressions. She was mesmerized for a minute, and then he pressed deeper, finding the line between pleasure and pain, and then he was beyond her vision again, her eyes rolling and closing, her head tucking into his shoulder, her back arching off the bed.

She longed to thrash away from him, such were the waves of pleasure that threatened to crest, but he held her. For once, Eleanor realized just how incredibly strong Alec was. She was wiry and strong herself, but he would always dwarf her. He could break her.

The wave threatened to crest again. His hands again tightened on her wrists. He was getting close. He kissed her, she kissed back with desperation, longing for him to finish what he'd started.

There were no more thoughts of other partners, his or hers. There was no Order, nor threat to Benec. There was only the connection of flesh to flesh, soul to soul, a binding chord that laced her to Alec in ways she could not understand. She offered herself to him without words. And he embraced her, taking what he desired from her body, and yet also holding that fragile thread of emotion, nurturing it with his kiss, his caress, with the look in his eye. And when the power of their joining washed over them, he held her tight to his chest, soothing her trembling body as the tears fell.

She let him feel the proof of her emotion. Perhaps he needed to be reminded of the power he had to break her. He didn't need his hands. He held her heart, which could break far more easily than her body. Alec shifted her in his arms, hugging her tighter, kissing the top of her head. *So he felt it then. Did knowledge of that power scare him as well?*

Chapter 26

Though she felt even more exhausted when she left Alec's chamber than she had when they arrived, she at least emerged clean, with combed and braided hair and fresh clothing. It felt strange to be in a dress again after weeks running around in men's clothes. Alec was already in the hall, working the crowd with fluid ease, as only he could do. He met her eye across the room and smiled, and she couldn't help but smile back. They still needed to talk, but she had more faith that the strains could be worked through.

Eleanor scanned the rest of the room, noting a few familiar faces as the household began to gather for the evening meal. The people from Neroche sat together at one long table. They all looked well, and a few of them waved to her. There was a larger group of strangers, men and women, who must be the pre-existing household of the castle. The women came up to her and bent their knees, heads bowed, and then went about their tasks. The men approached and bowed low. Eleanor felt awkward, for at Levan Manor she had thrown herself so much into the vast amount of work that she had become one with her household. Here, she was the Lady of the Manor. She was nobility.

She took a deep breath. As nobility, she and Alec had to sit at the head table. It was placed central to the room, overlooking the other tables. Two high-backed chairs were placed at the center for her and Alec. Thomas was already seated, glumly watching the scene from the right of Alec's place. Eleanor wondered if his frown was his normal expression. Two shorter-backed chairs were to the left, ready for guests of honor. Wilfred and Marie would sit there. Where there had been no social hierarchy at Levan Manor, now there was one.

Eleanor made her way across the room as platters of food were carried in and set on the tables. She stood beside her chair and waited until Alec excused himself from conversation and took his place next to her. Wilfred and Marie followed shortly after, once the children were settled at the table with old Guillaume. Benec seemed to like the grey-haired caretaker. That was good. He could use a grandfather figure watching out for him.

Eleanor's stomach twisted at the thought of her own grandfather.

All were seated but Alec, who raised his glass in toast and prayer. "Great thanks to God for our safe passage. May we have a peaceful winter together. To you!"

The cups and glasses tinged at all the tables, and then the conversation again buzzed around the room as people dug into the platters of food.

Thomas and Alec immediately got into speaking about matters of the fief. Thomas had things under control, but Alec still wanted to press forward with some minor repairs and fortifications. Eleanor wondered if Raganor's proximity was still weighing on his mind.

Wilfred leaned slightly towards Eleanor and whispered, "How did it go?"

She swallowed. "Well, Raoul confirmed a lot of what we suspected. But then I was kidnapped by the Lezays."

"Oh lord, there's more than one of them?"

"Yes. It was a game for them though, and we got a bit more information. Then we met a man on the road, Sir Simon of Bavaria, who told me a few of Alec's secrets."

"He has a lot of secrets."

"I've discovered that. How many do you know?"

"Not as many as he has." Wilfred took another bite, chewing thoughtfully. "I'll leave you to pursue that with him. So did you confirm your grandfather was involved with burning the manor?"

"Not directly. It's more complicated than that." She debated how much to tell Wilfred. She did not want him to learn about The Order, for fear it would put him in danger. And yet was not knowing dangerous, just as not telling him about Raganor had inadvertently revealed the manor's location?

Wilfred leaned forward, looking around her to get Alec's attention. "So will you return to Levan Manor in spring or stay here?"

"We haven't planned that far ahead yet," Alec admitted.

The castellan looked notably curious about this part of the conversation. Of course, his lord being in residence or across the channel affected his own plans, right down to his own accommodations.

Thomas offered, "Lord Cenric always throws a grand feast if you're interested in going. His castle is a short ride away. His messenger invited you last week."

Eleanor smoothed her skirts. She hated gatherings. And yet, being that they had just ridden across kingdoms looking for answers to questions that still largely remained unanswered, perhaps a social event would serve to further their knowledge of where their allies and acquaintances stood. After all, it wasn't just The Order that was roiling that winter. There were still whispers of King John's crown being given to his young nephew. Where better to learn more than the biggest social event in the county? Eleanor had been there during the years she had served Lady Gwen.

Alec seemed to read her thoughts, and he smirked slightly. "Well, if you want to go." He knew as well as she what the real purpose would be. Though he, of course, loved any occasion with a lot of people and copious amounts of ale.

"It's only two days away," Eleanor pointed out.

"If we leave early tomorrow, we'll still be there in time for church services on Christmas Day. Lord Cenric's manor isn't far. Though we'll have to spend the night there."

Marie piped in quietly from the end of the table, "Wilfred, I don't think I'll go. I'll stay with the children."

"Marie's been traveling more than she ever did," Wilfred explained. "I think we'll take it easy for a while. You two go. Have a good time. You should probably meet with Lord Cenric anyway."

"We should." Alec met Eleanor's eye. "We'll take Benec with us, too. He should learn how to travel, see what court life is about."

Eleanor nodded. She didn't want the boy far from her if it could be avoided. She stole a look at him as he played with his cousins at a nearby table. He was so innocent. May he never know men were searching across kingdoms to find him. May he be safe here in England, as Eleanor herself had been while similar men hunted her.

They finished the meal with jovial regaling of the past month's events, at least those they could talk about.

Afterwards, Eleanor tucked Benec into bed next to his cousins in Wilfred and Marie's room, just as she had since he was a baby. He felt most comfortable with his cousins nearby.

"Mama, you stay with me?" Benec asked, his tired eyes barely able to stay open. He yawned.

Eleanor's heart soared at the words. "For a little bit, mon cher."

And she did. Curled next to him on his tiny bed, she slept until dawn. She woke to Wilfred's heavy footsteps and pulled herself away from her slumbering son. Wilfred hesitated at the door, a finger to his lips. Eleanor glanced at Marie, who lay curled in the big bed across the room, lightly snoring. Extracted from the trundle bed, Eleanor quietly slipped out of the room after Wilfred.

"I'm sorry, I didn't mean to stay all night." She had slept sounder than she had in weeks.

"It's no trouble, my lady. We didn't want to wake you," Wilfred answered. "Even Alec didn't want to disturb the two of you. Benec missed you more than he lets on." Wilfred paused, facing her. "Be honest with me, Eleanor. How much danger is the boy in?"

She rubbed her forehead, then resolutely met Wilfred's gaze. "More than we know."

Wilfred nodded solemnly. "I didn't tell you last night—I didn't want to say anything in front of Marie, or Thomas for that matter. But on our way here we stopped in Sarum.

Lady Gwen warned that the king had made inquiries about the boy. Very general, she said. But still, despite your fame, why would the king care about your child? We're all petty nobles, not dukes or earls or people close to the king. He doesn't monitor every single citizen of his kingdom. So why Benec?"

A pit settled in Eleanor's stomach. Was it possible that even King John was tied to The Order? "I don't know."

Wilfred gave her a long look. "You've never been one to lie to me, Eleanor. Don't start now."

She closed her eyes. Wilfred was her dearest friend, one of few people she trusted. "I'm sorry. I can't tell you more. Not yet."

He nodded once. "That, I'll accept. Just don't lie to me. And you know the more you tell me, the better I can protect him. I don't want to make another mistake like I did with Raganor." He reached out to touch Eleanor's shoulder, then quickly let his arm drop again. "You know Benec means a lot to me. He is my nephew. And with the circumstances the last few years, he is more, to Marie and I both."

Eleanor nodded, any words that would have come choked with emotion.

Wilfred gave her a last empathetic look then headed off in the direction of the stables. Eleanor worked her way back to Alec's chamber, where he was still fast asleep in the big bed. He startled as she closed the door behind her, then relaxed back and yawned. He shot a look to the light that had begun to filter through the window, and then back to her.

She crawled into bed with him, tucking her cold feet next to his bare legs.

Alec turned towards her, looping an arm around her middle. His eyes drifted closed. "I didn't realize how exhausted I was."

"Me, too. Do you think the lord and lady of the castle get to sleep all day?"

"Hmm," he murmured. "I doubt it. But they're going to have to pound on that door before I get out of this bed."

Eleanor's eyes fluttered closed, and she was about to fall back into a content sleep, when the knock came. It persisted for a few minutes before Alec groaned and pulled away from her. Eleanor tucked deeper into the warm bed, listening to Thomas's morning greeting. Then he was gone, and Alec was shuffling around the room pulling his clothes on.

She felt him kiss her lightly.

"I love you," he whispered.

"Want me to get up?" she mumbled back.

"Sleep. You're only the lady of the manor, for once."

She opened one eye to glare at him, debating if that warranted the throwing of a pillow, then decided it was not. She nestled into the covers. "Well get to it, my lord. I'll get back to my needlepoint by noontime."

He laughed from across the room. "I'm afraid to ruin your plans, my lady, but you have to get ready for a party. We'll ride out at noon for Cenric's. And I fully expect that as your grand return to England, everyone will want to see if the Lady of the Tournament is still the fairest in the land." Alec slipped out of the room.

Eleanor rolled to her back, staring at the ceiling, all hope of sleep now evaporated like the morning dew. She'd retaken her role as a knight well enough, riding across France and fighting men. She hadn't thought about retaking her other role, as the beautiful Lady of the Tournament. When she'd last been in England, they'd sang about her beauty while reveling in the scandal of her immorality. In large part that had been just a show, but they didn't know that. Now she had to return to that society, plastering on her smile and keeping her chin up. She grimaced. This would be a greater test of endurance than any ride across Europe.

Chapter 27

Lord Cenric's grand castle came alive for the Christmas celebration. All the local nobility attended, including Lord Gawain and Lady Gwen. It was an impressive production. Pennants flew from all the towers. The great hall was decorated with holly and ivy, and red-dyed candles flickered in elaborate candelabras all over the castle. The hearth fires roared, so the room was warm, and the occupants could shed their bulkiest outer layers to showcase the embroidered and dyed gowns that boasted their wealth. The morning was spent in a long church service, but now the entire afternoon was devoted to celebrating.

Eleanor held Benec's little hand tight in her own as they watched dancers twirl to the lively sound of lute, fiddle, drums, and shawm. He was giddy with excitement, though overwhelmed enough to keep a clutch on her skirts. The room was loud enough that the woman next to her had to yell into Eleanor's ear to be heard.

"Quite the celebration, isn't it?"

Eleanor turned to see Lady Gwen, who smiled at her. She fought the urge to curtsey. They were equals now. "Lady Gwen," she acknowledged, bowing her head politely. "How are you?"

"Oh, I'm lovely, Lady Eleanor. Simply lovely. Why aren't you out there dancing?"

Eleanor made a face. "I'm not a dancer."

"Your husband seems to be in his element." Lady Gwen nudged Eleanor slightly, and they both looked over at Alec, who was in the midst of the revelry, a different woman on his arm every time the music changed.

Eleanor shrugged. She'd watched Alec throughout the afternoon, and he'd frequently caught her eye with a twinkle in his own. She'd continue to do what she was best at, observing. The wine was good, too.

Torchlight sparkled in Gwen's eyes as she turned back to her former maid. "Married life seems to be treating you well."

Thankfully, Eleanor was saved an awkward response by a sudden hush in the crowd. The two women stood on their tiptoes to see what was occurring. "God save the King" someone called out.

"Long to reign over us," echoed around the room. The entire crowd dropped to one knee. Eleanor pulled Benec tight to her side as he watched with wide eyes.

"Well, well. He made it," Gwen said, her normally enthusiastic expression somewhat dour.

Across the room, they could see a sandy-haired man with a simple gold crown work his way through the crowd. He smiled brightly and seemed surprisingly normal to Eleanor. He did not have the same degree of regal bearing as his late brother Richard. He waved everyone back to their feet and they obliged.

"Do you know the king?" Eleanor asked Gwen. She had heard many stories about him, not many of them good.

"Aye, I know him," Gwen replied distantly.

"You still believe he hates Alec and I?" Eleanor asked, referring to Gwen's warning to Alec.

Gwen nodded. "I still don't understand why, but I know he does. Perhaps your husband will yet smooth things over." They watched as Alec approached amidst a group of other knights and bowed to the king. John quickly turned his attention from the men, attracted to a table of delicacies not far away.

Gwen suddenly turned, her face bright. "Come, Lady Eleanor! I will teach you how to dance."

After a few minutes of embarrassing missteps at Lady Gwen's side, Eleanor was almost competent enough to enjoy herself on the dance floor. Gwen had commandeered little Benec, and they were now seated along the edge of the room eating sweets. The little boy had taken to her as if they were old friends, and occasionally his giggle rang out through the noise of the crowd. The music changed to a softer tempo, and the couples paired off in a line. Eleanor swallowed and eyed the middle-aged lord across from her. Why did everyone with a beard seem to look like Montag? She felt the skirts of the women next to her brush against her own as they spun past her towards the line of men and quickly stumbled to catch up.

Alec stepped in front of her, catching her fingers in his own. She glanced up in surprise. Her eyes widened even more as he guided her through the next steps, following the dancers next to them. He gave her a wink and suddenly dropped her hand, breaking off with the other men as the dance moved on. Eleanor did her best to follow the others.

Another knight stepped in next to Eleanor, offering his hand for the next steps. She hesitated, and he gave her a quizzical look. Forcing her fingers into his, she mused on the rough callouses there. His hand was strong but gentle. She glanced sideways at him in between steps. A knight? *Green and yellow, green and yellow.* She must remember his colors and find out his name. He gave her a smile when he caught her gazing at him, and she quickly looked away, relieved as the dancers split across the room once again.

Once again they came together, and she was partnered with someone new. She glanced around, her body now absently following the steps. How long would this go on for? Surely not until they'd changed partners a dozen times? The new man next to her was bald, wiry, and graceful on his feet. He smiled openly at her, his sweaty fingers clutching hers more firmly than the others. She frowned at him.

"Now, now, Lady Eleanor, why the face? I've waited all night to dance with you."

Eleanor looked away, her face still stubbornly locked in a frown. The man pulled her closer to him on the next spin, close enough that she could smell the wine on his breath, the scent of horse still in his clothes. This one was definitely a knight. She faced forward. The dance had to be almost over.

"You don't remember me, do you?" the man asked.

She couldn't help but look closer at him, his sharp blue eyes piercing her own with such intensity she had to look away only a moment later. There *was* something familiar about him.

"Sir Jacques of Brittany. It was a lifetime ago, Lady Eleanor."

Eleanor stiffened, her steps faltering. Jacques chuckled and caught her, scooping her along that they stayed in place. Mercifully, the music ended, and the dancers separated, their jovial conversation echoing through the room like a music of its own. Still Jacques stood before her, though he had released her hands and now crossed his arms, studying her from head to foot.

"It really has been a lifetime, hasn't it?" Eleanor said softly.

"I would say so," Jacques nodded. He stepped away into the crowd.

A new song began, and dancers separated as the new formation was made. Reluctantly, she allowed herself to be guided into the new line, concentrating to catch on to the new steps. Her first partner was again the knight with the calloused hands. She let herself breathe as she followed his lead.

"I'm glad you decided to join in this time," he said in a voice that seemed to rumble from somewhere deep.

Eleanor mused on his words for a moment then asked, "This time?"

The man chuckled. "I may not frequent the tournaments like you and your husband, but even in the north we've heard of the 'English Winter.' I was told you never mingled."

He gave her fingers a quick squeeze as the dancers separated, and she immediately fell into step with a beady-eyed old man that stared far too intently at her. She kept her mouth in a firm line and practically held her breath until they rotated again. Alec stepped into her arms, and she breathed a sigh of relief.

"Are we done yet?" she pleaded quietly.

Alec chuckled. "I thought you looked like you were enjoying yourself."

Eleanor groaned. A laugh rang out over the music, and she glanced at Lady Gwen, who was deep in conversation with someone. Benec was still comfortable on her lap, eating a cake. "How does she do it?" Gwen was the ultimate rose of the party, adored by all, even little Benec, who hardly knew her.

Alec smiled his crooked grin. "That's her talent. Pity yours involves a horse and a sword." She startled as his hand firmly squeezed her behind as he spun her on to her next dance partner, who was a more familiar face.

"Lord Cenric, how are you?" Eleanor asked politely. His hand was as roughly calloused as the rest of the knights. She expected no less, as he was the man who had trained Alec. He may be greyed, but he was still a man of vigor.

"I am well, my lady. Are you enjoying yourself?"

Lord Cenric spun Eleanor out and then in the return spin pulled her close. Eleanor gritted her teeth, fighting the urge to push away from her husband's lord. It was only part of the dance. She felt his breath against her hair. His clothes smelled of lavender and mint: strange for a man, but pleasant. Regardless, she felt herself stiffen in his arms.

"My, you are a defensive one, aren't you?" They followed the dance.

Eleanor's silence confirmed it.

The song ended, and Lord Cenric bowed to her, her hand still in his palm. His expression seemed amused as he left her. Eleanor wiped her sweaty palms on her skirts, looking for Alec.

The musicians picked up another tune, but Eleanor was well over the dancing. She brushed past the dancers and snatched her wine goblet off the table, filling it to the brim. Her hand shaking slightly with tension, she downed half of it in one go.

"I thought you didn't drink?" Jacques leaned against the table next to her.

"It's been a long day. Make that a year."

He laughed, some of his boyish charm returning to his features. Eleanor drained the rest of the goblet and refilled it.

"So how have you been, Jacques?" She narrowed her eyes at him, taking in the lines of his face, his balding head. Though he was her age, he'd already gone grey, at least in what was left of his hair. His body had filled out since his teenage years, though he did not have as large a frame as Alec.

"I've been well. My father continues to run our estate, and my brother is well placed to take over when father can't handle it anymore. All that is left is for me to travel to tournaments, offer my services as needed." He smirked. "A nomadic lifestyle has its benefits, I suppose."

Eleanor could read between his words. He was a mercenary. Judging by the quality of his clothing and the large gold ring on his finger, he was a skilled one. She mused, "You have a family of your own?"

He shook his head, biting his lower lip in amusement. "I hear you've been busy yourself though. How old is your little one?"

"He's almost two." Eleanor pointed to Benec and Lady Gwen.

Jacques watched them a long moment, his expression neutral. "Congratulations," was the automatic reply.

Her eyes flicked back to the crowd that still swirled around the dance floor. Where was Alec? She spotted him far across the room, animatedly talking with a few other men.

"It was good to see you, Lady Eleanor. God speed." Jacques tipped his cup to her and disappeared.

Eleanor frowned after him, thinking the conversation odd. She turned back to study the dancers again: Lord Cenric, King John, a few other lords she knew not by name but by title. They all looked preoccupied with themselves and each other. Alec looked over, a twinge of jealousy in his gaze. He'd been watching the whole time then, as always. She drained her cup and pushed off the table towards him.

Chapter 28

Alec thought Eleanor was gorgeous even when her hair was a mess, she had not bathed in days, and she smelled like a horse. This side of her, which he had not seen since before Benec's birth, was something even troubadours struggled to put into words. Her rich brown hair was plaited like a wreath around the top of her head, a red ribbon woven through it like a crown. It shown in the candlelight, as did her face, with her cheeks rosy, those lips red and full. And then there was her figure, which her burgundy dress did little to disguise. Though his hands knew what those curves felt like to hold in the dark, he had not seen her in a garment that so accentuated her femininity in months. No more thick, bulky wool. Tonight she was draped in a dress that accentuated her full breasts, lean waist, and a curve of hip that no male in the room had failed to notice.

The tournament beauty had returned.

Alec had noted her string of suitors. She had continually spurned each of them, much to his amusement. The latest, however, carried himself with such a casual posture that Alec suspected he was no stranger to Eleanor.

Jealousy bubbled within him as she approached, her attention distracted. Even though she had spurned her acquaintance, Alec hated that she had a past. He wished she knew no other men, that they could not even see her. He was gripped by a sudden urge to mark her as his own, to remind her she was his.

By the time she reached his side, he knew he was not masking his lust.

He offered her a hand, and she wordlessly took it, her expression a mix of trepidation and longing. Alec's mind raced as he felt his desire grow. He shot a glance at Lady Gwen, who still looked content to occupy Benec. She met his eye, a knowing smile creeping onto her lips. With an incline of her head Gwen gestured him out of the hall. Alec seized the opportunity and led Eleanor from the hall, scanning for an obscure place. His eye caught the alcove behind the stairs. The stonework curled around the alcove enough that it was only visible from one side, and the wooden staircase covered part of that. In the dim torchlight, it was a cave of flickering shadow. He pulled Eleanor forward.

"Where are you going?" she protested quietly. "Benec—"

"Didn't you ever want to know what it is like to be one of those couples in the stairwell?" Alec smiled, gently pushing her back to the wall and kissing her lips. Yes, the English Winter did melt for him. Her hips pressed into his. Her hands ran up his sides. He pressed into her, letting her feel what she was doing to him, which was getting more obvious by the second. "We'll be back before the song changes."

"But people will see..." She didn't pull away.

"Only if they look back here in the dark, and when they do, they'll only see me, not you." He slid his thigh between her legs and felt her gasp against his lips. His hands roamed her body freely, groping and caressing through the fabric of her dress. "I am so glad you're finally back in a dress, instead of in those breeches," he whispered against her neck as he left a trail of kisses. Her breath was faster now.

"I'm still mad at you," she breathed, but her eyes stayed closed, her head back against the wall.

"I know," he whispered back.

It would only take a moment. No one would know. But as Alec kissed Eleanor, he felt her withdraw. Maybe she still was as icy as the English Winter. He sighed, and rested his forehead against hers.

"I love you," he breathed.

She remained silent, then subtly straightened her clothes and her spine, effectively pushing him away. "I'm sorry," she whispered.

Alec took a step back, offering his hand once again, and led her back to the hall.

Eleanor was certain the evidence of what they had almost done would be written on her face like a prostitute's rouge. She dropped her head, furtively glancing up at the people around them. No one paid them much mind. She scanned the room for Benec, who was where they'd left him.

Alec squeezed her hand. "So who is he?"

She knew pretending ignorance of whom he meant was futile. "His name is Sir Jacques of Brittany. We knew each other a long time ago, when he was a squire."

"He studied under Montag?"

She shook her head. "No. It was after I left—with a lord outside of London, Sir William. I worked with him for a time."

"I knew you had formal training." He smiled and squeezed her hand, which was still laced with his.

"I'm not sure I would call it formal training. I was trying to disguise myself as a boy as long as possible. Sir William noted my ability with the horses and took me in as a groom. His squires—they fought constantly. So yes, I did have to learn a bit."

"And where did Jacques come in? You were friends?"

"Were. I beat him once in a swordfight which, ironically, initiated a friendship. Until he discovered I was a girl." She shook her head. "Worse than that, he discovered my name." She met Alec's gaze. "He is the only one other than you that ever figured it out. I ran after that. This is the first I've seen him since then."

"He wouldn't keep your secret?"

Eleanor thought for a moment. "I really don't know. I suppose he did, since Montag and Lezay didn't find me. It was more—everything changed between us when he found out. In part because I was his match with a sword, which for a knight-in-training was embarrassing. But he may also have been attracted to me." She shook her head. Her imagination was running too wild, her body still hot from Alec. Jacques had been a jealous friend, nothing more.

"He's definitely still attracted to you."

Eleanor's gaze snapped up. Perhaps Jacques' expression had held an eye-narrowing element of lust in it. But so did half of the appraising stares of the party attendees, excluding those who had already been swatted away from staring by their wives or knew her well enough to have been snubbed in the past. She'd heard the whispers behind her back.

Alec was looking down at her with a twinkle of amusement in his eye. "Do you think you could talk to Jacques?"

"I did already."

"He's from Brittany. I'm curious if he knows who the nobles there are supporting…their own Arthur or King John?"

What was this, a test to see if she could coax information out of people like his precious Giselle? She ground her teeth. Well, she wasn't Giselle. "No."

"Very well, I'll ask Lady Gwen what she can find out."

She looked at him. "You wouldn't."

Alec nodded his chin back to Jacques, who was next to Gwen, who sat to the side of the room with Benec playing in her lap. Eleanor would have left it at that, but that Jacques' gaze was not on Gwen, but Benec. When Jacques reached for Benec, Eleanor's feet were already in motion, carrying her towards the trio. When Gwen clung to the child and twisted away from Jacques, Alec pushed past Eleanor, parting the densc crowd with his large frame.

Eleanor saw the flash of metal, heard the scream, and the scene was blocked from her view as the crowd closed in to watch. Alec was ahead of her, and there were more shouts. When she finally pushed through the wall of people, her heart pounding and nerves firing that every sense was tuned on high, Jacques was being restrained by two men, blood spreading on his shirt and dripping onto the floor, and Alec was kneeling beside Gwen, who was curled in a ball next to the wall. A child's scream rang out over the chaos, cutting at Eleanor's heartstrings.

Alec pulled Benec from beneath Gwen's protective arms. He passed the boy to Eleanor without fanfare, and she knelt before him, searching him for wounds. He had a few drops of blood on him, but he himself didn't have a scratch. She pulled him tight into her arms, relief surging through her. When she turned back to Alec, he was still kneeling next to Gwen, who had not risen. Eleanor could see the clenched-nail grip Gwen held on Alec's forearm, but her face was tucked down, Alec's hand pressed to her cheek. Then Eleanor saw the blood streaming through Alec's fingers. He said something quietly to Gwen, and she seemed to shake her head and take a deep breath, and then she stood, Alec's hand still cupping her cheek.

The sight was ghastly. Half of her face was painted red, and it was beginning to flow down her neck to her crème-colored dress, which was already spotted with scarlet. Gwen kept a grip on Alec's forearm as he led her out of the hall. He pointed his chin at Jacques, who now looked like he was fading in and out of consciousness from whatever cut he had received. "Find Lord Cenric."

Eleanor shifted Benec in her arms, then led the way out of the hall towards Lord Cenric's quarters, where he had withdrawn just a few minutes ago. The two men pulled Jacques along, his feet stumbling and dragging in his delirium. Lord Gawain emerged from the crowd, leaning heavily on his cane.

"What on earth happened?" Gawain asked, scanning the room to piece it together.

"He attacked your wife," one of the men holding Jacques said.

"He what?" Gawain suddenly raised his cane and smashed Jacques over the head with a solid whack. Jacques went limp, and the men dropped him.

Eleanor stepped up, caught Gawain's arm as it raised for another strike, and forced him to meet her eye. "Go with Lady Gwen."

Gawain hesitated, as if shocked she was talking to him, much less touching him.

She gave his arm a little shake. "Go with Lady Gwen." Then she released him and pointed to where Alec was guiding her through the crowd.

"Gwen..." Gawain whispered, and hobbled after her as quickly as he could.

The two handlers heaved Jacques partway to his feet and resumed carrying him out of the hall. They were never going to make it up the stairs with him. Eleanor stepped ahead of them, opening doors until she found a vacant storage room.

"In here," she ordered, and held the door so they could deposit the barely-conscious man. "Get Lord Cenric. Quickly." The men hurried out, and Eleanor deposited Benec on his own feet. "Honey, I need you to sit in that corner over there. Can you do that?"

Benec sniffled and sat where she directed him.

Eleanor turned her attention to Jacques, searching for the source of his bleeding. Part of her wanted to finish the job and slit his throat for threatening her child, but the other part knew he was likely working for someone else. She needed to know who. She would do her part to save him, and he would know it. Better the devil you know than one unknown. "So, Benec, what did you think of the party? Did you have a good time with Lady Gwen?"

She looked up just long enough to see Benec nod. The bleed was coming from Jacques' chest, just below the right collarbone. Alec must have stabbed him. She looked around for something to plug the wound with and found a bundle of linen. She drew her dagger and cut a long strip and began pushing it into the wound.

"Look away, honey," she told Benec, her fingers working quickly. Slowly, the bleeding began to ebb. Eleanor sat back on her heels, wiping her forehead with a wrist. Her hands were stained red. She wiped them on a corner of Jacques shirt, since his was already ruined and her dress at least stood a chance of surviving. She looked to Benec, who watched her with wide eyes. With a ping of pain, she realized how much blood he would see in his future, should he follow in his parents' footsteps and become a knight. She opened her arms to him. "You were very brave, sweetheart." He shuffled to her and hugged her tight, tears again threatening.

There was a commotion down the hall as Cenric roared about being pulled out of bed by a brawl. Jacques blinked, consciousness returning. Eleanor leaned towards him, her voice urgent.

"Who are you working for?"

Jacques grimaced and closed his eyes.

She kicked his foot, and he flinched, opening his eyes to glare at her.

"You want another blade in you? Who are you working for?"

Cenric and his men were outside the door now. Jacques mumbled, "King John," but Eleanor had the distinct feeling he was lying. And yet, if he was, that was a dangerous claim.

"Easy enough to prove. Will the king pardon your assault on his friend Lady Gwen?"

"Aye," Jacques breathed and leaned back.

Eleanor gritted her teeth. She was certain he was lying. She couldn't say why, just a gut feeling. The man was a skilled mercenary after all. Discretion was his livelihood. But there was no time to press him further. Cenric burst through the storage-room door, stopping short at the sight of Eleanor kneeling next to Jacques.

"He attacked Lady Gwen," she volunteered. No one need know about Benec's importance. Jacques narrowed his eyes at her. She stared him down, willing him silent.

"So who stabbed him? You?" Cenric asked.

"Sir Alec tried to defend Lady Gwen," one of Cenric's men offered. "Jacques cut her pretty badly. Alec pulled him off her."

"Well isn't Sir Alec just the hero of the day. Where is he?" Cenric looked around.

"With Lady Gwen," the man answered.

"He's very good at healing wounds. You might want to have him look at Sir Jacques, too," Eleanor said.

"Jacques is going to have plenty more wounds until I'm done with him," Cenric said quietly. "Take him down to the dungeon."

The handlers moved to obey, and Eleanor stepped out of their way, Benec again in her arms.

Jacques gave her a last long look, as if she were the one being studied, the one that was going to be questioned down in the deepest part of the castle. He did not look afraid, only tired and resigned. Then they pulled him away, with Cenric already beginning to rant loudly about what he could possibly have been thinking.

King John, sided by a half-dozen men at arms, met them in the hall. Cenric quieted and greeted the king, who then followed the party towards the dungeon. At the top of the stairwell, the fair-haired ruler looked back at Eleanor, or more specifically, Benec. She held him tighter in her arms.

Then King John moved on. Eleanor again felt a shiver run down her spine. Perhaps what Jacques had claimed, that he worked for the King of England, was true. If so, then they had yet another front, the most powerful yet, to defend Benec against. Wilfred had warned of the king's curiosity. *What kind of boy holds this kind of power?* she wondered.

"You tired, honey?" she asked Benec, who already had his head against her shoulder. She carried him up the stairs to their small guest room, where she barred the door with a heavy beam. Alec would pound when he wanted in. And no one but him would gain admission. She put Benec to bed and curled around him, praying he would remember nothing of this dramatic Christmas.

Gwen was taking her injury well, though her jaw clenched against the pain and she kept a firm grip on Gawain's hand as Alec treated the wound and sutured it. She'd taken the blade across her cheekbone. A few inches lower and her cheek would have been severed—what nasty healing that would have been. As it was, it would heal if no fever set in, and Alec had confidence it would not. But she would be marred by a scar to mark her warrior woman soul.

A hard blow for one whose life had centered on being the beauty.

She was braver than he'd expected. Gawain's concern for her was equally impressive. He'd known she was more than she appeared in public, and that her marriage was complicated, but to see it all play out while he was an up-close bystander was something else.

"What were you thinking, stepping in front of a blade?" Gawain asked for a third time.

Now that Alec had finished most of his work, she replied, her voice tight as she tried to minimize the movement of her jaw. "I had to protect him."

Alec dabbed salve on the wound. "He isn't yours to protect." He glanced to Gawain, who'd gone quiet, shaking his head.

Gwen turned to Alec. "That boy is special. I don't know why, but from the first I saw him, I felt protective of him. I've never felt that for another child." Her voice trailed. "I usually don't like children..."

Gawain shifted. "Is it because it's *his*?"

Alec swallowed. He'd wondered the same himself, but to hear the comment from his liege lord was awkward. He avoided their eyes, feeling them burn into him.

Gwen spoke softly. "Perhaps."

Alec had an urge to leave the room. He stood. He took a last look at Gwen's wound, but froze when he saw her eyes, which studied him with a ferocity not unlike Eleanor's or Giselle's.

She saw he noticed. "Sit, Alec."

He looked to Gawain, his eyes pleading to be released. Did Gawain know what had transpired between Gwen and himself years ago? Alec had long suspected, but he couldn't be sure. Gawain motioned to the chair.

Alec acquiesced.

Gawain narrowed his eyes. "I never wanted to have this conversation, but in light of tonight's events, I feel we should." He took Gwen's hand, and she kept her gaze on Alec. "I know." His jaw clenched as he searched for words. "It would have been worth it, had it worked. But alas, we are still without progeny."

Alec stiffened.

"We will need an heir for Sarum, or King John will place whomever he chooses. We want someone who will be fair to our people. Someone we can raise, teach, and develop."

Alec swallowed, wondering what they would ask of him this time.

"Allow the boy to mentor with me." Gawain's eyes were earnest, his body leaning eagerly towards Alec. "I may not be young anymore, but if you are any indication, I am a good teacher. And I have others that will help me teach the boy." He looked to Gwen. "And my lady—I have never seen her care so much. Your son will be well taken care of."

"He is too young." Though, Alec could see the many advantages of this plan.

Gwen laid a hand on his arm. "Tensions are escalating. You and Eleanor may both be called to France, to fight. Perhaps as early as spring. Benec will be safer here. King John knows Gawain and I are loyal to him. You stand with us, trust the boy to us, and he will have to accept that you, too, are on his side."

"She's right," the king said as he entered, wiping at a speck of blood on his tunic. Gwen and Alec leapt to their feet. Gawain pushed up from his seat with a bit of a wince. King John looked down his nose at Alec. "With enemies around me, why would I trust *you*?"

Alec lifted his chin. "As I said when we met, Eleanor and I are loyal—"

"Yes, yes. Just words. Send the boy to live with Gawain. Prove you are willing to give up what you value most in order to serve me. Besides, with courage like Gwen's, who better is there to protect him?" He stepped to Gwen and admired Alec's work. Gwen kept her eyes averted, her face blank. "Well, Alec. If you ever quit the cutting business, at least you can take up sewing." He scanned the room. "I'll give you until spring. Then I want you fighting for me. I want the child in Sarum, far from King Philip and Eleanor's French roots, far from others who wish to make use of him, and I want pretty little Eleanor—stunning by the way, you should have told me—back in Aquitaine where she belongs."

Alec studied the king, mind calculating, knowing that as the king's order, they had no choice but to obey it. There were far worse things John could demand of them. Still, it was hard for the family to be ordered to split into three.

He was saved from answering by Gawain's indignant question, "And what of the man that did this to my wife?" He gestured to Gwen.

King John again turned to Gwen, his face unreadable. "You leave him to me." His eyes lingered. Gwen shifted uncomfortably beneath that gaze, and then the king left.

Gwen looked up to Alec with pained eyes. "Be careful."

Alec laid a hand on her shoulder. "You should rest, my lady."

It was minutes later, when Gwen was drifting off to sleep at her husband's side, that Alec realized the king *knew* other men were after the child. He straightened and looked to the door King John had passed through. How—and what—did the King of England know about his son?

Chapter 29

Eleanor woke to an empty bed. Well, almost empty, since little Benec didn't take up much space. She pulled away from him, careful not to wake him, and slipped out of bed. She'd slept fully dressed. The hearth was cold. Where was Alec? She unbarred the door and looked out into the hall. No one. All were asleep, recovering from a long night of excitement.

She set the bar back over the door, packed their few belongings into a satchel which she threw over her shoulder, and then picked up Benec. "Come on, little man. Let's go find your papa." His arms curled around her neck; his head nestled against her shoulder. Tears threatened as she held him like that for a moment, her heart swelling as if it too could wrap around him. This little boy was so much to her, regardless of the circumstances after his birth. She exhaled, steadied herself, and then rose to her feet. The fire in her heart burned as bright as if it was a tournament day.

She padded down the stairs, her arms getting more tired by the minute. Benec was getting big. Thankfully he still slept. He was exhausted. Where would Alec have taken Gwen? She checked the great hall, which was empty. She worked her way back to the entranceway, wondering which way to go next, when she saw Gawain.

"Lord Gawain," she called. He stopped and turned to her. "How is Lady Gwen?"

He thought for a moment, frowning. "She will be fine thanks to Alec. Though never the same."

Eleanor still didn't know the extent of Gwen's injury. "Where is she?"

Gawain pointed his cane. "Three doors down."

Eleanor followed his guidance and went ahead of him, knocking on the third door. A male voice bid entry, and she pushed open the door. The room was small and flooded with candlelight. Gwen sat on a bench next to the table, her head in her arms. Exposed was the injured cheek, which was cut from ear almost to her nose. It was neatly stitched shut, and Eleanor recognized the smell of Alec's healing balm, but Gawain was right. Gwen, the beauty of all of England, would never be the same.

Alec rose from a chair in the corner. "Are you alright?" He wrapped his arms around Eleanor and Benec both.

"We're fine. Is she?" Eleanor looked to Gwen.

"We gave her something for the pain, so she'll sleep. She said Jacques attacked her out of nowhere."

"It wasn't her he wanted."

Alec laid a hand on Benec's head. They both knew who the real target had been.

With a hand on her elbow, Alec guided her further from the sleeping Lady Gwen. As he relayed his conversation with the king, her heart sank.

"He's too young," she protested when he was through.

"Most men begin their training very early."

"He's separating us on purpose."

Alec inhaled. "I know."

That admission set a pit of fear in Eleanor's gut. The timing coincided with The Order's warnings—and the invitation to the ceremony on the spring equinox. She already knew she had to return to Aquitaine to meet The Order. They had questioned who to keep Benec with. Now they had a solution, but would Gawain be able to protect the boy?

As if reading her mind, Alec offered, "The king knows someone is after Benec. But I didn't get to ask him what he knows."

"How could he possibly know that?"

Alec shrugged.

Eleanor bit her lip. "Jacques...he said he's working for the king. If he was working for the king, then wouldn't King John just ask us to send the boy with him? Why attempt kidnapping? Why have Gwen and Gawain involved at all?"

"Do you believe Jacques?"

Eleanor thought a moment. "No."

"Neither do I. Or at least, what he told you is not the complete truth. He *could* be working for the king—he'd be a fool to be in England and not be. But that doesn't mean he doesn't have a second master, one that ordered Benec's capture from under the king's nose."

Eleanor rubbed her forehead. "I am so tired of half-truths." She was about to ask Alec what sort of punishment the king had set on Jacques, when Lady Gwen's eyes blinked open and she grimaced. She closed her eyes as even that subtle movement pained her. When she turned to look at Eleanor and Alec, Eleanor handed Benec to Alec and knelt at Gwen's feet as she had when she was a mere maid. Gwen's eyebrows shot up.

Eleanor didn't try to hide the emotion in her voice when she said, "Thank you, my lady. Thank you for doing what you could to protect my son."

Gwen reached out to her, cupping Eleanor's flawless cheek in her hand. Then she removed her hand and straightened. She looked to the sleeping boy still twined in Eleanor's arms. Moving her lips as little as possible, she said, "The boy is special. I will treat him as my own."

Eleanor felt a surge of emotion roll through her. Relief. Protectiveness. Jealousy. Gratitude. She ducked her head to hide the waves that washed over her.

Alec quietly said from her side. "The king has granted us a few more months before he will come here. It will coincide with our return to France."

Return to France without Benec? How could she? And yet the realistic part of Eleanor knew it would be best for the child. She knew he would be as safe as he could be at Sarum, particularly if she was to do her duty to her king while navigating the tumult of what The Order had planned for her.

Some of which even Alec did not yet suspect.

Gwen whispered, "I know you won't believe me, but I understand."

When Eleanor looked up, Gwen's eyes brimmed with tears. And somehow, that sincerity comforted her. Here was a woman who would act as Madame Brigitte had for Eleanor, an adopted mother, a protector, advisor, supporter. There may not be a blood tie, but Eleanor suddenly knew that Gwen would fulfill her role as all these vital things to the fullest of her ability.

Eleanor cocked her head to the side. She believed the sincerity, and yet she did not understand it. The woman owed her nothing. Owed her son nothing. "Why?"

Gwen gave a subtle shake of her head. "I just knew from the moment I saw him. I cannot explain it. As if what I longed for all these years, a hole deep within me, was somehow— though not filled completely—was at least covered over." She turned to Benec, who had woken and was now smiling at her. "And for whatever undeserving reason, he seems to have accepted me as well." She reached out a finger to the little boy, who took it, his sleepy eyes blinking at her.

Gwen looked back up at Eleanor. "I will not be you. I will not take your place. But I will have another place in his life."

Chapter 30

"Happy Christmas!" Wilfred greeted them with widespread arms in the entrance hall of what Alec had begun calling Earnblaec Castle.

Alec could only glare at him. He was in no mood for festivities, he hadn't slept in more than a day, and he still had things to do to make sure the manor was protected from whoever tried to kidnap one of his family members next. He pulled off his cloak and shook it.

"Oh, come on now. You're putting a damper on the holiday already? It's only the second day of Christmas. Now what happened?" Wilfred put his hands on his hips.

Benec spotted his cousins and joyfully squealed and wiggled to be put down. Eleanor obliged, and he took off running. Alec went to move past Wilfred, but Wilfred put out a hand to stop him.

"It might be your castle, but you can't storm in here like there's an army on your heels and not expect me to ask questions. My family is here, too. What is going on?"

Alec shoved Wilfred's hand away. How dare he lay a hand on him, this little groom he'd fed and raised for a decade?

"Hey, hey." Eleanor stepped between them. "He's right, Alec, we have to explain. It's for Benec's safety."

"I need to speak with Thomas," Alec grumbled. "Where is he?"

"In the solar," Wilfred offered.

Alec headed that way, listening in the background as Eleanor began an abridged version of what had happened at Lord Cenric's castle. When he got to the solar, he entered without preamble. Thomas looked up from his desk, papers and ledgers in hand despite the holiday.

"My Lord. How was the party?"

"Eventful. I want to lock down the castle, but do it discreetly. Can you manage that?"

Thomas rose to his feet. "Of course. Most of the household is already settled in for winter. Though there is still work to be done in the fields. Pruning, maintaining the sheep. Do we need to move the animals inside?"

"No. Not yet. I want a list of who leaves though. Who goes to market and where."

"I will have the porter start."

"Good. And don't admit any travelers, no matter who they are. Make some excuse...the plague is here or something. Send them on to the next location."

"Yes, my lord. May I ask what all this is about?" Thomas set his papers down, his brow furrowed.

"My wife and I have made a few enemies. Now they have followed us here. We do not want them causing havoc under our noses."

"Understood. I will enact the rules immediately."

Alec turned to leave, then hesitated, a hand on the doorframe. "Thank you, Thomas."

"My pleasure, my lord."

Alec made a circuit of the castle, but all seemed well. Eleanor and Wilfred were still in the entryway, deep in discussion.

"You told him what he needs to know?" Alec asked, feeling the fatigue drain him by the second.

"Yes," Eleanor said and put a hand on his arm. "Go. Sleep."

Alec nodded and wandered back to his room, where he collapsed into his big bed, and was asleep before he could even take off his boots.

The household was curious about having to state their travel plans to Thomas, but they did not protest. For the most part, their routines were uninterrupted. As a brutal, snowy winter settled over England, it left them content to stay within the warmth of the castle and its outbuildings. Turning visitors away was a more difficult task. Alec felt the cruelty of his inhospitality like a barb, even more so after having spent weeks living in those same frigid conditions at the mercy of strangers. He questioned his decision on a daily basis. How else, though, to avoid more assassins, kidnappers, or spies?

In the depths of January, they took a deep breath and a much-needed rest to celebrate Benec's second birthday. The little boy didn't know what the fuss was about, but he reveled in the attention. They finished a meal of ham and honeycakes, Benec's favorite, and then stretched out by the fire as the children played. Alec watched Eleanor laugh as she spoke with Wilfred and Marie. He could tell she was still anxious, but this moment was a good one. When she turned her gaze to him, her eyes sparkled. It did not linger on Alec though, but instead turned back to Benec. It was going to be hard for her to leave him in England.

Alec couldn't fathom where two years had gone. Benec could run with his older cousin, grew stronger by the day, was quiet when he was supposed to be, and though he didn't have a large vocabulary, he was gaining language skills every day. And fear—it was rather concerningly non-existent to the little boy, much to Marie's chagrin. Alec regretted not having found him a pony for his birthday. Well, a belated present would have to suffice. He studied the boy's features. Eleanor's mark on the child was evident in his face and hair color. What about a mark from the father?

Benec turned to Alec, conscious of the scrutiny, and smiled.

"Ahem," Thomas cleared his throat as he approached the fireside. "Sorry to intrude, my lord, but there are some visitors at the gate."

Alec frowned.

"I've been arguing with them for a while sir, but they refuse to move on." Thomas shifted from foot to foot. "I'll start shooting arrows at them if you wish, sir," Thomas offered, perhaps a bit too eagerly. Alec was starting to like the man for his unemotional efficiency.

"Hopefully that's not necessary." Alec sighed. He followed the castellan down to the entrance to the courtyard, only to be met by the bright, intense eyes of Giselle. His breath caught in his lungs. When he could turn his attention to her companion, he noted it was a mere boy, perhaps thirteen.

"What kind of lord refuses a noble lady in the depths of winter?" Giselle complained, though a smile played on her lips. As Alec looked closer, he noted she was, indeed, dressed like a noble woman, with a fur-trimmed cloak and a pretty, placid palfrey under her.

"I'm sorry, my lady." He turned to Thomas. "We'll make an exception. I know them. Thank you, Thomas."

Thomas nodded and returned to the castle.

Alec offered a hand to Giselle and helped her dismount. The boy dismounted from his own horse, his eyes looking high and low around the castle.

Alec handed the boy the reins to Giselle's horse. "Take them to the stable. The grooms will show you what to do."

"Thank you Marcarius," Giselle said, smiling like a proud parent.

Macarius headed out, still scanning around the manor, as if he'd never been to a castle before.

Just as Alec turned back to Giselle, Eleanor appeared in the doorway. Her face went from excited to confused to a masked look of indifference within seconds. She took a deep breath and approached them. Alec wished with his whole being that she had asked the questions she wanted to ask, that she knew everything. She had not, bottling up her conflicted, heartbroken emotions over his white lie. Now it all stood there in front of her.

She looked Giselle up and down. "Were you once nobility?"

Giselle lifted her chin. "No. But there is a convenience to travel as such, don't you think?"

Eleanor remained thin-lipped. Alec had never known her to travel as a noble woman. She traveled as a peasant, invisible. She traveled as a knight, so that people left her alone. Even when she'd dressed the part of Lady of the Tournament, she made no claim to be nobility. She and Giselle had no common ground.

"Giselle, what brings you here?" Alec asked.

She pulled back her hood, turning from Eleanor to Alec. Her hair shone blue-black even in the dreary winter light. "I didn't know where else to go. I found the boy in Harfleur, when he tried to pick my purse. He's pledged his loyalty and proven useful. We evaded the Lezays, skipped around, but then we ran into Raganor in Calais."

"You saw my grandfather?" Eleanor breathed.

"Yes." Giselle inhaled. "And he was most talkative."

A shiver ran up his spine. That meant Giselle had more information to relay.

"Before you ask, we are certain we lost him in Normandy and were not followed. We changed disguises several times. Macarius knows as much about listening and watching as I do. He'll be useful to us."

Alec looked in the direction the boy had gone. He hoped he could be trusted.

Eleanor sighed and slapped her hands on her thighs. "Well, you better come in." She turned into the manor.

Giselle and Alec lingered a few seconds longer.

"She hates me," Giselle mused. Turning to Alec, she said, "Which means you didn't tell her when I said you should."

"We were busy."

"Uhm-hmm." Giselle picked up her elaborate skirts and walked up the steps into the manor.

"Expensive dress, even for a noble woman," Alec observed.

"It was a present." She smiled. "From Macarius."

Chapter 31

Eleanor did her best to act the part of the lady. It was the most difficult feat she had yet done. Giselle had been courteous enough to her the prior summer. She'd willingly revealed what she knew of Eleanor's family, which had prepared Eleanor for the chaos that had followed. Still, she was not only a prostitute, she was a woman connected to Alec's past. His white lie had been brought to light, and still Eleanor was not satisfied. She could see there was something there—even if it was no longer love or lust—in the way they lingered when she walked away, speaking in lowered voices. She could see it in the casual way the other woman bore herself in Alec's presence, and how he got a distant look, deep in thought, whenever she spoke.

Yes, she simply *must* be a gracious host, if only to maintain her image as the lady of the manor. Thomas the Castellan watched, waiting for her cue as to where to house this newcomer. Private room? Or with the other maids? Did she need a place at all, if she was merely passing through? Eleanor hated these kinds of decisions, particularly when she didn't know the answers to all the questions herself. Surely, Giselle didn't expect to stay long? They had no need of her trade here.

Eleanor bit her tongue. Who was she, of all people, to judge? She had been faced with that hard choice between selling her body and starving herself. She'd scraped by, only by rare chance that she had the skills of a boy in regard to a horse and a sword. Giselle had her own story, her own reasons. And she wasn't openly plying the trade. She was a noblewoman, passing through, visiting an old friend.

Eleanor tasted blood on her tongue and forced herself to relax. Thomas awaited his orders from her side. They watched the woman float into the hall with the practiced airs of nobility. Dressed the part, if one placed her at a tournament, she would turn every head, draw the affections of every man. Her dark, angular features were just different enough from the pale-complexioned European women to turn heads. Her hair was the blue-black sheen of a raven's feather, and most of all, her eyes were deep liquid brown pools of curated expression. Only in her bearing did Eleanor catch the hints that alluded to a past beyond a noble upbringing. Didn't Giselle know to avert her eyes, to ignore the pennants hanging from the vaulted ceiling? It revealed she had spent little time in castles. Didn't she know not to pull on her skirts? Though if they had been made for her instead of stolen, she wouldn't have had to. At least after years of working in noble households, Eleanor could play the role. She folded her hands and straightened, thinking of her mother, elegant under any circumstance.

"Give her the spare room for guests, Thomas. Make sure there's a fire started."

"Aye, my lady," he agreed and bowed off to delegate what preparations must be done.

"Are you thirsty?" Eleanor asked stiffly and did her best to smile.

Giselle smiled lightly, as if she understood the inconvenience of her presence. "That would be lovely. Whatever you can spare."

Eleanor nodded, shooting her gaze towards Alec, and then went to fetch a bottle of wine. If she was going to play hostess, she might as well bring out the best.

Marie caught her in the hallway to the storerooms. "Who is she? A noble lady?" she asked in a hushed voice.

"An old friend of Alec's. Giselle."

The confusion that flitted over Marie's face mirrored Eleanor's emotions. Marie, born as common as one could be and still little exposed to the world of the nobility, knew little about concealing emotions. "She's awfully pretty," she blurted.

Eleanor sighed and put a hand on the young woman's shoulder. Words wouldn't come to explain the situation, so she merely squeezed Marie's shoulder. "At least we had a good afternoon. Can you let the cook know we have two extra guests? And if you see Wilfred, I have a feeling Alec might want to talk to him."

Marie nodded. "I'll make sure the children don't bother you." She hesitated. "Alec took her into the solar."

Eleanor nodded. The solar was a nice, dark, private room. But she couldn't think that way. "Thank you, Marie."

They parted, and Eleanor headed straight for the solar. The door was closed, and with one hand she undid the catch and shoved it open with her hip. They had no right to privacy; she had no need to knock. With a small degree of relief, she noticed the two of them were standing by the fire, a perfectly respectable distance apart. She set the wine on a side table and poured three glasses.

The room was awkwardly quiet.

"Well, don't stop talking on account of me," she mumbled to herself.

To her surprise, Giselle readily answered, "I think before we go any further, you should be able to ask whatever questions weigh on your mind."

"Oh, how gracious of you," Eleanor grumbled, her hands shaking as she plugged the bottle with its wooden topper. She turned to the two of them, a sweet smile on her face. She handed them their glasses. With her own in hand, she took a seat, swirling the liquid in the glass as she watched them. Neither looked fearful of talking, and yet they were not offering a place to begin. How far back did she want to know?

"You've been with my husband?" *Might as well be blunt.*

"Both of them," was Giselle's quick reply. Well, at least Eleanor could count on her to be honest.

"When?"

"It's been years since Alec and I had an intimate relationship. Before you. We keep in touch for other reasons. Rot—Rothulfus Lezay—was with me from the time I came to Alsace until Alec got me out of there."

Eleanor's brow furrowed. *Got her out of Alsace?*

Alec straightened, a warning look on his face. "One thing at a time, Giselle."

Giselle shot him a scathing look. "You didn't even tell her *that* yet?"

"We've been busy." Alec shot a worried look at Eleanor.

She took a long drink and clenched her fist. One piece of the story at a time. "How long were you in Alsace?"

"Most of my life. I left...maybe five years ago?"

"So you were with Lezay that whole time?"

"Yes."

"My uncle, too?"

"No. Never your uncle." There was something in Giselle's expression that alluded to more of a story, but it was irrelevant to Eleanor.

"And how did you meet Alec?"

"The usual way." She met Eleanor's eye, daring her to ask for details. Eleanor had a feeling she would tell her every touch, every caress, if she asked for it. Eleanor had to look away, taking another drink. She wished the wine was stronger.

"And how long did it go on for?"

"A few months."

"Months?" Eleanor shot a scathing look at Alec.

"Like I said, she introduced me to Lezay," Alec said. "After that, I owed her." He looked at Giselle, a shared look passing between them that turned Eleanor's stomach. "They realized she had passed on their secrets. There was punishment. When I could, I helped her escape."

Eleanor felt a twinge of nausea, and set her wine glass on the floor to place her elbows on her knees.

Giselle went on. "Alec and I were together in France until he returned to England. We kept in touch in the months that followed. That is, up until he found you."

Eleanor wearily lifted her head to look at Alec. "Is she the one you went to see that winter, when the villagers all talked about how you frequented the taverns and their whores?"

He met her eye. "Yes."

Giselle cut in, a single finger pointed. "But by that point, we had another arrangement. We were trading *information*. I was traveling city to city, independently I might add, and getting paid for what I learned by those who wanted to know. We both had reason to keep ears out for Rot, and I have plenty of my own reasons to find out about your family, and Raganor."

Eleanor pursed her lips. She could live with that answer. The two of them sounded adamant enough. "How often did you meet after we moved to Aquitaine? You were in Poitiers—"

"Monthly," Alec said calmly.

"All those trips—"

"I'm sorry, Eleanor. I promise you, we only talked."

"As if that matters..." She almost wished they had merely sweated together like two beasts in the rut. It somehow felt as great a betrayal, that while she had been whiling away making house in Levan Manor, trying to raise a child that didn't even know her, that Alec had sought Giselle for the value of her observant and investigative mind. She placed her forehead in her hands.

Giselle walked across the room and returned, the bottle of wine in hand. She wordlessly refilled Eleanor's glass.

She had to push this betrayal out of her mind. They'd had reasons. No wrong had been done. When she spoke again, her voice could not hide the waver. "You said you saw Raganor again."

Giselle took a deep breath. "He was in Calais. He had gotten word that you were coming here. But I convinced him to return to Aquitaine. He said he will wait for you there." She met Eleanor's eye. "He made it very clear that he wants to meet you."

Eleanor looked up at this strange woman, who somehow in the span of a few minutes had made her feel a spectrum of emotions. Now, Giselle was looking at her with the doting concern of a mother, though they were but a few years apart.

"If he wanted to meet her, why didn't he knock on the door instead of burning the manor's granary down?" Alec asked.

Giselle shifted her attention to him. "It was a distraction. He hoped to take the boy, but it sounds like he has been thwarted on several fronts. Of course, he doesn't do any of that sort of work himself these days." She didn't seem surprised that Raganor wanted a child, which gave Eleanor pause.

"Do you know why he wants Benec?" Eleanor asked.

Giselle looked at her with scrutinous eyes. "You don't?"

Eleanor met that scrutiny without wavering. Her fingers itched for her sword. How dare this woman enter her house and then insinuate she knew more about Benec than Eleanor herself?

The two women faced off from across the room before Alec's voice cut the long moment of silence. "We found out Benec is tied to The Order. That is why they want him. It has been a struggle to keep him safe. Thus why we have not been allowing travelers to stop here at the castle."

Giselle shrugged, her gaze distant.

"He wants to meet me?" Eleanor asked, leaning forward.

"The middle of March, in Poitiers. He said he'll wait where you saw him before." She looked Eleanor up and down. "And from what he told me, it sounds like you're joining them. You better figure out what you're getting into, because right now you don't seem like you're desperate enough to sell your soul."

Eleanor straightened. Giselle was right. She didn't want to join. She didn't want to be part of whatever darkness they reveled in. Nor did she see a way around it. She'd crossed a line into knowledge, and there was no turning back.

A knock sounded on the door.

Alec turned to Giselle. "No one else knows about The Order. All Wilfred Fyr Hors knows is that Benec has been threatened."

Giselle laid a finger to her lips and nodded once.

Alec called out entry. Wilfred came in, his brow furrowed with concern. Alec gestured towards Giselle. "Wilfred, meet my old friend Giselle. She will be our guest for a time."

The furrow in Wilfred's brow didn't ease. Eleanor leaned back in her chair, watching the trio and sipping wine. What an odd group. What an odd threat for such skilled individuals to be consumed by. What an odd day, at that.

Onions pervaded her dreams. Blood and pain, unwanted hands. She was fourteen again. Then her tormentor transformed to the old, dark-eyed man she'd seen in the marketplace, and she woke up, drenched in a cold sweat. Alec turned next to her, laying a hand on hers.

"You alright?" he asked.

But she didn't want his comfort. She didn't want to be touched. She gave him the obligatory *Yes* while slipping out of bed. He soon returned back to sleep. Eleanor wrapped a shawl around herself and padded out the door. She knew the corridors of the castle well now, even without a light. She wove her way downstairs and into the main hall, hoping there was still some weak ale left from dinner. She hadn't eaten much. Giselle's story still roiled within her. She could tell the woman had been through a lot, and yet she felt betrayed. That did not help her make a decision on how she felt about the woman.

A shadow flickered on the walls of the hall. Eleanor hesitated, disappointed. She didn't want to talk, even to say good evening. But the shadow turned towards her and beckoned.

"I figured you wouldn't be able to sleep either," Giselle said quietly. "It's always harder after you dig up the memories." She pulled her blanket tighter around herself, watching the flames, her long legs stretched out on a bench in front of her, skin exposed below the hem of her shift.

Eleanor sighed, searched the tables for the desired ale, and then approached the fire. She sat a bit away from Giselle, studying her.

She really was quite pretty.

"Are you still a prostitute?" she blurted out. It certainly had seemed like it last summer, in a shadowy brothel.

"Yes."

"Why? If you got out, why not stay out?"

"That's a complicated answer." Giselle hesitated for a moment. "What I do now is nothing compared to what I did. The money is better than any other profession for a single woman. We can't all inherit manors, I suppose." She smiled to soften her words, but still Eleanor felt them cut. "Your husband tried to convince me to work as a maid in a castle somewhere, but I can't see serfdom as a better life than what I have. And there's a certain excitement to it, I suppose. Particularly when its people's secrets I'm after."

"I couldn't do it."

"Why not?"

The question surprised Eleanor. "I—I just never could. I would have rather died. I almost did."

Giselle's dark eyes narrowed. "And I *could* for the same reason. I was dying. Starvation is a slow torture."

Questions floated through Eleanor's head, and yet she was too afraid of the answers to ask. There was one that she had to though. "You—and Lezay—more than once?"

"Rot? Oh, yes. I was his favorite." She studied Eleanor. "No, he wasn't gentle if that's what you want to know. I'm sorry for you if he was your first."

"You've been through far worse," Eleanor mused. She hesitated. "Sir Simon of Bavaria said he frequently visited you as well."

"Ah, yes. Simon." Giselle smiled. "I actually liked when he visited. He learned quickly not to talk about anything of importance though."

"And never my uncle?"

"Oh, definitely not. He was a bit put off by the fact that I was his father's pet."

"Raganor—"

"He brought me to Alsace. I suppose he saved my life. Not without cost." Giselle got a distant look in her eye, studying Eleanor as if she weighed how much to tell. "Your innocent ears won't want to hear more. Suffice to say, he is the most twisted man I have ever met, and there have been many. I was not happy to see him in Calais." She inhaled through her nose. "At least that's done."

"Did he hurt you?"

"Not this time. He's far more interested in you. That is the value of information."

They watched the fire awhile. Eleanor wondered what Giselle had told him, but in the grand scheme it didn't matter. Enough people had warned her that he found out everything.

The fire crackled before them. "How long will you stay here?" Eleanor asked.

"Just until the weather breaks. I'm told there's not much more of the world to travel going west, and yet I don't want to go east, ever."

"You don't want to go home?"

Giselle laughed. "What home? I was a child when I left. My family didn't want me, even if they are still alive. I don't even know what my mother tongue was. I know Langue d'Oc, English, German, a little Langue d'Oil. And I will never return to Alsace."

"Me neither," Eleanor chuckled.

Giselle smiled at that. "We aren't so different you know. We just took different paths into this room." She leaned towards Eleanor, her face a mask of serious concern. "Do you love Alec?"

"Yes," Eleanor answered quickly.

"Do you love him enough to die for him?"

Eleanor stammered.

Giselle dropped her voice. "That is the real reason I am here. You don't have much time to decide."

Eleanor sat as stunned as if she'd been slapped. Giselle knew about the bloodlines.

The woman rose to her feet.

Eleanor hurried after her, following her out of the hall.

"What do you mean?"

"Raganor says you already know what must happen." Giselle's posture seemed tense, her words clipped. "Really, after all Alec has done for you, you couldn't answer that question with an immediate, *yes*?"

"Of course I would!"

"It's too late. You hesitated. Do you even know what you have yet, Eleanor?" Giselle stopped. "Do you know what he is as a man? How rare that is?" Her voice shook for the first time that day. Even all the horrors she alluded to had not cracked this woman's resolve, though the thought of Alec now did.

Eleanor's knees felt weak. "You love him."

"Of course I do! And I *would* die for him. Worse yet, I would die for *you*, only because of him. Gathering this information you seek does not come without risks. You think you know too much about The Order to avoid joining." She pointed to herself, her voice shaking with emotion. "I know just as much, and I cannot join. I live as a nomad, reliant on the mercy of Raganor le Brun. Do you understand how thin of a line that is? I am The Raven; I cannot hide from him."

"Then stop meddling in this!"

Giselle laughed, a hint of madness in her voice. She was out of the hall now, heading up the stairs. "If I didn't meddle, where would you be?"

"I didn't ask for any of this!" Eleanor followed, two steps behind.

Giselle spun on her. "Neither did I."

Chapter 32

E leanor was frozen into place on the stairs. Giselle's footsteps faded into the castle. The darkness of the cold night encircled her like an icy blanket. Her flesh pebbled as the castle's draft reached its fingers through her thin night-clothes and shawl. Slowly, a hand on the wall to steady herself, she sank onto the stair. Within minutes her backside would be numb. So be it.

Her mind was as numb as her flesh.

In part, the shock of being scolded by a prostitute in her own home had incited her. But that shock had been immediately doused by the truth. For Giselle knew what Eleanor tried to avoid thinking about. If she was to join this order—as she had so foolishly claimed willing to do—then she needed to make a sacrifice. And that sacrifice had to be one of their accursed bloodlines. Alec was their natural choice. He didn't even know. She had been too cowardly to tell him, warn him. What was she afraid of? That he would choose to take his place as a member and lead *her* to sacrifice?

A shiver ran up her spine. *That was what Giselle wanted to know.* Would she, Eleanor, be willing to switch places with Alec? This stranger had seen straight through her cowardice and exposed it. Any loving wife would at least discuss the situation with her husband. Though the knowledge she bore was slowly eating at her, she had not brought herself to have that conversation with Alec.

I know who killed your father, and it wasn't the man you fought so hard to take revenge from. For Eleanor did know who had joined The Order around the time of Alfred of Homme's death, and she could only pray Alec never found out. And what did that make her? Selfish, at best.

A rushlight flickered down the corridor, and the soft scuff of feet reached her ears. Still, Eleanor didn't move. She stared, eyes unfocused, turning in her mind what she should tell Alec, questioning her own bravery. A round figure sat next to her on the stairs, the sweet scent of rosemary in the air. When a hand touched her knee, Eleanor looked up.

Marie's face was etched with concern.

Instead of reassurance, the image hit Eleanor like the blow of a lance. Wilfred. He was Alec's half-brother. The Order didn't know about him. But she did. There was a second option. And the thought of her dear friend, a man of exceptional character, father of at least two children by the woman next to her with a third on the way, having anything to do with The Order sent a wave of panic through her.

She felt her heart rate quicken. Her breath caught in her throat. She felt as if she had sinned by even thinking the thought.

"My lady?" Marie asked with concern.

Eleanor could only shake her head.

Marie squeezed her knee. "It's that woman, isn't it? There's something about her. No noblewoman acts as she does. Even you, who weren't always a noblewoman, act different. Though *you* can be whoever you wish. I've seen you do it enough times. What'd she do? You say the word, I'll have her out of this castle—"

Eleanor laid her hand over Marie's, quieting her. "It's not Giselle. Not entirely. She—" Eleanor thought, searching for a way to explain without revealing the complexity of the situation. "The truth is often hard to hear. That's all."

Marie remained quiet a long moment as Eleanor's thoughts continued to swirl. Even now, she felt guilty that Marie, and Wilfred for that matter, remained ignorant of the reasons behind the threats that surrounded them. How was that fair to this woman that had nursed and practically raised her son as her own? Didn't she have a right to know, that she could protect her family as Eleanor strove to protect her own?

As if reading her thoughts, Marie quietly said, "I know what the king ordered. With Benec. Wilfred told me." There was a catch in her voice. "You know I love him as one of my own."

"I do know. And I am grateful for it."

"Lady Gwen—I met her only briefly. Though I suppose a woman willing to take a blade for a child will be a good guardian."

"If I didn't think so, I would not let him go to her. King's order or not."

Marie nodded. "Aye. I know." She cleared her throat. "Wilfred means to go with you when you return to France."

This surprised Eleanor, and she turned to Marie, eyes narrowed in the dim light. The woman's face was earnest, her brow furrowed with determination. "Since it's a night of truth, I'll be out with it. I know you feel some jealousy towards me, for filling a role taken from you, in regard to your son. And if the role was reversed, I'd feel the same."

"Marie—"

"No, let me finish. I may be born common as a mule, but this has been weighing on me a long time. I feel that jealousy towards *you*, for what my husband feels he owes you. He will always be paying a debt to you. And in some ways, I will be that bystander, as you had to be with Benec."

Eleanor furrowed her brow. "He owes me no debt."

"Ah, but he does. For before you, he was as common as I. And you brought us both out of oblivion." She inhaled. "It was clear when we came back. I didn't want to come back; didn't want to see my family. They sent me away when they found out I was with child, to a man who didn't want me either. Now that Wilfred is a knight though, we are accepted again. Here, and everywhere we traveled. That is because of you, telling him he could be more. Because of you, he sought out his parentage. You are the one that helped him learn to fight. Otherwise, Alec likely would have bullied him as a groom forever."

Marie tightened her shawl. Eleanor followed suit. The damp draft was getting to them.

"But because of what you did for Wilfred, he feels you are his liege, perhaps more so than Alec. You need to know it. For if it came down to it, Alec may well revert to his old domineering lordship, at Wilfred's expense. It will be up to you to remind Wilfred to stay in his own light."

"He deserves his own light." Eleanor again thought of The Order. No, Alec must not know about his father's bloodline, lest he, too, come to Eleanor's realization of the third eligible member of the ancient organization.

"I want him to go with you," Marie said firmly. "He is most alive when he is a knight. And I know without doubt he will be faithful to me, return to me." She turned to look at Eleanor. "I won't be able to travel to Aquitaine until this next babe is out. Wilfred will have to leave before then. I don't know what the three of you have planned, but I can feel it. So when the time comes, I want you to look after him as your own. And in return, I will look after Benec for you. Even if Lady Gwen is his formal guardian."

Eleanor met those eyes, felt the sincere plea there. Marie, the sweet, quiet maid, was making the most earnest request she had yet made. It showed her courage. This young woman had a strength to match Eleanor's, only different.

She took Marie's hand and gave it a firm squeeze. "I give you my word."

Relief softened Marie's eyes, and she squeezed Eleanor's hand back, then dropped it. She rose to her feet.

"Then let's get to our warm beds, for I'm about frozen."

Eleanor let out a short laugh, quickly cut off by the greater implications of her oath. For without a second son of Alfred of Homme, the first son, Alec Earnblaec, was the one in danger.

And Alec didn't even know.

Chapter 33

Raoul set off for the Bergfried a month and a half in advance of the ceremony. It didn't matter that the weather in Alsace was still bitter. He intended to take his time, meet with members of The Order, and tend to some regular business that would allow for an extended time away from Brunstein.

He spent a few days at Leuwenstein, and while he did not outright apologize to Roric for his angry blow, he did smooth over the relationship with that volatile ally by the gift of two expensive destriers. Though he hated seeing pig-faced Elfroid on one of those gorgeous horses, it seemed worth the cost. The Lezays had assured him they still supported his plan to dissolve The Order.

From there he rode on towards France and made the regular stop at the Abbey of Saint Catherine, which happened to coincide with a bitter cold spell. The nuns fed him a warm meal in the entranceway and offered him a room. He was grateful and made a substantial donation. The cold lingered a few days, and when he grew tired of his tiny, cold room, he wandered his way into the library. It was a modest room, with only a few precious books, but Raoul figured it was as good a place as any to while away some time until traveling was more pleasant. He was thumbing through a massive illuminated copy of the New Testament when one of the nuns stopped outside the open door. He shot her a brief glance and a smile, then went back to his reading.

When still the woman had not left, he again looked up.

She had the most intense gaze of anyone he had ever met. It was as if she tried to peer through flesh and bone and see his soul. He felt worse than naked before her, as if he was dressed in all of his sins, as if she *knew* where he was going and what he had done to earn his place there. His eyes became locked on hers, unable to look away. She was dressed the same as any of the other nuns, her habit and veil plain and dark. She was middle-aged, with a face that belied she had seen pain and yet with a spark in her eyes that revealed she was beyond it.

There was a determination there, too. For what?

His skin itched under that stare. He bowed to the woman. "How may I help you, Sister?"

Her lips made a thin line. Fear sparked through her gaze and then faded. He thought she would turn and leave, as many of the shy sisters did, but she stayed in the doorway. Now it was Raoul's turn to study her more closely. Had he met her before, on a previous visit? Likely. There was something vaguely familiar about her.

The woman took a step towards him, hesitated, then took another. Raoul watched her, not sure what her intent was. Was he in trouble for violating the sanctum of their library? He had seen no guard.

The woman, now before him, raised her shaking hands to his face, searching his features. Then, with surprising strength, she curled those hands around his shoulders and pulled him into the strongest hug Raoul had ever felt in his life. There was love in that embrace, and not the kind of romantic love he had felt before in a woman's arms. This was stronger, unconditional, accepting. It was how Eleanor had once described her parents' embraces.

For a wild moment, he felt Eleanor's words echoing in his ears. *She's alive. Your mother is alive.*

Raoul's heart pounded. He didn't know if he should embrace this nun before him, or if such a movement would make her disappear. She pulled away before he could decide, her fingers again tracing his jaw. Her eyes were wet with tears, her fingers trembling, and yet now a smile was lighting on her lips. He felt his pulse in his ears now, his knees weak as willows.

He took a deep breath, which helped some. He met the woman's eyes, swallowed a few times, then finally forced out, "Are you my mother?"

She smiled and nodded once.

Still, he found it too hard to believe. This could be a taunting trick of the Lezays. She was too close to Brunstein. Too close, to have been dead all these years. Perhaps she was just a crazy nun, and he was just a lonely man. He narrowed his gaze. "Then what is your name?" he challenged.

She hesitated, and for a moment he thought he was right in all his doubts. The weight of disappointment pressed him, and he moved to push past her before she could see the hot tears that threatened.

She caught his arm.

"I was Lady Alenor of Tielo, once wife of Lord Montag le Brun. I am now Sister Mary. And your cousin, Lady Eleanor de Levan, told me that if her mother were alive, she would want to know." Tears streaked down the sister's face, the fear of rejection evident in her own pleading gaze. "So now I ask you, if your mother were alive, would you accept her?"

Raoul's hot tears broke free. He pulled his mother into his arms, curling them around her petite frame in a firm but gentle embrace. She curled her own around him, and when the sobs burst out of his chest, a well of emotion long suppressed, now broken, she rubbed his back as if he was the child she'd never been able to comfort.

They cried for the lost time. They cried for the joy of finding each other. They cried because it was safe for them to do so. And after their tears had run out, and their eyes were dried, Alenor led Raoul to a bench beneath a stained-glass window of a shepherd watching sheep, and they sat down.

"All this time, you were so close," Raoul said in awe.

Alenor nodded.

"I have been here before. Did you know it was me?"

She shook her head, opened her mouth to speak, closed it, shook her head again, and then cleared her throat. "Forgive me, I have not spoken freely in years. I took a vow of silence. It was only when Eleanor came, a few months ago, that it became clear some things were more important."

Raoul took her small hand in his own, and she squeezed with a firmness greater than her size.

"Raoul, my son—" Her voice caught on the words, but she pressed on, urgency now in her voice. "I know what your father forced you into. I know where you are going now. I could not let you leave without you knowing about me, and having my blessing."

Raoul could only begin to wonder at how she knew about The Order.

She met his eye. "The only question is, are you different than your father? Do you have the strength in you to fight this, to end this?"

"God, I hope so," Raoul said without hesitation.

Alenor then put her hands on his head, forcing him to bow chin to chest, then dropped her own head, her eyes closed. She did not speak, but Raoul felt the energy in her touch, the desperation in her breath as she prayed. When she released him, she was calm, her expression determined.

"May God guide you and save us all," she whispered. She met his eye. "When you return, visit again. We will talk more. There is so much to catch up on. But now you must go."

Chapter 34

Even if Eleanor had been ready to speak to Alec, he wasn't available. He was gone from her bed before she rose, regardless of how early she woke. They saw each other only in passing throughout the day, as Alec was often discussing matters of the estate with Thomas, or explaining his plans for a new building with the laborers. His list of duties seemed unending, and Eleanor couldn't help but wonder if his devotion to his manor was a discreet penance for what had happened to Lady Gwen or if it was his way of dealing with the anxiety that seemed to grip the entire household in a fist.

They didn't know there was a threat, and yet they knew there was something, so the rumors abounded, whispered behind hands, stifled when the lady of the manor passed by. It reminded Eleanor of when they had spoken about her at the tournaments, mocking her. She wasn't sure if they mocked her now or if it was only the situation. Then again, why would the household from Neroche have kept quiet about the mistress Alec had brought home from

Sarum and then followed to France to marry? That had to be the greatest story in years. They had plenty to whisper about.

As two maids again shut their mouths and hastened back to their chores, Eleanor longed to scream. Two things could calm her down: a ride out on Noir or holding Benec. The ride was out of the question; rain had turned much of the countryside into a mix of ice and mud. The horses weren't even being let out of the stable. That left Benec, so she set off in search of him, listening for the joyful sound of the children.

She found them in the main hall, playing at Marie's feet. Benec and Godfrey seemed to be fighting over a wooden toy, and Benec ended up getting hit over the head with it. He burst into tears. Eleanor stepped forward to console him, but before she could get into sight, Marie had picked him up and dried his tears. His arms held tight to Marie's neck, even as she scolded Godfrey. Eleanor stopped, a mere bystander, and then backed away, unnoticed.

She felt something pull in her chest. It hurt to breathe. She rubbed the spot and headed to the lord's room, her room, where, with the door firmly shut behind her, she gasped and doubled over. Tears spilled from her eyes, dropping to the floor as if the rain outside was dripping through the roof. Then she straightened, her hands on her hips, and forced her body back under control.

Why was her son being raised by another woman?

Because she was good to him.

But why was she good to him?

Because he loved her.

Why did he love her?

Because she'd nursed him when Eleanor couldn't.

Montag, Raganor, and The Order had taken that from her. It was common for noblewomen to hire wet nurses for their children. There never had been a discussion when Alec and Eleanor had asked Marie to care for the child after they got him back. The loss had seemed trivial, until it was compounded. The long hours of nursing, burping, then napping had been robbed from her, given to another. She held nothing against Marie. She was grateful for her. As Marie had said, Benec was as close to her as one of her own boys.

What was she, Eleanor, to him?

Her chest still felt tight, the emotion forced down by years of practice. She couldn't, wouldn't think like this. Her son still knew who his mother was. She would forever be the one that protected him until her dying breath. She went to the window and watched the rain splatter on the panes. She could not see anything beyond the glass, such was the layer of thin ice coating the castle.

Alec entered, his clothing soaked. He barely noted her as he pulled off outer layers and hung them by the fire, where they instantly began to steam. He was oblivious to her pain. Thus when she asked, "Where were you?", the words came out short and angry.

"Working," he grumbled. Still, he didn't look at her.

If someone had asked her why she said it, she would not have been able to explain. Perhaps it was just the raw emotion of a grey, rainy afternoon, but she blurted out in an accusatory tone, "Working with *her*."

Alec looked at her then, his eyes narrowed.

"What did she tell you this time? What was the cost?"

Alec didn't defend himself, which gave her heart yet another jolt. Was there an element of truth to her accusations? She stepped up to Alec and folded her arms, studying him now. "My lord...you *were* with her."

He ran a hand over his head, spraying ice crystals onto the hearth, which melted instantly in faint hisses of steam. When he turned to Eleanor, his expression was dark. "We were discussing other potential members of The Order. I didn't want to have the conversation near the household, so we went for a short walk." With hands on his hips, he surveyed her, the muscle in his jaw working furiously.

For some reason that short answer was what brought forth the emotion. The tears welled, and Eleanor fought quickly to blink them away. She met Alec eye to eye as closely as her stature allowed. "Then why not take me along?" Her voice was a pained whisper, like the sound was ripping itself from her chest.

"I thought she would speak more freely with me. From what I've seen the last few days, the two of you aren't exactly friends." His tone was level, the emotional walls up to full height.

Friends. No, she should think not.

He still stood with hands on hips, almost like his hand hovered near his sword, which infuriated her more.

Her face was hot, her hands now clenched at her sides. "You never even asked me." Always secrets with Alec. Half-truths. Yet he asked her to trust him? He didn't deserve it, not when he pulled tricks like this. The pain of that revelation welled up from deep inside her, washing over her like a flood. Betrayal floated on the current. Before she recognized her action, she had slapped Alec—hard—across his face.

He didn't even flinch.

A handprint was already glowing red on his left cheekbone; the muscle twitched as he pursed his lips in his own boiling anger. His hands had left his hips and were flexing and fisting, the sinews readying for battle.

Eleanor braced herself, defiantly matching his glare, readying for the retaliatory blow she deserved, but none came. He merely turned on his heel and left the room.

That infuriated her more.

"Alec Earnblaec, you get back here! We are not finished with this conversation!"

"Not much of a conversation, Eleanor, when you act like that."

Eleanor, desperate for anything to throw, snatched her comb off the side table and threw it at his retreating form, hitting him square in the back. He whirled around towards her, the full fury of a knight now in his posture. She grabbed a broom that stood against the corridor wall, giving it a mighty whirl towards his head. He ducked easily, pursuing her, forcing her to yield a few steps down the corridor. She attacked again, and he sidestepped. She swung, and this time he only had time to throw up an arm, which the broom handle cracked painfully—for both parties—against. Eleanor's eyes were blurred with tears now.

"Fight back you coward! You have a sword!" She again swung, and this time Alec caught the handle in a grip that wrenched the broom from her hands entirely. She staggered for her footing, almost falling into him, but then caught herself and readied to run. Instead of raising the broom against her though, Alec threw it across the corridor. It clattered against the stone. Eleanor's moment of hesitation was what allowed Alec to close the distance between them and grab her wrists. Instinctually, Eleanor twisted her arm like he had showed her, breaking the grip on one arm but failing against Alec's strong right hand. He pulled her into him, capturing her free arm before she could slap him again, and gave her a shake that forced her to meet his eyes.

"Stop!" he bellowed, the fury echoing around the corridor like a gong. Surely the whole castle heard now.

Eleanor stilled, avoiding his eyes, still struggling to pull away as the tears came. "You lied. You told me no more secrets."

Alec released her, stepping away, still tense with fury. "I didn't lie."

Eleanor held an arm over her stomach as the pain ripped through her, more mental than physical but there just the same. "But you did, and you can't see it. And it just keeps happening, again and again. This is my past and my future, Alec. I have a right to know. And when you put it all together…You. Just. Lie." Eleanor stepped away from him as a flower fades under frost.

He didn't pursue, just watched her with that infuriating, emotionless mask.

She wanted him to scream at her, hold her, apologize, explain it away, slap her, kiss her. There was only the numb, blank stare. Maybe he didn't care at all then. How could his emotion not be welling over like hers, when there was this much at stake?

"Alec, sometimes I wish you would just hit me. The physical pain—I think I could take that easier than indifference."

She spun on her heel and left him, not even the recognition of her departure on his face.

Eleanor didn't know where to go. The storm was still swirling outside. The lord's chamber was the last place she wanted to be. She strode through the castle, pacing off her fury, unable to remain still, and yet with no place to run. She passed Giselle, whose black hair still shone from the rain, just like Alec's. Marie met her in the main hall, only to step out of her way with one look. Eleanor ducked down a stairwell, slipped past one of the laborers, and found herself in the castle armory. She slammed the door shut with a bang that resounded through the thick walls.

She stood there in the doorway, fists clenched at her sides, her shoulders rising and falling with her breath as if she was fresh from a fight. She was. She hastily wove some errant strands of hair back into place as she stepped up to the long rack of swords. They were aged, from a generation or two before, but a slide of the finger warned that they had been stored sharp. She let her hand drift over the hilts, debating which one to try. Her eye caught the one given by Simon, with the golden E on the hilt—Edmond's sword. She slipped it off the rack and hefted it, rotated her wrist and heard it cut the air with a faint whistle.

There was a massive table on one end of the rectangular room, and an open area on the other. She stepped into this space, and let the blade swing. It didn't matter if there was no one to clash swords against. She fought her invisible foes, sometimes putting faces to them, sometimes not even caring. Lezay and Montag fell for a second time. Raganor tried his hand and failed. She parried with Edmond, releasing her fury at him for plying her heart and then leaving to die. When Alec's face popped into her head, she fought the hardest, until winded and sobbing she fell to her knees, the sword clattering away from her. The cold bit though her clothes as if they were sheer, cooling the sweat on her back. She fisted her hands and hunched over herself, feeling as if she would break.

But she didn't. Nothing broke. She didn't die. Her heart still beat stubbornly on. Her chest rose and fell with each life-sustaining breath. And eventually she stilled, wiped her eyes, and sat back on her heels. The sword still lay a few feet away. She stared at it, wondering if she was weak. Alec had not hurt her, not like her first husband, and yet here she was crying as if the world was ending because he went for a walk.

I don't trust anyone, she'd told him months ago. *But I love you*. And perhaps that was the very reason for the pain that radiated through her from head to fingertips, heart to toe, unlike a physical pain that stayed localized. Her muscles ached from sheer tension. She was dizzy from sleepless nights. All along, it was simple. She loved him. And by such, he had a power to hurt her he had not yet figured out how to control.

Eleanor reached for the sword, sliding it back across the thick plank floor towards her. Because she loved Alec, there was only one answer to Raganor's call. She would go to him. She would tell him her family would have no part of his dark order. And when he told her she didn't have a choice, she would make her choice. She would fight.

Ignorance would keep Alec and Wilfred away until it was over. All of them, Marie and Gwen included, would protect Benec. If she survived to return—she would have to decide then what to do. Let the next months determine her value, who she was.

Let these next weeks determine where she was supposed to be.

Chapter 35

Within hours of her explosive fight with him, she was gone. Alec had caught on to her plan too late—she must have already been packed—and by that point she was already swinging a leg over her massive destrier. She was dressed to run, fight. Clad in hauberk, helmet, tunic, and cloak, with sword and dagger both belted to her side, she looked the part of a knight. At least she paused in the courtyard, let him stare at her, stared back, her face a blank slate, as if all emotion had been drained, and the walls he had fought for years to breach had been rebuilt.

How had he hurt her so much?

This was more than just him walking with Giselle. She knew about Giselle. Why could she not see that there was nothing there but an alliance against a common, deadly enemy? What else had he done? Was there some deep secret she herself held that had pushed her to this extreme? The questions swirled in his mind in an endless loop, none of them being answered, for he could not bring himself to speak, to ask.

She had never left without him before. And he had a suspicion of where she intended to go.

"Take care of Benec," she said quietly, a tremor of emotion in her voice.

So she wasn't too far gone yet. "Stay—" he began, but she was already turning, her face set.

He took a step towards her, but Noir was fast.

He stared after her, only vaguely aware of footsteps running up behind him. Giselle stood at his side, breathless.

"Where is she going?" she asked.

"Away."

"Go after her!"

He felt numb. She hated him that much, that she would leave without even a final goodbye.

Giselle shook his arm. "Alec!"

He shrugged her off. "Leave me. You should not have come here."

Giselle stood immobile, staring after him as he stalked back into the manor, and he didn't care. Eleanor was gone.

He slammed the kitchen door, unclasping his sodden cloak in a fury that strained the toggles. His shaking hands moved to hang the fabric but missed the hook, the cloak falling to the floor. Alec turned his back to it, uncaring, and frowned deeper as he noted the man that sat at the table by the fire.

Wilfred poured a cup of ale and pushed it towards Alec, his eyes wide.

At least his bloody tongue was silent.

Alec let out a slow breath, which did nothing to quiet his temper, and snatched the ale from the table, pacing before the fire. He downed the cup in a few swallows, then filled himself another, resuming his pacing. Wilfred merely leaned back against the table and watched him.

"Too much water in this ale." Alec finished the second cup. He poured a third.

"What's the point? We all know you can drink a whole barrel and not feel a thing."

"Puts me to sleep at least. I'd take sleep over this nightmare."

"How is she?"

"Gone."

"Gone where?" Wilfred sat up a bit straighter.

Alec ignored the question. Why did everyone want to ask the one thing he wasn't sure of himself? Gone was gone. "It's never enough for her. We went over there, risking our bloody lives, all to help *her* regain *her* lands." Alec's voice boomed, making Wilfred wince. He gestured wildly in the easterly direction. "Now, that isn't enough.

I somehow betrayed her by omission, and she wants to go running into the wild again on her own." Alec palmed his forehead in frustration. Had she forgotten what had happened in Alsace? That thought made his pulse race. He whirled back toward Wilfred. "She looks for reasons to fight." Alec slammed the empty cup back on the table. He leaned on the edge, stilling.

He was so lost in his thoughts, reliving every little thing he could have done differently, that he forgot Wilfred was there.

Wilfred cleared his throat. "I think you're missing the thing she actually wants."

"Oh, what did I fail to give her?"

"She wants you to be honest with her."

"I am honest with her! My God, she knows more about me than any woman in the world!"

Wilfred shrugged. "Maybe that's the thing that isn't enough."

Alec stared at him, contemplating if he should knock him over the head like the childish groom he once was or if he should feel for fever to see if Wilfred had lost his mind entirely. The secrets he and Eleanor shared were enough to put all their lives at risk. What more could she possibly need to know?

"Alec, what *is* your story?" Wilfred shrugged as Alec shot him a bewildered look. "I know the Sir Alec Earnblaec from the tournaments, the man who moved me and Old

Guillaume to an obscure ruin yet provided for us. What about all the time before that?"

"You knew me then, too." Alec suddenly felt very tired.

"No, I knew that the young man I occasionally passed in the village was the son of my lord. You were not my master then, nor my brother."

Alec sighed and straightened. "I was a squire under Lord Gawain, knighted by Lord Cenric. I went to a few tourneys. I found out I was good. My mother died. Then my father went east on pilgrimage, and I didn't hear a word until I was told all our lands and titles were to be stripped from us." He grew silent.

"Then you tried to track our father. You went to France." Wilfred prompted, looking at him expectantly.

"Yes."

"Alec, what happened in France?"

Alec turned to the fire, staring into it blankly. At long last he spoke. "When my father—our father—left, I was a lost man." He slowly turned the cup in his hands, eyes unseeing. "I did not want him to go on pilgrimage. I wanted him to continue running Castle Homme, that I could attend tournaments, travel Europe, make a name for myself. But he had his own grief to deal with, and he left. I ran Castle Homme the best I could...I think I did a good job."

Wilfred shrugged. "I never noticed any difference in management."

"Good." The silence lingered in the air like a pre-storm fog. "Then Father didn't come home." He poured more ale, remembering the day the messenger from the king had arrived—the first he'd ever had contact from a king—only to hand over a sealed letter informing Alec that he was relieved of all titles and the management of Castle Homme. His father was a deserter who had abandoned his men in the Holy Land, there was a new lord arriving on the morn, and Alec had to vacate the premises. He cleared his throat. "I had nowhere to go, so I went to look for answers. I had enough from former tournament winnings that I could get into taverns...talk to people. No one paid me any attention. I—" he cleared his throat. "I used women to try to numb the grief for a while. Alcohol never was enough for me, though I gained a bit of a reputation for holding it, which won me a few bets to refill my purse."

Wilfred smiled. He had witnessed as much.

"I was looking for Father, but when you look for things, you find more than what you look for." He met Wilfred's eye, then looked away. "I thought I was at a dead end. I felt like a failure. I had lost everything I had worked my whole life to gain. All I could feel was a deep, barely contained rage that threatened to unleash at the slightest provocation. That is when I met the most beautiful woman. I was told I could do anything to her. No repercussions. No limits."

"Fie, Alec, I don't need the details—" Wilfred blanched.

"You should know this." Alec shot him a withered look that rooted Wilfred to his bench. When Wilfred's mouth was sufficiently clamped shut again, Alec pressed on. "Giselle was a whore at a brothel in Alsace. She gave me back the control I craved. Needed."

Wilfred's face turned pink and he looked away, studying a tapestry with rapt attention.

"What I hadn't counted on was finding a kindred soul. There was no other like her. An artist in every way, and probably the smartest woman I've ever met." He gave Wilfred a stern look. "And don't you ever repeat that to Eleanor."

"Nope," Wilfred mouthed, with a pop of his lips. He continued studying the tapestry.

"She already knows about Giselle by the way. That's why she's so mad at me. Again."

"I don't blame her."

Alec glared at him.

Wilfred threw his hands up in the air. "You've had a former amour living in your house, with your wife, for weeks. And you self-proclaim this other woman to be beautiful and smart. And if you've been honest with Eleanor, she knows this, which makes her feel unworthy of you. And if you haven't told Eleanor all this, then she senses your dishonesty, which makes her question *everything*."

Alec reached for the ale. Wilfred twitched as if to pull the pitcher away, but thought better of it.

"Easy there, Alec. The ale isn't free tonight. You may own it, but there's only so much."

Alec looked down into his cup sadly, musing that he was actually starting to see the sparkle of the torches. He was feeling the drink for once. He poured another cup, took his time drinking, then lingered with the cup in the air until the last drop fell onto his tongue.

"Giselle is the one that told me about Lezay. He had bragged to her about killing my father. I didn't believe her at first, but then I overheard him, too. He was so cocky, he felt he could boast about it in public, with no repercussions."

He reached for the ale. Wilfred pulled it away.

"You can have more after you finish the story," Wilfred promised.

"I wanted to kill him. I wanted my revenge. His boasting was the only proof I thought I'd ever find. Who would have believed me? So I figured I'd just kill him and accept my punishment in hell."

"Why didn't you?" Wilfred's brow was furrowed as he listened.

"Giselle. She said she liked me. Didn't want to see me drawn and quartered for murder. She told me about another client—a farmer—who found a body along the road. The man had a gold ring, with my crest on it. She catches details like that, even when she's..." He cleared his throat. "I met the man the next day, made it seem like it was a chance meeting, and through conversation he told me what he'd found. I bought him a few drinks, and he took me to the place my father was buried. The ring and the body were the proof I needed to clear my family name. I unburied my father, his corpse riddled with worms, and took him to the bailiff. I forced the bailiff to write and seal a letter to King Richard that my father was murdered. Sir Alfred of Homme never even made it to the Holy Land. He certainly didn't desert anyone. He didn't stab himself to death twelve times and then slit his own throat, that much was evident even with decay. I reburied him in Alsace. Delivered the letter to the king. You know the rest."

Wilfred sat stunned.

Alec thought for a moment, the ale making his head swirl. "No, you don't know the rest. Neither does Eleanor. The bailiff refused to do anything to Lezay. The Lezays were his lords, so effectively he was powerless to do anything more than inform my king of what he'd seen of the body. So again, I felt murderous. I wanted revenge. It was Giselle that told me about Lezay's wife, and gave me the idea to find her, use *her* to get back at Lezay. But I lingered at that brothel too long. Lezay suspected his favorite girl was talking. So I took Giselle with me." He reached for the ale, which Wilfred let him have. "I didn't expect to fall in love with Eleanor. I only wanted her for revenge. No wonder she still doesn't trust me."

The men were silent in thought a long moment, drinking until the ale pitcher was empty.

"You know, Eleanor told me on the road from Alsace that I killed the wrong man. That Lezay wasn't even the one that killed our father. Do you think she said that just for spite?"

"Eleanor isn't petty like that, Alec. Even when she's mad."

"What if she's right then? What if she's the one with all the secrets, and I'm the blind fool in the dark?"

Wilfred chortled. "You, a fool? Alec, not knowing every little secret does not make you a fool."

Alec groaned. His head felt fuzzy with drink.

Wilfred quietly ventured, "You realize she—Eleanor—never had a place to call home? You and I, we moved and traveled a bit, but we kept coming back to the same place. Eleanor never had that. Even as a young girl she was always on the move. She's a nomadic soul now, and I don't think she knows how to handle settling."

"That is what a wife must do."

"Is it?" Wilfred looked at Alec. "What does it matter where she goes as long as she keeps coming back to you?" Alec stared at him. "You're her only home, Alec. But that doesn't mean she has to physically be with you every moment. I'm sure she has a reason for leaving, and when she calms down, she'll be looking for you."

Alec was silent a long moment. "It took Lezay ten years to find her after she ran. She can disappear—she's done it enough times in the past. She blends in, becomes someone else..."

Wilfred gritted his teeth, deep in thought. "Then follow from a distance. You can disappear, too."

Chapter 36

"*C*orpse *with worms, bottled wine, come and take it, off the vine,*" Alec sang under his breath. He stumbled over a sack someone had left carelessly on the floor. Oh, right, he was in a storeroom; maybe it should be there. "*He takes the girl, on the floor, come and take it, at the door.*" Somehow he worked his way out of the storeroom and back into the main corridor, where he ran into Thomas. The castellan frowned, but kept his mouth shut and continued on his way. "Rude," Alec grumbled. He traced the stone, stumbling back towards what he thought was the direction of the stairwell, and his room beyond. "*Simple words, ever short, come and take it—*"

"What the bloody hell is wrong with you?"

Alec squinted at the blurry figure ahead of him. Skirts. Must be a woman. Hmm, better run the other way. He turned and stumbled again, this time falling to his knees. They cracked painfully, which brought back some awareness. He sat back against the wall and groaned, rubbing them. The woman's figure loomed in front of him, her hands on her hips. She kicked his foot, which also hurt.

"Ow." He glared at her, his eyes beginning to focus. Definitely a woman. Pretty, too. She spun on her heel and disappeared, only to return a few minutes later with a man. A bucket of ice-cold water splashed onto his face. He roared into awareness, shaking his head. "What the—"

Giselle squatted down in front of him, her brown eyes sparking in the torchlight. Why was there torchlight? Oh, it was dark already. He groaned. How had the afternoon disappeared? At least that meant bedtime was near.

She lightly tapped his cheek. "Alec, you fool. Get yourself together." She turned aside. "How much did he have?"

Wilfred answered, "Just one pitcher with me."

"And one after that, and one after that, and one—" Alec pressed his wet hair out of his eyes, then shook the droplets off his fingers. "Which one of you threw the water?"

"That was me," Wilfred growled. He grabbed Alec by the armpit and hauled him to his feet. "I take back what I said earlier about you not being a fool. You're an idiot."

Alec leaned against the wall and rubbed his forehead. Some semblance of normal thought was returning, though he wished it wasn't. "Where's Eleanor?"

"She's gone, remember?" Giselle said in a short tone. Her hands were back on her hips. "And you need to go after her."

"Why?"

Giselle shook her head. "You know why. Alec—she's going to go to Raganor."

Wilfred looked at Giselle with wide eyes. "He failed to mention that."

Alec dropped his hand and gave Giselle a hard look. He had rarely seen her show much emotion, at least not unintentionally. Now, the tension was radiating off of her. "How do *you* know this?"

She looked at him with steady eyes. "I told her Raganor wanted to see her, before—" She shot Wilfred a sideways look and pressed her lips in a line. "You only have a few weeks until the equinox. Where else would she go?"

Wilfred looked from one of them to the other, frustration evident. "What are you talking about? I thought the whole reason we traveled in England—in winter—was to get away from Raganor. To get away from France."

Giselle inclined her head towards Wilfred, but spoke to Alec. "He doesn't know?"

"Of course not. It's too dangerous."

"Alec...not all secrets should be kept. He is your brother. Even I know that."

"That has nothing to do with this!" She needed to stop speaking. It was making his head hurt. And he was getting cold. Ice water and cold air didn't mix well. Not to mention, his stomach didn't feel quite right.

Giselle was watching him with awe. "She didn't tell you."

"I'm a bit drunk, so you have to be more specific."

Giselle turned to Wilfred. "I need your help. We need to ride out of here. There is someone you both need to speak with."

Wilfred appeared bewildered, but pulled Alec to his feet and followed Giselle. She ordered a servant to gather provisions, sent Macarius to saddle their horses, and when they were in Alec's room, she packed for him, starting with his armor first. Wilfred helped her while Alec emptied his stomach into a basin. He had never been truly drunk in his life. It wasn't a pleasant feeling. Had he really overdone it that much? Probably. Eleanor left.

"Can't we wait until morning?" Alec groaned.

Giselle glared at him. "Morning is almost here, you fool. You've already wasted too much time."

"Where exactly are we going?" Wilfred asked.

"London. There we will meet Sir Jacques of Brittany."

Alec's head snapped up at that. "Jacques? That murdering, kidnapping—"

Giselle met Wilfred's gaze. "We will deliver Benec to Sarum along the way. That will make the king happy. Lord Gawain and his men at arms will protect him."

Wilfred caught her arm. "Jacques is the one that tried to kidnap Benec. What business do we have with him?"

Giselle looked from one of them to the other. "It is not my place to say. I'm sorry, but I am not supposed to know. Sacrebleu, I'll take a risk for you, Alec, but I'm not suicidal. Jacques will tell you everything. And I will disappear." Her gaze lingered on Alec. "After we reach London, you must not try to find me again."

Alec was too confused by the events unfolding to demand further answers.

Wilfred picked up his and Alec's saddlebags. "I'll tell Marie. It will be hard for her, but she's been preparing for this." He motioned to the window, where light was just cutting the horizon. "Dawn is starting to rise."

In a rush, they were out of Earnblaec Castle, riding into the dawn as if chased by a storm. Benec sat in front of Wilfred, his eyes bright in the early morning light. As ever, the child was taking the excitement with a calm beyond his years. Alec still fought the nausea of his hangover, head splitting. Perhaps they were *chasing* the storm, as somewhere out there, Eleanor was ahead of them, the fury of his betrayal lingering in the frost of her hoofprints.

Chapter 37

Eleanor's tears had dried miles back. The pounding of her heart now matched her horse's stride. The dark pit of doubt in her stomach churned like the waves on the coast, battering her inside. She was no stranger to running. This time felt different.

She was never destined to be a wife. She should have recognized that as a child. She was nothing like her mother, quiet and obedient, sweet and social. She could only remember little bits, but Alec's stories confirmed what she knew. Her mother was the perfect wife, the perfect woman. She may have carried around a dagger, but she'd never used it, not like Eleanor had.

She could still feel the heat of the blood on her hands. She glanced down, half expecting them to be red. They were clean, white, and though wrapped in thick wool, cold. The images of blood came back, and she longed to scream.

England had refused to let her go quietly.

Perhaps it was the brutality of the winter. Certain villages seemed hungrier than usual. The small amount of coin she had left would not last long, and thus she had to stretch her provisions as long as possible. Her belly rumbled, but the outlaws waiting for single travelers could not hear it. Despite her desire to put as many miles between Earnblaec Castle and herself as possible, those bandits seemed to press her ever onward. She had almost made it to Southampton when she was forced to draw blood.

It is amazing the speed at which blood dries. It is equally curious the lack of speed by which it liquifies again, washing away in cold running water, the clots dissolving to red smears, the smears to lines scrubbed out of knuckles, maybe even requiring the use of a determined fingernail. One may bloody their hands with haste, but there is nothing hasty about washing it away.

She should have given him something. She would have, but he had grabbed for her horse, a hungry look in his eye, half-crazed. Was it mere hunger? Was it too much drink? Or was he touched by the devil? There had been no way to find out. He had not given her the chance to ask, but made a grab for her saddlebags that had forced her to draw her sword. She only meant to scare him away, but he was not scared, such was his state of madness, like a wild beast, scratching and circling at her, waiting for a break in her defenses. She was almost away, but then he had thrown himself at her. On instinct, Eleanor blocked him with her sword. It was what she had trained for. There was no thought to it. Her body had reacted to danger as it was supposed to do.

He had impaled himself on the blade and died before she could even dismount to aid him. Was it murder? It depended on what the courts would say. She was a noblewoman, him a beggar. She had defended herself, but it is hard to claim defense when you have no scratch, and the other party is dead.

His blood was on her blade. And by her futile attempt to aid his injury, on her hands. Thus she had knelt by the river, scrubbed away the memory of the man's hungry gaze, and ridden on. The guilt followed her like the train of an unwieldy gown. She confessed in St. Michael's Church in Southampton, found little relief, then boarded the first ship to Harfleur. Perhaps she should have slowed then, allowed herself rest, but she had pressed south into unfamiliar land. Perhaps it was the fatigue that brought back the disturbing memories of her past. Perhaps it was grief, for losing her family to her family's dark secrets. Perhaps she had become a bit mad herself.

Thus it was no small reaction when circumstances prompted her to take up her sword a second time, her hands tight on her reins as she pulled Noir up. The black horse pranced, tossing his head in protest, and the focus it took to stay in the saddle brought her back to awareness.

There was a man in front of her, his hands raised in the air, and he was backing away.

"I only meant to warn you there isn't another place to stop for another day's ride. Of course you're welcome to travel on," he said.

Eleanor narrowed her eyes at him. Behind him was a two-story wooden building, a sign dangling in front of it with two crossed spears.

Still the man backed away.

Eleanor sighed and sheathed her sword. "I'm sorry."

He stopped, his back to the door. "You just looked a bit peaked is all. Business is slow; I haven't seen many travelers lately. And I mean it about it being a day's ride. Though perhaps you don't mind sleeping in the cold. Feels like snow again to me though."

"I don't have much. What are you charging?" Eleanor rubbed her forehead. She really needed a good night's sleep. And hot food. And Noir needed rest and a good bucket of oats.

"Knight-errant are you? Well, my rate's low this time of year."

"Fair enough," she agreed, and dismounted. A few minutes later, her horse tucked in the barn and the snow swirling outside, she was seated by the fire with her belly full of warm stew. She let her eyes drift closed and mused on just how exhausted she was. The peace of this quiet tavern soothed her anxious mind for the first time in over a week. Was death like this, warm and welcoming? She had always thought it to be cold and sharp, like a sword.

Like a bloody sword.

She squeezed her eyes together, pressing the tear that threatened away. This was not time nor place to cry. She was a knight today. The room swayed a bit, and she longed to sleep, her back against the wall, her face warm from the hearty fire before her.

Someone entered the tavern and greeted the innkeeper by name. His voice sounded vaguely familiar, but that was probably just her imagination. She was too tired. The two men spoke in low voices for a while, their tone light and friendly. Then she heard the man walk over and take a seat. Of course, the fire was the warmest place to be, but the inn was empty. Did he really have to sit across the table from her? She opened one eye, sure her expression was none too welcoming.

Simon smiled at her.

She didn't have the energy to do more than groan. "I'm armed, Simon."

"What are the odds of meeting you here?"

"And who am I?"

He chuckled. "Your horse is rather recognizable, my lady."

The tavern owner delivered Simon a bowl of stew, and he thanked him. He made a sound of enjoyment as he ate, as if he and Eleanor were old friends.

"The ground will likely be covered in snow tomorrow. Though not much," Simon observed.

Eleanor ignored him and closed her eyes again. She hadn't been aware of how many parts of her body ached from the long hours in the saddle.

"I wanted to apologize," Simon began. He let the silence linger until Eleanor squinted her eyes at him. "For killing Edmond."

"I hate you."

Simon studied her thoughtfully. "Where's Alec? Did you ask him about Giselle?"

Eleanor settled back in her chair. "I spent a few weeks with her."

"Well, now...if that's your taste..."

She again was forced to glare at him. "She told me all about you. Why are you here, Simon? Don't you have a grand castle and a family in Bavaria?"

He leaned towards her, his voice dropping slightly. "Same as you. It's only a few weeks away. It takes time to travel."

She exhaled through her nose. "Then you know why I'm here."

"But I don't understand why Alec isn't with you."

"Yes, you do." She looked down her nose. He knew about the bloodlines. He knew what The Order would force her to do. Or what they would force Alec to do.

And finally, all the games, all the layers of secrecy seemed to fall away. Simon looked at her with a steady gaze, respect obvious. And finally, she knew every question she asked would be answered.

"I don't need him to do what needs to be done," she said quietly.

"Then you intend to *protect* him? By what, allowing us to kill you? It won't work, Eleanor. There needs to be a sacrifice."

"And if there is none, what next? What do you do then? Kill each other? I don't know your rules, but none of it makes sense."

Simon absently turned his cup of ale. "You and Alec are the only two of the bloodlines currently eligible. The timing of Montag's death was rather...inconvenient. Raoul was recently inducted. Then after Lezay we took in Elfroid. We had just enough fellow knights to...complete it." He inhaled. "Then Montag died. We knew Alec was eligible, and when you became knighted, you became so as well. The first woman in centuries that qualified. Well, Raoul, as our de facto leader, refused to touch either of you. He delayed over a year, succeeded in convincing about half the members that we should dissolve everything. But there are no protocols for how to do this. He and I hoped that if we simply did not induct more members, eventually The Order would simply die out." He leaned back. "And then Raganor returned."

The fire in the hearth next to them cracked, its warmth settling over Eleanor like a blanket.

Simon stretched out his legs, also soaking in the warmth. "Raganor intends to bring The Order back to its glory days, as he calls them. Days of murder for power, the thirteen of us reaching our fingers ever broader. I think he envisioned an empire, but Montag held it away from him. He has convinced many of the older members, powerful men, that those days are not yet gone. But for his plans to continue, The Order cannot die. And there is a place to be filled."

Eleanor met his eye. "And no one but Alec and I is qualified?" She again thought of Wilfred, wondering if anyone knew he and Alec were half-brothers. She prayed not.

Simon shook his head. "Not until my son is knighted later this year." He pursed his lips. "And my son is not Raganor's first choice. He wants his own blood in power. And that is you. I heard the Lezays informed you of the curse, and how your parents broke it?"

Eleanor nodded once. They let the silence linger a moment.

"You see, I understand what you face, in longing to protect your son." Simon took a slow sip of ale, then leaned forward again. "Raoul intends to take the power from Raganor. If he succeeds, then all this will end."

"How?"

"The leader must become the sacrifice. And instead of the inductee drawing the blood, there must be a cut from every single member."

Eleanor's stomach churned.

"The last man to draw blood becomes the leader."

"And Raoul intends to be that man?"

Simon nodded. "You see though, in order for all members to be gathered, we need to hold an initiation ceremony. Which is why you must now pretend to be willing to join."

"How can I do that without a sacrifice?"

"Alec will be there. I promise you."

"No. He doesn't know what happened to his father. And not to mention, he and I had a fight—"

"Eleanor, this is out of your power. Other members of The Order will ensure he gets there. And he loves you. He will fight for you. He will play his role."

Eleanor's heart pounded. "You intend to make us go through with it…"

Simon shook his head. "Do you trust Raoul?"

Eleanor frowned. Did she? She once did. And yet he had let secrets linger between them that she had been forced to discover through difficult means. She hardly knew him anymore. And even if she did trust Raoul, could she trust Simon, the storyteller? The man that had killed Edmond?

"If you intend to meet Raganor, you should know that he will not kill you. He is a lot of cruel, twisted things, but he values his bloodline above all else. I can only recommend that you play his game as long as you can, and when it is time, know that you are not alone."

"And what if Raganor himself is dead? What becomes of your Order then?"

Simon's gaze flicked over her. "You intend to kill him yourself then. That is your plan." His eyes met hers. "Greater men than you have failed to bring down Raganor le Brun. I must say, you have more courage than I anticipated."

"There are only so many times my family can be threatened." Eleanor straightened, her exhausted mind struggling with the flurry of emotions all this information had brought forth.

Simon merely studied her. "Must be hard, lonely, being that strong all the time." He furrowed his brow. "It's an easy trap for a knight to fall into. Being in charge, in control, yet on alert with a thousand doubts." With a last slurp of his stew, he rose. "I will see you in a few weeks, Lady Eleanor. Now it is your turn to keep our secrets."

Chapter 38

Raoul watched the old man across the tavern. So far, he seemed oblivious to his presence. Raoul let his hood fall over his eyes a bit more, shrugging into the cloak as if he were cold, though the thumping blood in his veins actually had him quite comfortable. He'd been this way for the better part of an hour, as long as it took him to finish his stew and half a mug of ale. All that time, the man across the room had been deep in conversation with another familiar face, another member of the order that hailed from colder Nordic lands.

Raganor looked like Montag. Though his face was lined with age, his hair was only streaked with white, maintaining that dark color that matched Raoul's own. It was the eyes that reminded him the most of Montag. They were as dark as caverns, even from across the room. Big, empty holes full of monsters.

His imagination was getting the best of him. Raganor was only a man. He ate and drank like everyone else. He had a noticeable limp that required the use of a cane.

He smoked that pipe regularly, and even from across the room, Raoul could tell it was no ordinary substance in there. Whatever it was seemed to calm and invigorate Raganor all at once, at least judging by how animated the conversation was. Right now, it was quiet, and the pipe was out. The two men seemed to have reached some conclusion.

It was likely that the members of the order would all decide to proceed with the initiation. All his speeches about dissolving the organization had been for naught. One hour with Raganor, and the members were thirsty for blood again, even knowing there was a fifty-fifty chance their own descendants would be on the table. Why? Wealth. Power. Some men hungered for it, an itch that could never be satisfied. Raoul understood the urge. He enjoyed managing his estates, enjoyed leading men. But would he sacrifice his own child to maintain that? No. Did he want more, to rule the world as it were? No.

Raoul ducked his head into his shoulder as the Viking descendent walked past. Raoul was not recognized. Just another man in a crowded tavern. He'd dressed in plain clothes, taking a play from Simon's habit. When he raised his eyes back towards the table in the corner, Raganor was gone. His heart pounded. Where had he gone?

Raganor's cane smacked across the table with a ferocity that made Raoul flinch. "So busy trying to make people unaware, that you are caught unaware." Raganor smiled, but it lacked mirth. It was merely that his lips turned up. "I am glad we get to speak at last, Grandson." Raganor slipped into the chair across from Raoul.

Raoul pushed his hood back, meeting his grandfather's dark gaze. "How long did you know I was here?"

"Since you finished your dinner. I could feel your eyes on me. The mark of the family is on you. We stamp our sons well." Raganor leaned forward, a sparkle in his eyes. "So. What nagging questions have drawn you from your mountain refuge, across France, to sulk in a tavern like a vagabond?"

There was no point in hiding that this was not a chance meeting. "I got the letter, like everyone else. We're all headed to another initiation."

"Of course. There is a place that has gone far too long without being filled. I appreciate you waiting for my return, that I may select the new member."

"Of course," Raoul lied. He suspected Raganor saw right through it. Just in case he didn't, let him believe he was as loyal as ever. He tapped his knuckles on the table, feigning worry. "You see, we also had the dilemma of the potion. With Montag gone, no one was sure how to make it. Yet we know it is essential for the ceremony."

Raganor pursed his lips, likely weighing the truth in Raoul's words. He would not find fault. The master of the ceremony was the one to make the brew, which had been Montag in Raganor's absence. He had not taught another, whether it be for the security of his own position, or a desire to dissolve the order himself on his passing. Perhaps it was a mere act of insolence. Perhaps it was because Raoul had burned everything in Montag's study that could possibly have held the old potion recipe.

"We must remedy that," Raganor said quietly. His eyes raked over Raoul, studying him. Raoul made his face a mask of eagerness, letting Raganor see only what he wanted him to see. His years living with Montag had trained him for this moment, now the ultimate test, for if Raganor saw through him, there would be no other plan. "It would be good to keep the successor in the family."

"I hoped you would say that."

Raganor nodded slightly. "Fine then. I will teach you how to make it."

Raoul's smile was genuine.

Raganor pursed his lips. "I heard you brought back my banner, with the stag."

Raoul shrugged. "Welcome back."

The old man's eyes twinkled. "Will you be married under that crest? Or your father's?"

Raoul straightened. He could not admit that he didn't intend to marry. Not if he wanted Raganor to believe he wished to keep The Order alive as its next leader. "I haven't met the right woman yet."

"Well, we can surely remedy that." Raganor snapped his fingers at a passing tavern maid. She paused at the edge of the table, pitcher of ale in hand. Raganor slipped the pitcher from her hand with a touch of fingers as light as a caress. It sickened Raoul, as he knew what else those hands were capable of. The maid took her coin and walked away, a flush in her cheeks. Raganor poured the ale. "We will talk about what type of woman you like. But first, you must tell me more about your cousin. I hear she wishes to join us."

Raoul's mask of indifference slipped, if only for a second, and Raganor smiled. The trap had been set and closed without Raoul even knowing. He could now thrash about, or he could lay quietly and wait to be released.

"It sounds like you already know more than I do," he said carefully.

"Perhaps about the future. But you know her character. Do you think she is able to follow through? Is she a knightess, or is she a mere woman, playing a man's game?"

Raoul exhaled the stale breath he'd been holding. "For her son, she'll follow through. At any cost."

"As I hoped." Raganor's toothy grin flashed across the table like the snarl of a wolf.

Raoul forced his mask into place. This was going to be a difficult conversation to navigate. And they had the whole night to go.

Chapter 39

A few days later, in Poitou, Eleanor steeled herself, her nerves alive as she crossed the street. She took in every sound, every smell. Her eyes darted around, watching for anything or anyone that seemed out of place. She straightened her back as she pressed through the door to the Boars Head Tavern, instantly overwhelmed by the smells of smoke, body odor, and roasting meat. The volume of chatter seemed normal, and the tavern was as full as one would expect at noontime during a tournament day. She squinted as her eyes adjusted to the dim light, focusing on the man in the corner whose eyes were already on her. He was exactly where he had told Giselle he'd be.

With her lips in a thin line, she approached, stopping before him across his small table.

For a long moment they studied each other. Eleanor took in the deep lines of his face and the neatly trimmed grey beard, which did little to mask the black glare of the man's eyes or the twist of a cruel-looking mouth. She didn't miss how his gaze flicked over her from head to toe, lingering a second longer on her sword, and reflecting his amusement. She had no inclination to sit down, and he didn't offer. He merely stared her in the eye, pulling a long drag from his pipe.

"Rumor has it you are my granddaughter," Raganor said in a low, rumbling voice.

"If you are the father of my mother, so it would seem," Eleanor echoed.

"There isn't much of her in you." Raganor studied her emotionlessly. "Beauty, yes, but it is different. She was fair, delicate. You...you are dark, solidly built. Like me."

"Montag used to say I look like my father. He hated it."

"He was right. And I hate it, too." He took another long pull from his pipe, then motioned for Eleanor to sit. With the grace of a noblewoman, she obeyed.

"You've returned from Jerusalem for good?" Eleanor asked quietly.

"For now. I have missed quite a bit here in France it seems."

Eleanor bit her tongue and stayed quiet, her palms sweating. His dark gaze was unnerving.

"Drink?" Raganor motioned to a server, who quickly brought over a pitcher of ale before scurrying off.

"No, thank you."

Raganor poured himself a cup. Without looking at her, he casually said, "I hear your husband killed my son."

Eleanor stiffened. "He didn't."

"Oh?" Raganor leaned back in his chair, sipping his ale, watching her again with that unblinking gaze.

He was casual, emotionless. Mention of his son's death didn't stir a twinge of grief or regret from him. Eleanor narrowed her gaze. Alec was right, this man was the most dangerous sort. He did not feel. Instead of that knowledge frightening her, something clicked into place, just like it did on the battlefield. Her senses sharpened. The seconds slowed. She thought faster. She played his game.

"I killed him."

"Really now?" Raganor raised an eyebrow, but it was a scripted move. Eleanor suspected he already knew this.

"I'll do anything to protect my family," Eleanor said quietly.

The old brow furrowed. "Is an uncle not family?"

"He left me no choice. He threatened my son and my husband."

"Is an old grandfather family?"

"It depends on if that grandfather acts like family. Or if he acts like an enemy."

Raganor smiled in genuine amusement.

"At least the stories of you are true, Eleanor."

"I hope the stories about you are not," she replied, keeping her gaze steady, her face impassive.

"Oh, they probably are," Raganor said with a smirk. A glint returned to his eyes, like a spark of flame in a dark forest.

Eleanor frowned. "Why are you back in France?"

"I can't ally with my granddaughter? The famous Knightess of Aquitaine?"

"I do not align myself with men I do not trust, Lord Raganor." He exhaled a mouth full of smoke in her direction, and she blinked as it stung her eyes and nose but did not wave it away. Whatever drug was in that smoke was strong and gave her a heady, light feeling. She fought it, but it was distracting.

"If you do not trust me, and you do not wish to be my ally, then why did you agree to meet me? I must admit you are braver than your cousin. He sulked in a corner, hiding from me."

Eleanor hesitated, delaying the truth a little longer. "I didn't know you existed until a few months ago. Save Raoul, I did not know any other family still survived."

"Well, that's not truth now either, is it, Granddaughter?" Raganor's eyes grew blacker, his lips twisting cruelly. "Your son is your family." He exhaled another breath of smoke towards her absently, chewing the end of the pipe.

Eleanor felt a prickle up the base of her neck, that heart pounding tingle of danger. She listened to it and stood, hand on her sword. But her fingers trembled, and her legs felt weak. The panic quickened. "What is that?" she eyed the pipe dubiously, stalling as she waited for her legs to steady, one hand resting on the table in a manner she hoped appeared casual.

"Poppy, for my old aching joints. Laced with a few other things from the east. Extremely expensive. Once highly effective. Yet unfortunately I seem to have developed a tolerance for it over the years." He squinted at the pipe. "Once upon a time, a little wisp of this could put me to sleep. Now I may enjoy its pain-relieving benefits with little effect, though it takes a fortune of the stuff. How about you?" The black eyes stared into hers, and she dared not look away as her heart's pounding slowed, despite her conscious desire for her legs to run. "Why don't you sit back down, Granddaughter?" Raganor blew a last breath at her, searing her lungs, then set the pipe aside.

Eleanor had no choice but to obey as her mind and body swam in a fog. She dug her fingernails into her palms, using the pain to bring back focus. "Is this the part where you kill me?" Oddly, as her focus faded, the sounds of the tavern grew louder around her, more confused.

"Kill you? You are my blood. I have much better use for you alive." Raganor leaned back in his chair, appraising her. "Is it true you want to join The Order? I was pleased that Raoul was inducted, but he seems to prefer to take a more complacent role than what our family legacy requires." Eleanor's eyes grew wide, and she blinked rapidly at him. "I won't live forever you know. I need someone brave enough to take the place of leader. Now that Montag is gone—"

Eleanor shook her head. "He is gone years now."

"Like I said, your cousin has been complacent." He leaned forward. "He wishes to dissolve what our ancestors have spent centuries building. We need someone with ambition. You should join."

Eleanor shook her head again slowly. "I don't like the initiation." The drug was seeping into her bones. She wanted to panic, scream, run, but instead she felt like her body was too heavy to lift from the chair. This was not the plan. She had only intended to meet him, determine if his death was necessary. Even this meeting was beyond her. Raganor had been moves ahead of her. She should have listened to Simon, not hesitated. But wouldn't that make her just as dark as them?

"It's not as bad as it sounds. And here is the brutal truth, Granddaughter...you know too much. You either join us, or you will be part of the initiation in another way."

Perhaps she could yet reason with him. "If you are the leader, you can change the rules, change the initiation."

"But why? It has proven effective."

"Why? To stop murdering your fellow knights. I know what you expect me to do in the ceremony. And then you will in a few decades force my son to participate as well. You have the power to change all that. To use The Order for good instead of as a harbinger of death."

"You will understand the necessity of experiencing power over life or death in a few days. Regardless of what you choose—and I hope you will join us—you will gain that power."

"I don't want it." Eleanor found the strength to stand then, pushing back from the table. She stumbled a step before Raganor secured her in his arms.

"Too much ale," he said apologetically to the few patrons that noticed. They smiled and turned back to their own food and drink. Then, cane in hand, the other wrapped securely around Eleanor's middle with surprising strength, he pulled her through the back entrance and into the alley beyond. There a wagon waited, and before Eleanor could protest, her swords were unbuckled and she was laid gently amongst the cargo.

Her mind screamed in a moment of clarity, but it wasn't enough to combat the drug. Her tongue felt thick in her mouth, and she could only whisper, "Why?"

"Blood begets blood, Eleanor. You will see that our power comes from our bloodline, and due to your cousin's insolent chastity, you are the last of that bloodline able to breed. I am sure someone has told you the rarity that you are. Your boy is not enough. You will be inducted to the order, as the rarity you are, and I promise you, you will bear the most powerful heirs France, Europe, and the world have seen."

A tear streamed down Eleanor's face as she used the last of her strength to reach for him. But it wasn't enough. The wagon lurched forward and the drugs overcame her to a dark, terrifying blackness from whence she was not sure she would ever be able to awake.

Chapter 40

Much to Alec and Wilfred's frustration, Sir Jacques was not where Giselle said he would be. Giselle herself disappeared in London as she had promised, taking her loyal protegee Macarius with her. They wasted precious days looking for a man Alec had no desire to meet. He trusted Giselle though, and if she said Jacques knew something important, then he would have to be found. When Alec could delay no further, Wilfred split off to continue looking for Jacques—with plenty of reservations and protestations—while Alec crossed the channel for the fifth time in as many months in order to look for Eleanor.

She wasn't making things easy. Alec had been expecting it, and still his wife was so adept at her disguises that she had disappeared as soon as she left Earnblaec Castle. Now mind, she had Noir with her, who had the temper of the wind and the youth of Eden to speed them along, but it was her ability to transform that had thrown Alec off. He'd learned early on to start looking for Noir, not Eleanor. He made his way through Normandy and Brittany, riding in the shadow of her horse's reputation. From what Alec gathered in his travels, Eleanor had kept a steady lead on him by a few days. He was catching up, and from what everyone was saying, the "young man on a black horse" was doing just fine. She had made steady progress south. She had been cautious, which made him feel a bit more at ease. At least, until he got closer to Poitiers.

He now stood outside the tavern Giselle had told him to look for. Eleanor's giant black horse was in the stable. Was she inside?

He strode across the street, glancing around with heightened senses as he went. Perhaps they had underestimated Raganor. Everyone seemed ordinary. Too ordinary. He tucked into the smokey, dimly lit tavern, stepping to the side to study the guests. They all seemed engrossed in their own conversations. Nothing unusual, except Eleanor was not there. His eyes narrowed on the man in the corner, casually smoking a pipe. He caught a whiff of the exotic smoke and recognized it from that summer day in the market. Raganor.

Alec glanced around for Raganor's allies, but no one seemed connected to him. He stepped up to the man and stopped before him, hand casually on his sword, looking into his black eyes, which fearlessly met his own

"Have a seat, Sir Alec. It is about time we met."

An icy finger ran up Alec's spine, but he kept his face neutral. "Where is she?"

"How many times can a man misplace his family? First your son, then I hear the Lezays took your wife, and now you once again seem to have lost her. If I had your misfortune, I would stop letting them out of my sight. Have a seat, and I'll tell you where she is."

He was calm, too calm, but panic was what he wanted from Alec. So Alec sat, glaring, and waited.

Raganor eyed him emotionlessly, but his silence alerted Alec that he had not expected the calm, calculating man that was now seated with him. The Le Bruns were used to meeting fire with fire, not with ice. Alec had lived long enough with Eleanor to learn how to manage it.

"Is it true you love my granddaughter?" Raganor asked.

Alec blinked, the question catching him off guard as intended. "Yes."

"You've done a great deal for her rise in station. I don't know if you're a fool to allow a woman to surpass you in power, or if you're so arrogant you haven't realized she has."

Alec kept his face neutral, waiting.

Raganor again grew silent, blowing the smoke of his pipe into Alec's face. Alec fisted his hands in annoyance beneath the table.

"Why have you only had one child? Have you tired of her?"

"No." The man didn't deserve a further answer. He didn't need to know Eleanor had almost died and would likely never have another child. Thus, her loyalty to and ferocious protection of Benec.

Raganor chewed his pipe, the smoke swirling around him. Finally he yielded. "You are everything they warned me of, Sir Alec. I must admit, you may actually be up to my standard."

"For what?"

"The Order."

"What Order?" Alec allowed the corner of his lip to curl in amusement.

Raganor blew another breath of smoke Alec's direction.

"You're wasting my time," Alec finally insisted. "Tell me where my wife is. Did she meet you?" Another puff of smoke fanned his face, and he refused to blink as he glared at the old man.

"We met. She's traveling on."

Alec rose, hand on his sword, his anger controlled but visible now. Eleanor hadn't traveled on, since her horse was still in the stable.

Raganor eyed him up and down with something akin to surprise, then masked it once again behind indifference. "Castle Bergfried. The initiation begins in two days. You both need to decide if you want to join...or not."

"I'm not one of your bloodlines."

"Interesting. She didn't tell you."

Alec suspected this was just another ploy to confuse and delay him. He didn't have time for this. "Where is Castle Bergfried? What dutchy?"

Raganor shook his head, his face twisting not in a smile but some toothy snarl. "It lies not in a dutchy nor a kingdom. It lies where there is no law. Where the mountains meet the river, where the forest cannot grow, where the beasts of farm and field waste to nothing. The wealth there comes from the ground, in the form no man or nation would refuse." Raganor stood, meeting Alec eye for eye. "Follow the road to the end. Have your decision made before you enter."

For once in his life Alec was thoroughly confused. He hid the furrow of his brow too late, and Raganor seemed satisfied. He turned and exited the tavern, Alec quick on his heels. The old knight easily mounted his horse, the weakness in his legs non-extant while mounted. Alec looked for his own horse, which was still tethered where he had left him.

"How is she traveling if her horse is here? Raganor, how is she traveling!"

But the old man was cantering off down the road, heading north.

Alec cursed, mounted Ches, and followed him, but no sooner had he gotten to the edge of town when he lost the man. Had he doubled back? Stabled somewhere? Alec cursed, spinning his horse around in a wild circle. Raganor had disappeared. He was not on the north road; no one was. Alec ran a hand through his hair, pulling it, trying to concentrate. For all his travels, he had never heard of a Bergfried that was its own entity. Two days. That meant it had to be relatively close if Eleanor was also going to be there in that time. Who would know?

Raoul. The Lezays.

Alec groaned. They were a week's ride away.

Unless...unless they were headed to the ceremony as well. They had to be at one of the taverns nearby, just like Raganor. Alec didn't have time to check every one though. He had to find someone who knew everything, everyone.

Slowly Alec turned his horse back into the city, weaving the narrow streets until he came to a tavern with a broken sign dangling with the image of what was supposed to be a swan but more closely resembled a dying, brown goose. He dismounted, gritting his teeth. His horse secured, he wiped his sweaty palms on his breeches and pushed open the door. The overwhelming smell of perfume and wine filled his nostrils, overpowering the stench of sweat and sex.

The madame met him at the door, her face gaudy with paint. "Ah, sir, welcome. May I take your cloak?"

Alec made no move to unfasten it, holding off her eager hands. She seemed put out, but smiled encouragingly anyway.

"What are you in the mood for today, sir?"

"Is The Raven here?"

The madame eyed him suspiciously, but there was a flicker in her eyes that gave Alec hope that Giselle had indeed returned to Poitiers.

"The Raven flew. She doesn't work anymore."

"I'm an old friend."

She laughed. "You all are though, aren't you? I've got plenty of other lovely girls."

A young teenage boy ducked out of sight into a back room, but not before Alec recognized him as Macarius. Alec held out a coin to the madame worth more than his supper. "Please? I need to speak with her."

The woman's eyes narrowed on the coin, then flicked back towards him. She quickly pocketed it and leaned towards him, whispering. "Listen here, this is how this will go. You go out the back and down a block, outside the livery. I'll give her your name, and if she has a mind to see you, she'll meet you there. Otherwise, I don't want to see you in here again, clear?" Her eyes flicked around. "It's bad for business, having a girl here not working. The gentlemen get the itch for something they can't have."

Alec thanked her and did as she instructed. A few anxious minutes later, a woman with a shawl pulled over her head approached him.

"If you had anyone follow you, and you lead any one of them to me—"

"This is the third time you've returned to Poitiers, Giselle. You've made yourself predictable."

"I had to pick up the money I left here. I wanted to be out of this town days ago, but my horse has an abscess. It is the absolute worst week to be here. I walked into a nest of vipers. I can't leave until they do."

"Do you know where the ceremony is? Raganor described the Bergfried. But I don't know the area."

"You spoke with him?"

"Yes."

Giselle cursed. "So he's in town. The Lezays are a block down the street. I think I even saw Simon. All I need is the dead to start walking, and it's like a grand little reunion. Should have just bought another horse—"

"Giselle, please." He could not voice his urgency. If she didn't know the answer, he would stop at nothing to find it, but it might still be too late. Though if other members of The Order were in town, he had options. Like torturing it out of Elfroid Lezay.

"You go to her, and only one of you will come back alive."

"Who told you that?"

"You know how the ceremony works. Think about it. They've been luring you both all along."

Giselle didn't know about the bloodlines though. His lack of bloodline disqualified him. That meant there was a chance. "I have to get her out of there, before they use her."

Giselle's brow wrinkled. "Didn't you find Jacques?"

"No. Wilfred is looking. Would have been a lot easier for you to just tell us what is so important. And maybe I would have found my wife before it came down to this."

She reached out a hand and placed it on his arm. "You love her enough to die for her?"

"Yes."

"No hesitation..." Giselle mused. She looked both awed and saddened.

Alec grasped her arm, lightly. "If you know where she is, you must tell me."

"South." She closed her eyes. "There is a river, A small horse-trail follows it into the mountains. The Bergfried sits on top of the hill. Once you leave the woods, they will be watching you."

Alec gave her arm a squeeze. "Thank you." He turned to run back to his horse.

"Alec—" Giselle looked pained as she watched after him. "I hope she's worth it."

Alec looked back at her, his pulse racing. "She is."

Chapter 41

Raoul watched Alec and Giselle from the shadows, trying to judge what their relationship was. If Alec was being unfaithful to Eleanor, Raoul was quite tempted to change his plan and let the man die. But the conversation was chaste, emotional perhaps, but brief. Alec walked away with new determination. Raoul suspected he knew where he was headed. That would have to wait. First, he needed to speak with the dark-haired beauty standing outside the livery, watching Alec go as if it would be the last time she ever saw her lover.

They must have been lovers. Of course they were. She was The Raven after all.

Jealousy burned in the pit of Raoul's stomach like a brand. At the same time, a sorrow weighed on his shoulders that made his feet too heavy to lift. He could only stand where he was, watching the woman watch Alec. This was his own fault after all. He could have been the one that got her out of Alsace. He could have married her and damned the family name, run off in the name of love like his aunt and uncle had done ages ago. He had done nothing, and then it had been too late, and she had disappeared.

Her brown eyes found his, and their gazes locked. She recognized him instantly, as she tended to do, but that recognition did not register but for the lingering gaze, daring him to approach. Daring him to look away, pretend he didn't know her, pretend the past didn't exist or matter.

But all that did.

He took the first leaden step forward, then another. All the while, Giselle held his gaze. When he was in front of her, he still was as speechless as a child.

Then he bowed to her, holding it low until he could compose the emotion contorting his face. When he stood, a single tear was sliding down her cheek, unbidden. He had a hope it was for him, not Alec. He reached out, hesitated, then cupped her cheek in his palm, wiping the tear with his thumb.

Giselle threw herself forward, her arms tight around him. He held on to her as if the very wind could pull them apart. Then she pulled away from him and slapped him.

He smiled.

Her hands went to both sides of his face. Her gaze searched his, and he could only hope she saw everything she needed. He could not put it into words.

"You still love me." A statement, not a question.

"With all my heart," Raoul breathed.

"Then come back for me this time. After you save them. After you kill *him*. It is the only way we will all be free."

"You have feelings for Alec."

"I do. But his heart belongs to Eleanor. As does yours. So you know what you must do, for both of them. Then come back to me."

Raoul pulled her towards him, kissed her as if she was a rose in full bloom. "Stay hidden. Raganor is here." He hesitated. All these years. They had so much to talk about. So much to heal between them.

"I know." Her eyes said it all. She pulled her shawl higher up her head, covering more of her dark hair. "Hurry, before Alec bursts into something he's not ready for. He doesn't yet know who he is."

It didn't take Raoul long to catch up to Alec. He was buying provisions, checking his equipment one last time before riding out. Eleanor's horse was tethered next to Alec's. Raoul suspected where Eleanor was, and why she wasn't with Alec. Under the circumstances, their separation had been inevitable.

"I need to talk to you, Alec," Raoul called out. He stood in front of Alec's horse, hoping man or beast didn't have a mind to run him over.

"I'm a bit busy, Raoul. You see, your grandfather just kidnapped my wife. Why people think they need to continue to force her places is beyond me."

"That is why we need to talk."

"I am sick of *talking*! We had all winter to talk, and still you roll in your secrets and half-truths and refuse to tell me what I need to know. Now I know she is in danger, and I know where she is, and I am going to get her back, take her home! To hell with your secret organization." He adjusted his horse's reins and prepared to mount.

Raoul pulled the reins away from him, forcing Alec to stay on the ground. "Damn your pride, Alec. I'm trying to save your wife. Push aside our differences long enough to listen."

Alec straightened, glowering at Raoul like a feral horse debating the benefits of attacking a rough handler.

Raoul continued, meeting that glare with one of his own. "Do you love her?"

"Of course I do."

"Do you love her enough to die for her?" he said more gently.

Alec narrowed his eyes. "That is the second time I have been asked that today. Yes."

"It is too late to keep her out of the ceremony. They will use her, one way or another. They have to. She can join us, and she will be bound to silence by her own deeds in a way there is no coming back from. Only if she joins us will she survive. If she does not wish to join—you will be the one to kill her. I tell you this, for you must understand. You are past the point of rescuing her."

Alec glowered. "I *will not* be the one to kill her. I have no idea what you are talking about. I will get her out of there—"

"No. If you get her out, they will hunt her, kill her later."

Alec thought for a moment. "Even if it is years later, that is how it works, isn't it? That is why Raganor had her father killed in tournament. He saw part of the ceremony."

"Yes. Sometimes it takes us years to track down those who find us, but they all die in the end."

Alec's hand clenched into a fist. "Then she must join."

Raoul inhaled. "She needs a sacrifice. You must volunteer."

"I thought the sacrifice had to be one of the bloodlines." Alec furrowed his brow.

Raoul looked Alec in the eye. How had they gone this long and no one had told him? Roric Lezay said he'd told Eleanor. Had she failed to tell Alec? Was she hoping to keep him away, or was she so desperate to join that she was willing to do it, kill her husband? Giselle even knew...hadn't she told Alec? Raoul hesitated to the point where Alec looked annoyed and started adjusting his reins again. He had to know, even if Raoul took the brunt of his fury. And fury there would be, for Raoul was the absolute last person who should inform Alec of his ancestry. How he took this news would reveal everything, if he could handle the task Raoul had in mind or if everything would unravel.

"Alec, you *are* one of the bloodlines. You are an Earnblaec, the son of Sir Alfred of Homme. And he was a sacrifice."

Alec's brow furrowed, then he started to shake his head. "No, Lezay killed my father. It was highway murder. I heard him bragging about it."

Raoul kept his gaze level. "Lezay was there, with the whole Order. But the initiate dealt the last cut that day." He closed his eyes. "It was me."

Emotion roiled off of Alec in waves. *Let him snap*, Raoul prayed. *Let him kill me now, that I will not have to watch what is to come.* But then there would be yet another place available, another initiation...

"No—" Alec shook his head, brow furrowed. Suddenly the confusion lifted. "You traitorous, two-faced, lying bastard!" The air shook with the volume of his words, and Raoul could only smile weakly.

He decided keeping Alec focused on the present risks, not the past's grievances, was key. "If you are her sacrifice, Eleanor will be allowed to proceed with the ceremony. I think the two of you have the potential to pull a trick no one has ever been able to do. There is a chance—and I do not guarantee anything—that the potion to drug you will not work. I am the one making it, and there is a key ingredient I will omit. If you trust your wife to play along—for we cannot tell her this plan—then you may both be able to fight free. I, and several others, will back you and ensure Raganor falls, and we can regain control of the order. But if the potion works, if I am wrong and it puts you into a deep sleep, she will be forced to kill you. Or they will kill you both."

"She couldn't do that."

"She would to protect your son. Without the two of you, he is vulnerable. Different branches of The Order have already been fighting over who will educate him. They will want his allegiance. How many times have you had to fend off his capture?"

Alec stilled, fists balled at his sides.

Raoul had to make Alec understand what Eleanor, Giselle, Simon, and even the Lezays knew. This was bigger than Eleanor. Bigger than little Benec. This was about ending an ancient society that put power over morality, wealth over humanity. There was a heart of evil to The Order, and Raganor Le Brun was beating it. Only when he fell could the others speak out, do what needed to be done to dissolve or refashion the group to something of light.

Raoul was poised to be the one to do it. But everyone had to be gathered. Eleanor and Alec had to play their parts. Even if there was no guarantee that things would go to plan. If things had gone to plan, the other members would never have been stirred to another ceremony.

Anything could happen once the ceremony began. And Eleanor was a wildcard. Once Raoul knew a ceremony was inevitable, he had intended to speak with her, but Raganor had, of course, beat him to her.

"I ask you again, are you willing to die for your wife?"

Alec glared into Raoul's eyes. The depth of hatred coursed through him like a wave of burning oil. It took all of Raoul's resolve not to flinch back. Yet, he felt he deserved it, and if this final phase of his plan worked, he may yet be redeemed.

"Yes," Alec said evenly.

Raoul smiled lightly, somberly. "Then we all stand a chance. I promise you, neither of you will be without allies in that room." It was going to be a hell of a fight, and someone, even if it wasn't Eleanor or Alec, was bound to die. But if they could succeed, The Order could be dissolved forever.

Alec needed time alone. He needed to contemplate the possibility of his death. He tried to draw the courage to picture it being at Eleanor's hand. He couldn't. He also needed to somehow accept that Eleanor and Raoul were the ones keeping the secrets this time. He had sought revenge on the wrong man for the wrong thing. All along it had been Eleanor's beloved cousin, Raoul, who had killed his father. How long had she known?

It explained her actions over the past months, her withdrawal from him. She was right. She'd said in the Vexin forest that he'd killed the wrong man. That meant she'd kept this secret for months. He should have spoken to her, asked *her* things, not Giselle. What did she fear in telling him? That he would kill her cousin as he had Lezay? He scoffed. She was right on that. Did she somehow think he would stay away if he didn't know? Then she didn't know him like she should. He rubbed his forehead. Then there was the curse, and Benec, and the impossibility of bloodlines ever crossing to create progeny, which meant his son was not his son, a thought which required more space in his head than what was available at the present time.

The initiation was looming. Two days.

For all her anger at him, for all her independence and even despite her innate desire to protect their child, he could not picture her doing it. She was strong, but there were deeds that morality—love—required more strength *not* to perform. She was that kind of strong. She would fret and plan and do anything in her power to avoid the grisly task. Alec knew this. He would have to trust this. And if Raoul were to also be trusted, his insane plan might just work.

Still, just in case it didn't, Alec had to find his peace with God.

The cathedral of Poitiers was a massive building. He was familiar enough with the place that he knew the alcove he needed to head to, the shrine to St. George. He knelt there for some time, all too aware of the value of the minutes passing, and what they could mean for Eleanor. This was more important. He became lost in his prayer, pleading for a sign that Raoul's plan would work. He only vaguely recognized the rustle of clothing as someone joined him in the alcove. When he blinked his eyes open and rose to his feet, he looked. There, side by side, lips moving silently and eyes closed, were none other than Sir Wilfred Fyr Hors and Sir Jacques of Brittany.

Alec stifled his surprise and stepped back. He waited.

Wilfred was the first to rise, and when he turned to Alec, a smile played on his lips. He joined Alec as they waited for Jacques. When he too rose, his face was stoic. Alec dared not shed blood in a church, particularly when he was so desperate for God's assistance, but his hand still fell to the sword on his hip.

Wilfred clapped a hand on his shoulder. "He's with me. And we're with you."

Alec was too bewildered to form a question.

Wilfred smiled, a knowing look in his eye.

Jacques cleared his throat. "For the sake of time, let's cut this to the point. Your wife saved my life on Christmas, though she had every right to end it. I owe her. And I not only work for King John, I work for Lord Raganor le Brun. I know what he is capable of. I am sick of it. For Eleanor's sake, I will stand with you to end this."

"You are already a member?" Alec asked quietly.

"Yes. For many years."

Alec turned to Wilfred. "Then—you know?"

"Jacques found it necessary to tell me everything on our journey from England. I wish *you* had told me. Have you forgotten I am your brother?"

"Well—no…"

Wilfred smiled. "You miss my point. I am your brother. I am descended of the bloodline, even if I am a bastard. I have every right to be included in this little group, the same as you or Eleanor."

"Raoul just told me about our father. I didn't know the Earnblaecs are a bloodline, that he was a sacrifice." Alec realized that Jacques, too, as a member, must have been there. He closed his eyes to steady the anger that roiled. There was no point in letting emotion have a play now. "So what is your plan?" Alec asked. He did not trust Jacques.

"We go to the Bergfried. You have the hardest role." Jacques met Alec's eye with a seriousness that was reassuring. "As you are able, act the part. You will have to take the burns to be convincing. That will be painful, I am certain. If Raganor reacts as the other old members, the Dark Ones we call them, that part of the ceremony becomes euphoric, as if they are the ones drugged. He will be most vulnerable then. In the right moment, we will act, and Raganor will fall. Do you think you are man enough to last that long?" Jacques looked him up and down, judging.

Alec nodded once. It was getting even harder to trust him, but at least this plan seemed to complement Raoul's. And he would not tell him anything about Raoul's intentions, just in case.

Jacques continued. "I am going to ride ahead of you. I do not want to be seen with you." He looked Alec in the eye. "But I give you my word, Alec. You and Eleanor have allies. You are not going to be in the Lion's Den alone."

He seemed genuine. And as yet, it seemed as if he was not aware, at least entirely, of Raoul's very similar desire to pull The Order apart. Perhaps there was yet to be a power struggle for the new leadership. Alec turned to Wilfred. "What about your family? Marie and the children? You don't have to go."

Wilfred met his eye, not a trace of fear or hesitation evident. "Alec, I am a knight. This is what I was born to do. This time is even more important, for we fight true evil. Marie knows that. And she may not be as fiery as Eleanor, but Marie is the strongest person I know. She will manage, and she will thrive, regardless of what happens here. Knowing that is what gives me the courage to be here. I do this as much for her, for my sons, as you do for Eleanor and yours. We will pull this group apart from the inside out."

Alec looked at the two men, then turned back to the cross beneath which he had prayed. If this was an answer to a prayer, it could not be clearer.

To vanquishing evil then.

Chapter 42

E leanor blinked her eyes open. Her mind remained foggy, though now it seemed her other senses functioned again. She was in a stone room, with a stone floor, stone ceiling. She squinted. It was round, as was the opening above her head where a dim light shined in through the domed ceiling. She realized it was daylight but overcast. She tested her arms and legs, and they moved on her command. With a sigh of relief, she recognized she was not bound. She sat up slowly, clenching the edge of the stone bench she was on as a mild dizziness came and went. At least nothing hurt. Not even her normal aching muscles. She looked around the room a little more closely. A doorway straight ahead, doorless. The room was maybe fifteen horses wide, windowless but for the round hole in the ceiling, and unfurnished but for the central slab she sat on. She looked down and suddenly leapt to her feet in terror, pressing her back to the wall, staring. She'd woken on an altar.

Her heart pounded so loudly in her ears that she didn't hear the footsteps coming from the doorway until it was too late. Raganor stood in the entry, one hand on his sword, the other on his cane, his black eyes glittering with an excitement that sparkled more than the gloomy sunlight. "You're awake!"

"Where are we?" Eleanor said quietly, trying to check her panic.

"This is the Bergfried. The Order will begin arriving shortly." Raganor smiled, but there was no warmth in it. "Have you decided in which capacity you would like to participate?"

"I don't want to participate at all."

Raganor shook his head, and she knew they had already been through this. The first time she'd woken in the back of the wagon, the driver had told her if she obeyed he would let her stay conscious. Of course she had fought him. She was just about to steal the horse and wagon when Raganor had ridden up. He'd promptly killed the driver—she knew now not to underestimate his strength despite his age—and then turned the sword on her. Faced with death, Eleanor suddenly very much wanted to live. She thought of Alec, Benec, and her friends. It was easy to be brave and say you were willing to die for someone. It was another thing entirely to do so in a foolish manner or without a fight. So she had stilled herself, obeyed Raganor. She let him bind her wrists. She rode in the wagon next to

him for several hours as he gave her a long description of
the ceremony to come. Even then, when he asked how she
would like to participate, she told him she wouldn't.

She'd thought about fighting him then, ending it all.
As if he read her mind, he told her his death would
stop nothing, only require another member to have to
be initiated. Remembering Simon and Raoul's plan, she
stilled her hand. But Raganor didn't trust her, and when
the pipe came out for a second time, she could not avoid
the smoke, and thus ended up asleep in the back of the
wagon again. That is, until she woke in the round room
of the Bergfried.

Now he was asking her for a final time how she would
like to participate, and she knew that if she did not decide
this time, he would make the decision for her. Really,
his intention was clear. There was only one answer. He
wanted her as their newest member, regardless of who had
to die to place her in that position.

Raganor strode to the altar, stroking it affectionately.
Eleanor stiffened her spine against the wall of the circular
chamber. The cold stone chilled her as much as his
presence.

Raganor's yellowed teeth flashed. "A thousand years
ago, there existed a brotherhood of men. Some were
kings, some warriors, some tradesmen. All powerful,
all ambitious, and all desiring one thing...power by the
cooperation of multiple kingdoms. When they met, they

met as equals. They cooperated, regardless of what their allies wished. It was a group that transcended all other hierarchies. Thirteen men. Sometimes the troubadours called them the Knights of the Roundtable. But do not mistake our Order with the legends of King Arthur. We are more than that."

Raganor paced, watching Eleanor out of the corner of his eye. She kept her face as emotionless as possible. "For these centuries past, we have continued to hold thirteen members, all of the original bloodlines. The Le Bruns are descended from the original founder. It gives our family a bit more—prestige shall we say?"

"I thought it was a round table?" She looked around the round room.

"Blood has its own power, regardless of how we try to equalize things. Men aren't created equal."

Eleanor bit her tongue to keep from arguing back. She wasn't even a man, so where did that leave her?

Raganor looked to the altar. "When we induct new members, to keep our number at thirteen, we put them through the ceremony. Each member stands witness for the others, knowing the sins each has committed in their dedication to the cause. It inspires a transformation as it pulls our new members into the brotherhood." Raganor whirled towards Eleanor, spryer on his feet than his age should allow. "You do not want to die, Granddaughter. Join us."

Eleanor swallowed, forcing herself to meet her grandfather's black eyes. So dark they were, as if they had no pupils. She blinked, forcing herself to be brave. Taking Montag's life had been different than what was being asked of her. She and her family had been threatened. To take an innocent man's life in cold blood was such a greater crime; of course that was why they did it. It made sense that every member would seal his lips for all the others after they witnessed such a thing. Raoul...he had done it, too. To Alec's father. The thought made her sick. Sicker still was the thought of who Raganor expected her to kill.

Eleanor's stomach churned. "Alec doesn't know."

"Sir Alec Earnblaec will come." Raganor smiled. "He loves you."

Eleanor paled, but still stubbornly shook her head.

Raganor looked out over the valley. "Love makes fools of the bravest men."

"He won't do it. And neither will I. Then what will you do?"

"We kill you both. Wait for the next two progeny to be knighted. Simon's two boys will be ready in the next year or so. Won't that be fun...two brothers. I wonder who will fill what role. And of course, without you, your son will be raised by me. He will certainly be made ready for the task of leading The Order, unlike you or Raoul."

Eleanor fisted her hands, her back to the wall. Let Alec not come. Let him take Benec and hide. And yet she knew him better than that. He would come.

Raganor left her, the click of his cane echoing down the corridor. Eleanor leaned her head against the wall, shaking. Then she slowly slid to the floor. It had seemed so simple to cut the head off the monster. Now she understood why no one, even Montag, had yet done it. Raganor wasn't just a man; he was a force. Perfectly ruthless, blinded by power, and with enough men backing him to be invincible, she had greatly underestimated him. She knew that alone she could not bring him down.

Nor could she kill Alec. Would he kill her to spare himself? She lingered on that thought, thinking back to his anger a few weeks ago. Maybe he could do it. He would have to.

The distant whinny of a horse sounded from outside.

She pulled herself to her feet and straightened her clothes and hair. She would act until the very last moment. She had to. She had to hope that if her own plans failed, Raoul's would not.

She was not confined, so she walked out, following the passageway into a huge circular courtyard. The Bergfried tower loomed overhead, practically carved into the stone of the mountain they stood on. The air was chill and damp, the wind whistling through the stonework of the towers around her. A thin line of river wound through the valley below. She stepped to the wall and could see the small dots of riders in the distance, headed their way. She glanced to the sun, but it was obscured, making it impossible to tell how many hours of daylight remained. She wrapped her arms around herself, continuing to study the fortress, which even in its opulence was perhaps only a quarter of the size of Brunstein.

Perhaps that was the problem. In its simplistic layout, it was a fortress, and there was no escape.

The wind gusted up around Eleanor, lifting the strands of wild dark hair that had worked loose from their plaits. The air was damp with fog, a smell of rot from mud and decayed vegetation appropriate as the talk of death in the air. For months, she had warred within herself, wondering what her new role in life would be, at times so frustrated she did not care if she lived or died. Now, with the possibility at her feet, she cared. She remembered who she was, the knightess that did not give up, the woman that sang with the resilience of a sword, standing strong no matter how many blows came crashing down. She would defend and protect until that dying breath. And that would not come today.

There was no escape. This Bergfried had only one path in and out, and there were members of The Order riding that path at this very moment. She would not risk her life scaling a sheer cliff. No, she would have to stay and see this through, however the coming events played out. That thought gave her a sense of peace, and her pounding heart steadied. The decision was made. She would trust Raoul until it was time to act, and then she would fight if need be.

She looked to Raganor, who stood only a few feet away, watching the riders come, his cloak swirling around him. The man may be old, but as his demonstration with the wagon driver had shown, he did not appear easy to kill. It was obvious where Montag and Raoul's size came from. Even lean with age, Raganor towered over Eleanor. And she knew better than to underestimate that cane. One blow to her head could compromise everything.

"Where is my sword?" she asked Raganor, gauging his reaction.

"In the upper tower. There is also a dress for you. It is not becoming for a woman to dress in a man's clothes." He did not look at her, his gaze locked on the riders below.

Eleanor did not question further, but turned from him and entered the tower at the back of the courtyard, which rose even higher above the valley. The stairs spiraled up to a series of rooms, one of which did indeed have a green dress carefully laid across the bed, with Eleanor's sword and dagger next to it. She plucked up the blades, instantly grateful for the familiar feel of their handles. The room was basic, though the bed looked as if it would provide needed sleep, and a basin of fresh water sat across the room. On the table next to it was a decanter of wine and a bowl of bread and dried fruit. She ate and drank readily, knowing she would need all the strength and sustenance she could get.

Hooves clattered on the cobbles of the courtyard. She peered through the window. The first to reach the courtyard was an elaborately dressed, dark haired man who spoke to Raganor in rapid Spanish. The other was a man with a size as grand as her Uncle Montag's. He had a long blond beard and blond hair, which was braided back from his temples. He was dressed only in his tunic, as if he was hot, though a fur coat was strapped to the back of his saddle. Their greeting to Raganor was professional and deferential. Raganor was obviously their leader. They put their horses away and headed towards the tower as Eleanor watched a third rider crest the hill into the courtyard. Her heart pounded with a mix of trepidation and relief at the familiar face. Simon.

She watched him greet Raganor with a great show of respect when she felt eyes on her. She turned to see the blond man standing in the doorway, his eyes raking over her from head to foot.

The Spaniard whispered something and laughed as he sidled past and continued up the staircase. Still the blond stared.

"You don't deserve this room," he said, his accent thick and voice deep.

Eleanor shrugged. "You're welcome to it."

"No. It is for the inductee. We shall see how brave you are, if you can burn a man until the flesh stinks and melts, then listen to him scream as you administer the cuts to kill."

The food in Eleanor's stomach turned to stone.

"I told Raganor you don't have it in you," the Norseman continued. "He thinks you'll be the leader. I will not let a little girl be in charge over me. You will be dead on that table, if not tomorrow, then when Raganor is dead."

"At first I was told The Order is about cooperation, joining together to accomplish great deeds. From what I've seen, all you want to do is kill each other. Why not just end it all?"

The Norseman's eyes shown with an eager spark and he raised a fist. "Power." Then he turned and continued up the stairwell. A few seconds later, Eleanor heard a door shut.

She hastened to her own door, intent on shutting it, but Simon caught it with a hand.

"He's still alive, I see." Simon's eyes twinkled.

"You could have warned me about the pipe."

"What pipe?" Simon inclined his head. He looked genuinely ignorant.

"Oh, never mind." Eleanor moved to shut the door a second time, then paused. "News of Alec?"

"Everything is running to plan."

That did not reassure her.

Simon smirked. "The members will arrive overnight into tomorrow afternoon. Then it will begin just before dark. I suggest you sleep while you can." He eyed the room behind her. "And maybe bar this door? Raganor has been playing matchmaker with every member of the order that isn't already locked into marriage. More than a few want a glimpse of the knightess."

He continued on, and Eleanor hastily did as he said and barred the door. She returned to the window, belting her blades to her waist. On impulse, she snatched the dress off the bed and threw it out the window, watching it flutter down to the rocks below. When she looked back to Raganor, he was watching her, an amused look on his face. She shut the window and turned away. She poured more wine. She would need her strength.

Chapter 43

Raoul arrived at the Bergfried at high noon on the day of the ceremony. Only a few hours until it would all be over, for better or worse. About half the order was already there. The Lezays and their quiet friend Heinrich stood to one side of the courtyard, watching him with wary eyes. One of the Spanish lords was deep in conversation with the big Norse prince, both of them dressed in their finery as if they were heading to a tournament. Simon stood off to the side by himself, plainly dressed as ever, his back pressed into a corner of the stone parapet as if he were invisible. To most of the others, he likely was. And then there was Eleanor, arms folded across her chest, her clothes lending the image of just another man within the group, though her unbound hair flew wildly around her in the cold wind like tendrils of black silk.

She turned to look at him, her expression pained, and then looked away. Raoul instantly felt guilty. Raganor likely had told her what was to come, and the role she would have to play. She didn't know there were any other plans. He could only imagine her sense of his betrayal in not explaining everything the day she'd ridden across kingdoms to ask. He had hoped it wouldn't come to this. He had to speak with her, lest she refuse to start the ceremony.

Two more knights cantered up, letting out a cheer as they scanned the courtyard. Jacques and one of the old veterans from the east. Raoul didn't know where they stood in the proceedings. Likely both with Raganor. Raoul suspected Jacques was one of the spies that gave Raganor his power.

Jacques' face fell as his gaze landed on Eleanor. "Why is a woman here?"

"Meet our newest inductee," Elfroid said from across the courtyard, bitterness evident in his tone. Raoul doubted his gift of a destrier had been enough to secure the other man's loyalty; he would have to be wary of Elfroid.

"Since when do we allow women to join?" Jacques protested. The look of distain he raked over Eleanor convinced Raoul that he was indeed on Raganor's side. Nothing to do about it. They'd fight it out soon enough.

"We have always allowed women to join, since the days of old." Raganor's voice boomed. "We just have not had a woman worthy for centuries. She is a knight."

The men stood straighter in his presence, and the courtyard went silent. More men rode through the gate, including the King of England. They tied their horses. As the men greeted each other, Raganor mingling amongst them, Raoul made his way to Eleanor.

"Alec must be the sacrifice. He must take the potion," he whispered.

She looked at him, her face blank. Good, at least she knew to feign indifference.

Raoul continued to scan the small group of men, as if they spoke of the weather. "This is your best chance. Your only chance. Alec *must* be the one."

"I cannot kill him."

"Now is not the time to fall in love."

"Who said it was now?" she looked up at Raoul, forcing him to meet her gaze. Raoul stared into her eyes, then gave a slight nod.

"Trust me. Everything will change tonight." Raoul looked to Raganor, who started making his way directly to them. His only grandchildren.

"Does he want me dead?" Eleanor asked.

Raoul shook his head. "I don't think he cares, as long as there is someone's blood on the ground." He looked at her pointedly. "Don't let it be yours." With that he turned and entered the passageway into the round room. The rest of the men followed suit, quieting their conversations as they entered that sacred space.

—◦❖◦—

Eleanor stood with Raganor, looking over the castle walls, her hair whipping around her, the blood thrumming in her veins. Could she trust Raoul, or was he only looking out for the family blood like Raganor wanted? Surely, some plan must emerge that would leave her a way out. But the sun was setting, even though the thick, gloomy cloud cover masked any glorious sunset. It was as if the very sky itself knew the dismal deeds about to be performed.

She shivered slightly. "He's not here." Even as she said the words, she saw another rider emerge from the forest below. He had a spare horse in tow that looked quite familiar, even from a distance. Noir.

"Have you made your decision?" Raganor looked out over the valley, his cloak swirling in the wind.

Eleanor took a shaking breath. What choice did she have? If Alec was there, then Raoul's vague plan was the best gamble. She could back out at the last minute. Though that would end in her own death and the fulfillment of Raganor's fantasy of raising Benec. "I will join."

Raganor's face broke into a wide grin. "Then let us begin."

Chapter 44

Eleanor looked around the room at the faces surrounding her. She felt like a treacherous queen at Raganor's side as his loyal subjects watched him expectantly, shooting looks at her with various degrees of distain, curiosity, admiration, and downright loathing. Her sword was in her hand, tip to the ground, mirroring the men that joined the circle.

Her eyes lingered on Raoul, willing him to meet her eye. He remained staring stubbornly ahead, his face grim, chin lifted in subtle defiance. Beside him was Simon, who had no trouble meeting her gaze. He stared openly, one lip curled in subtle mirth. His eyes sparkled when he noticed her return gaze. She held that gaze for a while, wondering if he had told her the truth or if his amusement was because she believed his lie. On the opposite side of the circle was Jacques. How had they not realized he was one of The Order? Perhaps he was the slyest member of all. Had she been a fool to save his life?

A glance at her grandfather made her shiver. He stood alert, a slight smile on his face, as if he had heard something. Eleanor's ears strained. Where was Alec? She didn't know what to pray for. She did not want him to come. And yet, if he did not, what would these men do with her? As they all had continually reminded her, she knew too much. Her eyes stared into the burning hearth near the altar in the center of the room. Sparks flared, rising towards the hole in the ceiling that took away the faint column of smoke. There was another sound, perhaps the logs shifting. But perhaps not, as the men of the room straightened, each head turning towards the corridor.

Alec appeared.

His sword was drawn, but he did not hold it to attack. He was alert yet calm. Dressed in full knightly regalia, the black hawk emblazoned on his green tunic somehow made him appear even larger, stronger.

Eleanor's heart pounded on.

Eleanor was the first one Alec saw. She looked as beautiful as ever, strong, straight-backed. There was a determination in her face that reassured him. He did not know what she knew of what was to unfold, but he knew she would fulfill her role in it, no matter the cost. Now he could only hope that Raoul and Jacques had not lied to him, that they had not merely seduced him to this place to ensure their own dark plans would rise to fruition. He longed to go to Eleanor, to tell her everything, but he stilled his feet. There would be time enough for that after this was finished.

He scanned the rest of the faces, many of which he recognized. King John eyed him with quiet recognition. Ah, so he was a member as well. That explained his interest in Benec. Which side was he on though? Then there was the crippled Sir Jean fil de Jean, who had been nearly killed by Wilfred in the melee a few years back. He seethed with a look of pure hatred; there would be no ally there. The two Lezays and Sir Heinrich watched with curiosity. Elfroid avoided his gaze. Where did his true loyalties lie, with his family or with Raganor, who promised power? Raoul stood to the far left, his frown deepening by the minute. Simon and Jacques looked indifferent. The circle was finished out by several grizzled men of obvious wealth. A richly dressed Spaniard and a tall blond man that reminded Alec of Viking tales stood among them.

Kings and lesser knights, together as equals in a circle of power, with Raganor the only man breaking that line. Alec let his gaze fall back to Raganor. The old man's eyes simply sparkled with excitement.

"You told me I could join." Alec met those eyes, which were black as the night that had fallen outside.

"We would take you only if Eleanor declined. She has accepted. The sacrifice *must* be you."

Alec looked to Eleanor, his eyes boring into hers. She stood straight as an arrow, her eyes locked to Alec's. "So this initiation she must pass...she has to murder me in front of all of you? In front of my own king?" He again looked to King John, who avoided his gaze. Even a king did not have power here.

"Every man here is witness to the others' crimes, and them his own. It ensures our existence remains secret, and that our bonds to each other remain as thick as the blood spilled." Raganor straightened, the darkness of his soul reveling at the thought, unable to hide his eagerness.

Alec grew silent, the circular room starting to feel like it was closing in around him. Though he had been told what to expect, he felt the finality of Raganor's words as if they were fresh. At least half of this group yearned for blood. Even if Raoul and Jacques had told him the truth, would they be strong enough to fight off the others? Were their alliances as strong as they thought? His palms sweated, his mind steaming and coming to the same conclusion each time.

He turned to Eleanor. "For your future, I accept."

She blinked at him, then closed her eyes. When she met his gaze again, there was a spark of ice there, his English Winter. Even if he could count on no one else in the room, he knew then that he could count on her.

Raganor turned to Eleanor. "Do you wish to join The Order?"

Eleanor's voice was steady. "Yes."

Raganor lit up with excitement, swirling towards Alec, his cloak fluttering around him like bat wings. In a second, he had snatched Alec's sword from his hand. He threw it carelessly against the foot of the altar. He rubbed his hands, limping back towards Alec. "Shall we begin?" He gestured toward the altar.

Would you die for him? Make sure he takes the drink. Protect your son. Two bloodlines. One must be the sacrifice. Would you die for him? Protect your son. Give him the drink.

Eleanor felt dizzy as she stood in front of Raoul. He held the cup in his hands. As she reached for it, his strong hands lingered on hers, giving her a squeeze that brought her out of her panicked circle of thought and forced her to meet his eye.

Make sure he takes the drink, Raoul had warned.

She gritted her teeth and took the cup. Who did she trust? There was no time left now to make the decision. She quickly turned and approached Alec, the chants of the men around her increasing in volume. Alec sat on the edge of the stone slab, watching her expectantly, no trace of fear in his eyes.

He could not be that fearless.

She halted in her steps. Was he that brave? Did he know something she did not? Who did she trust?

Under Raganor's direction, she acted her role. She gave Alec the drink, her hands shaking. He laid back on the stone, his muscles relaxing, eyes closing as if his body would mold into the altar. She knew that body so well. Every scar, every curve of muscle. She knew what those hands felt like on her bare flesh. She knew what his sweat tasted like, what he smelled like after weeks on a horse or fresh out of a stream.

She looked away.

Someone took the cup from her hands and replaced it with a red-hot iron. The heat radiated down the metal to her hands, and she focused. This part Raganor had described carefully. She could not falter. The quicker the better. He was drugged; he would not feel anything. She hoped.

How could you not feel flesh burn and sizzle?

A few of the knights rolled Alec onto his stomach. His body was limp. Was he dead? No, he breathed. The timbre of the chant grew, and Eleanor stepped forward. She lifted the iron, red tip glowing, and lowered it for the first mark on his shoulder blade. The flesh smoked, a hiss barely audible over the voices. Alec flinched. She drew the iron back, alarmed. No, he was still. He had not cried out. He felt nothing. She took the next hot poker and made the second mark. Hardly movement, but it was there.

She scanned the circle. No one else seemed to have noticed. Perhaps this was normal, an involuntary reaction. She took up the third. This was a visible flinch, and yet still he did not cry out. Eleanor shot a look at Raoul. He gave her a subtle nod, his lips continuing the chant with the others. It was then that she realized what Raoul had done; he had altered the drink.

Alec felt everything.

Eleanor sucked in a quick breath, her senses sharpening. Yes, they had a plan. And apparently this was part of her role. She reached for the next iron, and then the next, making the series of burns as quickly as she could until the constellation was complete. The smell of burned flesh turned her stomach, but there was no time for that now. She felt the bloodlust surge through her veins as it had the night she had fought Montag. The whole room knew what the next part of the ceremony would be.

She reached for the stimulant, a sharp smelling herb, and held it at arm's length, her nose burning from it. Alec was rolled onto his back, and then she held out the bundle to him.

"Wake," she said quietly, no longer certain if he would know what reactions he was expected to have to these drugs.

He blinked his eyes open, and she discarded the bundle into the fire, where it sparked and filled the room with a diluted, sweet smell. The effect on the knights of the room was immediate. Their eyes sparkled; their feet shifted with the energy. Now was the crux of the ceremony, the thirteen cuts, the very last of which would take Alec's life.

She picked up her sword and approached the altar, positioning herself as Raganor had instructed. The chant cut off, silence ringing in the room. No one moved to stop her. She dared not look at Raoul.

"Do it!" Raganor shouted, the anticipation of blood lacing his words with a darkness that seemed to reach its fingers towards her hand.

Would you die for him? Giselle's question echoed.

Eleanor leaned over Alec and pressed her lips to his, one last time. She felt the stubble of his beard against her lips, tasted the sweat that beaded there.

And Alec's lips moved against hers, with all the promises he had made her. *Protect. Hope. Persevere.*

She smiled down on him, then let the hilt of the sword slip down to his right hand. As one, she stepped back as he burst to his feet, roaring like a lion let out of a cage.

Raoul's heart hammered in his chest as he watched Eleanor slide across the stone altar and pluck Alec's sword from its base. As one, they met Raganor's furious attack. Raoul should have expected it. She had timed the moment beautifully. As the rest of the members stirred to action by

Raganor's scream of "Kill them!" he and Simon entered the fray, swords flashing as they held back those they could from Alec and Eleanor. Raoul registered another man run in from the corridor. He moved to stop him but was distracted by the Spaniard, who swung a flash of metal towards Raoul's head.

Simon shouted from somewhere to his right, "We have an invader!"

"He's with us!" Jacques' voice carried across the room.

Raoul looked over, his opponent equally distracted. Jacques was fighting two of Raganor's most loyal supporters.

The Spaniard growled at Jacques. "You traitor!"

Jacques smiled, shoving back his other opponent, the big Norseman.

Alec's back felt like it was on fire, and the drugs had made everything sharper, the initial haze now burned away. That was why the sacrifice had to be done quickly. In their cruelty, the potion was designed to dull the senses only long enough to let the victim be harmed, that in the final moments before death, during death, the senses would rush back a thousand-fold. He was supposed to have his neck open already, feeling his blood run from his body, hearing the drip of it onto the stone, seeing every spark reflect in his tormentors' eyes. But he was whole. And now he sensed every movement of the men around him as they debated what to do in this change of events. He saw every twitch of Raganor's muscles.

Raganor's face warned Alec of his action as he brought his sword swinging up toward Alec's middle. Alec leapt back with a champion's agility, ready again for the man to attack. Raganor pursued, stalking Alec.

Alec blocked another blow, spinning away towards Eleanor. Eleanor fended off a weak attack from Jean fil de Jean. As Raganor raised his sword again, Alec swung hard, knocking the blade aside, then slammed into him with his shoulder. The old man tripped on his bad leg, falling hard into a cluster of fighting men. He yelped in pain as swords grazed him.

Alec made it to Eleanor's side, fighting back-to-back with her as they defended themselves from their attackers, bruising and cutting a few. Alec arrested his blow in time to merely wound the half-heartedly fighting King John. What would the aftermath of this fight be like? How many of the other men in this room were kings or equally as powerful?

"This is madness! Stop now!" Alec shouted.

Eleanor shouted from next to him. "You will all be dead, and then what? You will kill more of your own children to fill your places?" She staggered backwards after blocking a particularly hard blow from Elfroid.

No one was listening.

Raoul noticed that a few members fell back, the King of England among them, unsure who to fight. Meanwhile the fight in the center of the room was gaining intensity. Eleanor shoved off an opponent, pleading for the men to stop. Alec was distracted by Elfroid, who had betrayed his family to fight for Raganor. Raganor sidestepped towards Raoul, his limp noticeable though his legs held their strength. His shirt was cut in several places, crimson running. He had a gash over one eye that highlighted his furious expression. Raganor's focus was taken by the outsider who had entered their ranks and locked swords with him. He did not notice the blade Raoul stuck out, and when Raganor turned to avoid the outsider's blow, he impaled himself on Raoul's blade. The other man, unaware of his opponent's injury, pulled him back and shoved him across the altar, delivering a stab to Raganor's mid-torso.

"Stop!" Raoul bellowed.

The stunned Order obeyed, watching their leader struggle for breath. Not one of them moved to aid. Raoul knew what he had to do to take the leadership. One last slice across Raganor's neck, end his reign of terror, hasten his merciless death. His mother's words echoed, *Let it end with you.*

Raganor's black eyes met his, the cold glint yielding to fear, then fogging over. The old man fought, the reality of his death finally making him afraid. What did he see?

Make the blow, Raoul, his mind warned.

Eleanor looked back and forth between him and Raganor. Did she know the final deed? The outsider, who Raoul now recognized as Wilfred, stood alert, as if expecting Raganor to leap back off the altar. The Norseman stepped forward, expression resolved, hungry to take the title himself. Jacques stopped him.

"Someone has to claim the power," the Norseman protested.

"No." Jacques said, fire reflecting in his eyes. "Who among us wants *this* to continue? Who wants to see the next generation die at each other's hands as we have been forced to?"

The room again fell silent. The Norseman stepped back. Raoul stepped forward.

The dying man's gaze fell on him. His lip curled in the corner, a final challenge, a question of whether Raoul was truly a Le Brun. Did he deserve the family name? Raoul lifted his sword, meeting the old man's gaze. Behind him he heard a scuffle; he ignored it. He laid his blade along Raganor's neck, let it settle there.

A line appeared as thin as a blade of grass, as if made by a single sheet of parchment. The blood welled, spilled in a drop, then two. It was enough. It was the final blood. There was nothing in the traditions that said the final cut had to end the life. It only had to be made. And it was.

Raoul turned his sword point down and stood as he had when the ceremony had begun. The scuffle behind him had quieted, and he knew either Jacques or Simon had kept the other bloodthirsty members off his back. He let his voice find all the strength of his ancestry and let his words resonate within the round chamber. "We let the order die with him."

Eleanor stared at her cousin's back, noting the steel in his resolve, noting that Raganor still heaved for breath on the altar despite the line of blood that dripped from his neck. She wasn't sure what Raoul had done or why it was important, but the action had stilled the room of powerful men around her. One by one the other knights followed Raoul's lead and placed their sword tips down, starting with Simon and Jacques, then Roric Lezay, then Heinrich, and all the rest, even Raganor's allies. They formed a circle not unlike how the evening had begun and waited. With a glance between them, Alec, Eleanor, and Wilfred followed suit.

It did not take long, as the man on the altar before them shuddered, then stilled.

It was done. Raganor had not had as many allies as he thought.

Chapter 45

The quiet settled over the group as a fog settles in a valley. Eleanor felt as if she had to hold her breath, as even that was too loud. She flinched as Raoul began a chant, which when echoed by the members of The Order in their deep voices, made the room vibrate. She could not understand the words, but the intent was clear. There was power in those words. There was mourning and darkness. Then the song changed as Raoul carried on alone. The members stared at him, their eyes wide. They did not follow this song. It was as if they did not know it. It was as if Raoul sang to the sun, the urgency and power in his words making him appear larger than the man he was. What a group of twelve had created, Raoul now carried alone. Eleanor watched as his eyes closed in concentration. One by one, the members averted their eyes, like dogs submitting to the alpha. Whatever his words, the members understood that he alone knew them. It was the last part of tradition he needed to finalize his claim as Raganor's heir.

Eleanor longed to step back into the shadows of the room, but she felt as if she was rooted in place, loathe to make any sound lest she distract Raoul. She looked to Alec, who watched Raoul with his usual, observant gaze. It was as if he knew exactly what he was witnessing. Wilfred's eyes had dropped like the rest of the group. Only Simon was left, watching Raoul with a clenched jaw. Then with the subtlest shake of his head, he let his eyes drop. As quickly as it had started, the chant cut off, the last note echoing in the chamber.

After only a heartbeat, the members turned as one and filed out without speaking. The trio remained staring after them, then at Raoul, who continued to face the altar and his grandfather's corpse. After a long moment, he turned to face Eleanor. His shoulders sagged as if the burden of power he had just accepted was a physical weight. There was a hint of a smile there, too, however faint.

He placed a finger to his lips, then waved them into the corridor. Once they were out of the round chamber, Raoul exhaled. Then he pulled Eleanor into his arms, his body trembling with emotion.

"I underestimated you, cousin," Raoul whispered to her, his voice thick. "I could not have done it without you." He pulled away from her. "Or you, Sir Alec Earnblaec." He held out his hand, and Alec clasped it. "I wish I had explained sooner, but I had hoped it wouldn't come to this."

Alec straightened. "Am I right in what I just saw? Are you now the leader of The Order?"

Raoul smiled and lifted his chin. "I am. And better yet, as the leader, I now have power to dissolve it."

"How?" Wilfred asked.

Raoul released Alec's hand and shook Wilfred's as well. "Sir Wilfred. Your contribution was so valuable. My cousin is lucky to have you as a friend." He released Wilfred's hand. "How, you ask? There were two parts to declaring my leadership. The last blood, which I drew. And that chant. There's not a member here who's ever heard it. None were here when Raganor took power all those years ago. They assumed it lost, and that power would transfer another way, perhaps by blood alone. But they cannot deny those words. There is history in that chant, an age of it and more. We are an organization birthed from history itself, from tradition. There is no question that I am meant to be leader." Raoul released Wilfred and began to stride out of the corridor towards the courtyard beyond.

"Did you get it from Raganor?" Eleanor asked, only a stride behind him.

"I found it in Montag's study, the night you killed him. I burned it that very night, after committing it to memory."

Alec rolled his shoulders, his burns shining in the torchlight. "You needed all this just to prove you are their leader?"

Raoul stopped, facing Alec. "They would have fought each other for years if I did not make it clear. They would have chosen the blood-born heir, the child of three bloodlines, if I did not make it clear that I am now the one in power."

"Benec," Alec said.

"Yes, Benec. That is why everyone wanted him. But now they have another leader." Raoul turned to head into the courtyard, then hesitated. "Think of me what you will, but I did not relish killing my own grandfather, monster though he may have been. I still wish there had been another way." He stepped out into the moonlight.

The members of the order were scattered around the courtyard in small groups, many deep in conversation. They turned to Raoul as he emerged, the trio trailing him.

Raoul raised his hands in greeting. "You know what has happened. You know what I now want."

The Norseman spat on the ground. "Was it even thirteen cuts? Or was it only half done?"

Raoul smiled. "I have no doubt that if you count, there will be thirteen. All of you contributed. He allowed himself to be passed among us."

Eleanor could tell by the members' faces that Raoul was right. Each of them remembered a moment when their blade had grazed Raganor. She knew her own had as well.

"Where'd you get the chant from? It's been lost." The group turned towards Elfroid, whose whining voice had called from the back of the courtyard. When they shifted back to Raoul, a few hands fell to swords.

"Lord Montag had it among his papers. It was written not in his hand but that of Raganor himself." Raoul paced towards the group, placing himself in their midst, as if challenging them to attack. No one moved. "You know what I want. I want this to be the last we see each other. I want tonight to be the last night blood is spilled in this organization's name. I want this to be the last time power becomes a greater priority than humanity. Let us leave as friends, no longer bound to each other's selfish desires. No longer bound to darkness."

"Sounds good to me." Simon shrugged from his place leaning against the wall.

"We still have secrets to keep," King John pointed out. He pointed at the trio. "They now know everything about us. They know who we are." The King pointed at Wilfred. "And that man isn't even one of the bloodlines."

"Ah, but he is. Sir Wilfred Fyr Hors is the bastard of Sir Alfred of Homme," Jacques cut in, looking entirely pleased with himself. He met the king's gaze with an easy familiarity. "He is one of your knights, as are the other two. And they all are of our ridiculous bloodlines, not that that matters anymore."

"You are so quick to let centuries of tradition fall," Elfroid said.

"Does anyone *want* to continue this? Do you *want* to watch your sons and grandchildren die?" Raoul shouted over them all. They quieted. "We agreed after Montag that we were done. This dies with us. Raganor tried to threaten you otherwise, and he has received the death of thirteen cuts. *He* was the sacrifice tonight. Does any man here challenge that?"

A rumble of dissent echoed around the courtyard.

Raoul spun around, his arms wide. "Anyone who wants to take my place, take me back to the altar now. But you need each member to administer a cut. And I know half of you will not."

Eleanor watched each member take a step back, recognizing the restrictions of their own traditions.

Elfroid alone stalked forward. "Without you, the blooded child would come to power."

Eleanor glared at the man who once thought he could intimidate her. "And with him in power, you and your family would be nothing." She stepped forward. "My son is a child of the Levans, the Le Bruns, and the Earnblaecs. He will inherit *everything*. And when he does, the Lezays will be a mere memory of nobility." With her face a mere handsbreadth from Elfroid's, she breathed, "I assure you, it is in your best interest if this Order is dissolved long before my son becomes a man."

She met Elfroid's eyes without blinking, the similarity to his uncle only a memory. Before her was a mere man, a man without the grit and courage of the men who had come before him. She was more than him. He would have cowered had he lived through what she had. With a blink of his eyes, she saw him finally recognize that as well. She backed away, returning to Alec's side.

Raoul's voice again reached everyone's ears. "I wish you all peace. This is over. There are plenty of good causes to take up, should you find yourself needing more than a life of luxury in your castles. They call for more crusaders. Our original oaths were to defend the defenseless, a noble cause. Go home now to your families. Hug your children close. Be at peace."

As the knights broke off, some of them riding down into the dark valley in an eager desire to return home, Eleanor felt Alec lace his fingers through hers. She turned to him. He was still bare-chested in the cold, the light of the torches in the courtyard illuminating the contours of his body, the body that she had just harmed. His thumb circled hers in a gentle caress.

"I'm so sorry," she breathed. It was an understatement. How could she explain how she wished she had taken his place, that she had allowed their roles to be reversed. She closed her eyes as he cupped her cheek with his palm. She was a coward. She was undeserving of him, just like Giselle had implied. Even as she wished reversal, she knew she would not have been able to tolerate it like he had. He had not called out from the burns. He had handled the potion with whatever alteration Raoul had done.

Both of his hands now lifted her face, and she forced her eyes open. She could face him. He deserved that.

"I see you," Alec breathed. His eyes met hers, the veil that so often covered his emotion lifted. The love she saw there was so raw, her breath caught in her throat. "I always have. I always will. It is you I chose, and I would choose you again." His eyes shone in the darkness, but then they were hidden as he pulled her into his arms, folding her into him in a way no one else could.

"I love you," she breathed into his chest.

"I trust you," he replied.

The words caught her off guard, and she pushed away slightly to look at him. His lips turned into a light smile. She realized then how much it had taken for him to lay there helpless, being weakened by drug and injury, trusting that she would somehow empower him to fight back. Raoul and Simon, with their carefully constructed plan, had in turn trusted that this love was powerful enough to throw things off in the necessary moment. And she, Eleanor, had had to trust all of them to support her.

Alec squeezed her fingers and turned back to the knights that remained.

Jacques held out his hand. "Glad you two saw it through."

Alec and Eleanor both shook it.

"Are you done trying to kidnap my son?" Eleanor blurted out.

Jacques bowed to her. "As you are now part of what is left of The Order, Benec is under my protection." He smiled, a twinkle in his eye, and went over to King John, who stood next to his horse.

The king gave Alec a nod. To Eleanor he said, "Get your son. And report on how your manor fairs in Aquitaine. I'd appreciate a barrel of your wine when you next return to England." Before they could respond, the king had mounted his horse and ridden away, Jacques following close behind.

Simon stepped up to fill their place. He hesitated, then held out his hand to Eleanor, who took it with a steady grip. "I have to hand it to you, you aren't bad with a sword." He shot a sideways look at Alec. "Could the two of you use a squire? I have a twelve-year-old who thinks he knows everything there is to know."

"Send him." Eleanor smiled.

Simon's hand still clasped hers, and his face sobered. "You forgive me yet?"

She nodded. He had offered his apology enough times, in enough ways, to show he meant it. His actions that evening spoke even louder than his words. It was time to let it go, and the relief Eleanor felt as she did took an invisible weight off her shoulders she hadn't known was there.

"Thank you," Simon whispered. He stepped away with a final nod to Alec.

Raoul, Wilfred, and the Lezays were deep in discussion across the courtyard. They were some of the last members remaining. Eleanor took a deep breath. She felt Alec's strong presence at her shoulder.

Raoul's face had a pained expression, which he turned towards Alec.

Wilfred stood next to him, his brow furrowed. "Can we move beyond this?" He motioned to the circle of men.

There was so much history in that last group of knights. Raoul had killed Alec and Wilfred's father. But he was Eleanor's loyal cousin. Alec had killed Rothulfus Lezay, the brother of Roric and uncle of Elfroid, thinking he was the man to seek his revenge upon. Though he had been innocent of that crime, Rothulfus Lezay had hurt Eleanor. But because Alec had sought him out, Alec had met Eleanor. Did he have the energy to long for revenge against Raoul, who had just proven himself so loyal to his wife? Did the Lezays, for that matter, still want to avenge Rothulfus?

Alec swallowed. He met Raoul's gaze, which offered a willingness to accept punishment. He turned towards Roric, who appeared ready to move on. Elfroid, he was busy staring at Eleanor, that hungry look still in his eye, like a mad bear leashed and saving its energy for the fight.

Well, you couldn't live life without at least a few enemies. Alec stepped up next to Eleanor, reminding the Lezays they were a force united.

"If we are in agreement, I am willing to put the past behind us," Alec said.

Raoul breathed a sigh of relief, as did Wilfred and Eleanor. Roric nodded his head, then held out his hand to Alec.

"Let us move forward," Roric agreed. They shook.

Elfroid crossed his arms, a smirk turning a corner of his lip.

Alec turned to Raoul, and held out his hand. "If you had not joined, you would not have been in a position to end things as you have. And I cannot change the blood in my veins." Alec felt an ache in his chest as he said the words. It was some comfort that at least his father had been on the right side of the table, not the dark side like Raganor had. The men clasped hands in a strong grip.

It was a night of rebuilt alliances indeed.

—◆—

They decided to stay at the Bergfried that night. Alec was exhausted from his wounds and the lingering effects of the potion. Eleanor was keen to treat him. She showed him to the room she'd been granted and then returned back downstairs to care for their horses and gather his belongings from his saddlebags.

Every time Alec closed his eyes the scene replayed. Fire. Blood. The rational part of his brain told him the images would dim in time, but he knew too he could not erase them; the energy behind them was too strong, too powerful. The drugged potion had amplified them. The pain that still radiated across his back would not allow him to forget. Even for just a moment, he needed reprieve.

Alec splashed cold water on his face from a basin in the corner of the room. The water turned red as it dissolved the blood crusted on his hands. Right. They had fought, too. It probably wasn't his blood at least. He stared at it a moment, then looked away, finishing his washing blindly. He dried his hands on a cloth, then buried his face in it, the dampness of the water cooling his burning, tired eyes.

The door clicked open softly behind him, and he spun, nerves tingling.

"Just me," Eleanor said softly, entering and closing the door behind her. She watched him from the doorway, sadness in her eyes as she studied his back, his jar of healing balm in one hand. "Alec…"

He let out slow breath and turned away from her, replacing the cloth on its hook by the basin. Eleanor's fingers brushed his arm, and he yielded to her as she pulled him into an embrace. Her tears wet his chest. Slowly his arms wrapped around her. He buried his face in her hair, then lower, into the crook of her neck. He felt a shudder run through his body, the emotion threatening to break through, but the tears didn't come. He was too exhausted for that. Too numb. His lips deftly kissed her soft skin.

"Alec, I missed you," she breathed. "I love you."

He kissed her forehead, his own eyes damp. "Eleanor, I will spend the rest of my life reminding you I love you. Can you promise me one thing?"

She squeezed his forearm.

"Even if our paths separate in the future, if we end up kingdoms apart, don't ever leave me again."

She let out a rare giggle, then with a stoic, serious face, turned to him. With a light kiss she whispered, "That I can promise."

Slowly the layers of pain and betrayal between them fell to the floor. Her walls crumbled a stone at a time under his caress. He felt it in how she moved, how she breathed, and eventually in how she melted into and around him. And when they were done, bound once again to each other as man and wife, Alec knew he and Eleanor shared something in their bond that resounded with its own power.

With Eleanor in his arms, his body yielded mercifully to sleep, the images of the day for a few hours at least, forgotten.

Chapter 46

Alec couldn't tell if it was the remnants of the potion or the thoughts stirring in his head, but by morning he was worse for wear. He slept late, and still woke with a throbbing headache, as if he had drunk an entire barrel of ale the night before. The burns on his back, despite balm, still felt tight and when he moved, they burned anew.

His bed was empty, which despite the promises of peace the night before made him nervous. He forced himself to his feet with a few unmanly groans and dressed. Within a few minutes, he found Wilfred, Eleanor, and Raoul digging a grave just outside the fortress. He sat on a rock and watched them.

"How are you?" Eleanor came to him, her calloused fingers gently brushing his face as she pulled him to a soft kiss.

Alec shook his head. It was agony, but it could be worse. At least he was alive. "Almost done?"

"Yes," Eleanor said softly. Raganor was wrapped in a white cloth, neatly bound.

"The things we do for family," Raoul grumbled, rhythmically throwing shovels of dirt.

That reminded Alec of something. He blurted out, "Raoul, is it true that if two of the thirteen bloodlines marry, they will be childless?"

Everyone froze in their work, staring at him.

Raoul took a deep breath. "As far as I know it is true. But you and Eleanor broke the curse."

Alec inhaled sharply. If that was true, then why wasn't Eleanor pregnant again? Wilfred would soon have three children by Marie in almost the same amount of time. And it wasn't as if he and Eleanor hadn't had plenty of opportunity...

Eleanor was shaking her head. "No. No, Alec don't you go back to that. I was hurt after Benec. That's all. If there ever was a curse, like Raoul said, we broke it."

Wilfred stopped digging and looked at Alec, his brow furrowed. "You think Benec isn't yours?"

Eleanor answered, "He was early. After Edmond..." She shot an embarrassed look at Raoul. "I told Alec I didn't know. Things have changed now. I am certain. Alec, I have no doubt Benec is yours."

Wilfred leaned on his shovel, smiling. "I hate to be the one to tell you, Alec, but that child is all yours. You ever look at his ears?"

Alec scrunched his face. "What? His ears?"

Wilfred laughed. "Alec, they look exactly like yours, right down to the wrinkle. I know because they're mine, too, and my son's. And I bet if you think hard, you'll remember our father's looked the same. Apparently, we Earnblaec's stamp that one trait pretty well." Alec's old doubts rose, and Wilfred cut off his words. "Oh no, don't you go back to that either. We clarified that little fit of jealousy years ago, back in Neroche." Wilfred went back to digging, and Alec shut his mouth, looking lost.

"That's not true. Your first son doesn't have any wrinkle at all to his ears. They're huge."

Wilfred dug the spade a little harder into the ground. "Godfrey isn't my son."

Everyone but Wilfred stopped digging and stared. He continued to rhythmically plunge the spade into the earth. "Not mine. And I have no doubt. I have morals. I was a virgin when I married."

"But she..." Eleanor stammered in confusion.

"You'll have to talk to Marie about who the sire is, but it isn't me. My other son...that one is all mine. And by the time I get home, there might be a daughter waiting for me as well. And I *will* be a father to all of them. And Alec, your son—he is all yours. So you better own it."

Eleanor took Alec's hand in her own.

Wilfred hesitated mid-dig. "Eleanor, is it true that your father survived the ceremony, like Alec just did?"

"Yes."

"Then I don't know what you're worried about. Eleanor, *you* are the one that broke the curse, if ever there was one." Wilfred chuckled to himself and went back to digging.

"Maybe its true love that breaks the curse," Raoul said to Wilfred as they dug. The two men looked at the bewildered couple next to them and laughed.

Eleanor twined her fingers into Alec's and smiled. He wrapped his arm around her and kissed her forehead, sighing out his relief.

The hole dug, they buried Raganor without much ceremony. Raoul managed to get out a prayer for his soul, and then they filled the hole and placed stones over it. There was no chapel on the hill, no hallowed place to bury him, so instead he rested on the ridge overlooking the river. It was a peaceful spot at least, and one belonging to The Order that Raganor had led his whole life.

Wilfred glanced at the sun as it rose to its height in the sky. "Where do we go from here?"

"I might go propose," Raoul said quietly.

Heads turned towards him.

"I've been in love a long time, to a woman whom while Raganor was alive would never have been able to marry me. Now Raganor is gone, Montag is gone, and I completed my quest, so she might just say yes."

"Your quest?" Eleanor asked.

"I had to save the two of you," Raoul smiled but kept his eyes averted.

"Who else knew of all this madness?" Alec asked.

Raoul glanced up at him, a challenge in his eye. "Giselle."

Alec felt Eleanor's fingers tighten on his arm and looked down at her. Her eyes held worry. Did she still think she was second? He placed a kiss on her forehead, and she inhaled. He turned back to Raoul. "Good luck, my friend." He extended his hand, and Raoul shook it.

"Raoul, will we be invited to the wedding?" Eleanor asked, her mood now lighter.

"Of course."

"You should invite your mother, too," Eleanor said, a smile playing on her lips.

"I will."

Eleanor looked ready to argue, but stopped short. "Wait, you will? Have you found her?"

Raoul relayed to them his meeting with Alenor. "I must thank you, Eleanor. I didn't realize how I longed for family that cared, until all of a sudden I found it."

Eleanor reached a hand to him and squeezed his shoulder. As her hand dropped she looked around the group, her eyes lingering on Alec. "I am glad we all found it."

Chapter 47

Eleanor's heart pounded the entire ride back to Sarum, England. She prayed constantly that Jacques and the rest of The Order had kept their word and left Benec alone. Not that they could have traveled as fast as Alec, Eleanor, and Wilfred, who had the haste of worry to drive them. She prayed Lady Gwen was healing and had not changed her mind about the boy. She prayed Lord Gawain was strong enough to protect him. She prayed King John would not change his mind and order her to leave Benec in England.

The journey did not take long. The gates to Sarum opened for them with a fanfare of trumpets. Lady Gwen met them in the courtyard, her beauty in the spring sunshine as radiant as ever. The line of a faint scar followed the contour of her left cheek, but more noticeable was the little hand that clutched hers, belonging to a two-year-old child as handsome as his father.

Benec's eyes widened. He danced from foot to foot. Eleanor blinked away tears as he let out a shriek of joy and pulled away from Gwen, running towards Eleanor with the strength of a pony. She knelt as he crashed into her, his arms tight around her neck. Eleanor's eyes blurred with tears as she kissed his hair. Her little boy had not forgotten who she was, not at all.

"I missed you, Mama," Benec said, his words steady.

Eleanor looked up at Alec in wonder. He smiled down at them.

Gwen walked over, her skirts dusting the cobblestones. "He is a bright child, Lady Eleanor. A good boy."

Eleanor looked up to Gwen. "Thank you, my lady."

Gwen reached a hand down to her and pulled Eleanor to her feet. Benec shifted out of Eleanor's arms and returned the handshake Alec offered him, then beamed up at Alec. "Papa, you're tall."

They laughed.

"I have a feeling you will be too one day." Alec ruffled the boy's hair.

Eleanor squeezed Gwen's arm. "I mean it. Thank you."

"Truly, it is my pleasure." Gwen looked down at Benec with a hint of sadness. "King John sent a message that you will be taking Benec back to France. I hope you visit England often."

"We will," Eleanor replied. "And humble as it may be, you are always welcome at Levan Manor."

"I may very well take you up on that. I'm not sure I can stand another English winter." Gwen smiled and led the way to Sarum Castle. Wilfred followed at her side, asking for news of Earnblaec Castle and Marie. "Oh, your wife is doing just fine. Gawain and I took Benec to visit just last week. She's fit as a horse and almost as round as one."

Wilfred let out an audible sigh of relief, then continued his inquiries as they entered the castle.

Eleanor paused on the path before the massive doors of the castle, turning back to look over the plains of Sarum. The sun was warm against her face, the breeze gentle in her hair. Alec stopped next to her.

"It's like the day we met," Alec noted quietly.

"Did you know then how this would turn out?" Eleanor looked at Benec, who snuggled into her shoulder, then to Alec, his handsome face not much different than it had been four years ago when they'd stood at this same spot under very different circumstances.

"I never would have guessed." He smiled, taking her hand in his own. "After all, I didn't even know your name."

Eleanor smiled. She wrapped her free arm around Alec as he pulled her and Benec into a gentle embrace. Then they laughed as Benec, not to be left out, threw his arms around them both, almost pulling himself out of Eleanor's arms in the process. Alec was there to help her rebalance the boy's weight. She closed her eyes and breathed in the spring air, sweet with mint, flowers, her husband, and her son.

Here was family. Here was home.

About the author

When J.A. Stein isn't dreaming up stories of centuries past, you can find her training horses like those in her novels. Or perhaps you won't find her at all, as she frequently disappears into America's stunning wilderness to chase adventure. She loves to read anything with a plot and makes it a goal to write stories that can't be put down.

She holds a bachelor's degree in English. Her debut novel *Knightess* is a winner of a 2023 Royal Dragonfly Literary Award in the New Author Fiction category.

Dear Readers

I owe you your own thank you page, as assuming you've made it this far, you've been with me on this journey for a while now. Without readers, my dream of being a writer was just a dream. It is wild to think that I now have four novels out, and not only are people willing to read them, they are willing to buy them and even anticipate my next release. That just amazes me. I am so glad you can find entertainment, escape, distraction, and joy from these crazy stories that bounce around in my head. And I must say, I am grateful that with every bit of feedback, you set the bar higher and challenge me to stretch my imagination a little further to see just what I am capable of. I promise you, I'm not done yet. I am hopeful that this "conclusion" is just the beginning of an even broader adventure. **Thank you for reading along with me on this journey!**

To help me stay on my toes and give me that ever elusive confidence boost, I need your help. If you could take a few minutes of your time to **review this book,** it is a huge help. I don't have a massive marketing team or budget behind me, so the main way people hear about my work is by word of mouth. Reviews are the best, as they show readers across the *world* if my stories are worth reading. You can review on any retailer site, Goodreads, or BookBub.

There are perks for *you* if you follow me, too! Check out my very varied reading list on Goodreads or my recommendations of some favorites on BookBub. If you subscribe to my YouTube channel (@AuthorJAStein), you'll get writer tips, book trailers, backstory on my inspiration, and glimpses of my wild farm life. Subscribe to my website blog for updates on upcoming projects, releases, writer tips, and signings. I try to do a lot of signings to compensate for my lack of social media. If you're in the area, come chat with me. I'll give you a bookmark! And best of all, be sure to subscribe to my newsletter, ***Tournament Whispers***, which releases monthly. This will get you the Password to access **bonus chapters!** Subscribe soon so you can get caught up.

Thank you again! And keep reading.

Sincerely,

J.A. Stein

www.authorjastein.com

authorjastein@gmail.com

YouTube @AuthorJAStein

Acknowledgements

This book was my toughest challenge to date. Four years, twelve massive draft changes, tens of thousands of cut words, and then an amazing team to help me get it all together. I feel like I have been on my own quest to finish this trilogy, which in itself was a bit of an ambitious undertaking for a first-time author. I am so grateful for the people I have met along the way. Their input gave the story its polish, and their care for my writing proves that you should never be afraid of reaching out to make new connections.

To my editor Gail Delaney, thank you again for your scrutinous eye. You keep me on track, and I am so grateful you have such attention to detail.

To my cover designer Laura at Venom Co., thank you for bringing my ideas to life in such a beautiful way. I love opening your drafts and saying "wow".

To Marsha, thank you for riding this trilogy all the way through. You gave me the confidence to bring *Knightess* into the light. Without you, I'd probably still be rewriting

Eleanor's initial story, and we never would have discovered where else she could go.

To Robin and Richard, thank you for sharing your eye for historical details. You challenge me and my research in all the right ways.

To Melissa, your balance of positive and constructive feedback helped me get this book where it needed to be. I am so glad I introduced myself at book club. It is wonderful to have a local author friend who "gets it".

Orwigsburg Library Book Club...without you I'd likely still be the unknown-one-book-author. Thank you for giving me a chance and encouraging my writing. The support of a group of strangers, many now turned friends, has meant the world. I hope you enjoy this one as much as the last!

And finally, to my mom, who I can always trust to give me honest feedback, even if it means I have to rewrite the ending (again), my great thanks that you are still my biggest cheerleader. And to my husband, my sincere thanks for all those nights I made you watch the TV on mute or you brought me dinner so I could finish "just one more chapter".

Also by J.A. Stein

When a warehouse developer approaches Bill Fogel about buying the farm that has been in his family for generations, the offer seems too good to refuse. After all, almost all the neighboring farms have sold, leaving Bill's farm an island in a sea of concrete. The decision stirs up old memories, including a legend of gold. As his adult grandchildren investigate, the Fogels will have to decide what matters most: financial security, the family, or the farm.

"JA Stein is a wonderful writer. I could not put this book down. The subject is one that is close to my heart as I was raised on a farm in southern Schuylkill County...The issue facing family farms is real now in this area, but it is also a warning to other parts of the country." -Donna, Amazon Reader

Winner of a 2023 Royal Dragonfly Literary Award. In J.A. Stein's authorial debut, Eleanor is hiding from her past working as a maid. When Sir Alec discovers her secret, will she again change personas and hide, or will she step into the light and become the woman she was born to be, even if it means she must fight?

"I could not put this down!" -Amazon Reader

Eleanor's story continues in *Lady of the Tournament*, which not only continues the saga with a new revelation, but also serves as a prequel showcasing her parents' story and all they overcame.

"Another epic love story that could easily take your breath away." -Melissa Roos, Author